Wash This Blood Clean
From My Hand

Fred Vargas

Wash This Blood
Clean From My Hand

TRANSLATED
FROM THE FRENCH
BY
Siân Reynolds

ALFRED A. KNOPF CANADA

Library and Archives Canada Cataloguing in Publication

Vargas, Fred
Wash this blood clean from my hand / Fred Vargas ; Siân Reynolds, translator.

(The Commissaire Adamsberg series)
Translation of: Sous les vents de Neptune.
ISBN 978-0-676-97798-1

I. Reynolds, Siân II. Title. III. Series: Vargas, Fred. Commissaire
Adamsberg series.

PQ2682.A697S6813 2007   843'.914   C2006-905393-6

Typeset in Minion by Palimpsest Book Production Limited,
Grangemouth, Stirlingshire

First Edition

Printed and bound in the United States of America

2 4 6 8 9 7 5 3 1

To my twin sister, Jo Vargas

Will all great Neptune's ocean wash this blood
Clean from my hand?

Macbeth, II.ii

I

LEANING HIS SHOULDER AGAINST THE DARK BASEMENT WALL, JEAN-Baptiste Adamsberg stood contemplating the enormous central heating boiler which had suddenly stopped working, two days before. On a Saturday, October 4, when the outside temperature had dropped to one degree Celsius, as cold air had arrived from the Arctic. The *commissaire* knew nothing about heating systems, and was examining the silent tank and pipework, in the hope that his benign gaze would either restore the boiler's energy or perhaps conjure up the engineer, who was supposed to be there but hadn't turned up.

Not that he felt the cold, nor was he distressed by the situation. On the contrary, the idea that the north wind should sometimes come funnelling down from the polar ice cap to the streets of the 13th *arrondissement* of Paris gave him the sensation that he was only one step away from the frozen wastes, that he could walk across them and dig a hole to hunt seals, if he felt like it. He had put on a pullover under his black jacket, and if it was up to him, he would have waited patiently for the repairman to come, while watching for the whiskers of a seal to pop up out of the ice.

But in its own way, the powerful heating system down in the basement was a full-time participant in the handling of the cases that poured in all day long to the Paris Serious Crime Squad, as it conveyed its warmth to the thirty-four radiators and twenty-eight police officers in the building. The said officers were at present shivering with cold, huddled into anoraks and crowding round the coffee machine, warming their gloved hands on the white beakers. Or else they had simply left the building for one of the nearby bars. Their files were consequently frozen solid too. Important files, dealing with violent crimes. But the boiler wasn't concerned with all that. It was simply waiting, in lordly and tyrannical fashion, for the man with the magic touch to arrive and kneel in front of it. So as a gesture of goodwill, Adamsberg had gone downstairs to pay it brief and unsuccessful homage, and in particular to find a quiet dark place where he could escape from the complaints of his colleagues.

Their curses at the cold, since the inside temperature was, after all, about 10 degrees, did not augur well for the vote on the proposed DNA profiling course in Quebec, where the autumn was turning out severe – minus 4 yesterday in Ottawa, and it was already snowing in places. They were being offered two weeks' full-time study of genetic imprints, using saliva, blood, sweat, tears, urine and other excretions, now captured on electronic circuits, classified and broken down. All body fluids had become battleground weapons in criminology. A week before the planned departure date, Adamsberg's thoughts had already taken off towards the Canadian forests, which he had been told were immense and dotted with millions of lakes. His second-in-command, *Capitaine* Danglard, had reminded him crossly that they would be staring at computer screens, not gazing out over lakes. Danglard had been angry with him for a year now. Adamsberg knew why, and was waiting patiently for the grumbling to subside.

Danglard was not dreaming about lakes, but praying every day that some urgent case would keep the entire squad back home. For weeks he had been imagining his imminent death, as the plane blew up over the Atlantic. But since the heating engineer had failed to arrive, he had cheered up somewhat. He was hoping that the unforeseen breakdown of the boiler and the sudden cold snap would put paid to the absurd idea of travelling to Canada's icy wastes.

Adamsberg put his hand on the tank and smiled. Would Danglard have been capable of scuppering the boiler, since he was well aware that it would spread alarm and despondency? And then making sure that the technician didn't turn up? Yes, Danglard would have been quite capable of that. His fluid intelligence could slip into the narrowest mechanisms of the human mind. As long as the mechanisms were those of reason and logic. And it was precisely along that watershed, between reason and instinct, that Adamsberg and his deputy so diametrically differed, and had done for years.

The *commissaire* went back up the spiral staircase and crossed the large room on the ground floor where people were walking about slowly, heavy shapes bundled up in extra sweaters and scarves. Nobody knew quite why, but they called this the Council Chamber, presumably, Adamsberg thought, because of the full-scale meetings and consultations that took place there. Alongside it was the similarly named Chapter Room, where smaller gatherings were held. Where the names came from, Adamsberg did not know, but probably from Danglard, whose encyclopedic knowledge seemed to him sometimes to be unlimited, and almost toxic. The *capitaine* was capable of sudden outbursts of information, as frequent as they were uncontrollable, rather like the snorting of a horse. It could take a trifle – an unusual word, an imperfectly formulated idea – for him to launch into an erudite and not always well-timed lecture, which could be stopped by a warning gesture.

Shaking his head, Adamsberg communicated to the faces that looked up as he passed that the boiler was still showing no signs of life. He walked into Danglard's office. His deputy was finishing off various urgent reports with a gloomy air, just in case the disastrous expedition to Labrador went ahead as planned, although of course he would never reach Canada, on account of the mid-Atlantic explosion, caused by the fire in the left-hand engine, which would have been knocked out by a flock of starlings. The prospect gave him a cast-iron excuse for opening a bottle of white wine before six o'clock. Adamsberg perched on a corner of his desk.

'Where are we in the D'Hernoncourt case, Danglard?'

'All sewn up. The old baron has confessed. Full confession, crystal clear.'

'Too crystal clear by half,' said Adamsberg, pushing the report aside and picking up the newspaper which was lying neatly folded on the desk. 'A family dinner turns into a bloodbath, and we have an old man who stumbles and stutters and can't express himself. Then all at once, he starts expressing himself with absolute clarity. No light and shade. No, Danglard, I'm not signing that.'

Adamsberg noisily turned over a page of the newspaper.

'What's that supposed to mean?' asked Danglard.

'Go back to the beginning. The baron's stringing us along. He's protecting someone, his daughter, I would guess.'

'And you think the daughter would let her father take the rap?'

Adamsberg turned over another page of the paper. Danglard disliked the *commissaire* reading the newspaper he had just bought. He would give it back to him all crumpled and out of order, and then it wouldn't go back into shape properly.

'It has been known,' Adamsberg answered. 'Aristocratic traditions, or more likely, a reduced sentence for an old man in poor health. I'm just saying we don't have any light and shade here, and it's not credible. His change of heart is too obvious. Life's never as simple as that. Someone, somewhere, isn't telling the truth.'

Overcome by weariness, Danglard felt a sudden urge to pick up his report and fling it in the air. And to snatch away the newspaper which Adamsberg was carelessly disassembling. Whether Adamsberg's instinct was right or wrong, now Danglard would have to go and check the baron's damned confession, on the sole pretext of a half-baked hunch outlined by his boss. The said hunch belonged, according to Danglard, to a primitive species of jellyfish, without feet or tentacles, top or bottom, a sort of transparent being, floating in the water, which was a major source of infuriation, not to say disgust, to his precise and rigorous mind. He *would* have to go and check, because these jellyfish hunches had an unfortunate habit of turning out to be right, thanks to some kind of clairvoyance which defied the most sophisticated logic. It was this clairvoyance

4

which had taken Adamsberg to one success after another, and brought him to his perch on this table, in this post, as the unlikely and dreamy head of the Serious Crime Squad located in the 13th *arrondissement* of Paris. A clairvoyance which Adamsberg himself denied, and called it just, well, people, life.

'You couldn't have mentioned it a bit earlier, could you?' Danglard asked. 'Before I'd typed out the whole report?'

'It only came to me in the night,' said Adamsberg, abruptly closing the newspaper. 'I was thinking about Rembrandt.'

He folded the paper up hastily, thrown off balance by a sick feeling that had suddenly come over him, something like when a cat jumps on to your shoulders with its claws out. A feeling of shock and fright, sending sweat down the back of his neck, despite the cold air of the office. It would pass, surely, it was passing already.

'In that case,' said Danglard, picking up the report, 'we'll have to stay here to clear this up. There's no choice really, is there?'

'Mordent can take care of it while we're away, he's very reliable. And where are we now anyway with the Quebec expedition?'

'The prefect of police is waiting for a reply from us by two o'clock tomorrow afternoon,' said Danglard, grimacing with anxiety.

'Good. Call a meeting of the eight officers scheduled to do the course for ten-thirty in the Chapter Room. Danglard,' Adamsberg went on after a pause, 'you don't have to come with us, you know.'

'Oh no? The prefect has drawn up a list of people supposed to go, and I'm number one on the list.'

Just then, Danglard didn't look like one of the outstanding members of the squad. Fear, as well as cold, had removed his usual dignified air. Ugly and ill-served by nature – his own verdict – Danglard normally chose to compensate for his shapeless features and stooping shoulders by dressing with faultless elegance, hoping to impart some kind of English charm to his bulky outline. But today, wearing a tense expression, a fur-lined jacket, and a sailor's cap, he was making no attempt at style. Particularly since the cap, which must have belonged to one of his five children, had once had a pompom on top; Danglard had done his best to remove it, but you could still see its ridiculous red woolly stump.

'You could always say you'd caught a chill because the heating broke down,' Adamsberg suggested.

Danglard blew into his gloved hands.

'I'm coming up for promotion in a couple of months,' he muttered, 'and I can't afford to miss it. I've got five kids to feed.'

'Show me the map of Quebec, then. Where is it we're going?'

'I've already told you,' replied Danglard, unfolding a map. 'Here,' he said pointing to a spot several kilometres outside Ottawa. 'To some godforsaken place called Hull-Gatineau, where the GRC has put one of its annexes of the National DNA Data Bank.'

'The GRC?'

'Told you that as well,' repeated Danglard. '*Gendarmerie royale du Canada*, or if you prefer, RCMP: Royal Canadian Mounted Police, the Mounties. They're on horseback, with boots and red coats, like in the good old days when the Iroquois were still a force to reckon with on the banks of the St Lawrence.'

'They still wear red coats?'

'Just for the tourists these days. If you're so impatient to get there, you ought to know what you're getting into.'

Adamsberg gave a broad smile and Danglard dropped his eyes. He didn't like Adamsberg smiling when he himself had decided to be in a bad mood. Because, as they said in the Chat Room (the broom cupboard that contained the coffee machine and snack dispenser), Adamsberg's smile pulverised objections and would melt the ice of the Arctic. And Danglard felt himself melting too, just like a girl, which since he was over fifty, put him out of temper.

'I do know that the Mounties or whatever you call them have a base on the Ottawa River,' Adamsberg remarked. 'And that you get wild geese there.'

Danglard swallowed a mouthful of white wine and smiled grimly.

'Canada geese, I expect you mean,' he pointed out. 'And the Ottawa isn't really a river. It may be much bigger than the Seine, but it's just a tributary, a feeder for the St Lawrence.'

'Well, all right, a feeder. You know too much about it to back out now, Danglard. You're part of the expedition, and you'll come with us. But just reassure me it wasn't you that sabotaged the heating system the other night, or murdered the repairman to stop him getting here.'

Danglard looked up indignantly.

'Why would I do that?'

'To petrify our energy and freeze our intentions of going on a Canadian adventure.'

'Me? Sabotage? What the hell are you talking about?'

'Just a little mini-sabotage. Better a broken-down boiler than a mid-air explosion. That's the real reason you don't want to come, isn't it?'

Danglard suddenly banged his fist on the table and drops of wine splashed on to the reports. Adamsberg jumped. Danglard could mutter, grumble and sulk in silence, all very controlled ways of expressing his disapproval, if he had to, but he was above all a courteous and polite colleague, whose goodwill was both limitless and discreet. Except on one topic, and Adamsberg stiffened in anticipation.

'My real reason?' said Danglard bitterly, his fist still clenched on the table. 'What the fuck do you care about my real reason? I'm not in charge of this squad, it's not me that's taking us all over there to fool about in the snow like idiots, for Christ's sake.'

Adamsberg nodded. It was the first time in all their years that Danglard had said 'fuck' to his face. OK. He wasn't upset, thanks to his own abnormally mild and unconcerned nature, which some people called indifference and lack of interest, and which could get on the nerves of anyone who tried to penetrate the cloud.

'Let me remind you, Danglard, that this is an exceptional chance to collaborate with one of the best systems in the world. The Canadians are light years ahead of us on this one. We'd look like idiots if we turned it down now.'

'Don't make me laugh. Don't tell me it's your professional work ethic that's making you take us out to the icefields.'

'Of course it is.'

Danglard downed the rest of the wine in a gulp and glared at Adamsberg with an aggressive tilt of his chin.

'What other reason would there be?' Adamsberg asked, softly.

'*Your* reason. Your real reason. Let's hear about that, instead of accusing me of sabotage. What about *your* sabotage?'

Aha, thought Adamsberg. We're getting there at last.

Danglard stood up abruptly, opened a drawer, took out the wine bottle and poured another large helping into his plastic cup. Then he began to pace round the room. Adamsberg folded his arms and waited for the storm to break. It would be no use arguing with this combination of anger and wine. The anger was about to explode, one year on.

'Come on, Danglard, out with it.'

'OK, you asked for it. Camille. Camille is in Montreal, and you know it. And that's the only reason you want us to fly the fucking Atlantic.'

'That's what all this is about?'

'Precisely.'

'It's none of your business, *capitaine.*'

'Oh no?' shouted Danglard. 'A year ago, Camille disappeared. She flew out of your life, thanks to one of those diabolical acts of sabotage that you're so good at. And who wanted to find her? Who was it? You or me?'

'Me.'

'And who tracked her down? Found her? Gave you her address in Lisbon? You or me?'

Adamsberg got up and closed the office door. Danglard had always venerated Camille, whom he protected and cherished as if she were a work of art. There was no way he would stop doing that. And his protective adoration was on a collision course with Adamsberg's dishevelled way of life.

'You,' he replied, calmly.

'Exactly. So it *is* my business.'

'Not so loud, Danglard. I can hear you perfectly well, there's no need to shout.'

This time, the special timbre of Adamsberg's voice seemed to do the trick. Like some sort of magic medicine, the *commissaire*'s voice patterns seemed to wrap his interlocutor in softness, releasing the tension, or producing a feeling of serenity or even complete anaesthesia. *Lieutenant* Voisenet, who had trained as a chemist, had often raised the matter in the Chat Room, but nobody had been able to identify what soothing ingredient it was that went into Adamsberg's voice. Thyme, royal jelly, beeswax, all of them? At any rate, Danglard dropped his voice somewhat.

'And who,' he went on, less loudly, 'went rushing off to Lisbon, and ruined all the good work in about three days?'

'I did.'

'That's right, you did. An act of pure folly.'

'But not your business.'

Adamsberg got up, and fired the plastic cup into the rubbish bin, bang in the middle. As if he was aiming for it. He walked out evenly, without turning back.

Danglard pursed his lips. He knew he had overstepped the line, trespassed too far on to forbidden territory. But exasperated by months of disapproval, exacerbated by the Quebec business, he had been unable to hold back. He rubbed his cheek with his rough woollen gloves, hesitating, and weighing up those months of heavy silence, of lies, and possibly of betrayal. Good or bad. Between his fingers, he caught sight of the map of Quebec spread out on the table. What was the point of getting worked up? In a week's time he would be dead, and so would Adamsberg. The starlings would have been sucked into the left-hand engine, which would have burst into flames, and the plane would have exploded over the Atlantic. He picked up the bottle and took a swig of wine. Then he picked up the phone and called the heating engineer.

II

ADAMSBERG CAME ACROSS VIOLETTE RETANCOURT AT THE COFFEE machine. He stood back, waiting for his heftiest officer to take her cup from the machine's udder – since in his mind the drinks dispenser was a kind of dairy cow, tethered inside the Crime Squad's offices, like a silent mother watching over them all, the reason he was so fond of it. But Retancourt slipped away as soon as she saw him. Hey ho, thought Adamsberg, putting his plastic cup under the spout, it really isn't my day.

His day or not, *Lieutenant* Retancourt was a rare bird. Adamsberg had absolutely no complaints about this statuesque woman of thirty-five, 1.79m tall, and weighing 110 kilos, who was as intelligent as she was strong, and capable, as she had reminded him, of channelling her energy in any direction. And indeed, the range of actions which Retancourt had accomplished in the past year, displaying a striking force of terrifying proportions, had made her one of the pillars of the squad, its all-purpose 4 x 4 war-machine, whether for brainpower, tactics, administration, combat or marksmanship. But Violette Retancourt did not care for Adamsberg. She showed him no hostility; she simply avoided him.

Adamsberg picked up his plastic beaker of coffee, patted the machine gently as a sign of filial gratefulness, and returned to his office, hardly allowing Danglard's outburst to enter his mind. He did not intend spending hours of his time calming his deputy down, whether it was over Camille or a Boeing 747. He would simply rather not have learnt that Camille was in Montreal, something which he hadn't known, and which

10

now cast a slight shadow over the Quebec trip, to which he had been looking forward. He would rather Danglard had not revived those images which he had expelled into the corners of his eyes, into the gentle miasma of oblivion, where the sharp jawline, the childlike lips and the pale skin of Camille, daughter of the north, had become greyed-over and misty. He would rather his deputy had not revived the memory of a love which he was gradually and gently allowing to fall apart in favour of the different landscapes offered by other women. There was no getting away from it, Adamsberg was a compulsive chaser after girls, a collector of young bodies, and, naturally, that was something that upset Camille. He had often seen her put her hands over her ears after one of his escapades, as if her melodious lover had scratched his nails on a blackboard, introducing an unbearable dissonance into the delicate scoring laid out for him. Camille was a musician, which explained it.

Sitting sideways on his office chair, he blew on his coffee, looking at the noticeboard covered with reports, urgent messages and, in the centre, notes about the objectives of the Quebec expedition. Three sheets of paper, neatly lined up and attached with three red drawing pins. Genetic fingerprints, sweat, urine, computers, maple leaves, forests, lakes, caribou. Tomorrow he would sign the mission orders, and in a week's time he would be taking off for Canada. He smiled and sipped his coffee, feeling settled and even happy.

Then suddenly, he experienced once more that cold sweat on the back of his neck, the same dread coming over him, the cat jumping on to his shoulders. He bowed his head under the shock, and carefully put the coffee cup on the table. The second sudden turn in less than an hour, an alien feeling of trouble, like the unexpected arrival of a stranger setting off an alarm or a panic button. He forced himself to stand up and take a few steps. Apart from the shock and sweat, his body seemed to be behaving normally. He ran his hands over his face, relaxing the skin and massaging his neck. A sort of convulsive defence reflex. The sharp bite of some distress, a warning of a threat, making his body react to it. And now he was able to move more easily, but was still left with an inexpressible feeling of sorrow, like a dark sediment that the wave leaves behind when it ebbs.

He finished his coffee and put his chin in his hands. He had many times failed to understand his actions, but now for the first time he felt he had lost touch with himself. It was the first time that he had reeled for a few seconds, as if some stowaway had slipped into his head and taken charge. For of that he was certain. There was a clandestine passenger aboard. Any sane person would have explained that this was absurd, and suggested he was coming down with flu. But Adamsberg diagnosed something very different, the brief intrusion of a dangerous unknown being, who wished him no good.

He opened the cupboard and took out an old pair of trainers. This time a short walk and a few moments daydreaming would not help. He would have to run, for hours if necessary, straight down towards the Seine, then along the embankment. And as he ran, he would try to shake off his pursuer, throwing him into the waters of the river, or perhaps transferring him to someone else, why not?

III

CLEANSED, EXHAUSTED AND SHOWERED, ADAMSBERG DECIDED TO EAT A
meal at the *Liffey Water*, a dark bar whose noisy atmosphere and acrid
smell had often punctuated his excursions round Paris. He understood
not a word uttered by the other customers, who were almost exclusively
Irish, so the pub offered the unique advantage of a warm human ambiance
along with complete solitude. He found his usual table, sticky with beer
and smelling of Guinness, and recognised the barmaid, Enid, whom he
asked to bring him some roast pork and potatoes. Enid served the dishes
up using an ancient metal fork, which Adamsberg liked, with its polished
wooden handle and three irregular prongs. He was watching her put his
meat on the plate, when the stowaway in his mind suddenly returned,
but now with the force of a rapist. This time, he seemed to detect the
attack a fraction of a second before it struck. Fists clenched on the table,
he tried to resist the intrusion. He tensed his whole body, calling up
different thoughts, imagining red maple leaves. Nothing worked, and the
sense of dread swept through him like a tornado destroying a field,
sudden, unstoppable and violent. And then carelessly, it abandoned its
prey, going on to wreak havoc elsewhere.

When he was capable of unclenching his hands, he picked up his knife
and fork, but could no longer touch the food. The deposit of distress that
the tornado had left behind had taken away his appetite. He apologised
to Enid and went out into the street, walking at random and without any
sense of purpose. The memory flashed into his head of a great-uncle,

who when he was ill, would go and curl up in a ball in some hollow rock in the Pyrenees until it was over. Then the old man would uncurl and come back to life, the fever having passed from him and been swallowed by the rock. Adamsberg smiled. In this huge city he could find no den to curl up in like a bear, no hollow in the rock that would drain the fever and eat his stowaway alive. Perhaps in any case the stranger had jumped on to the shoulders of one of his Irish neighbours in the pub.

His friend Ferez, the psychiatrist, would no doubt have tried to identify the mechanism that was provoking the intrusion. He would try to probe the hidden chagrin, the unavowed pain walled up inside Adamsberg and shaking its chains like a prisoner, causing these sudden sweats, clenched muscles and a singing in his ears that made him flinch. That's what Ferez would have said, with the sympathetic pleasure he took in unusual cases. He would say, now what were you talking about when the first cat jumped on to your shoulders? Perhaps about Camille? Or about Quebec?

Adamsberg stopped on the pavement, searching his memory, trying to think what he had been saying to Danglard when the first cold sweat had broken out on his neck. Rembrandt, yes, that was it. He had been thinking about Rembrandt, and the absence of shades of dark and light in the D'Hernoncourt case. It was just then. So, it was well before any talk of Camille or Canada. Above all, he would have had to explain to Ferez that never before had any worry of that kind made a vicious cat spring on his back. This was something new, never experienced, quite unprecedented. And the shocks had recurred at different times and in different circumstances, without any apparent link between them. What connection could there be between his kindly Enid and Danglard, between the table at the *Liffey Water* pub and his own bulletin board? Between the noisy crowd in the bar and his quiet office? None at all. Even someone as quick on the uptake as Ferez would be quite lost. And he would refuse to believe that an alien had climbed on board. Adamsberg ran his hands through his hair, then rubbed his arms and legs energetically, trying to revive his body. He set off once more, making an effort to use his normal inner resources: walking round quietly, observing passers-by with detachment, letting his mind float like a log on the surface of the river.

The fourth tornado pounced on him about an hour later, as he was going up the boulevard Saint-Paul, a few yards from home. He flinched under the attack, and leaned against a lamp post, freezing like a statue as the wind passed over him. He closed his eyes and waited. Less than a minute later, he slowly lifted his head, shifted his shoulders, and flexed his fingers in his pockets, but was then assailed by the feeling of profound unease the storm had left in its wake for the fourth time that day. A distress which brought tears to his eyes, a sorrow without a name.

He had to put a name to it. To this red alert, this torture he was undergoing. Because the day that had begun so normally, with him walking in as he did every day to his headquarters, had left him a changed man, unable to contemplate resuming his routine. An ordinary human being in the morning, and by the evening a nervous wreck, paralysed by a volcano that had opened up under his feet, its fiery mouth containing an undecipherable enigma.

Peeling himself away from the lamp post, he examined his surroundings, as he would a crime scene of which he was himself the victim, seeking to identify the killer who had stabbed him in the back. He retreated a metre or so and stood again in the exact spot where he had been at the moment of impact. He looked along the empty pavement, the darkened shop window on the right, the advertising hoarding on the left. Nothing else. Only the advertising poster was clearly visible through the dark, since it was lit up inside its glass case. That must have been the last thing he saw before the assault. He looked at it carefully. It was a reproduction of a classical sort of painting, with a strip across it announcing 'Nineteenth-century paintings in the academic tradition. Temporary exhibition. Grand Palais, 18 October–17 December.'

The painting depicted a muscular figure with pale skin and a dark beard, sitting comfortably on a huge shell in the middle of the ocean, and surrounded by nymphs. Adamsberg stared for a long moment at the picture, trying to work out what it might have done to unleash the whirlwind, in the same way as his conversation with Danglard, his office armchair and the smoke-filled *Liffey Water* bar. But surely a man can't fall from normality into chaos with a snap of the fingers. There must be some kind of transition, some way through. Here, as in the D'Hernoncourt case, what was missing was the set of nuances, the bridge between the two river banks, one deep in shadow, the other brightly sunlit. Sighing with frustration, he bit his lip and peered out into the darkness, in search of a cruising taxi. He hailed one, climbed into the cab and gave the driver the address of Adrien Danglard.

IV

HE HAD TO RING THE BELL THREE TIMES BEFORE DANGLARD, BEFUD-dled with sleep, opened the door. The *capitaine* gave a start at the sight of Adamsberg, whose features seemed to have become more drawn, the nose more arched, the dark shadows under his high cheekbones more pronounced. So the *commissaire* had not been able to relax as quickly as usual after a tense moment. Danglard knew he had overstepped the line, earlier in the day. Ever since, he had been mulling over the possibility of a confrontation, a reprimand perhaps. Or a punishment? Or worse. Unable to stop the deep waves of pessimism, he had been thinking about his growing fears all through supper, trying not to let anything show in front of the children, about this concern or indeed about the aeroplane engine. The best distraction was to tell them another story about *Lieutenant* Retancourt, which would certainly amuse them, especially since this massive woman – who seemed to have been painted by Michelangelo, a painter whose mighty genius had not been at its best in rendering the supple uncertainties of the female body – had the name of a delicate wild flower: Violette. That day, Violette had been talking quietly with Hélène Froissy, who was suffering from an unhappy love affair. Violette had emphasised one of her remarks by bringing the palm of her hand down sharply on the photocopier, and it had immediately started working again, after having been stuck for five days.

One of the older children had asked what would have happened if Retancourt had banged Hélène Froissy's head instead of the photocopier.

Could she have sent her unhappy colleague's mind off in a more positive direction? Could Violette change people and things by knocking on them? All the children had then tried their luck with the family television set, which was also out of order, to test their strength. Danglard allowed them only one go each, but alas, no image appeared, and the youngest one had hurt his finger. Once they were all in bed, his pessimism had once more overtaken him with dark forebodings.

Faced with his superior officer, Danglard scratched his chest in a gesture of illusory self-defence.

'Quick, Danglard,' whispered Adamsberg. 'I need you. There's a taxi waiting.'

His head cleared by this sudden return to calm, the *capitaine* hurriedly pulled on a jacket and trousers. Adamsberg evidently wasn't bearing a grudge, his anger being already forgotten, swallowed up in the clouds of his habitual indulgence or indifference. If the *commissaire* had come to fetch him late at night, it must mean the squad had another murder to deal with.

'Where are we going?'

'Saint-Paul.'

The two men went downstairs, Danglard trying to tie his tie as well as putting on a thick scarf.

'Is there a victim?'

'Just get a move on, *mon vieux*, it's urgent.'

The taxi dropped them off by the poster. Adamsberg paid the fare, while Danglard was looking in surprise down the empty street. No flashing lights, no technical team, just a deserted pavement and sleeping buildings. Adamsberg caught his arm and pulled him hurriedly towards the advertisement. Without letting go, he pointed to the picture.

'Danglard, tell me, what's that?'

'I beg your pardon?' said Danglard, in puzzlement.

'The painting, for God's sake. I'm asking you what it is. What's it about?'

'But where's the murder?' asked Danglard turning round. 'Where's the victim?'

'Here,' said Adamsberg pointing at his own chest. 'Just give me an answer. What is it?'

Danglard shook his head, half shocked, half confused. Then the surreal absurdity of the situation seemed so funny to him that a pure feeling of hilarity swept away his black mood. He felt full of gratitude to Adamsberg, who not only seemed to be overlooking the earlier insults, but was also quite involuntarily offering him a moment of exceptional extravagance this evening. Only Adamsberg was capable of squeezing ordinary life to extract these escapades, these shafts of weird beauty. So what did it matter that he had been woken up in the middle of the night and dragged off in the freezing cold to stand looking at a picture of Neptune?

'Who's that man?' Adamsberg was repeating, without letting go of his arm.

'Neptune rising from the waves,' Danglard said with a smile.

'Are you sure?'

'Yes. Neptune, or Poseidon if you prefer.'

'Is he the god of the sea, or of the underworld, or what?'

'They're brothers,' Danglard explained, delighted to be able to give a midnight lesson in mythology. 'Three brothers, Hades, Zeus and Poseidon. Poseidon reigns over the seas, with all their storms and calms, but also over what lies under the sea, the vasty deeps.'

Adamsberg had let his arm go by now and was listening hard, his hands clasped behind his back.

'In the picture,' Danglard went on, moving his finger across the poster, 'we see him surrounded by his court and his demons. Here are Neptune's benign actions, and here is his power to punish mortals, represented by his trident and the evil serpent who drags men under the sea. This is an academic painting, sentimental and unremarkable. I can't identify the painter. Some artist long forgotten, who did pictures for the walls of bourgeois householders and probably . . .'

'So that's Neptune,' Adamsberg interrupted in a thoughtful voice. 'OK, Danglard, thanks a million. Go home, go back to bed. My apologies for waking you up.'

Before Danglard could even ask what it was all about, Adamsberg had stopped another taxi and pushed his deputy inside. Through the car window, he watched his *commissaire* walking away slowly, a thin, dark, stooping figure, steering a slightly irregular course through the night. He smiled, automatically put his hand to his head and found the remains of the pompom on his woolly hat. Suddenly anxious, he touched it three times for luck.

V

BACK HOME, ADAMSBERG LOOKED THROUGH HIS HAPHAZARD COLLEC-
tion of books to find one that might tell him more about
Neptune/Poseidon. He found an old schoolbook where on page 67 the
sea god appeared in all his glory, brandishing his divine weapon. He
looked at it for a moment, read the little caption describing the bas-relief,
then still holding the book, he collapsed on to his bed, fully dressed but
worn out with exhaustion and worry.

He was woken at about four in the morning by a cat miauling on the
rooftops. He opened his eyes in the darkness and stared at the lighter
rectangle of the window opposite his bed. His jacket, hanging from the
window catch, looked like a broad-shouldered, motionless silhouette, an
intruder who had crept into his bedroom to watch him sleeping. It was
the stowaway who had penetrated his secret cave and wasn't letting him
escape. Adamsberg closed his eyes then opened them again. Neptune and
his trident.

This time, his arms started to tremble, and his heart beat faster. This
was nothing like the previous four attacks, but sheer stupefaction and
terror.

He took a long drink from the kitchen tap and splashed cold water on
to his face and hair. Then he opened all the cupboards, looking for some
alcohol, the stronger the better, a liqueur, anything. There must be something of the kind, the remains of an evening with Danglard, for instance.
In the end, he found an unfamiliar earthenware bottle and uncorked it.

Sniffing the neck, he looked at the label. Gin, 44 degrees proof. His hands holding the heavy bottle were trembling. He filled a glass and drank it straight off. Twice. Adamsberg felt his body loosen up and let himself fall into an old armchair, leaving only a reading lamp alight.

Now that the alcohol had deadened his muscles, he could start thinking, begin again, and try to face the monster that the image of Neptune had finally called up from his own vasty deeps. The stowaway, the dreadful intruder. The invincible and arrogant killer, whom he used to call 'The Trident'. The murderer who always escaped, and who, thirty years earlier, had thrown his life off course. For fourteen years after that, Adamsberg had been chasing after him, following his tracks, hoping each time to catch him and then losing his moving target. He had run, fallen headlong, and run again.

And had ended by falling once more. In the course of this pursuit, he had given up hope and, above all, had lost his brother. The Trident had escaped, every time. He was a Titan, a devil, a Poseidon from hell. Raising his three-pronged weapon and killing with a single blow to the belly. Leaving his impaled victims with three bloody wounds in a straight line.

Adamsberg sat up in the chair. The three red drawing pins in his office, the three bleeding holes. Enid's long three-pronged fork, echoing the trident's three points. And Neptune raising his trident-sceptre. These were the images which had given him such pain, dredging up a great sorrow, and then, in a single stream of mud, liberating his resurrected anguish.

He ought to have guessed, he thought now. He ought to have linked these violent shocks to the long and painful trajectory of his pursuit of the Trident. Because no other living being had caused him more pain and dread, distress and fury than this man. Sixteen years earlier, he had had to close up the gaping wound the killer had made in his life, seal it up, cover it over, and forget about it. And suddenly, without rhyme or reason, it had opened up under his feet.

* * *

Adamsberg stood up and paced round the room, with folded arms. On the one hand, he felt relieved and almost peaceful, since he had identified what lay at the eye of the cyclone. The tornadoes would not catch him out again. But this sudden reappearance of the Trident alarmed him. This Monday 6 October, he had risen up like a ghost bursting through the walls. It was a troubling revival, an inexplicable return. He put the bottle of gin back in the cupboard and carefully rinsed out the glass. Unless, that is, he did somehow know, unless he did understand why the old man had risen from the past. Between his calm everyday arrival at the office and the spectre of the Trident, there was some missing connection.

He sat on the floor, back to the radiator, hugging his knees and thinking of his great-uncle, curled up like that in the rocks. He needed to concentrate, peer into the deepest recesses of his mind without giving up. Return to the first appearance of the Trident, the initial tornado. So, he had been talking about Rembrandt while he explained to Danglard what he saw as the flaw in the D'Hernoncourt case. He tried to relive this scene again. Although he always found it difficult to remember words, images invariably imprinted themselves on his memory like pebbles on soft mud. He saw himself sitting on the corner of Danglard's desk, and he saw the grumpy face of his deputy, under the sailor's cap with its remains of a pompom. He saw the plastic cup of white wine, and the light falling from the left. And he was talking about light and shade. How was he sitting? With arms folded? Hands on knees? Hands on the table? Or in his pockets? What had he been doing with his hands?

He had been holding a newspaper. He had picked it up off the table, and had been leafing through it, without really reading it, during their conversation. Had he really not been reading it? Or had he seen something there? Something so powerful that a tidal wave had surged up out of his memory?

Adamsberg looked at his watch. Five-twenty in the morning. Getting quickly to his feet, he smoothed down his rumpled jacket and left the house. A short time later, he was neutralising the alarm on the front entrance and walking into the Crime Squad offices. The hall was freezing cold. The engineer who was supposed to have come at seven the previous evening had still not arrived.

He saluted the duty officer and slipped quietly into his deputy's office, avoiding telling the night shift he was in the building. He switched on the desk lamp and looked for the paper. Danglard was not the sort of man to leave it lying around and Adamsberg found it in the in-tray. Without bothering to sit down, he turned the pages looking for a Neptune-type incident. It was worse than that. On page 7, under the headline 'Girl murdered with three stab wounds in Schiltigheim', there was an indistinct picture of a body on a stretcher. And despite the fuzziness of the photograph, it was possible to make out that the girl was wearing a light-blue sweater, and that there were three wounds in a straight line across her abdomen.

Adamsberg went round the table to sit in Danglard's chair. Now he held that last missing piece of the jigsaw, the three puncture-wounds he had fleetingly glimpsed. The bloody signature, seen so many times in the past, and denoting the actions of the murderer, actions lying hidden in his memory and buried for over sixteen years. The photograph, briefly registered, must have awoken the memory with a jump, triggering the terrible feeling of dread and the sense that the Trident had returned.

He was quite calm now. He tore out the page, folded it and put it in his inside pocket. The elements were all there and the attacks would not be able to trouble him again. Any more than the Trident would, the killer whom he had mentally exhumed because of a mere echo from a briefly-seen press photograph. And after this shortlived misunderstanding, the Trident could be dispatched back into the cave of oblivion where he belonged.

VI

THE MEETING OF THE EIGHT DESIGNATED MEMBERS OF THE QUEBEC mission took place in a temperature of 8 degrees, in a gloomy atmosphere rendered even more sluggish by the cold. The whole project might have foundered had it not been for the crucial presence of *Lieutenant* Violette Retancourt. Without gloves or hat, she gave no sign of discomfort. Unlike her colleagues, whose clenched teeth made their voices tense, she spoke in her usual strong and well-tempered tones, heightened by the interest she considered the Quebec mission to represent. She was backed up by Voisenet, from behind a thick scarf, and young Estalère, who professed an admiration without reserve for the versatile *lieutenant*, as if devoting himself to some powerful goddess, a mighty Juno combined with Diana the huntress and twelve-armed Shiva. Retancourt spoke eloquently, cajoling, giving examples and concluding. Today she had visibly channelled her energy into persuasion, and Adamsberg, with a smile, let her take the lead. In spite of his disturbed night, he felt relaxed and back on form. He didn't even have a hangover from the gin.

Danglard observed the *commissaire*, who was tilting his chair backwards, apparently quite restored to his usual nonchalance and having forgotten both his irritation of the previous day and even their nocturnal conversation about the god of the sea. Retancourt was still speaking, challenging negative arguments, and Danglard felt he was losing ground: an irresistible force was propelling him in through the doors of a Boeing condemned to be hit by a flock of starlings.

Retancourt won the day. At ten past midday, the decision to go on the RCMP course in Gatineau was carried by seven to one. Adamsberg closed the session and went to convey their decision to the prefect of police. He caught up with Danglard in the corridor.

'Don't worry,' he said. 'I'll hold the string. I'm good at it.'

'What string?'

'The one that holds the plane up,' Adamsberg explained, pinching his thumb and forefinger together.

Adamsberg gave a nod to confirm his promise and walked off. Danglard wondered if the *commissaire* was mocking him. But he had looked serious, as if he really thought he could hold the strings to keep planes in the air and stop them crashing. Danglard touched his pompom, which had now become a calming talisman. Curiously, the idea of the piece of string and Adamsberg holding it, brought him some reassurance.

On one street corner near the office was a large brasserie where the atmosphere was cheery, but the food was terrible, while on the opposite side was a small cafe where the seating was less comfortable, but the food was good. The fairly crucial choice between the two was faced almost every day by the staff of the Crime Squad, who were torn between eating well in a dark and draughty restaurant, and the comforting warmth of the old brasserie, which had kept its 1930s-style seats but had hired a disastrous new chef. Today the heating question won out over any other considerations, so about twenty officers headed for the *Brasserie des Philosophes*, a rather incongruous name since about sixty Paris *flics*, little given to conceptual acrobatics, ate there most days. Noting the direction taken by the majority, Adamsberg took himself to the under-heated cafe known as *Le Buisson*. He had eaten hardly anything in twenty-four hours, since abandoning his Irish meal when the tornado had struck.

As he finished the day's special, he pulled out of his inside pocket the crumpled page from the newspaper and spread it on the table, curious about the murder in Alsace which had provoked such a tumult in his head. The victim, Elisabeth Wind, twenty-two years old, had probably been killed at about midnight, when she was returning home on her bike from Schiltigheim to her village, about three kilometres away, a trip she made every Saturday night. Her body had been found in undergrowth about ten metres from the road. The first indications were that she had been knocked unconscious and the cause of death was the three stab wounds in the abdomen. The young woman had not been sexually assaulted, nor had any of her clothing been removed. A suspect was being held, one Bernard Vétilleux, unmarried and of no fixed address, who had quickly been discovered a few hundred metres from the scene of the crime, dead drunk, and fast asleep by the side of the road. The *gendarmes* reported that they had conclusive proof against Vétilleux, but according to the accused man, he had no memory of the night of the murder.

Adamsberg read through the article twice. He shook his head slowly, looking at the blue sweater, punctured by three holes. It was impossible, absolutely impossible. He, of all people, was well placed to know that. He ran his hand over the article, hesitated, then took out his mobile phone.

'Danglard?'

His deputy replied from the *Brasserie des Philosophes*, his mouth full.

'Can you get me the name of the *commandant* of *gendarmes* for Schiltigheim in the Bas-Rhin *département*?'

Danglard had the names of all the police chiefs of every town in France at his fingertips, but was less good on the *gendarmerie*.

'Is this as urgent as the Neptune business?'

'Not quite, but let's say it's not far off.'

'I'll call you back in about fifteen minutes.'

'While you're at it, don't forget to call that heating engineer again.'

Adamsberg was finishing a double espresso, much less impressive than the kind from the office dairy cow, when his deputy called him back.

'*Commandant* Thierry Trabelmann is the name. Have you got a pen?'

Adamsberg wrote the telephone number on the paper tablecloth. He waited until after two o'clock had struck on the old clock in *Le Buisson* before calling the Schiltigheim *gendarmerie*. *Commandant* Trabelmann sounded somewhat distant. He had heard of *Commissaire* Adamsberg, some good, some not so good, and was hesitating over how to handle him.

'I have no intention of trying to take this case over, *Commandant* Trabelmann,' Adamsberg assured him at once.

'That's what they always say, and we all know what happens. The *gendarmes* do all the dirty work and as soon as it gets interesting, the *flics* come in and take over.'

'All I want is to check something.'

'I don't know what bee you've got in your bonnet, *commissaire*, but we've got our man, and he's firmly under lock and key.'

'Bernard Vétilleux?'

'Yes, and it's rock solid. We found the murder weapon a few metres away from the victim, just chucked into the grass. It corresponded exactly to the wounds, and it had Vétilleux's fingerprints on the handle, clear as daylight.'

Clear as daylight. As simple as that. Adamsberg asked himself quickly whether he was going to follow this up or beat a retreat.

'But Vétilleux denies it?'

'He was pissed out of his mind when my men brought him in. Could hardly stand up straight. He can deny it all he likes, it won't make a blind bit of difference. He can't remember a thing about the night, except that he'd drunk himself silly.'

'Does he have a record? Any violence in the past?'

'No. But everything has to start somewhere.'

'The newspaper said there were three stab wounds. With a knife?'

'A carpenter's awl.'

Adamsberg was silent for a moment.

'Bit unusual?'

'Well, not all that. These homeless characters carry all kinds of tools around with them, an awl can be handy for opening tins or forcing locks. Don't get worked up, *commissaire*, we've got our man, I'll guarantee you that.'

'One last thing, *commandant*,' said Adamsberg rather quickly, sensing Trabelmann's impatience. 'Was the tool brand new?'

There was a silence from the other end.

'How did you know?' asked Trabelmann suspiciously.

'It *was* new, then?'

'Affirmative. But what difference does that make?'

'Trabelmann, can you do me a big favour? Send me the photographs of the body, close-ups of the stab wounds.'

'Why would I do that?'

'Because I'm asking you nicely.'

'And that's all?'

'I'm not trying to take over from you,' said Adambserg. 'You have my word.'

'So what's eating you?'

'A childhood memory.'

'Oh, in that case,' said Trabelmann, suddenly respectful, and dropping his guard, as if childhood memories were a sacred reason and an unquestionable open sesame.

VII

THE ELUSIVE HEATING REPAIRMAN HAD ARRIVED, AND SO TOO HAD FOUR photographs from Trabelmann. One of them showed the wounds of the victim very clearly, taken from directly above. Adamsberg had worked out how to use his computer, but he couldn't enlarge the images without Danglard's help.

'What's all this?' muttered Danglard, sitting down at Adamsberg's screen.

'Neptune,' said Adamsberg with a half-smile. 'Leaving his mark on the blue of the sea.'

'But what is it?' asked Danglard again.

'You always ask me questions, but you don't like my answers.'

'I prefer to know what I'm dealing with.'

'These are the three wounds of Schiltigheim, the three marks left by the trident.'

'Neptune again? Is this some kind of obsession?'

'No, it's a case of murder. A girl has been killed with three stab wounds from a carpenter's awl.'

'Trabelmann sent these to us? Has he been taken off the case?'

'Absolutely not.'

'So . . . ?'

'Well, I don't know. I won't know anything until I can get this picture enlarged.'

Danglard frowned as he set about working on the images. He did not at all like that 'Well, I don't know', one of Adamsberg's most used expres-

sions, which had many times led him off on to meandering paths, sometimes into complete quagmires. For Danglard, it presaged the quicksands
of thought, and he had often feared that one day Adamsberg would be
swallowed up into them without trace.

'The papers say that they've got the killer,' Danglard pointed out.

'Yes. With the murder weapon and his prints all over it.'

'So what's bothering you?'

'Call it a childhood memory.'

This reply did not have the same calming effect on Danglard as it had
had on Trabelmann. On the contrary, the *capitaine* felt his apprehension
growing. He made the maximum enlargement of the image and sent it
to print. Adamsberg was watching as the page emerged in stops and starts
from the machine. He picked it up by a corner, waved it quickly in the
air to dry, then switched on the desk lamp to examine it closely. Danglard
watched, puzzled, as he reached for a long ruler, took measurements one
way then the other, drew a line, marked the centre of each wound with
a dot then drew another parallel line and took more measurements.
Finally, Adamsberg put down the ruler and paced round the room, still
holding the photograph. When he turned round, Danglard saw on his
face an expression of pain and astonishment. And while Danglard had
seen this expression many times in his life, it was the first time he had
encountered it on the normally phlegmatic face of his superior officer.

The *commissaire* took a new file out of the cupboard, put his newspaper cutting and photograph in it, and wrote on the outside 'Trident
no. 9', followed by a question mark. He would have to go to Strasbourg
to see the body. This would hinder the urgent steps to be taken for the
Quebec trip. He decided to entrust these to Retancourt, since she was
well ahead of everyone else on the project.

'Come back to my place, Danglard. If you don't see what I'm going to
show you, you won't understand.'

* * *

Danglard went back to his office to pick up his bulky leather briefcase, which made him look like a British schoolteacher or perhaps a priest in civvies, and followed Adamsberg across the Council Chamber. Adamsberg stopped beside Retancourt.

'Can I see you at the end of the day?' he said. 'I'd like you to relieve me for something.'

'No problem,' said Retancourt, scarcely lifting her eyes from the filing cabinet. 'I'm on duty till midnight.'

'Fine, see you later then.'

Adamsberg was already out of the door when he heard the silly laugh of *Brigadier* Favre and his nasal voice saying:

'He needs her to relieve him, does he? Big night tonight, Retancourt, the deflowering of the violet! The boss is from the Pyrenees, so he likes mountains. The bigger the better.'

'One minute, Danglard,' said Adamsberg holding back his deputy.

He returned to the Council Chamber with Danglard behind him, and went straight over to Favre's desk. There was a sudden silence. Adamsberg caught hold of the metal table and gave it a violent shove. Papers, reports, photographic slides went flying with a crash as it toppled over. Favre, still holding a beaker of coffee, sat stock still, without reacting. Adamsberg took the back of the chair and tipped it backwards, so that the coffee spilled over the *brigadier*'s shirt.

'Take back what you just said, Favre, apologise, and say you regret it. I'm waiting.'

'Oh, shit,' thought Danglard putting his hand over his eyes. He saw from his stance how tense Adamsberg was. In the last two days, he had seen more new emotions overtake his boss than in years of working together.

'I'm waiting,' Adamsberg repeated.

Favre leaned forward to try and recover a little of his lost dignity in front of his colleagues, who were by now stealthily moving towards the epicentre of the confrontation. Only Retancourt, the butt of Favre's insulting words, had not budged. But she had stopped filing papers.

'Withdraw what?' Favre said hoarsely. 'It was the truth, wasn't it? You *are* an ace mountain climber, aren't you?'

'Favre, I'm waiting,' said Adamsberg once more.

'Oh bollocks,' muttered Favre, starting to get to his feet.

Adamsberg grabbed Danglard's black briefcase, took out a bottle of wine and smashed it against the metal table leg. Splinters of glass and wine flew all over the room. He took a step towards Favre, the broken bottle neck in his hand. Danglard tried to hold back the *commissaire*, but Favre had pulled out his service revolver and was pointing it at Adamsberg. Dumbstruck, the rest of the squad had frozen in their tracks, staring at the *brigadier* who had dared to level a gun at his boss. And staring too at their *commissaire principal*, whom they had seen angry only twice in the whole year, and then it had blown over very quickly. Everyone was searching for a quick way to defuse the confrontation, hoping that Adamsberg would recover his usual detached manner, drop the bottle and walk away with a shrug of his shoulders.

'Drop the gun, you fucking idiot,' said Adamsberg.

Favre threw down the revolver with an insolent look, and Adamsberg lowered the bottle. He had the unpleasant feeling of having gone over the top, the secret certainty that he had looked ridiculous, without being sure whether he or Favre had come off worst in that respect. He loosened his fingers. At that moment, the *brigadier*, in a furious outburst, straightened up and threw the jagged base of the wine bottle at him, cutting Adamsberg's left forearm as cleanly as a knife.

Favre was quickly overpowered, put on a chair and held fast. Then faces turned to the *commissaire*, waiting for his instructions in this unprecedented situation. Adamsberg made a gesture to stop Estalère who was reaching for a telephone.

'It's not deep, Estalère,' he said, his voice back to its usual calm, and holding his arm up against his body. 'Just tell the police doctor to come over, he can handle it.'

He nodded to Mordent and gave him the top half of the broken bottle.

'Put this in a plastic bag, Mordent. It's evidence that I started the fight. Attempt to intimidate a subordinate. Pick up his Magnum and the base of the bottle, as evidence for a charge of aggression without intention to . . .'

Adamsberg ran his other hand through his hair trying to think of the right words.

'Yes, there bloody was intention,' shouted Favre.

'Shut up, you dope!' cried Noël. 'Don't make things worse for yourself. You've done enough damage.'

Adamsberg looked at Noël in surprise. Normally Noël would smile and back up the crude sallies his colleague came out with. But a gap had opened up between Noël's tolerance and Favre's aggression.

'Without intention to cause grievous bodily harm,' Adamsberg went on, making a sign to Justin to take down his words. 'Motive for the confrontation, *Brigadier* Joseph Favre's insulting remarks regarding *Lieutenant* Violette Retancourt and defamation of character.' Adamsberg looked round to count the number of officers in the room.

'Twelve eye-witnesses,' he added.

Voisenet had made him sit down, pulled back the sleeve from his left arm and was applying first aid.

'Confrontation proceeded as follows,' Adamsberg continued in a tired voice. 'Superior officer issued a reprimand, accompanied by a show of violence and intimidation, without making physical contact or injuring any part of the body of the said Joseph Favre.'

Adamsberg clenched his teeth while Voisenet pressed a cotton pad on his arm to stop the bleeding.

'Brandishing of service weapon and sharp implement on the part of the *brigadier*, occasioning slight injury caused by a piece of glass. You can do the rest, write the report without my signature, and send it to the disciplinary tribunal. Don't forget to photograph the state of the room.'

Justin got up and came over to the *commissaire*.

'What shall we say about the bottle of wine,' he whispered. 'Do we say you took it out of Danglard's bag?'

'We say I picked it up off the table.'

'Reason for the presence of a bottle of wine in the office at three-thirty in the afternoon?'

'A little party at midday,' suggested Adamsberg, 'to celebrate the squad's decision to go to Quebec.'

'Ah yes,' said Justin in relief. 'Good idea.'

'What do we do about Favre?' asked Noël.

'Suspension from duty and confiscation of his gun. The magistrate can decide whether he was an aggressor or whether it was a case of self-defence. We'll deal with the rest when I get back.'

Adamsberg rose to his feet, leaning on Voisenet's arm.

'Be careful,' Voisenet said to him. 'You've lost an awful lot of blood.'

'Don't worry,' said Adamsberg. 'I'm going to the police doctor right away.'

Leaning on Danglard's arm, he went out leaving his officers stupefied, unable to collect their thoughts or, for the moment at least, to pass judgment on what had happened.

VIII

ADAMSBERG HAD GONE HOME WITH HIS ARM IN A SLING, AND PUMPED full of the antibiotics and painkillers that Dr Romain, the staff doctor, had made him swallow. The cut had needed six stitches.

His left arm being numb because of the local anaesthetic, he opened his bedroom cupboard clumsily with one hand, and called Danglard to help him pick up a box file from the lower shelf where it was sitting among old pairs of socks. Danglard put the box on a coffee table and the two men sat down facing each other.

'Can you take out the papers, Danglard? Sorry, I can't do anything with this arm.'

'Why in heaven's name did you break the bottle?'

'Are you defending that scumbag?'

'I agree, Favre's full of shit. But when you smashed the bottle, you drove him to violence. He's that kind of character. And as a rule, you're not.'

'Well, maybe when I come across that kind of character, I change my habits.'

'Why didn't you simply suspend him, like you did last time?'

Adamsberg made a gesture of impotence.

'Pressure?' suggested Danglard cautiously. 'Neptune?'

'Could be.'

Meanwhile Danglard had pulled eight files out of the box, all labelled with a title: 'Trident no. 1', 'Trident no. 2', and so on up to 8.

'And talking of the bottle in your briefcase, things are going too far on that front.'

'And that's none of *your* business,' said Danglard using the *commissaire*'s own words.

Adamsberg nodded agreement.

'Anyway,' Danglard went on, 'I've made a new resolution.'

Touching his pompom, but deeming it best not to mention that, he announced, 'If I get back from Quebec alive, I'll only drink one glass at a time.'

'Of course you'll get back, because I'll be holding the string. So you can start on the new regime right now.'

Danglard nodded vaguely. In the commotion of the last few hours, he had forgotten that Adamsberg would be keeping the plane in the air. But just now, Danglard had more confidence in his pompom than in his superior officer. He wondered fleetingly if a sawn-off pompom was quite as powerful as the real thing, a bit like asking whether a eunuch was still potent.

'I'm going to tell you a story, Danglard. I warn you, it's a long one. It lasted fourteen years. It began when I was ten, it exploded when I was eighteen, and went on simmering until I was thirty-two. Don't forget, by the way, that people sometimes fall asleep when I'm talking to them.'

'No chance of that today,' said Danglard. 'But is there a chance of a little drink? I'm feeling a bit shaken after all that.'

'There's some gin, behind the olive oil, in the top cupboard in the kitchen.'

Danglard came back looking happier, with a glass and the heavy earthenware bottle. He helped himself, then went to put the bottle back.

'See,' he said. 'I'm starting. Just one glass at a time.'

'That stuff's 44 per cent proof.'

'It's the thought that counts.'

'Oh well, that's different then.'

'Yes, it's different. And is that any of your business?'

'All right, I'm poking my nose in, like you did. Even when they're over, accidents leave their traces.'

'Very true,' said Danglard.

Adamsberg let his deputy take a few sips.

'In my village in the Pyrenees,' he began, 'there was this old man. When we were kids we called him "the Lord and Master". Grown-ups called him by his name and title: Judge Fulgence. He lived alone in *Le Manoir*, a big house surrounded by trees and walls. He didn't socialise with anyone, he didn't talk to anyone, he hated us boys and we were scared stiff of him. We would gang up to look out for him at night, when he went into the forest to take his dogs for a walk, two great big alsatians. How can I describe him to you, Danglard? I was just a kid of ten or twelve at the time. He seemed old to us, very tall, white hair brushed back, the best cared-for hands in the village, and the most elegant clothes ever seen there. As if the man were coming back from the opera every night, according to our parish priest – and priests are supposed to be indulgent on principle. Judge Fulgence always wore a white shirt, an expensive tie, a dark suit, and a grey or black woollen cape, short or long, depending on the season.'

'A dandy then, a poser?'

'No, Danglard. A very cold fish. When he walked into the village square, old men sitting on benches would greet him with respect, in a murmur that ran round the edge of the square, and every conversation stopped. It was more than respect, it was fascination, almost cowardice. Judge Fulgence left behind him a trail of slaves, never bothering to spare them a glance, like a ship ploughing on and leaving a wake behind it. You would have thought he was still dispensing justice in the olden days, sitting on a stone bench with the poor peasants crawling at his feet. But above all, people were afraid of him. Old and young, everyone was afraid. And nobody knew exactly why. My mother forbade us to go near the Manor, so of course we dared each other to get as close as we could. We tried some new trick every week, to see if we had balls, I suppose. The worst part, was that although he was getting on, Judge Fulgence was a man of striking beauty. Old women would whisper, hoping that heaven wasn't listening, that he had the beauty of the devil.'

'Perhaps that's just the imagination of a twelve-year-old?'

With his good arm, Adamsberg felt among the files and pulled out two black and white photographs. He leaned forward and threw them on to Danglard's knee.

'Take a look, *mon vieux*, and tell me if that's just the imagination of a child.'

Danglard studied the photographs of the judge, one three-quarters profile, the other full profile. He whistled softly.

'Impressive, isn't he? Film star looks?' said Adamsberg.

'Yes, very,' said Danglard, putting the photographs back.

'But no woman in sight. A loner. That's how he was. But the way we kids were, we couldn't leave him alone. Saturday nights, we'd dare each other to do something. Pull stones out of his walls, write graffiti on his gate, or chuck rubbish into his garden, jam jars, dead toads, birds. That's how children are in the country, Danglard, and that's the way I was too. In our gang there were boys who would put a lighted cigarette in the mouth of a toad, and after two or three breaths it would explode, like a firework, guts all over the place. I just used to watch. Am I boring you?'

'No,' said Danglard, swallowing a tiny sip of gin, trying to make it last with a mournful look, as if he had no money for more.

Adamsberg wasn't concerned on that score, since he had observed Danglard fill the glass to the brim in the first place.

'No, no,' said Danglard. 'Go on.'

'Nobody knew anything about his past or his family. We only knew, and this was like a warning bang on the gong, that he had once been a judge. Such a powerful judge that his influence still ran in the land. Jeannot, one of the most daring boys in our gang—'

'Sorry, can I just ask,' said Danglard with a concerned look. 'The toad, did it really explode, or was that just a figure of speech?'

'It really exploded. It would puff up to the size of a melon and then suddenly, bang, it exploded. Where was I?'

'You'd got to Jeannot.'

'Yes, so Jeannot, bit of a daredevil, we all looked up to him, climbed right over the wall of the Manor. And when he got among the trees, he chucked a stone through a window of the Lord and Master's house. Well, the upshot of that was, Jeannot got hauled in front of a court in Tarbes. When his trial came up, he still had the scars from where the alsatians had almost torn him to pieces. The magistrate gave him six months in an approved school. Just for a stone, thrown by a kid of eleven. That was how powerful Judge Fulgence was. His arm was so long that he could just bend the entire judicial system any way he liked with a wave of his hand.'

'But how did the toad manage to smoke the cigarette?'

'Danglard, are you listening to me at all? I'm telling you about a man sent by the devil, and you're fussing about the blasted toad.'

'Yes, of course I'm listening, but I was curious about the toad smoking.'

'Well, it just did. If you put a lighted cigarette in its mouth, the toad would begin to swallow smoke, not like a chap leaning nonchalantly up against a bar, no. Like a toad, puffing and puffing without stopping. Puff, puff, puff, and then bang, it exploded.'

Adamsberg waved his good arm in the air to illustrate the toad's entrails flying about. Danglard followed the curve with his eyes and shook his head as if he was registering something of great importance. Then he apologised again.

'Carry on,' he said, taking another mouthful of gin. 'So, Judge Fulgence was powerful. Was Fulgence his first name or his surname?'

'His surname. Honoré Guillaume Fulgence.'

'It's an odd name, Fulgence. It comes from the Latin *fulgur*, thunderbolt, or lightning strike. I suppose it suited him down to the ground.'

'I think that's what our old priest used to say. In our house we were non-believers, but I spent a lot of time in the priest's house. First of all because there was sheep's cheese and honey to eat there, which is very good to eat combined. And then he had masses of leatherbound books. Most of them were religious, of course, with big illuminated pictures, red and gold. I just loved those pictures. I copied dozens of them. There wasn't much else to copy in our village.'

'Was everyone old in your village?'

'That's what it seems like when you're little.'

'But why, when they gave him a cigarette, did the toad start puffing at it, puff, puff, till it burst?'

'Oh for heaven's sake, I don't know, Danglard,' said Adamsberg raising his arms in the air.

The instinctive movement brought a spasm of pain. He quickly lowered his left arm and put his hand on the dressing.

'Time for another painkiller,' said Danglard, looking at his watch. 'I'll fetch it.'

Adamsberg nodded, wiping sweat from his forehead. That bastard Favre.

Danglard disappeared into the kitchen with his glass, made a lot of noise with cupboards and taps, and came back with some water and two tablets for Adamsberg. Adamsberg swallowed them, noting out of the corner of his eye that the level of gin in the glass had magically risen.

'Where were we?'

'You were talking about the old priest's illuminated books.'

'Yes. There were other books there too, poetry, picture books. I would copy and draw things from them and read a bit here and there. I was still doing it at eighteen. One evening I was sitting at his big kitchen table with its greasy surface, reading and scribbling, when it happened. That's why I still remember, word for word, a bit out of a poem. It's like a bullet embedded in my skull that I can't get out. I'd put the book back and gone out for a walk on the mountainside at about ten o'clock. I climbed up to the Conche de Sauzec.'

'Eh?'

'Sorry, a little hill overlooking our village. I was sitting there on a rock, repeating to myself these lines I'd just read and that I was sure I would have forgotten by the next day.'

'And they were?'

'What god, what harvester of eternal summertime,
Had, as he strolled away, carelessly thrown down
That golden sickle in the field of the stars?'

'It's by Victor Hugo.'

'Ah. And who asks the question?'

'Ruth, the woman who bares her breast.'

'Ruth? I always thought I asked the same question myself.'

'No, it was Ruth. Hugo wasn't to know you would come along. It's the end of a long poem, *Boaz asleep*, it's famous. But tell me something. Did it work for frogs too? Puff, puff, bang? Or was it just toads?'

Adamsberg threw him a look of despair.

'Sorry, sorry,' said Danglard, gulping another mouthful of gin.

'I was reciting this to myself anyway, because I liked the sound of it. I had just done my first year as a probationer at the police station at Tarbes. I was back in the village on leave. It was late August, the nights were beginning to get cool, and I started off home. I was washing my face at the sink as quietly as I could – there were nine of us in a couple of rooms – when Raphaël came rushing in like a madman, with blood on his hands.'

'Raphaël?'

'My younger brother. He was sixteen.'

Danglard put the glass down, open-mouthed.

'Your *brother*? I thought you only had sisters. Five of them.'

'I did have a brother, Danglard, almost like a twin, we were so close. It must be almost thirty years ago now that I lost him.'

Stunned, Danglard maintained a respectful silence.

'He was seeing a girl from the village, in the evenings, up by the water-tower. It wasn't just a teenage fling, they really loved each other. Lise, the girl, wanted to get married as soon as they were of age. But that was a nightmare for my mother, and as for Lise's family, they were furious. They really didn't want their little girl to get involved with the likes of our Raphaël. We were the lowest of the low. And her father was the mayor. So you see.'

Adamsberg stopped for a moment before he could carry on.

'Raphaël grabbed my arm and said: "She's dead, Jean-Baptiste, she's dead, she's been killed." I put my hand over his mouth, washed the blood off him and pulled him outside. He was crying. I asked him over and over, "What happened, Raphaël, tell me for God's sake." He just kept saying: "I don't know, I don't know." Finally he said, "I found myself on my knees, up there by the water-tower, with blood all over me, and this big screwdriver in my hand, and she was dead, Jean-Baptiste, dead, with three stab wounds in her stomach." I begged him not to shout, or cry, I didn't want the family to hear. I asked him if the screwdriver belonged to him. "I don't know, it was just in my hand." "But what were you doing before that, Raphaël?" "I can't remember, Jean-Baptiste, I swear to God. But I know I'd gone out and got drunk with my pals." "Why?" "Because she was pregnant. I was beside myself, but I'd never have touched a hair of her head." "But then what happened, Raphaël? Between drinking with your pals and the water-tower." "I went through the wood to meet her as usual. And because I was frightened, or because I was drunk, I was running and I hit my head on the sign." "What do you mean?" "The sign to Emeriac, it must have been across the path. Next thing, I found myself by the water-tower. Three red wounds, Jean-Baptiste, and I was holding this screwdriver." "And you can't remember what happened in between?" "No, not a thing. Maybe the blow on my head made me go out of my mind, or maybe I am out of my mind, or maybe I'm a monster. I can't remember . . . I can't remember hitting her."

So I asked him what he had done with the screwdriver. He'd left it up there, by her body. I looked at the sky and I thought, we're in luck, it's going to rain. Then I told Raphaël to wash himself properly, to get into bed, and if anyone asked him later, to say that we'd been playing cards in our little backyard since quarter-past ten, when he left his friends – have you got that, Raphaël? We were playing *écarté*, you won five games and I won four.'

'Providing a false alibi,' remarked Danglard.

'Absolutely, and you're the only person who knows about it. I went running up there and Lise was lying just as he had described, with those stab wounds in her stomach. I found the weapon, sticky with blood up to the hilt, and the handle covered with bloody fingerprints. I pressed it on to my shirt to get its measurements, then I put it under my coat.

It was raining a bit by then, enough to muddy the footprints near the body. I went and threw the weapon into a pool in the Torque.'

'The what?'

'The Torque, the river that runs nearby and forms big pools, we call them *launes*. Anyway I threw it in where the water's quite deep, and chucked a lot of stones on top of it. It wasn't going to surface for some time.'

'False alibi, plus concealing material evidence.'

'Exactly, and I've never regretted it. I've never, ever, had the slightest remorse. I loved my brother better than myself. Do you think I was going to let him go down?'

'That's for you to say.'

'But something else I can say, is that I'd seen Judge Fulgence out that night. Because while I'd been up on the mountain earlier, on the Conche de Sauzec, I could see down into the valley, and I'd seen him going past. It was him all right. I remembered that later, while I was holding my brother's hand to get him off to sleep.'

'Could you really see that well?'

'Yes, you could see the path through the trees, silhouettes stood out against it.'

'Did he have the dogs? Was that how you recognised him?'

'No, it was because he was wearing the summer cape. His outline was like a triangle. Most of the men in the village were stocky and much shorter than him. It was the judge for sure, Danglard, walking along the track to the water-tower.'

'Raphaël was out that night too, and so were his pals. Who were blind drunk. And you were out yourself.'

'Never mind. Listen to the rest, and you'll understand. The next day, I climbed the wall of the Manor and went poking about the outbuildings. And in the barn, with a lot of spades and shovels, I found a three-pronged garden fork. A trident, Danglard.'

Adamsberg raised his right hand with three fingers up.

'Three prongs, three holes in a row. Look at the photo of Lise's body,' he said, taking it out of the file. 'Look at that straight line of puncture marks. How could my brother, who was in a state of panic and very drunk, possibly have made three stab wounds in a perfectly straight line?'

Danglard examined the picture. It was true that the wounds ran in an absolutely straight line. He understood now why Adamsberg had been using a ruler to measure the Schiltigheim pictures.

'How did you get hold of this picture? You were just a trainee policeman, a probationer.'

'I pinched it,' said Adamsberg calmly. 'The fork was a very old garden tool, Danglard, it had a handle that was polished and decorated, and the crossbar was rusty. But the prongs were clean and shiny, without a trace of soil or a mark of any kind. Cleaned, polished, smooth as could be. What does that tell you?'

'Well, it's suggestive, but it's not clear proof of anything.'

'It's as clear as the water in the pool. As soon as I saw that fork, the evidence exploded in my face.'

'Like the toad's guts?'

'If you must. An outpouring of vice and wickedness, the real insides of the Lord and Master of the Manor. But then there he was at the barn door, watching me, holding his two dogs on the leash, the terrifying dogs who had torn Jeannot to bits. And when Judge Fulgence was watching you, Danglard, even when you were eighteen years old, it put the fear of God into you. He asked me what I thought I was doing, with that contained anger in his voice that was second nature to him. I said I'd come to play a trick on him, to unscrew the bolts in his workbench. I'd done that kind of thing so often over the years that he believed me, and with a royal wave of his hand he pointed to the way out and said, "I'll count to four, young man, to give you a start." I ran like crazy towards the garden wall, because I knew that on the count of four he would unleash the dogs. One of them got hold of my clothes, but I was able to pull myself free and get over the wall.'

Adamsberg pulled up his trouser leg and showed a long scar on his calf.

'Judge Fulgence's teethmarks are still there.'

'His dog's, you mean.'

'Same thing.'

Adamsberg took a sip of the gin from Danglard's glass.

'At the trial, they took no account of my having seen Fulgence in the woods. I was too subjective a witness. But in particular, they didn't accept the trident as the murder weapon. And yes, the spacing of the prongs was exactly the same as the wounds. That coincidence held them up a bit, and they took expert evidence again, because they were terrified of the judge, who was starting to make threats. But their second examination relieved them. The depth of the perforations didn't correspond. They were too deep by half a centimetre. What cretins! As if it wasn't easy enough to have plunged the screwdriver into each of the wounds and then put it in my brother's hand. They weren't just fools, they were cowards. The examining magistrate in charge of the case was just a lackey in the hands of Fulgence. They preferred to believe it was the work of a kid of sixteen.'

'And did the depth of the wounds correspond to the screwdriver?'

'Yes. But of course I couldn't suggest that, since the weapon had mysteriously disappeared.'

'Yes, very mysteriously.'

'Raphaël had everything stacked against him. She was his girlfriend, he met her there regularly every night, and she'd just announced she was pregnant. According to the magistrate, he was panicked by the news, so he killed her. But you see, Danglard, there was vital evidence missing, if they were going to convict. No weapon, because it had disappeared, and no witness to testify that Raphaël was up there at the time. And he wasn't there, because he had been playing cards with me, since leaving his friends. I swore that under oath.'

'And as a policeman, your word counted double?'

'Yes, I took advantage of that. I lied from start to finish. And now if you want to go and fish the murder weapon out of the pool, go ahead.'

Adamsberg looked at his deputy through half-closed eyes and smiled a little for the first time since he had been speaking.

'You'd be wasting your time of course,' he said. 'I went and pulled it out later and threw it into a dustbin in Nîmes. Because water is not to be relied on, nor is its god.'

46

'So he was acquitted then, your brother?'

'Yes. But the rumours went on, getting worse and worse. Nobody would speak to him in the village, they avoided him, out of fear. And he was haunted by this black hole in his memory, and didn't know whether he really had done it or not. Do you see, Danglard? He honestly didn't know whether he had murdered the girl he loved. So he dared not go near anyone. I ruined half a dozen cushions, trying to prove to him that if you stab someone three times, you simply can't do it in a straight line. I must have given hundreds of demonstrations. But it was no good, he was completely destroyed, he kept his distance from everyone. I was away in Tarbes, I couldn't hold his hand every day. And that's how I lost my brother, Danglard.'

Danglard passed him the glass and Adamsberg swallowed two mouthfuls.

'After that, I had just one idea in my head, to bring the judge to justice. He left our region, because he too was affected by rumours surrounding the case. I wanted to track him down, and get him prosecuted, so as to clear my brother's name. Because I knew, and I was the only one who knew, that Fulgence was guilty. Guilty of the murder and guilty of destroying Raphaël too. I followed him relentlessly for fourteen years, all over the country, chasing him through press reports and archives.'

Adamsberg put his hand on the files.

'Eight murders, eight people stabbed, with three wounds in a row. Between the years 1949 and 1983. Lise was killed in 1973. All eight murders had been solved, eight culprits easily caught, virtually weapon in hand. Seven poor sods in jail, as well as my brother, gone to perdition. Fulgence always escaped. The devil always escapes. Read the files, take them back home with you, Danglard. I'm going to the office to see Retancourt. I'll call round at your place late tonight, OK?'

IX

ON HIS WAY HOME, DANGLARD MULLED OVER WHAT HE HAD LEARNT. A brother, a crime and a suicide. An almost-twin brother, accused of murder, driven from the world, and dead. A drama so traumatic that Adamsberg had never spoken of it. In such circumstances, what credence could be given to his accusations, based simply on having seen the silhouette of the judge on a woodland path, and having found a garden fork in his barn? In Adamsberg's place, he too would have desperately sought a culprit to take the place of his brother. And instinctively, he too might have pointed the finger at the well-known hate-figure of the village.

'I loved my brother better than myself.' It seemed to Danglard that Adamsberg had somehow been holding Raphaël's hand in his, ever since the night of the murder. He had removed himself in this way from the world of ordinary people for the last thirty years, since he could not join it without risking letting go of that hand, abandoning his brother to guilt and death. In that case, only the posthumous clearing of Raphaël's name and his return to the world would release Adamsberg's fingers. Or alternatively, Danglard told himself, clutching the briefcase tightly, recognising his brother's crime. If Raphaël really had been the killer, his brother would have to face it one day. Adamsberg couldn't spend his entire life chasing a false phantom, in the shape of a terrifying old man. If the dossiers led in that second direction, he would be obliged to hold the *commissaire* back, and force him to open his eyes, however brutal and painful that might be.

* * *

After supper, once the children were in their rooms, he sat down at his table, in an anxious frame of mind, having lined up three beers and three files. The children had all gone to bed too late. He had had the badly-timed idea of telling them the story of the toad that smoked cigarettes, puff, puff, puff, bang. The questions had come in thick and fast. Why did the toad smoke? Why did it explode? What size melon did it look like? Did its guts fly very high in the air? Would it work for snakes? Danglard had in the end had to forbid them to carry out any experiments along these lines: they were not to put a cigarette in the mouth of any snake, toad or salamander, lizard, pike or in fact any creature whatsoever.

But finally, by eleven o'clock, the schoolbags were all packed, the dishes had been washed and the lights were out.

Danglard attacked the dossiers in chronological order, memorising the names of the victims, the place and time of the crime, and the identity of the perpetrators. Eight murders, all committed, he noted, when the number of the year was uneven. But after all, odd or even years are a fifty-fifty matter, and can hardly be called a coincidence. The only thing that really linked these various murders was the unshakeable conviction of the *commissaire* that they were connected; nothing immediately suggested that they were the work of the same man. Eight murders, all in different regions of France: Loire-Atlantique, Touraine, Dordogne, Pyrenees. True, one could imagine that the judge had moved about a lot, to avoid being traced. But the victims were also very diverse, in age, sex and appearance: young, middle-aged and old, male and female, fat and thin, blond and dark. That didn't seem to fit the obsessional pattern of a serial killer. And the weapons were different in each case: kitchen knives, sharpened screwdrivers, carpenters' awls, hunting knives, flick knives, chisels.

Danglard shook his head, feeling somewhat discouraged. He had been hoping to follow Adamsberg's lead, but such a variety of circumstances created a serious obstacle.

It was true that the wounds did present converging features: in every

49

case there were three deep perforations inflicted somewhere on the torso, below the ribs, always preceded by a blow on the head sufficient to render the victim unconscious. But then in all the murders committed in France in half a century, what were the chances of finding three wounds to the abdomen? Very high. The abdomen offered a large, easy and vulnerable target. And as for the three blows, that was not so unusual either. Three blows to make sure of killing the victim. Statistically, the number of cases with three stab wounds was high. It couldn't be called a signature or a mark of identity. Just three blows, more or less the norm in murder cases.

Opening his second can of beer, Danglard looked attentively at the wounds. He had to do his homework conscientiously, so as to be certain one way or the other. It was unquestionably the case that the three wounds were in a straight line, more or less, in all the murders. And it was true that anyone dealing three separate frenzied blows would be most unlikely to place them in a straight line. That certainly pointed towards a fork or trident. And the wounds were all deep, which could also be explained by the force of a tool with a handle, whereas it was rare for a knife to penetrate three times up to the hilt. But the detailed reports appeared to wipe out that train of thought. The blades used varied in width and length. Furthermore, the spacing between the perforations varied from one case to another, as did the alignment. Not by very much, sometimes just a third or a quarter of a centimetre, with one of the wounds slightly out of line. But such differences appeared to rule out the use of the same weapon in every case. Three very similar blows, but not similar enough to point to a single weapon and a single hand behind it.

What was more, all the cases had been cleared up, the guilty parties having been arrested and sometimes even having confessed. But with the exception of one other teenager just as vulnerable and mixed-up as Raphaël, all those found guilty were individuals on the margins of society, homeless tramps or vagrants, habitual drunkards, and all, at the time of arrest, had presented with a spectacularly high alcohol count in their bloodstream. It would hardly have been difficult to extract confessions from people already so disturbed, and who had so quickly given up on themselves.

Danglard pushed away the large white cat sitting on his feet. The cat was warm and heavy. He hadn't changed the cat's name since Camille had left it with him the year before, when she took off for Lisbon. Then the kitten had been a fluffy little ball with blue eyes, and he had called it Snowball. It had grown up sweet-natured, without scratching the furniture or the walls. Danglard could never look at the cat without thinking about Camille, who was similarly not very good at self-defence. He picked up the cat under the stomach, took one of its paws and scratched at the little pad. But the little claws did not come out. Snowball was a one-off. He put it down on the table and finally let it return on top of his feet. If that's what you want, stay there.

None of those arrested, Danglard noted, could remember having committed the murder. That amounted to an astonishing run of cases of amnesia. In his career in the police, he could think of only two cases where there had been loss of memory after a murder, both caused by a refusal to consider the dreadfulness of the act, as the perpetrator went into denial. But that kind of psychological amnesia could hardly explain eight cases. Alcohol on the other hand, that might do it. As a young man, when he had been a serious drinker, he could recall waking up with no memory of the night before, so that his friends had had to fill him in on it the next day. He had started to cut back after being told that he had stood up on a table in Avignon, stark naked, and declaimed, to much applause, a passage of Virgil. In Latin. He was already starting to put on weight, and the thought of what he must have looked like appalled him. Very merry, according to his friends (male), quite charming according to his friends (female). Yes, alcohol-induced amnesia was something he knew about, but it was unpredictable. Sometimes, if you drank yourself silly, you could remember everything afterwards, and sometimes you couldn't.

Adamsberg knocked twice quietly at the door. Danglard took the cat under his arm and went to open it. The *commissaire* glanced at the cat.

'OK on that front?' he asked.

'As well as can be expected,' said Danglard.

Subject closed, message understood. The two men sat down at the table and Danglard put the cat back to sit on his feet before explaining the doubts he had about this genuine or false string of murders. Adamsberg listened to him, his left arm held tight across his body, his right hand propping up his cheek.

'I know,' he interrupted. 'Do you think I haven't had all the time in the world to analyse and compare the measurements of the wounds? I know them all by heart. I know how deep they were, the form they took, and all the deviations and differences from case to case. But you have to realise that Judge Fulgence has absolutely nothing in common with an ordinary mortal. He would never be so stupid as to use the same weapon every time. No, Danglard. This man is powerful. But he kills with his trident. It's the emblem and sceptre of his power.'

'Well, it has to be one thing or the other,' objected Danglard. 'Either it's a single weapon or several. The wounds have differences.'

'It comes to the same thing. What's so striking about the differences is that they're *tiny*, Danglard, absolutely tiny. The space between the perforations, in whatever direction, may vary. But the variation is always small. Look at them again. Whatever the distribution, the maximum length of the line is never more than 16.9 centimetres. That was the case when my brother's girlfriend, Lise Autan, was killed, and I know the judge used the trident then: 16.9 with a space of 4.7 centimetres between the first wound and the second, and 5 between the second and the third. Look at the other victims. Number 4, Julien Soubise, killed with a knife: 5.4 centimetres and 4.8, in a total length of 10.8 centimetres. Number 8, Jeanne Lessard, murdered with a chisel, 4.5 centimetres and 4.8 centimetres, total length 16.2. The longest totals are when the weapon was a chisel or a long screwdriver, and the shortest with a knife, because the blade is thin. But the total is never greater than 16.9 centimetres. Now how do you explain that, Danglard? Eight different murderers, each killing the victim with three blows, in a straight line never longer than 16.9 centimetres? Since when has there been a mathematical maximum limit for stabbing someone in the stomach?'

Danglard frowned, without speaking.

'As for the other type of variation,' Adamsberg went on, 'the width of the tines, that's even smaller, never more than 4 millimetres, even when the weapon was a knife, and less if it was some kind of pointed tool. The widest perforation is 0.9 centimetres. Not more, never any more. That was the width of each wound in the case of Lise. How do you explain that? By the use of a ruler? By some sort of agreement among killers? These suspects were all roaring drunk, what's more, so wouldn't you think their hands would be unsteady? And they suffered from amnesia. And all of them were confused. Yet not one of them contrived to stab outside a thin rectangle 16.9 centimetres by 0.9 centimetres. Is that some kind of miracle, Danglard?'

Danglard reflected quickly, and conceded that the *commissaire*'s argument was persuasive. But he still couldn't see how all the murders were perpetrated with a single weapon.

'Well, look,' said Adamsberg doing a rapid sketch. 'Take a three-pronged agricultural fork. Here's the handle, here's the reinforced crossbar and here are the three prongs. The handle and the crossbar stay the same, but the prongs change. Do you get it, Danglard? *The prongs were changed.* But of course they couldn't exceed the extent of the crossbar, 16.9 centimetres long, and the perforations 0.9 centimetres across in this case.'

'You mean to say that our man takes off the metal prongs every time, and solders some other blades on?'

'Yes, you've got it, *capitaine*. He can't change the original implement. He's neurotically attached to it, as serial killers often are, and that attachment is the clearest proof that we're dealing with a psychopath. The weapon has to be the same one, for him that's an absolute necessity. The handle and the crossbar are the soul and spirit of the weapon. But to evade detection, the judge modifies the prongs every time, by fixing on blades from knives or screwdrivers or whatever.'

'That's not so easy, to solder blades.'

'Yes it is, Danglard, it's quite simple. And even if the solder isn't all that firm, the weapon is only going to be used once. To penetrate vertically, not to dig the earth.'

'Well, in that case, if you're right, the murderer would have to get hold of four knives or something similar for every killing: three to take off the points and attach them to the trident, and one to put in the hands of the poor sod who's going to take the rap.'

'Exactly. And that isn't so complicated either. That's why in virtually every case, the weapon found on the spot was an ordinary everyday one, and above all brand new. A brand new implement, belonging to a tramp, is that likely?'

Danglard rubbed his chin reflectively.

'He didn't do it that way for your brother's girlfriend, did he? According to you, he stabbed her with the fork, then pushed the screwdriver into the wounds.'

'Same thing for case number 4, where the scapegoat was another teenager, also in a small village. Probably the judge thought that finding a brand new weapon in the possession of a youngster might seem suspicious, and the trick would be discovered. So he chose an old screwdriver, longer than the prongs on the trident, and mutilated the wounds with that.'

'I suppose that makes sense,' Danglard said.

'It makes sense, because it fits together like a jigsaw. Same man, same implement. Because I checked, Danglard. When the judge moved out, I went and searched the Manor. Most of the garden tools were still in the barn, but not the fork. He'd taken his precious instrument with him.'

'But if all this is so obvious, why on earth wasn't he found out before this? You said you were after him for fourteen years?'

'For four reasons, Danglard. First of all, forgive me, but everyone reasoned exactly the same way you're doing, and stopped right there. The weapons were different and so were the wounds, so there was no connection between these murders. Secondly, the geographical regions of each inquiry were quite far from each other, and as you know, communication between different police forces isn't all it might be. And next, because every time, there was an ideal suspect ready on hand, with the evidence sitting right beside him. Finally, don't forget that the judge was powerful and virtually untouchable.'

'OK, but when you put this dossier together, why weren't you listened to?'

Adamsberg gave a wry smile.

'Because I had zero credibility. Every magistrate on these cases knew I had a personal axe to grind, and they thought my accusations were obsessive and subjective. They all thought that I would have dreamed up any scenario to clear Raphaël's name. And you think that too, don't you, Danglard? And what was more, my whole hypothesis implicated this powerful man. I was never allowed to get anywhere. "Adamsberg, just get it into your head that it was your brother that killed that girl. His disappearance proves it, if nothing else." Then I would be threatened with a libel suit.'

'Right, so you were blocked,' Danglard summed up.

'What about you, *capitaine*, are you convinced? Do you understand that the judge had already killed five other victims before he attacked Lise, and two more afterwards. Eight murders, stretching over some thirty-four years. He's no ordinary serial killer, he has a cold-blooded, meticulous plan, stretching over an entire lifetime, measured, programmed, scheduled. I found out about the first five crimes by searching the police records, and I may have missed something. As for the next two after Lise, by then I was following the judge's movements and watching the press. Fulgence knew I would never give up, so I forced him to keep moving. But he kept slipping through my fingers. And you must see, Danglard, that it's not over. Fulgence has risen from the grave to kill a ninth victim in Schiltigheim. It's his signature, I know it. Three blows in a straight line. I'll have to go there myself to check the measurements, but you'll see, Danglard, the line won't be longer than 16.9 centimetres. The weapon was brand new. The suspect is some poor old wino, a vagrant, and he can't remember a thing. It's all there.'

'All the same,' said Danglard, pulling a face, 'if you include Schiltigheim in the sequence, that gives us a series of murders spread over what? Fifty-four years? I'd say that was unprecedented in the annals of crime.'

'The Trident is an unprecedented character. A monster, exceptional in all respects. I don't know how I can persuade you of that. You never met him.'

'All the same,' said Danglard again, 'you're suggesting he stopped in 1983 and then started again twenty years later. That just doesn't make sense.'

'Who says he hasn't killed in the interval?'

'You do. You said you had watched the press like a hawk. And then nothing happens for twenty years.'

'That's quite simply because I stopped looking in 1987. I told you I tracked him for fourteen years, but not for thirty.'

Danglard looked up in surprise.

'But why? Did you get fed up? Did someone lean on you?'

Adamsberg stood up and walked about for a moment or two, his head hanging down towards his injured arm. Then he came back to the table, supported himself with his right hand and leaned forward towards his deputy.

'Because in 1987, he died.'

'*What* did you say?'

'He died. Judge Fulgence passed away, about sixteen years ago, of natural causes, in Richelieu, the last place he was living, on 19 November 1987. The death certificate indicated a heart attack.'

'Good God, are you sure?'

'Of course. I heard about it straight away and I went to his funeral. The press was full of obituaries. I saw his coffin lowered into the grave and saw the monster buried under the earth. And on that terrible day, I despaired of ever being able to clear my brother's name. The judge had got away from me for good.'

There was a long silence, which Danglard did not know how to break. Out of countenance, he automatically smoothed the files on the table with his hand.

'Go ahead, Danglard, say something. Say what you're thinking.'

'Schiltigheim,' murmured Danglard.

'Precisely. Schiltigheim. The judge has come back from hell, and I've got a chance to catch him again. Do you understand? *One more chance.* And this time he isn't going to get away with it.'

'If I'm reading you right,' Danglard said hesitantly, 'he's got a disciple, a son perhaps, or an imitator.'

'No, that's not it at all. He wasn't married, he has no children. The judge is a solitary predator. Schiltigheim is his work, not some copycat crime.'

Anxiety stopped the *capitaine* speaking for a moment. He wavered, then opted for sympathy.

'This recent murder has unsettled you. It's a terrible coincidence.'

'No, Danglard, no, it's not.'

'*Commissaire*,' Danglard began carefully, 'the judge has been dead for sixteen years. He's nothing but dust and bones.'

'So what? Do you think I give a damn? It's the Schiltigheim girl that matters to me now.'

'Good grief,' exclaimed Danglard, running out of patience, 'what do you believe in? The resurrection of the body?'

'I believe in actions. It's him all right and one more chance for me to catch him. And I've had signs too.'

'What do you mean "signs"?'

'Signs, warnings. The barmaid, the poster, the drawing pins.'

Danglard stood up as well now, this time really alarmed.

'Great God in heaven, "signs"? Are you turning into a mystic? What are you chasing after, *commissaire*? A ghost? A zombie? And where does the creature live? In your mind?'

'I'm going after the Trident. Who was living not far from Schiltigheim quite recently.'

'But he's dead! Dead!'

Under his *capitaine*'s thunderstruck gaze, Adamsberg started to put the files back in his briefcase, carefully, one by one.

'The devil snaps his fingers at death, Danglard.'

Then he picked up his coat and, waving his good arm, said goodbye.

Danglard sat down again, in desperation, and raised the can of beer to his lips. Adamsberg was a lost soul, caught up in a spiral of folly.

Babbling about drawing pins, a barmaid, a poster and a zombie. It had gone much further than he had realised. Mad, doomed, carried off by some evil wind.

After a few hours sleep, Danglard arrived late at the office. A note had been left on his desk. Adamsberg had taken the train to Strasbourg that morning and would be back the following day. Danglard spared a sympathetic thought for *Commandant* Trabelmann and prayed he would be indulgent.

X

FROM A DISTANCE, ACROSS THE FORECOURT OF STRASBOURG RAILWAY
station, *Commandant* Trabelmann looked short, thickset and tough. Setting
aside the military haircut, Adamsberg concentrated on the *commandant's*
round face and detected in it both determination and a sense of humour.
There was perhaps some chink of hope there for opening the impossible
dossier he was bringing. Trabelmann shook hands, giving a brief laugh, for
no reason. He spoke loudly and distinctly.

'Battle wound?' he said, pointing to the arm in the sling.

'A difficult arrest,' Adamsberg confirmed.

'How many does that make?'

'Arrests?'

'Scars.'

'Four.'

'I've got seven. There's not a *flic* in the regular police who can beat me
for stitches,' concluded Trabelmann of the *gendarmerie*. 'So, *commissaire*,
you've brought along your childhod memory, is that it?'

Adamsberg pointed to his briefcase with a smile.

'It's all in here. But I'm not sure you're going to like it.'

'Well. It costs nothing to listen,' said the other, opening his car door.
'I've always enjoyed fairy stories.'

'Even ones about murder?'

'Do you know any other kind?' asked Trabelmann, as he started the engine. 'Cannibalism in *Little Red Riding Hood*, attempted infanticide in *Snow White*, the ogre in *Tom Thumb*.'

He braked at a traffic light and laughed again.

'Murders, nothing but murders everywhere,' he went on. 'As for Bluebeard, he was the original serial killer. What I used to like in the Bluebeard story was the fatal spot of blood on the key, that would never come off. It was no use trying to wash it or scrub it off, it kept coming back like a mark of guilt. I often think about that when a criminal gets away. I say to myself, all right, my boy, run all you like, but the blood-stain will come back and then I'll catch up with you. Don't you do that?'

'The story I've got here is a bit like Bluebeard. There are three blood-stains in it that are wiped out and then keep coming back. But it's like in the stories: only people who believe in them can see them.'

'I've got to go round by Reichstett to pick up one of my men, so we've got a bit of a drive ahead of us. Why don't you start telling me your story now? Once upon a time there was a man . . .'

'Who lived alone in a huge manor with two dogs,' Adamsberg went on.

'A good start, *commissaire*, I like it!' said Trabelmann with a fourth burst of laughter.

By the time they had reached the small car park in Reichstett, the *commandant* was looking more serious.

'All right. Your story's got some convincing elements, I won't deny that. But *if* it was your man who killed our Mademoiselle Wind – and I'm saying *if*, please note – that would mean he's been going round the country with this all-purpose trident for fifty years or more. Do you realise that? How old was your Bluebeard when he started on his killing spree – still in short pants?'

Different style from Danglard, thought Adamsberg, but the same objection; naturally.

'Not quite.'

'Come on, *commissaire*, out with it, what's his date of birth?'

'That I don't know,' Adamsberg prevaricated. 'I don't know anything about his family.'

'Yeah, but come on, he can't be a young man by now, can he? He's got to be between seventy and eighty minimum, am I right?'

'Yes.'

'Do I have to tell you how strong you've got to be to overcome an adult, and then stab them with a weapon?'

'The trident gives the blow extra power.'

'Maybe so, but the killer then dragged the victim – and her bike – off into the fields, about ten metres off the road, and there was a ditch to cross and a bank to climb over. You know what it's like pulling a dead-weight along, don't you? Elisabeth Wind weighed 62 kilos.'

'Last time I saw this man, he wasn't young, but he still seemed very strong physically. He really did, Trabelmann. He was over one metre eighty-five, and he gave an impression of vigour and energy.'

'An "impression" you say, *commissaire*,' said Trabelmann, opening the back door for the *gendarme*, and saluting him briefly in military style. 'And when might that have been?'

'Twenty years ago.'

'Well, you've given me a laugh, Adamsberg, I'll say that for you. Mind if I call you Adamsberg?'

'Feel free.'

'We're going straight to Schiltigheim, bypassing Strasbourg. Pity about the cathedral, but I guess you won't be bothered about that.'

'Not today, no.'

'I'm not bothered about it, full stop. All that old stuff's not for me. I've seen it a million times, mind you, but it's not my kind of thing.'

'What is your kind of thing, Trabelmann?'

'My wife, my kids, my work.'

Simple.

'And fairy stories. I do like stories.'

Not quite so simple, Adamsberg corrected himself.

'But stories are old stuff too, aren't they?' he said.

'Yeah, even older than your madman. But keep going.'

'Can we stop at the mortuary?'

'You want to get out your tape measure, I suppose. No problem.'

Adamsberg had reached the end of his story by the time they reached the Medico-Legal Institute. When he forgot to stand up straight, as at this moment, he and the *commandant* were about the same size.

'*What?*' shouted Trabelmann, stopping dead in the middle of the hall. 'Judge Fulgence? He's your man? *Commissaire*, you must be out of your mind.'

'You've got a problem with that?' asked Adamsberg calmly.

'For crying out loud, you know who he is, don't you? Fulgence? This isn't a fairy story. It's as if you told me Prince Charming had started spitting fire instead of the dragon!'

'He's as handsome as Prince Charming, yes. But it doesn't stop him spitting fire.'

'You realise what you're saying, Adamsberg? There's been a book written about Fulgence's cases. It isn't every judge in France gets a book written about him, is it? Respected, famous, a pillar of the justice system.'

'Not fond of women or children, though. Not like you, Trabelmann.'

'I'm not going to compare myself with him. An eminent man like that. Everyone in the profession looked up to him when he was on the bench.'

'Feared, rather, Trabelmann. He handed down heavy sentences.'

'Well, justice has to be done.'

'He had a long arm too. When he was in Nantes, he could strike the fear of God into the assizes at Carcassonne.'

'Because he had authority, because his views commanded respect. Well. As I said, at least you've given me a laugh, Adamsberg.'

A man in a white coat hurried up to them.

'Please, gentlemen, show some respect.'

'Morning, Ménard,' said Trabelmann.

'My apologies, *commandant*, I didn't see it was you.'

'Let me introduce a colleague from Paris, *Commissaire* Adamsberg.'

'I've heard the name,' said Ménard, shaking hands.

'He's got a remarkable sense of humour,' said Trabelmann. 'Ménard, we need to see the caisson containing Elisabeth Wind.'

Ménard carefully pulled up the mortuary sheet to display the body of the young victim. Adamsberg looked at it without moving for several seconds, then gently lifted the head to examine bruises on the neck. After that, he concentrated on the puncture wounds in the abdomen.

'As I recall,' Trabelmann said, 'the line of wounds runs to about 21 or 22 centimetres.'

Adamsberg shook his head doubtfully, and took a tape measure out of his bag.

'Can you help me, Trabelmann? I've only got one good hand.'

The *commandant* ran out the tape measure. Adamsberg put one end at the outside edge of the first wound and measured the exact length from there to the outside edge of the third.

'16.7 centimetres, Trabelmann. I told you, it's never much more than that.'

'Matter of pure chance.'

Without replying, Adamsberg used a wooden ruler as a marker and measured the maxium width of the wounds.

'0.8 centimetres,' he announced, snapping the tape measure back in its case.

Trabelmann, looking slightly bothered, contented himself with a slight twitch of his head.

'I suppose you can provide me with a note of the penetrative depth of the wounds, back at the station?' asked Adamsberg.

'Yes, I can – along with the awl, and the man who was holding it. And his fingerprints.'

'But will you at least do me the favour of taking a look at these files?'

'I'm no less professional than you, *commissaire*. I don't leave any lead unexplored. Ha!'

Trabelmann laughed again, for no reason that Adamsberg could detect.

* * *

At Schiltigheim *gendarmerie*, Adamsberg put the bundle of files on the *commandant*'s desk, while an officer brought him the murder weapon in a sealed plastic bag. The tool was of a standard make and brand new, except for the dried blood on the shaft.

'If I'm following you rightly,' said Trabelmann, sitting down at the desk, 'and that's a big if, we would need to look for someone buying four of these, not just the one.'

'Yes, but it would probably be a waste of time. The man in question' – Adamsberg dared not pronounce the name of Fulgence again – 'would never make the elementary mistake of walking into a hardware store and buying four identical tools. That would attract attention to him in the most amateur way. That's why he chooses ordinary cheap makes. He can get them from several different shops, spacing out his purchases.'

'That's true, it's what I'd do too.'

Once back in the office, the *commandant*'s tough persona was becoming more established and his sense of humour was vanishing. Perhaps it was because he was now sitting behind his desk, in his official surroundings, Adamsberg thought.

'He might have bought one of these in Strasbourg in September, another in Roubaix in July, and so on,' he said. 'We've got no chance of following that lead.'

'That's that, then,' said Trabelmann. 'Well, do you want to see the suspect? Another few hours in here and he'll be confessing. I'm warning you, when we picked him up, he had the equivalent of about a bottle and a half of whisky inside him.'

'That's why he can't remember anything.'

'The amnesia is what's getting you worked up, isn't it? Well I'll tell you something, *commissaire*, it doesn't surprise me one bit. Because by saying he can't remember a thing, and pleading temporary insanity, this character's sure to get ten or fifteen years knocked off the sentence. Worth a try, isn't it? And everyone knows that. So I believe in your killers and their amnesia about as much as in your Prince Charming turning into a dragon. But go ahead, Adamsberg, take a look at him yourself, if you want to.'

* * *

Bernard Vétilleux, a gaunt man in his middle years, with an unhealthily puffy face, lay sprawled across the bed in his cell. He watched without displaying the remotest interest as Adamsberg walked in. This or any other cop, why should he give a shit? Adamsberg asked if he was prepared to answer some questions, and he agreed.

'But I ain't got nothing to say,' he said in a voice without expression. 'I dunno what happened, can't remember.'

'Yes, I know. But before all that, before they picked you up on the road?'

'Don't even know how I got there, guv. Don't like walking. Couple of kilometres is a long way for me.'

'Yes, but before that,' repeated Adamsberg. 'Before you were on the road, what were you doing, can you remember?'

'Yeah, I remember that, course I can. I haven't forgotten the rest of my bleedin' life, have I? Just how I got to be on the fuckin' road and all that stuff after.'

'I know,' Adamsberg repeated patiently, 'but before that.'

'I was drinking, wasn't I?'

'Where?'

'At the counter, to start with.'

'What counter?'

'In the bar, *Le Petit Bouchon*, by the greengrocer's. See, I know where I *was*, at least.'

'Then what?'

'Then they chucked me out, as per usual, I was broke. But I was so pissed I couldn't even hold my hand out. So I looked for somewhere to kip down. Because it's bleedin' cold here, I tell you. And my usual spot, these other so-and-sos had pinched it, and they had dogs with 'em. So I had to move on, and where I went was in this playground I know, with a sort of plastic cube-thing the kids play in. It's a bit warmer in there, it's kind of like a dog kennel. Little door, and on the floor there's soft stuff like moss, only not real moss, so the kids don't get hurt.'

'What playground was this?'

'It's got ping-pong tables, it's by the bar, 'cause I don't like walking, I told you.'

'And after that? You were on your own there, were you?'

'Ah no, there was this fella, wasn't there, he was after the same pitch. Bugger that, I thought. But I changed my mind pretty quick, 'cause this guy he had a couple of litres with him. My lucky day, seemingly, so what I said was, you want to come in here, you share the hooch. And he said OK, you're on, fair enough. Piece of luck.'

'Remember anything about him, what he looked like?'

'Can't remember everything, can I? I'd had a skinful already, and it was pitch dark. Anyway you don't ask questions, someone comes along with some booze. I wasn't interested in him, just his bottles.'

'Come on, surely you can remember something about him. Try. Just tell me anything you noticed, what he talked like, how he drank. Was he big or small, old or young, does anything at all come back?'

Vétilleux scratched his head as if to try and get his mind working, then sat up on the bed and looked at Adamsberg through red-rimmed eyes.

'They don't give me nothing in here.'

Adamsberg had come forearmed, with a small hip flask of brandy in his pocket. He looked meaningfully at Vétilleux, indicating the officer on guard at the cell door.

'Ah,' said Vétilleux, catching on.

'Wait a minute,' mouthed Adamsberg, silently.

Vétilleux got the message immediately and nodded.

'Come on, I'm sure your memory's not that bad,' Adamsberg continued. 'Tell me about this other man.'

'Oldish,' said Vétilleux, 'but kind of youngish too. Can't say exactly what I mean. He wasn't decrepit. But old.'

'Clothes?'

'Looked just like any other wino on the streets, wanting a place to shelter. Old coat, scarf, couple of woolly hats, gloves, tucked up against the cold, you gotta, haven't you, unless you want your balls to freeze off.'

'Glasses? Beard?'

'Nah, no glasses, could see his eyes under his cap. No beard neither, but he hadn't shaved for a bit. He didn't smell, mind.'

'What do you mean?'

'I wouldn't share a kip with a guy who smells, it's just a thing with me. I go to the showers twice a week, I don't like smelling bad. And I don't piss in the kids' playground either. Just because I like a drink don't mean I'm going to be nasty to kids, does it? They're nice, they talk to me. They say "ain't you got no mummy or daddy?" They're OK, kids are, till the grown-ups get at them. So I don't piss in their playground. They respect me, I respect them.'

Adamsberg turned to the duty guard.

'Officer,' he said, 'would you mind fetching me a couple of aspirin and some water. It's for the pain,' he added, lifting the bandaged arm.

The officer nodded and went out. Vétilleux shot out his hand to snatch the hip flask, and put it in his pocket. When, a minute or so later, the officer came back with a plastic cup of water and the aspirin, Adamsberg forced himself to swallow them.

'Now then,' said Vétilleux, pointing to Adamsberg's cup. 'That reminds me. The guy who shared with me, he did something funny. He had a cup just like that. And he had his bottle, and I had mine. He didn't drink it straight from the bottle, see. So he was a bit la-di-da, bit of a toff.'

'Are you sure about that?'

'Yeah, course I am. And I said to myself, *he's* seen better days, I'll bet. There's people like that, you know. Some woman chucks 'em out, they start drinking, then it's downhill all the way. Or their business goes bust or something. No guts. Giving up just because you've lost your woman or your job. Me, I'd carry on. But then me, it's different, s'not that I haven't got guts. But no way I could go downhill, see, 'cause I was already bottom of the pile. It's not the same, is it?'

'No, I see,' Adamsberg agreed.

'Mind you, I'm not setting myself up to judge anyone, but there's a difference. And when my Josie left me, maybe it did give me an extra push. But I was already drinking by then, and that's *why* she left me, you wanna know. Can't blame her, I'm not judging her. Or anyone really. Except for those rich buggers who never even throw me a coin. Yeah, I've gone and dumped sometimes on their doorsteps, people like that. But I wouldn't do it in the kids' playground.'

'Are you sure this other man had seen better days?'

'Oh yeah, easy to see. And not so long ago, I'd say. 'Cause once you're down and out, you don't go round with your own cup for long. Maybe you hang on to it for three, four months, then you just drink from any old bottle like everyone else. Except I won't drink with guys who smell bad, that's different, that's just me, I don't like smells, I'm not judging them.'

'So you think he hadn't been on the streets that long? Three or four months?'

'How would I know? But I'd say not long. My guess is some woman's chucked him out, he finds himself with nowhere to go, something like that.'

'Did you talk to him much?'

'Nah, not a lot. Just stuff like nice drop of wine, bloody cold outside, that sort of thing.'

Vétilleux had his hand resting on his thick sweater, over the shirt pocket where he had slipped the flask.

'Did he stay long?'

'Don't ask me that, time don't mean much to me.'

'What I'm saying is, did he go away again? Or did he sleep there, same place as you?'

'No idea. That's when I must have passed out. Or gone walkies, I don't know.'

'And after that?'

Vétilleux opened his arms and dropped them again.

'Found myself on the road, in the morning, *gendarmes* all over me.'

'Did you dream? Remember seeing anything, smelling anything, any sensations at all?'

The man frowned, looking puzzled, his hand on his worn old sweater, and his long nails scratching at the wool. Adamsberg turned to the guard, who was stamping his feet to keep his circulation going.

'Officer,' he said, 'could you fetch me my briefcase? I need to make some notes.'

With the rapidity of a reptile, Vétilleux abandoned his slouched pose, whipped out the flask, undid the top, and swallowed several mouthfuls. By the time the officer was back, the whole thing was back under the pullover. Adamsberg admired such skill and dexterity. Practice had perfected the reflexes. Vétilleux was not stupid.

'There was one thing,' he said, with a little more colour in his cheeks. 'I dreamed I was in a nice comfortable place all warm, ready to doze off. But I was fed up because I couldn't use it.'

'Why not?'

'Because I wanted to throw up.'

'Does that usually happen? Do you throw up often?'

'Nah, never!'

'Do you usually dream you're in a warm place?'

'Listen, mate, if I spent every night dreaming I was warm, I'd be in heaven.'

'Do you own a carpenter's awl?'

'No, how would I, not unless that guy gave it me. The one who'd seen better days. Or maybe I pinched it? How do I know? All I know is I must've killed that poor girl with it. Maybe she fell off her bike in the road, and I thought she was a bear or something and went for her, how do I know?'

'Is that what you think?'

'They say my prints are on it, and I was right there, near her.'

'But why would you have dragged the bear, and the bicycle, off the road?'

'Someone like me, when I've drunk that much, who knows what's going on in my head? All I know is I'm really sorry, because personally I wouldn't hurt a soul. I don't hurt animals, why would I hurt people, know what I mean? Even if I was a bear. Not even afraid of bears. Lot of bears in Canada. They go round the dustbins, like I do. Wouldn't mind that, going round the dustbins with the bears.'

'Vétilleux, if you want to know something about bears . . .'

Adamsberg bent close to Vétilleux and whispered in his ear.

'Don't say anything, don't confess,' he hissed. 'Just keep mum, nothing but the truth, you can't remember a thing. Promise me.'

'Hey!' said the guard. 'Sorry, *commissaire*, but no whispering to the detainee.'

'My apologies, officer. I was just telling him a risqué joke about bears. Poor guy hasn't much to distract him.'

'Even so, *commissaire*, I can't permit it.'

Adamsberg gave Vétilleux a silent look, and made a sign indicating 'Understood?'

Vétilleux nodded.

'Promise?' Adamsberg mouthed.

Another wink, from those red-rimmed but watchful eyes. This cop had given him a hip flask, he was on his side.

Adamsberg got up and on his way out squeezed Vétilleux's shoulder lightly with his good hand, meaning 'I'm going now, but I'm counting on you.'

On the way back to the office, the guard asked Adamsberg if, with respect, sir, he would mind telling him the story about the bear. Adamsberg was saved by Trabelmann's appearance.

'So what do you think?' asked Trabelmann.

'He had quite a bit to say.'

'Ah, did he now? Not with me. He just sits there in a heap, sort of collapsed.'

'Yes. It's a warning sign. Don't take this the wrong way, *commandant*, but with an alcoholic as far gone as he is, depriving him of drink too suddenly is dangerous. He might just die on you.'

'I do know that, *commissaire*. He gets a glass of wine with every meal.'

'If I were you, I'd triple the dose. Believe me, *commandant*, it would be best.'

'Right you are,' said Trabelmann without taking offence. 'And in all this chat from him,' he went on, sitting down at the desk, 'did anything interesting turn up?'

'Not stupid. He catches on fast, and he's even fairly sensitive.'

'Could be. But once a guy starts drinking like that, he's had it. There are men who beat their wives, but they can be meek and mild until nightfall.'

'But Vétilleux doesn't have any form, does he? Never been in any fights? Did the Strasbourg police confirm that?'

'Affirmative. No, he'd never given them any trouble. Until now. Are you going to tell me you're on his side?'

'I listened to him.'

Adamsberg rapidly recounted the interview with Vétilleux, naturally leaving out the hip flask bit.

'One possibility that can't be ruled out,' he concluded, 'is that Vétilleux was bundled into the back of a car. He says he felt warm and comfortable, but at the same time he felt sick.'

'So *commissaire*, you've dreamed up a car, a trip out to the countryside, and a driver, just because "he felt warm". And that's it?'

'Yes. That's it.'

'You make me laugh, Adamsberg. You make me think of the guys who pull rabbits out of hats.'

'The rabbits really do come out of the hats though, don't they?'

'You're thinking about this other wino, I suppose?'

'A la-di-da wino who drank from his own bottle and carried a plastic cup around with him. A wino who'd seen better days. And was "oldish".'

'But a wino all the same.'

'Possibly, but not definitely.'

'Tell me something, *commissaire*. In all your career, has anyone ever been able to make you change your mind?'

Adamsberg took a moment to try and think honestly about the question. 'No,' he admitted finally, with a touch of regret in his voice.

'That's what I was afraid of. So let me tell you you've got an ego the size of a kitchen table.'

Adamsberg squeezed his eyes shut without replying.

'I'm not trying to pick a quarrel, *commissaire*. But in this case, you've come here with a load of your own dreamt-up ideas that nobody else has ever believed. Then you try and rearrange the facts till they suit you. I don't say there aren't some interesting things in your version. But you don't look at the other side, you don't even listen to it. And I've got a suspect who was found drunk, a few feet away from the victim, with the weapon at his side and his fingerprints all over it. Do you hear what I'm saying?'

'I perfectly understand your point of view.'

'But you couldn't give a damn about it, could you? And you'll carry on with your own theory. Other people can just take a running jump, can't they, with their work and their ideas and impressions. Just tell me one thing. There are killers still walking the streets all over France. Cases we've never solved, you or me, sacks of them in the archives. And you don't bother yourself with them. So why this one?'

'When you read dossier no. 6, for the year 1973, you'll see that the teenager who was brought to trial was my brother. It ruined his life and I lost him.'

'That's your "childhood memory", is it? You might have said so earlier.'

'You wouldn't have listened to the rest of the story. You'd have said I was too closely involved, that it was too personal.'

'Affirmative. Nothing like having one of your relations in the shit, to send a policeman off the straight and narrow.'

He pulled out dossier no. 6 and put it on top of the pile with a sigh.

'Listen, Adamsberg,' he said. 'Because of your reputation, I'll look at your dossiers. So we'll have had a full, frank and impartial exchange of information. You've had a look at my patch, I'll look at yours. Fair enough? I'll see you again tomorrow morning. There's a perfectly good hotel, a couple of hundred metres up the road on the right.'

Adamsberg walked for a long time along country roads, before checking into the hotel. He couldn't blame Trabelmann, who had been very cooperative, all things considered. But the *commandant* wouldn't go along with him, any more than anyone else. Everywhere, he had had to face incredulous stares; everywhere, he had had to carry the weight of the judge on his shoulders, alone.

Because Trabelmann was right in one respect – about him, Adamsberg – he would not abandon his theory. The measurements of the wounds in this case were once more within the limits of the original trident. Vétilleux had been picked out, followed, and plied with a litre of wine by the man with the cap pulled over his eyes. Who had taken good care not to touch any of his companion's saliva. Then Vétilleux had been taken by car and dropped off close to the scene of the crime, which had already been committed. The old man had only had to press the weapon into Vétilleux's hand, and throw it down beside him. Then he had driven off, disappearing calmly from the face of the earth, leaving his latest scapegoat in the hands of the zealous *Commandant* Trabelmann.

XI

ARRIVING AT THE GENDARMERIE AT NINE O'CLOCK NEXT MORNING, Adamsberg saluted the duty officer, the same one who had wanted to know the story about the bear. The officer indicated with a gesture that the storm signals were hoisted. And indeed Trabelmann had lost all his conviviality of the previous day. He was standing waiting in his office, his arms folded and his back ramrod-stiff.

'What the fuck are you playing at, Adamsberg?' he said in a voice tense with fury. 'Paris police think the *gendarmes* are a bunch of idiots, or what?'

Adamsberg stood facing the *commandant* without speaking. In this kind of situation, it was best to let people have their say. He guessed what had happened. But he had not imagined Trabelmann would have worked so quickly. He had underestimated him.

'Judge Fulgence died sixteen years ago!' Trabelmann shouted. 'He's dead, dead and buried, kaput! This isn't a fairy story, Adamsberg, it's science fiction. And don't tell me you didn't know. Your notes stop in 1987.'

'Yes, of course I know. I went to his funeral.'

'And you've made me waste a whole day on your crazy story? Just to tell me that this figment of your imagination killed the Wind girl at Schiltigheim? You didn't think for one minute that a stupid *gendarme* like Trabelmann might have checked up on the judge's current whereabouts?'

'It's true, I didn't think you would have got that far yet, and I apologise. But if you took the trouble to check the record, at least it means that you were intrigued enough by the Fulgence story to follow it up.'

'What the hell is your game, Adamsberg? Are you on a ghost hunt? I hope not, or you shouldn't be in the police force, but locked up somewhere. So why the fuck did you come all the way out here?'

'To take the measurements, to get a chance to question Vétilleux, and to tell you about this possibility.'

'Perhaps you thought he had an imitator? A disciple? A son?'

Adamsberg had the impression he was going back through his conversation with Danglard of two days before.

'No, I don't think he has a disciple, and he had no children. Fulgence is a lone wolf.'

'Do you realise you're standing there with a straight face and telling me you're out of your tiny mind?'

'I realise you think that, *commandant*. May I have permission to see Vétilleux once more before I leave?'

'No, you may not!' shouted Trabelmann.

'Well, if you want to go ahead and hand an innocent man over to the courts, that's your business.'

Adamsberg had to go round Trabelmann to pick up his files. He pushed them clumsily into his bag, which took him a little time, one-handed. The *commandant* did not make a move to help, any more than Danglard had. Adamsberg offered to shake hands, but Trabelmann kept his arms firmly folded.

'Well, we may meet again one day, Trabelmann. When I bring you the judge's head on a trident.'

'Adamsberg, I was wrong.'

The *commissaire* looked up in surprise.

'Your ego isn't as big as a kitchen table, it's the size of Strasbourg Cathedral.'

'Which you don't like?'

'Affirmative.'

Adamsberg headed for the exit. In the office, the corridors and the hall, silence had fallen like a shower of rain, stifling all movement, voices or footsteps. Outside the doors, he saw the young duty officer, who took a few steps alongside him.

'*Commissaire*, that story about the bears?'

'Don't come with me, officer, or you might lose your job.'

He winked quickly at the young man and went off on foot, without any car to take him to the station. But unlike Vétilleux, the *commissaire* was not put off by a few kilometres; the walk was barely long enough for him to rid his mind of the new enemy whom Judge Fulgence had added to Adamsberg's collection.

XII

THE PARIS TRAIN WAS NOT DUE TO LEAVE FOR ANOTHER HOUR, SO Adamsberg decided, as if in defiance of Trabelmann, to pay a visit to the cathedral. He walked all the way round the outside, since according to the *commandant*, his ego was equal to the colossal dimensions of another era. Then he explored the nave and the side aisles, and took the trouble to read the notices. 'A Gothic edifice in the purest and most radical style.' What more could Trabelmann ask for? He looked up to the top of the spire, 'a masterpiece, soaring to a height of 142 metres'. Adamsberg had only just reached the regulation height to qualify for the police force.

In the train, when he went to the bar, the rows of miniature bottles brought his thoughts back to Vétilleux. By now, Trabelmann was no doubt pressing him to confess, like a dumb beast going to the slaughter. Unless, that is, Vétilleux was heeding his instructions, and resisting the pressure. It was odd how much he blamed the unknown Josie for having left Vétilleux, thus letting him slide down the slope, considering that Adamsberg himself had abandoned Camille at a moment's notice.

Back in the office, he was surprised by the smell of camphor, and stopped in the Council Chamber, where Noël, his shirt unbuttoned and his forehead resting on his arms, was having his neck massaged by *Lieutenant* Retancourt. She was kneading his flesh from the shoulders to the nape of the neck, with long circular movements which seemed to have reduced Noël to a state of childlike bliss. He jumped, when he realised the *commissaire* was in the room, and buttoned his shirt up hastily. Only Retancourt showed no embarrassment, and calmly put the top back on the tube of ointment, while briefly greeting Adamsberg.

'I'll be with you right away,' she said. 'Noël, no sudden neck movements for two or three days. And if you need to carry something heavy, use your left hand, not your right.'

Retancourt came over to Adamsberg, while Noël quickly left the room.

'With this cold snap,' she explained, 'you tend to get a lot of muscle spasms and stiff necks.'

'And you can cure them?'

'I'm not bad. I've prepared the dossiers for the Quebec mission, the forms have been sent off and the visas are ready. The plane tickets should be here the day after tomorrow.'

'Thank you, Retancourt. Is Danglard about?'

'He's waiting for you. He got a confession from the D'Hernoncourt daughter yesterday. The lawyer is going to plead temporary insanity, which seems to be pretty much the case.'

Danglard got up when Adamsberg walked in, and held out his hand, looking rather embarrassed.

'Well, at least you're prepared to shake my hand,' said Adamsberg with a smile. 'Trabelmann has stopped doing that. Pass me the D'Hernoncourt report to sign and congratulations on tying up the case.'

While the *commissaire* was signing the report, Danglard observed him closely, to see whether he was being ironic, since Adamsberg himself had refused to accept the baron's confession, and had told them to follow an alternative lead. But no, there was no sign of a sneer on his face, and the congratulations seemed to be sincere.

'So it didn't go too well at Schiltigheim?'

'Well, in one respect it went very well. A brand new carpenter's awl and a line of wounds 16.7 centimetres long and 0.8 wide. I told you, Danglard, always the same crossbar. The suspect is a poor homeless tramp, harmless and alcoholic, the ideal fall guy. Before the murder, an old man came along and gave him the fatal push. A so-called companion of the streets, but one who took his wine from a cup and wouldn't drink out of the same bottle as a down-and-out.'

'And in other respects?'

'Not good. Trabelmann's taken against me. He thinks I just follow my own nose and take no notice of anyone else. He regards Judge Fulgence as a national treasure. And in fact I'm a national treasure too, but not quite the same way.'

'What do you mean?'

Adamsberg smiled before replying.

'Strasbourg Cathedral. He says my ego is as big as the cathedral.'

Danglard gave a low whistle.

'One of the pinnacles of Gothic architecture,' he remarked, 'the spire reaches a height of 142 metres, built in 1439, the crowning achievement of Jean Hultz . . .'

With a gesture, Adamsberg interrupted the flow of erudition.

'Still,' concluded Danglard, 'that's quite something, isn't it? A Gothic edifice for an ego, an e-Gothic ego trip. Trabelmann's a bit of a joker, is he?'

'Yes, he can be. But just then he wasn't joking, and he kicked me out as if I was a complete time-waster. I have to say in his defence that he looked up the judge's dates and found out he had been dead sixteen years. He didn't like that. Some people get put off by that kind of thing.'

Adamsberg raised his hand again to ward off a comment from his deputy.

'Did it do any good?' he asked. 'The massage Retancourt gave you?'

Danglard felt his irritation mounting once more.

'Yes, I guessed,' Adamsberg confirmed. 'Your neck looks pink and you smell of camphor.'

'I had a stiff neck. It's not a crime, far as I know.'

'On the contrary. It's perfectly in order to get yourself treated and I admire Retancourt's talents. But if you don't mind, and since all that is signed off, I'm going for a walk. I'm tired.'

Danglard made no comment on the contradiction, which was typical of Adamsberg, nor did he try to have the last word. Since Adamsberg obviously wanted to have the last word, let him have it. This kind of verbal sparring wasn't going to resolve their quarrel.

In the Chapter Room, Adamsberg beckoned Noël over.

'Where are we with the Favre business?'

'He's been questioned by the *divisionnaire*, and suspended until the inquiry has concluded. You're to be questioned tomorrow at eleven o'clock in Brézillon's office.'

'I saw the note.'

'There wouldn't be any problem, if you hadn't smashed the bottle. Given the way he is, he couldn't know whether you were going to attack him with it or not.'

'Neither did I, Noël.'

'*What?*'

'Neither did I,' Adamsberg repeated calmly. 'At the time, I'm not sure what might have happened. I don't think I would have attacked him, but I'm not certain. Stupid bastard that he is, he just made me furious.'

'For Christ's sake, *commissaire*, don't say anything like that to Brézillon, or you've had it. Favre would be able to plead legitimate self-defence and as for you, who knows where it could go? You'd have lost all credibility, all authority, do you realise?'

'Yes, Noël,' Adamsberg replied, surprised by the level of solicitude unexpectedly being shown by his *lieutenant*. 'At the moment, I'm all on edge. I'm dealing with a ghost and it isn't easy.'

Noël was used to incomprehensible remarks from his superior officer, so he made no comment.

'But not a word to Brézillon,' he added anxiously. 'No introspection or attacks of conscience. Just say you broke the bottle to intimidate Favre. That you were going to drop it, naturally. That's what we all thought, and that's what we'll say.'

The *lieutenant* looked directly at Adamsberg, waiting for his agreement.

'Yes, very well, Noël.'

Shaking hands, Adamsberg had the curious feeling that their positions had momentarily been reversed.

XIII

ADAMSBERG WALKED THE COLD STREETS FOR A LONG TIME, HUGGING his coat round him, and still carrying his overnight bag. He crossed the Seine, then started walking uphill to the north, without any destination in mind, his thoughts jangling in his head. He would have liked to return to that moment of calm, three days earlier, when he had put his hand on the cold tank of the heating system. Ever since then, he seemed to have been at the centre of a series of explosions, like the toad with its cigarette. Several toads in fact, going off at short intervals. A cloud of entrails thrown in the air and raining down images of blood. The sudden appearance of the judge from the depths, the idea of the dead awakening, the three stab wounds in Schiltigheim, the hostility of his closest colleague, his brother's features, the spire of Strasbourg Cathedral (142 metres), the prince transformed into a dragon, the bottle brandished in Favre's face. And his outbursts of rage, against Danglard, against Favre, against Trabelmann, and insidiously, against Camille who had left him. No, that was wrong, he was the one who had left Camille. He was getting things the wrong way round, like the prince and the dragon. Getting angry with everyone. So, what you mean, Ferez would have said calmly, is that you're angry with yourself. Oh, go fuck yourself, Ferez.

He stopped walking when he realised that as he had zigzagged through the chaos of his thoughts, he had reached the point of wondering whether if you stuffed a dragon into the doors of Strasbourg Cathedral, the whole thing would explode, puff, puff, bang. He leaned against a lamp post, looked around to make sure no posters of Neptune were lying in wait for him, and passed his hand across his eyes. He was worn out and the injured arm was making him feverish. He swallowed two painkillers without water and looking around, saw that he had arrived at Clignancourt.

His way ahead was clear. Turning right, he set off for the tumbledown house of Clémentine Courbet, tucked away in a little sidestreet near the fleamarket. He had not seen the old woman for a year, since the case of the painted door signs. And he had not known if he would ever see her again.

He knocked at the wooden door, suddenly feeling happy, hoping the grandmotherly figure would be at home, bustling about in her kitchen or her attic. And that she would recognise him again.

The door opened to reveal a large woman in a flower-print dress covered with a faded blue overall.

'Oh, *commissaire*, I'm sorry, I can't shake hands,' Clémentine said holding out her forearm. 'I'm in the middle of cooking.'

Adamsberg shook the old woman's arm, and she wiped her floury hands on her apron before returning to the stove. He followed her in, feeling reassured. Nothing seemed to surprise Clémentine.

'Now come on in, put your bag down, and make yourself comfortable.'

Adamsberg sat on a kitchen chair and watched her at work. A sheet of pastry was rolled flat on the wooden table and Clémentine was cutting out rounds with a glass.

'Cookies for tomorrow, m'dear,' she explained, 'because I'm fresh out of them. Help yourself from the tin, there's a few left. And then can you pour us out two little glasses of port, that won't do you any harm.'

'You think I need it, Clémentine?'

'You're in trouble. Did you know, I've got the boy married now?'

'To Lizbeth?' asked Adamsberg, pouring out the port and helping himself to a biscuit.

'Yes, just a while back. What about you?'

'Ah well, I'm afraid it's the opposite for me.'

'Oh, now surely she wasn't giving you the run around, a nice man like you?'

'On the contrary.'

'Your fault then, was it?'

'Yes, my fault.'

'Well, it's very wrong of you,' announced the old woman, absorbing a third of her port. 'A lovely girl like that.'

'How do you know she's lovely, Clémentine?'

'I spent some time in your police station, m'dear. And in there, my word, they do gossip, they talk, you find things out.'

Clémentine put the biscuits in the oven of her old gas cooker, shut the creaking door, and watched them anxiously through the smoke-stained glass window.

'You know what it is, don't you, with men who run after girls, they cause trouble when they think they're in danger of being hooked, don't they? And then they blame their poor sweetheart.'

'What do you mean, Clémentine?'

'Well, now, if they've really fallen for someone, it makes it more difficult to run around. So the poor sweetheart, they take it out on her.'

'And how do they do that?'

'What do you think, m'dear? They let her know good and proper that they're cheating on her, right and left. And it's not going to stop. So then the wee girl, she starts crying, and oh no, he doesn't like that a bit. Of course not, nobody likes making people cry. So then, he walks out.'

'And what happens next?' asked Adamsberg, hanging on her words as if the old woman were recounting him some fantastic epic.

'Well, then he's in trouble, isn't he? Now he's lost his true love. Because running around's one thing, and loving someone's another. Not the same at all.'

'Why not?'

'Because running around doesn't make a man happy. But being in love stops him running. So the man, he goes first one way then the other, and never really happy either. And the poor girl pays for it, but then after that, so does he.'

Clémentine opened the oven door, glanced in and shut it again.

'You're quite right, Clémentine.'

'Takes no magician to tell you that,' remarked Clémentine, wiping the table. 'I'm going to start the pork now.'

'But Clémentine, why does he still keep running after other girls?'

The old woman stopped, resting her large fists on the table.

'Because it's easier, that's why. You love someone, you've got to give something, haven't you now, but if all you want's a good time, you don't have to. Would you like beans with your pork chop, I've topped and tailed them myself?'

'You're asking me to supper?'

'It's supper time, isn't it? Man's got to eat, you're all skin and bone.'

'But I can't take the pork chop you were going to eat yourself.'

'Ah, but I've got two.'

'You knew I was coming?'

'I'm not a fortune teller, m'dear. But I've got a friend staying just now. Only she won't be in till late. And I was a bit bothered, tell you the truth, about the chops. I would have eaten the other one tomorrow, but I don't care to eat pork twice running. Don't know why, I just don't. I'll put a bit more wood on the stove, can you watch my oven?'

The sitting room, which was small and crowded with armchairs covered in faded fabric, was heated only by a fireplace. For the rest of the house there were two woodburning stoves. The temperature in the sitting room, when he went in was not more than 15 degrees. Adamsberg laid the table while Clémentine banked up the fire.

'We won't eat in the kitchen,' Clémentine forestalled him, bringing in the plates. 'For once when I've got fancy company, we're going to be nice and comfy in the sitting room. Drink your port, it'll buck you up.'

Adamsberg obeyed unquestioningly and indeed soon found himself perfectly comfortable at the table in the sitting room, his back to a blazing fire. Clémentine filled his plate and poured, without asking, a full glass of wine for him. She tucked a flowery napkin under her chin and gave one to Adamsberg who did the same.

'I'm going to cut up your meat, m'dear,' she said. 'With that arm, you can't do it. Is that what you're thinking about?'

'No, Clémentine. I'm not thinking much at all at the moment.'

'Ah, not thinking, that can get you into trouble. You must try and put your thinking cap on, my little Adamsberg. You don't mind if I call you that, my dear?'

'No, no, of course not.'

'Now then, that's enough of my fussing. What's been happening to you? Apart from your sweetheart.'

'I've just been going for everybody at the moment.'

'That's how you hurt your arm?'

'Yes.'

'Not that I'm against a good fight now and then, it calms things down sometimes. But if it's not your usual way, you must put your thinking cap on. Maybe you're unhappy on account of the girlfriend, or maybe it's something else, or maybe it's everything at once. Not going to leave that pork, are you? You just clear that plate, please. You don't eat and then you're surprised you're all skin and bone. I'm going to fetch the rice pudding.'

She put a dessert bowl in front of Adamsberg.

'If I had hold of you a week or two, I'd soon fatten you up. Is it something else that's bothering you?'

'A dead man come to life, Clémentine.'

'Ha. If that's all it is, it's easier than love affairs. So what's he done?'

'He killed eight people in the past, and now he's started again. With a trident.'

'And when did he die?'

'Sixteen years ago.'

'And where did he start again?'

'Near Strasbourg, last Saturday night. A young girl.'

'She hadn't done him any harm, the young girl?'

'She didn't know him at all. He's a monster, Clémentine, a handsome but very frightening monster.'

'You'll be right about that. Killing nine people you don't know? No, that's no way to carry on.'

'But nobody will believe me. Nobody at all.'

'Sometimes people don't want to listen, and you can't make 'em. And if you try, you'll end up with your nerves all frazzled.'

'Yes, Clémentine, you're right.'

'So we won't bother with all those other people, who won't believe it,' said Clémentine, lighting her roll-up cigarette. 'And you're going to tell me all about it. Let's pull our chairs up closer to the fire. We weren't expecting it to be so cold, were we? It's from the North Pole, they do say.'

Adamsberg took over an hour to explain all the facts carefully to Clémentine, without knowing quite why he was doing it. They were interrupted only by the arrival of Clémentine's friend, a woman almost as old as she was, about eighty. Unlike Clémentine, she was thin, fragile and vulnerable-looking, her face a network of fine wrinkles.

'Josette, this is the *commissaire* I told you about before. Don't be afraid, he's not the nasty one.'

Adamsberg noted Josette's dyed ash-blonde hair, her tailored suit and pearl earrings, the remnants of a long-lost bourgeois existence. By contrast, on her large feet she wore a pair of tennis shoes. Josette made a timid greeting and scuttled away into the so-called office, which was littered with computers belonging to Clémentine's grandson.

'What's she afraid of?' asked Adamsberg.

'And you a policeman,' sighed Clémentine.

'Sorry.'

'We're talking about your worries, my dear, not Josette's. It was a good idea to say you were playing cards with your brother. The simple ideas are often the best. And tell me now, did you leave that screwdriver in the pool? Because sooner or later, someone would fish it up.'

Adamsberg carried on, regularly feeding the fire and blessing whichever fair wind had driven him to take refuge with Clémentine.

'Stupid idiot, your *gendarme*,' Clémentine concluded, throwing away her cigarette end into the fire. 'Anybody knows Prince Charming *does* sometimes turn into a beast. He can't be very bright, not to see that.'

Adamsberg relaxed back on the old sofa, holding his injured arm across his stomach. 'Ten minutes shuteye, Clémentine, and then I'm on my way.'

'I can see he's worn you out, this dead man walking. And you're not out of the wood yet. But follow your hunch, my little Adamsberg. It might not be all right, but it might not be all wrong either.'

By the time Clémentine turned round from stirring the fire, Adamsberg had fallen into a deep sleep. The old woman picked up a tartan rug from a chair and placed it over him.

She met Josette on her way to bed.

'He's sleeping on the sofa,' she explained. 'He's got a tale to tell, that one. What bothers me, he's all skin and bone, these days, did you see?'

'I wouldn't know Clemmie, I've never seen him before.'

'Well, I'm telling you, he needs feeding up.'

The *commissaire* was drinking his morning coffee in the kitchen with Clémentine.

'I'm so sorry, Clémentine, I didn't realise.'

'No trouble, my dear. If you slept, it was because you needed to. Now eat up another piece of bread. And if you're going to see the boss, you better get smartened up. I'm going to give your jacket and trousers a bit of an iron, you can't go in there with them all crumpled like that.'

Adamsberg passed his hand over his chin.

'Take one of my boy's razors from the bathroom,' she said, carrying off his clothes.

XIV

AT TEN O'CLOCK, ADAMSBERG LEFT CLIGNANCOURT, WELL BREAK-fasted, shaved, with his clothes ironed, and his mind temporarily smoothed out by Clémentine's exceptional care. At eighty-six, the old woman was capable of giving herself without stinting. And what could he do? He would bring her a present from Quebec. They probably had some nice warm clothes there you can't get in Paris. A cosy bearskin jacket or some elkskin slippers – something unusual, like Clémentine herself.

Before presenting himself to the *divisionnaire*, he tried to go over *Lieutenant* Noël's anxious warnings, which Clémentine had backed up. 'Telling lies to yourself, that's one thing, but telling lies to the *flics*, well, sometimes you have to. No point giving yourself the third degree over a matter of honour. Honour, that's your own business, nothing to do with the cops.'

Divisionnaire Brézillon appreciated, from the point of view of statistics, the results achieved by *Commissaire* Adamsberg, which were much better than those of his other police chiefs. But he had no great sympathy for the man, or for his manner. Nevertheless, he well remembered the terrible fallout from the recent affair of the painted door signs, which had reached such proportions that the Ministry of the Interior had been on the point of making him resign as the scapegoat. Being a man of the law, extremely attentive to the scales of justice, Brézillon knew what he owed Jean-Baptiste Adamsberg, who had solved that case. But this set-to with a subordinate was embarrassing, and especially surprising on the part of someone who was usually such a cool customer. He had listened to what Favre had to say, and the obtuse vulgarity of the junior officer had deeply displeased him. He had heard six eyewitnesses, who had all doggedly defended Adamsberg. But the detail of the broken bottle was particularly serious. Adamsberg was not without enemies in the police disciplinary commission, and Brézillon's voice would swing the balance.

The *commissaire* gave him a sober version of the events. The broken glass had been intended to frighten Favre after his insubordination, simply a warning shot. 'Warning shot', was a term that had come to Adamsberg as he walked back to headquarters, and he thought it fitted his economical dealing with the truth. Brézillon listened to him with a grave face, and Adamsberg sensed that he was on the whole inclined to help him out of this mess. But it was clear that the matter was not closed.

'I'm giving you a serious warning, *commissaire*,' said Brézillon, taking his leave. 'The committee won't give a ruling for a month or so. In that time, I don't want to see the slightest stepping out of line, no fuss or bother, no escapades. Keep a low profile, hear me?'

Adamsberg nodded agreement.

'And congratulations on the D'Hernoncourt case,' he added. 'Your arm's not going to stop you leading the team to Quebec?'

'No, the police doctor's given me all I need.'

'When do you leave?'

'Four days from now.'

'No bad thing. Time for your name to be forgotten for a bit.'

With this ambiguous dismissal, Adamsberg left the Quai des Orfèvres: 'Keep a low profile.'

Trabelmann would have laughed at that. The spire of Strasbourg Cathedral, 142 metres high. 'At least you gave me something to laugh about, Adamsberg, there's that about it.'

* * *

By two o'clock, the seven other members of the Quebec mission were assembled for their technical and disciplinary briefing. Adamsberg had distributed reproductions of the different ranks and badges of the RCMP, though he had not yet memorised them himself.

'Generally speaking, try to avoid mistakes over rank,' he began. 'Learn these insignia off by heart. You'll be dealing with corporals, sergeants, inspectors and superintendents. Don't mix them up. The officer who will be meeting us is Superintendent Aurèle Laliberté, that's all one word, not La-space-Liberté.'

There were a few chuckles.

'That's exactly what you have to avoid. No sniggers. Québécois surnames and first names are different from French ones. You may find officers called Lafrance or Louisseize. You may meet officers younger than you, with first names you don't find these days in France, like Ginette and Philibert. And no mocking of the accent. When French-Canadians speak quickly, you may have difficulty following. And they use different expressions. So no stupid remarks please, or you'll discredit the whole mission.'

'The Québécois,' interrupted Danglard, in his gentle voice, 'consider France as their mother country, but they don't much like the French, or trust them. They find us arrogant, condescending and mocking, not entirely wrongly, because a lot of French people treat Quebec as if it was some kind of backward province full of country bumpkins and lumber-jacks.'

'I'm counting on you,' Adamsberg added, 'not to act like tourists, and especially not like Parisian tourists, talking in loud voices and criticising everything.'

'Where are we staying?' asked Noël.

'In a building in Hull, which is about six kilometres from the RCMP base. You'll each have a room with a view over the river and the Canada geese. We'll have some staff cars between us. Over there, no one walks anywhere, they all drive.'

The briefing lasted another hour or so, then the group dispersed in a contented buzz of voices, with the exception of Danglard who dragged himself out of the room like a condemned man, pale with apprehension. If by some miracle the starlings didn't get into the starboard engine on the way out, the Canada geese would find their way into the port engine on the way back. And a goose is bigger than a starling. Well, everything's bigger in Canada.

XV

ADAMSBERG SPENT MOST OF THE SATURDAY TELEPHONING ESTATE agents on the long list he had drawn up for the country round Strasbourg, leaving out the city itself. It was a tedious task, and he had to ask the same question every time. Had an elderly man, living alone, rented or bought, at some time unspecified, a property on your books, or more precisely a large isolated mansion? And if so, had the said tenant or owner either given up the lease, or put the property on the market very recently?

Until he had given up the chase, sixteen years earlier, Adamsberg's accusations had sufficiently worried the Trident to make him leave the region after a murder, thus slipping through the policeman's fingers. Adamsberg wondered whether, even after his death, the judge had retained this prudent reflex. The various residences Adamsberg had known about previously had all been grand and isolated mansions. The judge had acquired a considerable private fortune, and had usually bought his new lodgings rather than rented, since Fulgence preferred not to have a land-lord spying on him.

Adamsberg could easily guess how he had acquired his wealth. Fulgence's remarkable talents, his penetrating analysis of the law, his exceptional skill and memory for precedents, all accompanied by his striking and charismatic looks, had brought him fame and popularity. He had the reputation of being 'the man who knows everything', rather like St Louis sitting under his oak tree dispensing justice. And he was as

93

well-known to the general public as to his colleagues, who were outflanked or irritated by his excessive influence. As a respectable magistrate, he never formally overstepped the boundaries of the law or the professional code of conduct. But if he so chose during a trial, it took only a subtle expression or gesture on his part for it to be known what he thought, and the rumour would quickly circulate, so that juries followed him unanimously. Adamsberg imagined that the families of many a suspect, or even other magistrates, might have made it worth the judge's while for the rumour to go one way or the other.

He had been doggedly telephoning estate agents for over four hours without any positive sighting. Until his forty-second call, when a young man told him he had handled a gentleman's residence, set in parkland, deep in the country between Haguenau and Brumath.

'How far is it from Strasbourg?'

'About twenty-three kilometres to the north as the crow flies.'

The buyer, a Monsieur Maxime Leclerc, had bought the property, known as *Das Schloss*, the Castle, about four years earlier, but he had put it on the market only twenty-four hours ago, for urgent health reasons. He had moved out very quickly and the agency had just picked up the keys.

'Did he give them to you himself? Did you see him?'

'He got the cleaning woman to leave them with us. Nobody at the agency has ever clapped eyes on him. The sale was carried out by his lawyer, by correspondence, and by sending the ID papers and signatures to and fro by post. M. Leclerc was unable to do it in person, as he was recovering from an operation.'

'Ah,' said Adamsberg, simply.

'It's quite legal, *commissaire*. If the papers are certified in order by the police.'

'And the cleaning lady, do you have her name and address?'

'Madame Coutellier in Brumath. I'll get her number for you.'

* * *

Denise Coutellier had to shout into her phone to rise above the sound of children playing.

'Madame Coutellier, can you describe your employer for me?' asked Adamsberg, also at the top of his voice, in unconscious imitation.

'Well, you see, *commissaire*,' she said, 'I never used to see the gentleman face to face. I would go in for three hours on Mondays and again on Thursdays, same time as the gardener. I left a meal all ready for him and I got in groceries for the other days. He told me he would be away a lot, he had business to see to. He was something to do with the trade tribunal.'

Of course, thought Adamsberg. A spectre is invisible.

'Were there any books in the house?'

'Plenty of them, *commissaire*. What they were I couldn't say.'

'Newspapers?'

'He had them delivered, a daily paper and the *Nouvelles d'Alsace*.'

'Did he get much mail?'

'I couldn't say, sir, and his desk was kept locked. I expect with the tribunal papers and all that, it had to be. I was surprised when he left so suddenly. He left me a very nice letter saying thank you and good wishes, with all kinds of instructions and a generous final payment.'

'What instructions?'

'I was to come back this Saturday and do a thorough clean of the house, however long it took, because the *Schloss* was going to be sold. Then I had to take the keys to the agency. I've just got back from there now.'

'Was this note handwritten?'

'Oh no. Monsieur Leclerc always typed his messages, I suppose because he'd do that in his job.'

Adamsberg was about to hang up when the woman went on:

'It's not easy to describe him, because I only ever saw him the once, and then not for long. And that was about four years ago.'

'When he moved in, you mean? You saw him then?'

'Of course. You can't work for someone you've never seen, can you?'

'Madame Coutellier,' said Adamsberg, quickening his voice, 'can you be as precise as possible?'

'Has he done something wrong?'

'On the contrary.'

'I was going to say, that would surprise me. Such a nice careful gentleman, so particular. It's a pity his health has let him down. Let me see, as far as I remember, he was about sixty. He was, well, just normal-looking.'

'Try, all the same. Height, weight, colour of hair.'

'Just a minute, *commissaire*.' Denise Coutellier hushed the children and came back to the telephone.

'Not all that tall, rather plump, with a good colour. His hair, oh I think it was grey, going a bit bald on top. He was wearing a brown corduroy suit and a tie, I always remember what people wear.'

'Hang on, I'm just noting all this down.'

'But you know, now you ask me, I'm not all that sure,' cried the woman, who was having to shout again. 'Memory can play tricks on you, can't it? I said just now he wasn't very tall, but I may have got that wrong. Because his suits were bigger than I remembered him. Let's say they would fit a man of about one metre eighty, not seventy. Perhaps it was because he was plump, so I thought he was smaller. And I said he had grey hair, but when I was cleaning the bathroom or doing the laundry, I only found white hairs. But then of course he probably turned whiter over the four years, old age comes on quickly, doesn't it? So that's why I'm saying my memory may be playing me false.'

'Madame Coutellier, are there any outbuildings in the chateau?'

'There's the old stables, a barn, and a summer house. But that was empty and I didn't have to go there. He kept his car in the stables and the gardener used the barn for his tools.'

'Can you tell me the colour or the make of his car?'

'No, I never saw it, *commissaire*, because the gentleman was always out when I was working there, and I didn't have any keys for any of the outbuildings.'

'In the house itself, madame,' said Adamsberg, thinking of his precious trident, 'did you have access to all the rooms?'

'Yes, except for the attic which was kept locked. M. Leclerc said it wasn't worth wasting my time up there in all the dust.'

Bluebeard's lair, Trabelmann would have said. The locked room, the chamber of horrors.

Adamsberg looked at his watch. Or rather at his watches. The one he had bought himself about two years before, and the second one which Camille had given him in Lisbon, a man's watch that she had won at a street fair. He had wanted to put it on, to celebrate their finding each other again, and yet a day later, he had left her. Since then, curiously, he had not removed this second watch, a sporty waterproof model, with all sorts of buttons, chronometers and dials that Adamsberg couldn't work. One of them apparently told you how long it would take after the flash before you were struck by lightning. Very handy, Adamsberg thought. But he hadn't abandoned his own watch, which had a worn leather strap and joggled against the second one. So for a year now, he had had two watches on his wrist. All his colleagues had pointed this out, and he had informed them that he too had noticed. He had kept his two watches on the go, without really knowing why, which meant a bit of extra fiddling at bedtime and in the morning, taking them off and putting them back on.

One of the watches said one minute to three, the other four minutes past. Camille's was always faster than the other, and Adamsberg had never bothered to check which was right, or to set them properly. He liked them to be different and calculated what the average was between the two, assuming that to be the right time. It was therefore one and a half minutes past three. He had just time to catch the train back to Strasbourg.

The young man from the estate agent had astonished-looking green eyes, which reminded him of Estalère. He picked Adamsberg up at the station in Haguenau at 18.47 and drove him out to the *Schloss* once inhabited by Maxime Leclerc, a large property surrounded by a pine forest.

'No nosy neighbours to spy on one here then?' said Adamsberg, as they visited each of the rooms in the deserted house.

'Monsieur Leclerc had specified that he valued his peace and quiet above everything else. He was a very solitary gentleman. We come across people like him in this job.'

'What do you think? Did he dislike other people?'

'Perhaps he'd had an unhappy life,' suggested the young man, 'and preferred to live in an isolated place. Madame Coutellier said he had a lot of books. It takes them that way sometimes.'

With the young man's help, since his arm was still in a sling, Adamsberg spent some time taking fingerprints, from places which he hoped Madame Coutellier had not dusted too energetically, on the doorhandles and latches and on light switches. The almost empty attic had a floor of rough wooden planks, which made it difficult to detect changes. But the first six metres did not look as if they had remained entirely untouched for four years, and there seemed to be slight irregularities in the thickness of the dust. Under one beam, a vague line was discernible on the dark floor, where it was slightly lighter. It was probably too uncertain to base anything on, but if the man had put a trident down anywhere, it could have been there, where the handle had left a fleeting trace. Adamsberg paid special attention to the huge bathroom. Madame Coutellier had been very thorough in her cleaning that morning, but the size of the room left him some leeway. In the narrow gap between the foot of the handbasin and the wall, he found a little dust, containing several white hairs.

The young man, patient and amazed, opened up the barn for him, and the stables. The earth floor had been brushed, removing any trace of tyres. Maxime Leclerc had vanished with the ethereal evanescence of a ghost.

The windows of the little summer house were covered with grime, but it wasn't abandoned as Madame Coutellier had thought. Just as Adamsberg hoped, a few signs betrayed that it had been used on occasion. The dust on the floor had been disturbed, there was a clean wicker chair, and on the only shelf there were traces which could have been left by piles of books. It was most likely here that Maxime Leclerc had hidden away for the three hours on Mondays and Thursdays, reading in his armchair, out of sight of the cleaning lady or the gardener. The armchair and solitary reading reminded Adamsberg of the way his own father would read the paper, smoking a pipe. A whole generation of men had smoked pipes, and he remembered very clearly that the judge had owned one, a meerschaum, as his mother had said admiringly.

'Can you smell it?' he asked the young man. 'The smell of sweet pipe tobacco?'

Here, the table, the chair, the doorhandles had all been very carefully wiped, with a thoroughness which was eloquent. Unless, that is, as Danglard would have said, nothing at all had been wiped, because dead men leave no prints, do they? Although apparently they read books, like other people.

It was after nine o'clock when Adamsberg sent his guide home, the young man having seen it as his duty to drive him to Strasbourg station, since trains did not stop at Haguenau so late in the evening. As it happened, he had a train leaving in six minutes, so had no time to go and see whether a dragon had managed to block the main door of the cathedral. People would have noticed, Adamsberg said to himself.

On the return journey, he took notes, putting down in any order the details he had noticed in the *Schloss*. The four years Maxime Leclerc had spent there appeared to have been marked by the utmost discretion: it was as if the house's owner had evaporated, significantly, into thin air.

The plump man whom Madame Coutellier had met could not have been Maxime Leclerc himself, but one of his henchmen instead, entrusted with this brief task. The judge exerted power over a considerable cohort of people, a fragmented network which he had built up over his long years on the bench. A suspended sentence here, a light sentence there, a fact pushed under the carpet, so that the accused would emerge either with an acquittal or a much reduced prison term. But by the same token, he would join that collection of men in his debt, whom Fulgence would later use for some purpose. This network extended into the criminal world as well as into the bourgeoisie, business circles, the magistrature and even the police. Procuring false identity papers in the name of Maxime Leclerc would present no problems for the Trident, and he could dispatch his accomplices all over France if need be. Or he could assemble a group to help him organise a midnight flit. None of his hostages could escape from the judge's thrall without revealing the original deception and risking a fresh trial. It must be one of these ex-accused who had come along to impersonate the house's owner for the cleaning lady. Then Judge Fulgence had taken possession of the *Schloss* under the name of Leclerc.

Adamsberg could understand why the judge would make plans to move out. But the abruptness of the operation surprised him. Such extreme haste in abandoning the house and putting it on the market seemed to fit uneasily with Fulgence's normal powers of prediction. Unless, that is, something unexpected had cropped up to surprise him. It certainly wasn't any inquiry from Trabelmann, who had no idea who he was.

Adamsberg frowned. What was it that Danglard had said about the judge's name, his identity? Something in Latin, like the village priest. Adamsberg felt unable to telephone his deputy who, whether because of Camille, the living dead, or the Boeing, was becoming more and more hostile to him every day. He decided to follow Clémentine's advice, and put his thinking cap on. It must have been in his flat, after the bottle incident. Danglard was knocking back the gin and had said the name Fulgence suited the judge 'down to the ground'. And Adamsberg had agreed.

Fulgence, *fulgur*, lightning, that was it, *l'éclair*. Le Clair, Leclerc, sounded the same. And if Adamsberg was not mistaken, Maxime must mean 'the biggest', like maximum. The biggest flash of lightning. Judge Fulgence wouldn't be satisfied with a humble pseudonym.

The train was braking to enter the Gare de l'Est in Paris. Pride comes before a fall, thought Adamsberg. That's how he would get him. If his own cathedral was 142 metres high, something which had yet to be ascertained, Fulgence's must reach to the sky. Laying down the law up there, throwing down his golden sickles in the fields full of stars. Throwing

Adamsberg's brother, like so many others, before the courts and then into prison. He suddenly felt very small. 'Keep a low profile,' Brézillon had ordered. Well, he would do just that, but he did have in his bag a few white hairs from a dead man's head.

XVI

ON TUESDAY 14 OCTOBER, THE EIGHT MEMBERS OF THE QUEBEC mission were waiting to board their Boeing 747, take-off scheduled for 16.40, estimated arrival time midnight, or 18.00, local time. Adamsberg knew just how much that term 'estimated', repeated by the reassuring voices over the loudspeakers, was piercing Danglard with sick apprehension. He had been watching him attentively for the couple of hours that they had been waiting at Roissy-Charles-de-Gaulle airport.

The rest of the team was regressing into teenage behaviour, disoriented by the unusual context, as if they were off on a school trip. He glanced at *Lieutenant* Froissy, a sharp-witted woman, but still subject to an attack of depression, occasioned by an unhappy love affair, according to what he had heard in the Chat Room. Although she was not joining in the rather infantile rowdiness of her colleagues, the break from routine seemed to distract her and he had seen her smile a few times. But the same could not be said for Danglard. Nothing seemed to rouse the *capitaine* from his sombre prognostications. His long and already lethargic body seemed to have become almost invertebrate as the time of departure approached. His legs no longer appeared able to carry him, and he had shrunk back into the curved metal seat, as if it were moulded to him. Adamsberg had seen him three times fish in his pocket and produce a pill which he then thrust between his bloodless lips.

Danglard's colleagues, since they were aware of his fear of flying, were being deliberately discreet. The scrupulous Justin, who always hesitated to give an opinion, in case he offended someone or altered their ideas, was by turns re-telling standard jokes and pretending frantically to revise the ranks and insignia of the Québécois police. He was the opposite of Noël, who always rushed in where angels fear to tread. Any kind of movement was a good thing as far as Noël was concerned, so he was looking forward to the trip, as was Voisenet. The ex-chemist and naturalist was hoping to pick up plenty of scientific information on the visit, but also to explore the geology and fauna of Canada. In Retancourt's case, there was no problem of course, since she was adaptability personified, always adjusting to the demands of any situation. As for the young and timid Estalère, his large green eyes with their perpetual look of amazement were always on the alert for some new surprising curiosity. In short, Adamsberg thought, they all found some form of release or advantage in the expedition, which contributed to the noisy collective excitement.

All except Danglard, that is. His five children had been left in the care of his generous neighbour on the sixth floor, along with the cat, and on that front everything was under control, except the prospect of leaving them orphans. Adamsberg tried to think of some way of rescuing his deputy from his increasing panic, but the growing coolness between them left him little room for manoeuvre in trying to comfort him. Or perhaps, Adamsberg thought, he ought to try a different tack: provoke him and force him to react. What better way than to tell him about the visit to the phantom of the *Schloss*? That would certainly make Danglard angry, and anger is much more stimulating and distracting than fear. He had been thinking about this for a moment or two, smiling to himself, when their flight for Montreal-Dorval was called, bringing them all to their feet.

They were seated in a compact group in the middle of the plane, and Adamsberg saw to it that Danglard was seated to his right, as far as possible from a window. The safety instructions which were mimed by a smiling flight attendant, explaining what to do if there was a loss of pressure, or a landing on water, and how to evacuate the aircraft via the escape chutes, did not help at all. Danglard fumbled under his seat for his lifejacket.

'Don't bother,' said Adamsberg. 'If there really was any trouble, you'd be sucked out through the window without even being conscious, and disappear like the toad. Puff, puff, bang.'

This kind remark failed to bring a smile to the *capitaine*'s face.

When the plane stopped to rev up to full power, Adamsberg really thought he was going to lose his deputy, just like the damned toad. Danglard survived take-off by clinging to the armrests. Adamsberg waited till the plane had finished its ascent before trying to distract him.

'Look,' he explained, 'you have your own TV screen. They put on some good films. There's a cultural channel too. See here,' he added, consulting the programme. 'There's a documentary about the precursors of the Italian Renaissance. That's for you, isn't it? The Italian Renaissance?'

'Already know all that stuff,' muttered Danglard, his expression fixed, his fingers still gripping the armrests.

'Even the precursors?'

'Know all that too.'

'If you switch on your radio, there's a debate about Hegel's aesthetics, it says here. What about that?'

'Know all about that too,' Danglard repeated gloomily. So if neither the precursors nor Hegel could captivate Danglard, the situation was indeed desperate, Adamsberg thought. He glanced at his neighbour on the other side, Hélène Froissy, who had turned towards the window and was already fast asleep, or else lost in sad thoughts.

'Danglard, do you know what I did on Saturday?' Adamsberg asked.

'Don't give a damn, Adamsberg.'

'I went to visit the last known residence of our deceased judge, near Strasbourg, a residence that he left like a thief in the night, six days after the Schiltigheim murder.'

In the *capitaine*'s distraught features, Adamsberg thought he could detect a slight flicker of interest.

'I'll tell you about it.'

Adamsberg dragged out his account, omitting none of the details, the Bluebeard's attic, the stable, the summer house, the bathroom, and taking care to refer to the owner only as 'the judge', 'the dead man', or 'the spectre'. Although the tale did not quite manage to provoke anger, it did stimulate a sort of irritable interest on the *capitaine*'s face.

'Interesting, eh?' said Adamsberg. 'A man who's invisible to everyone, an impalpable presence?'

'Just some recluse,' Danglard objected in a distant voice.

'Yes, but a recluse who systematically wipes out all his traces? Who leaves behind, and then only by accident, a few stray hairs, snow-white incidentally.'

'You can't do anything with those hairs,' muttered Danglard.

'Yes, I can, Danglard, I can compare them.'

'With what?'

'With those in the judge's grave, in Richelieu. I'd just have to apply for an exhumation. Hair survives a long time, so with a bit of luck . . .'

'What's that noise?' interrupted Danglard in a changed voice. 'That whistling sound?'

'It's just the cabin pressure, it's normal.'

Danglard subsided in his seat with a long sigh.

'But I couldn't remember what you told me about the meaning of "Fulgence",' Adamsberg said, untruthfully.

'It comes from *fulgur*, lightning or a thunderbolt,' Danglard could not resist replying. 'Or from the verb *fulgeo*: to shine, dazzle, light up. In a figurative sense to be brilliant, illustrious, to shine forth brightly.'

Adamsberg registered mentally the new meanings his deputy was reeling off with erudition.

'And what about "Maxime"?'

'Don't tell me you don't know that,' grumbled Danglard. 'It's *maximus*, of course, the biggest or most important.'

'I didn't tell you the name our man used when he bought the *Schloss*. Would you like to know?'

'No.'

In fact, Danglard was perfectly aware of the efforts Adamsberg was making to distract him from his panic, and although he found the *Schloss* story irritating, he was grateful for this kindness. Only another six hours twelve minutes to go. They were over the Atlantic by now and would be for some time.

'Well, it was Maxime Leclerc. What do you say to that?'

'That Leclerc is one of the commonest surnames in France.'

'You're just trying not to see it. Maxime Leclerc: the biggest, the most brilliant, the most dazzling. The judge couldn't resign himself to some ordinary name.'

'You can play games with names just as you can with numbers. You can make them mean anything you like. There's no end to it.'

'If you weren't so wedded to your bloody rationality,' Adamsberg insisted, trying to be provocative, 'you'd have to admit that I've got some interesting things to say about this Schiltigheim business.'

The *commissaire* at this point stopped a benevolent attendant who was passing with a tray of glasses of champagne, unnoticed (remarkably) by the *capitaine*. Since Froissy had refused hers, he took two glasses and placed them in Danglard's hands.

'Drink these,' he ordered. 'Both of them, but one at a time, like you promised.'

Danglard made a slight nod of gratitude.

'Because from my point of view, it may not be all right, but it may not be all wrong.'

'Who says?'

'Clémentine Courbet. Remember her? I went to see her.'

'If you're going to start quoting the sayings of Clémentine Courbet as your new bible, the whole squad is going to hell in a handcart.'

'Don't be so pessimistic, Danglard. But it's true, one can play with names ad infinitum. Mine for instance. Adamsberg, Adam's mountain, the First Man. That's good, isn't it? And on a mountain as well. I wonder. Perhaps it was because of that, that ...'

'The stuff about Strasbourg Cathedral,' Danglard cut him off.

'Got it in one. And what about your name, Danglard, what does it mean?'

'It's the name of the traitor in *The Count of Monte Cristo*. A real bastard.'

'That's interesting.'

'Actually, there's more to it,' added Danglard, having downed the two glasses of champagne. 'It was originally D'Anglard, and Anglard comes from the Germanic Angil-hard.'

'And that means? You'll have to translate it for me.'

'Angil has two roots, meaning "sword" and "angel". As for hard, it means, well, "hard".'

'So you're a sort of inflexible angel with a sword. That's a lot better than the poor old First Man waving from the top of a mountain. Even Strasbourg Cathedral would be impressed by an Avenging Angel. Anyway, its door's blocked.'

'What do you mean?'

'By a dragon.'

Adamsberg glanced at his watches. Another five hours forty-four and a half minutes to go. He thought he was doing quite well, but how much longer could he carry on? He had never had to talk for seven hours running before.

Suddenly all his good work was interrupted by a set of red signals going on at the front of the cabin. 'What's the matter?' asked Danglard in alarm.

'Seat-belt sign.'

'Why are they putting on the seat-belt sign?'

'Oh, just a bit of turbulence that's all, it's going to be a bit bumpy.'

Adamsberg prayed to the First Man on his mountain to see to it that the turbulence was minor. But the First Man obviously didn't give a damn about him. Unfortunately the turbulence was particularly rough, making the plane plummet into air pockets several metres deep. Even the most blasé passengers stopped reading their books, the cabin crew were obliged to take their seats, and a young woman screamed. Danglard had closed his eyes and was hyperventilating. Hélène Froissy looked at him anxiously. On a sudden inspiration, Adamsberg turned to Retancourt who was sitting behind the *capitaine*.

'Retancourt,' he whispered, between the seats, 'Danglard's in a bad way. Can you do some kind of massage to send him off to sleep? Or can you think of any other way of knocking him out, or sedating him, or something?'

Retancourt nodded, which didn't altogether surprise Adamsberg.

'Yes, I can,' she said, 'as long as he doesn't know it's me.'

Adamsberg nodded.

'Danglard,' he said, taking his hand, 'keep your eyes shut, one of the cabin staff is going to look after you.'

He signalled to Retancourt that she could start.

'Undo his top three shirt buttons,' she whispered, loosening her seat-belt.

Then, with her fingertips moving in a rapid pianistic dance, Retancourt set to work on Danglard's neck, following the spinal column and moving to the temples. Observing the manoeuvre as the plane continued to lurch, Froissy and Adamsberg looked by turns at Retancourt's hands and at Danglard's face. The *capitaine*'s breathing seemed to slow down, then his features relaxed, and less than fifteen minutes later, he was asleep.

'Did he take any sedatives?' Retancourt asked, slowly removing her fingers from the *capitaine*'s neck.

'A cartload,' Adamsberg replied.

Retancourt looked at her watch.

'He probably didn't sleep a wink last night. He should sleep for at least four hours now, we can relax. By the time he wakes up we'll be over Newfoundland. Being over land is more reassuring.'

Adamsberg and Froissy exchanged glances.

'She is so amazing,' whispered Froissy. 'If she had boyfriend trouble, she'd just crush it like an insect underfoot.'

'Love affairs are never insects, Froissy. They're always walls, ten metres high. It's no dishonour to find them hard to climb.'

'Thanks for that,' Froissy whispered.

'You know, *lieutenant*, Retancourt doesn't like me.'

Froissy did not dissent.

'Has she ever said why?' he asked.

'No, she never says anything about you at all.'

A steeple of 142 metres can wobble, just because the incredible hulk Retancourt never finds it necessary to mention you, thought Adamsberg. He glanced at Danglard. Sleep was bringing the colour back to his cheeks and the turbulence was subsiding.

* * *

The plane was on its final approach when the *capitaine* woke up, looking surprised.

'It was the flight attendant,' Adamsberg explained. 'She's a specialist. Luckily, she's going to be on the return flight too. We land in twenty minutes.'

Apart from two brief scares when the undercarriage came down and when the air brakes went on, Danglard, still under the effect of his soothing massage, managed to get through the ordeal of landing reasonably well. When they arrived, he was fresh and rested, whereas everyone else was looking rather dazed. Two and a half hours later, they had all been allocated rooms. Because of the time difference, the course was not scheduled to begin until two o'clock the following afternoon.

Adamsberg had been given a two-room apartment on the fifth floor, as clean and new as a show flat, with a balcony. A Gothic privilege. He leaned on it for a long moment to look down at the immense Ottawa River which flowed down below between its wild banks, and on the far side the lights of the skyscrapers of Ottawa city.

XVII

THREE CARS BELONGING TO THE RCMP PARKED IN FRONT OF THE building next day. They were easily recognised by their gleaming white doors marked with the head of a bison, looking half placid and half determined, surrounded by maple leaves and surmounted by the British Crown. Three men in uniform were waiting for the visitors. One of them, whom Adamsberg recognised by his epaulettes as the superintendent, leaned towards his neighbour.

'Which one would you say was the *commissaire*?' he asked his colleague.

'The little guy, in the black jacket.'

Adamsberg could more or less hear what they were saying. Brézillon and Trabelmann would have been pleased: the little guy. At the same time, his attention was distracted by some small black squirrels hopping about in the street, as lively and unperturbed as sparrows.

'No kidding,' said the superintendent, 'the one who's dressed like a hobo?'

'That's the one. Don't let it get to you.'

'Not the big slouch with the good suit?'

'No, it's the dark one. And he's a big shot over there. So no personal remarks.'

Superintendent Aurèle Laliberté nodded and moved towards Adamsberg, holding out his hand.

'Welcome, *commissaire principal*! Not too jet-lagged?'

'I'm fine, thank you,' replied Adamsberg carefully. 'Delighted to make your acquaintance.'

They shook hands all round in an embarrassed silence.

'Sorry about the weather,' Laliberté said in his booming voice, with a big grin. 'Frosts're early this year. In you get, it's a ten-minute drive up to HQ. We're not going to kill you with work today,' he added, inviting Adamsberg to sit beside him. 'Just a little looksee.'

The RCMP base was situated in a wooded park which seemed to stretch as far into the distance as a French forest. Laliberté drove slowly, and Adamsberg almost had time to study all the trees.

'You've got a pretty big place here,' he said, impressed.

'Yup. As we say here, we've not got a lot of history, but we sure have plenty of geography.'

'Are those maples?' he asked, pointing out of the car window.

'Sure are.'

'I thought they had red leaves.'

'Not red enough for you, eh, *commissaire*? They're not like the one on the flag, they come in all colours, red, yellow, orange. Or it'd be boring. So, you're the boss of the group, right?'

'Er, yes.'

'Say, for a *commissaire principal*, you don't put on a lot of style. They let you go round dressed like that in Paris?'

'In Paris, the police isn't the army.'

'No need to take offence, Jean-Baptiste. I call 'em as I see 'em, better you know that right off.' Laliberté had started to call Adamsberg by his first name already. 'Here's the RCMP, this is where we get out,' he said, applying the brakes.

The Paris contingent stood in a group in front of the giant cubes of brand new brick and glass, surrounded by flaming red trees. A black squirrel was guarding the door, nibbling at something. Adamsberg lagged behind to have a word with Danglard.

'Do they all use first names round here?'

'Yes, it's their normal way of speaking.'

'Should we do the same?'

'Do what you feel comfortable with. People adapt.'

'He called you "a big slouch". What did he mean?'

'A sloppy-looking character.'

'I see. As he says, he calls 'em as he sees 'em.'

'So it seems,' Danglard agreed.

Laliberté showed the French team into a huge meeting room – the equivalent of the Council Chamber – and did some rapid introductions. The Québécois team consisted of Mitch Portelance, Rhéal Ladouceur, Berthe Louisseize, Philibert Lafrance, Alphonse Philippe-Auguste, Ginette Saint-Preux and Fernand Sanscartier. Then the superintendent spoke firmly to his officers. 'You're each gonna link up with one of the members of the Paris squad. We change partners every two or three days. Get stuck in, but no need to break any records. They're not dummies, but they're on a steep learning curve, this is new to them, so no rushing at it. And no snarky jokes if they don't understand, or don't speak the way we do. Just because they're French doesn't mean they're not up to the job. I'm counting on you.'

It was in fact, much the same kind of pep-talk Adamsberg had given his team a few days earlier.

During the rather tedious tour of the premises, Adamsberg took care to locate the drinks machine, which supplied 'soups', but also cups of coffee about the size of a glass of beer. He scanned the faces of his temporary colleagues. He felt an immediate rapport with Sergeant Fernand Sanscartier, the only unpromoted officer, whose chubby pink face, with its wide-open innocent-looking brown eyes, seemed to mark him out as a number one good guy. He would have liked to be partnered with him, but for the first three days, hierarchy had to be observed, so he would be working with the energetic Aurèle Laliberté. The French visitors were allowed to leave at six, and shown out to their official cars, which were equipped with snow tyres. Only the *commissaire* had a car to himself.

'So why do you wear two watches?' asked Laliberté, as Adamsberg seated himself in the driving seat.

Adamsberg hesitated.

'Because of the time difference,' he explained suddenly. 'I've got to follow some enquiries back home in France.'

'Can't you do it in your head like everyone else?'

'It's quicker this way,' Adamsberg prevaricated.

'Suit yourself. OK, welcome to Canada, man, and see you tomorrow, nine sharp.'

Adamsberg drove slowly, looking at the trees, the streets, the people. Once out of Gatineau Park, he entered Ottawa's twin town of Hull, which he would not personally have called a town: it was spread over kilometres of flat land, divided up in a grid plan of clean and deserted streets, lined with wood frame houses. There was nothing old or decrepit in sight, not even the churches, which looked like the icing sugar ornaments on wedding cakes rather than Strasbourg Cathedral. No one seemed to be in a hurry, and most people seemed to drive around in big pick-up trucks, capable of carrying several cubic metres of timber.

There appeared to be no cafes, restaurants or department stores. Adamsberg spotted a few isolated shops, all-purpose corner stores, which sold a bit of everything, one of them a hundred metres from their residence. He enjoyed walking over to it, feeling the snow crunching under his feet, and watching the squirrels which did not move away at his approach. A significant difference from sparrows.

'Where will I find a bar or a restaurant?' he asked the cashier at reception.

'All the late-night stuff's downtown,' she replied kindly. 'It's about five kilometres, you'll have to take the car. Bye, have a nice evening now.'

The downtown area was not large and Adamsberg had walked round it in under a quarter of an hour. He went into a cafe called the *Quatrain*, but found he was interrupting a poetry reading attended by a silent and intense audience, so he tiptoed out again, closing the door carefully. One to tell Danglard about. In the end he went into an American bar called *Les Cinq Dimanches*, a huge overheated saloon, decorated with the stuffed heads of caribou and bear, and sporting Québécois flags. The waiter brought him some food in a leisurely way, chatting about this and that.

The plateful was big enough for two. Everything's bigger in Canada, and more easy-going.

At the far end of the bar, a hand waved to him. Ginette Saint-Preux, carrying her plate, came and sat down at his table without embarrassment.

'Do you mind if I sit here, Jean-Baptiste?' she asked. 'I'm dining alone too.'

Ginette, who was very pretty, chatty and vivacious, started firing questions at him. What did he think of Quebec? Was it very different from France? Flatter? Oh really? What was Paris like? What was work like there? Fun? And what about you? Oh, really? She had children and 'hobbies', especially music. But for a good concert, you had to go to Montreal, would that interest him? Did he have any hobbies? Oh really? Drawing, walking, dreaming? Funny hobbies. How could you do those in Paris?

At about eleven o'clock, Ginette asked about his two watches.

'Poor you,' she said, getting up. 'Of course with the time difference, it's five o'clock in the morning for you now.'

Ginette had left on the table a green brochure, which she had been rolling up and unrolling during their conversation. Adamsberg unfolded it sleepily, his eyes drooping with fatigue. Some Vivaldi concerts in Montreal, between 17 and 21 October, a string quintet, with flute and harpsichord. Ginette must have some energy, to drive four hundred kilometres, just to listen to a quintet.

XVIII

ADAMSBERG DID NOT INTEND TO SPEND HIS ENTIRE CANADIAN VISIT with his eyes fixed on test tubes and barcodes. By seven in the morning, he was already outside, drawn by the river. Or rather the tributary as Danglard called it, the immense tributary of the St Lawrence, home of the Ottawa Indians. He walked along the bank until he reached a footpath. A sign informed him that it was the 'Portage trail used by Samuel de Champlain in 1613'. He started off along it, happy to be following in the footsteps of men of long ago, Indians and travellers, carrying their canoes on their backs. The track was not easy to follow, as the path often dipped more than a metre into hollows. The landscape was spectacular: foaming waters, noisy waterfalls, colonies of birds, red-leaved maples along the banks. He stopped in front of a commemorative tablet planted in a clearing, giving a potted history of Champlain's achievements.

'Hey, good morning!' said a voice behind him.

A young woman in jeans was sitting on a flat rock overlooking the river, smoking an early-morning cigarette. Adamsberg had detected a Parisian accent.

'Morning to you,' he replied.

'French,' stated the woman. 'What are you doing here? Tourist?'

'No, work.'

The young woman inhaled and threw the rest of her cigarette into the water. 'I'm lost. So I'm just waiting.'

'Lost? Literally?' asked Adamsberg carefully, while looking at the inscription on the Champlain stone.

'I met this guy? In law school, in Paris? Canadian. He said why didn't I come out here with him and I said yes. He seemed like a regular chum.'

'Chum?'

'Friend, boyfriend. The idea was to live together.'

'I see,' said Adamsberg, retreating.

'And after six months, what do you think the chum did? He dumped Noëlla and she found herself all washed up.'

'Noëlla, that's you?'

'Yes. In the end, she found a girlfriend to take her in.'

'I see,' said Adamsberg again, having already listened to more than he needed to.

'So I'm waiting,' she went on, lighting another cigarette. 'I'm making some quick bucks working in a bar in Ottawa, and as soon as I've saved up enough, I'm going back to Paris. Not very bright, eh?'

'Why are you out here so early?'

'She comes to listen to the wind. She comes here often, morning and evening. I tell myself that even if you're lost, you have to find somewhere to be. I've chosen this stone. What's your name?'

'Jean-Baptiste.'

'And your other name?'

'Adamsberg.'

'And what do you do?'

'I'm a cop.'

'That's a laugh! Here they call them pigs. My chum, he'd say, oh-oh, here come the pigs, and you wouldn't see him for dust. Are you working with the Gatineau cops?'

Adamsberg nodded and took advantage of the sleet that was beginning to fall, to get away.

'Bye for now,' she said, without budging from her stone.

* * *

At two minutes to nine o'clock, he was parking in front of the RCMP. Laliberté gave him a hearty wave from the doorway.

'Come on in!' he shouted. 'What about this weather! Hey, man, what have you been up to, with all that mud on your pants?'

'I fell over on the portage path by the river,' explained Adamsberg, rubbing at the marks.

'You been out walking already? No kidding?'

'I wanted to see the river, the rapids, the trees, the old portage.'

'Hey, an outdoor freak,' cried Laliberté with a laugh. 'So you took a dive?'

'A dive? In the river? No, sorry, I don't always understand, you mean a fall?'

'Right, don't apologise, I won't take it personally. Hey, call me Aurèle. I mean, yeah, how d'you come to fall?'

'The path's steep in places, I slipped on a stone.'

'No bones broken at least.'

'No, no, I'm fine.'

'One of your men is here already, the big slouch.'

'Don't call him that, Aurèle, he knows what it means.'

'How come?'

'He reads books. He may look sloppy, but there's not an ounce of slackness in that head. Only he does find it a bit hard getting up in the morning.'

'Let's grab a coffee while we wait,' said the superintendent heading for the machine. 'Got some change?'

Adamsberg took a handful of unfamiliar coins from his pocket and Laliberté extracted the right one.

'Decaff or regular?'

'Regular,' Adamsberg chose, hopefully.

'This'll set you up,' said Aurèle, handing him a huge plastic cup full of very hot coffee. 'So you go out for a breath of fresh air every morning, do you?'

'I go walking. Morning, daytime, evening, doesn't matter when. I just need to walk.'

'Right,' said Aurèle with a smile. 'Or perhaps you're on the lookout for a girl?'

'No, I'm not. But since you mention it, there was one, funnily enough, sitting by the Champlain stone, at eight in the morning. Seemed a bit odd.'

'Pretty weird, I'd say. A chick on her own, on the trail, could be a hooker. Nobody goes there. Don't get hooked, Adamsberg. It could be big trouble.'

Usual conversation of men round the coffee machine, thought Adamsberg, here or anywhere else.

'OK, off we go,' concluded the superintendent. 'No more talk about girls, we've got work to do.'

Laliberté gave out instructions to the teams of two in the big room. Danglard had been assigned to the innocent-looking Sanscartier. Laliberté had paired the women with each other, probably out of a feeling that it would be more correct, allocating the large Retancourt to the slim Louisseize, and Froissy to Ginette Saint-Preux. Today's task was on-the-spot collection. They would visit eight houses belonging to public-spirited citizens who had agreed to take part in the experiment. Each officer had a DNA collection kit. They would place their samples on a special card for collecting body fluids, said Laliberté, holding this object high in the air as if it was a sacred Host. It neutralised any bacterial or viral contamination, without the need for freezing.

'A new technique, which gives us an economy, one, of time, two, of money, three, of space.'

While listening to the strict instructions of the superintendent, Adamsberg was leaning forward on his chair, his hands in his pockets, which were still damp from the walk. His fingers encountered the green brochure he had picked up from the table, in order to return it to Ginette Saint-Preux. It was by now damp and crumpled and he took it out carefully, trying not to tear it. Discreetly, he spread it out on a table with the palm of his hand, to smooth it back into shape.

'Today,' Laliberté continued, 'we will collect, one, sweat, two, saliva, and three, blood. Tomorrow, tears, urine, snot and dirt from under the nails. And semen from those citizens who have agreed to fill a test tube.'

Adamsberg gave a start, not because of the public-spirited citizens and their test tubes, but because of what he had just read on the damp brochure.

'Check properly,' Laliberté said loudly, turning to the Paris team, 'that the codes of the cards correspond to those on the kits. As I always say, you have to remember three things: rigour, rigour and more rigour. That's the only way to get the job done.'

The eight teams moved towards the cars, armed with the addresses of the citizens who were obligingly lending their homes and their bodies to the series of samples. Adamsberg stopped Ginette as she went by.

'I wanted to give you this back,' he said, handing her the green brochure. 'You left it in the restaurant but I thought you'd be needing it.'

'Goodness, yes, I wondered where I'd put it.'

'I'm sorry, it's got wet.'

'Never mind. I'll take it to the office. Can you tell Hélène I'll be right back?'

'Ginette,' said Adamsberg, holding her back by the arm and pointing to the brochure. 'That Camille Forestier, the viola player, is she always in the Montreal quintet?'

'No, she isn't. Alban told me their viola player's on maternity leave. She was already six months pregnant when they needed to start rehearsals.'

'Alban?'

'The first violin, a friend of mine. He met this Camille Forestier, who's French, and auditioned her. She was good, so he took her on at once.'

'Hey, Adamsberg,' called Laliberté, 'get a move on there.'

'Thanks, Ginette,' said Adamsberg, joining his partner.

'What did I say?' said the superintendent, as he climbed into the car, laughing once more. 'Always after the ladies, aren't you? And with one of my inspectors too, on your second day here. Fast worker or what?'

'It's not what you think, Aurèle, we were talking about music. Classical music,' added Adamsberg, as if 'classical' somehow lent respectability to their conversation.

'Music, my eye!' laughed the superintendent, switching on the engine.

'Don't play the little plaster saint with me. You saw her downtown last night, right?'

'It was quite by chance. I was eating at the *Cinq Dimanches*, and she came over to my table.'

'Drop it with Ginette, she's married. And happily married.'

'I was just giving her back a concert programme. You can believe me or not, please yourself.'

'No need to take offence. Only kidding.'

By the end of the long day, punctuated by the loud voice of the superintendent, and when all the samples had been taken from the public-spirited Jules and Linda Saint-Croix, Adamsberg got back into his official car.

'What are you doing tonight?' asked Laliberté, putting his head through the window.

'I'm going to look at the river again, go for a walk. Then go downtown for something to eat.'

'You're real antsy, Jean-Baptiste, you gotta be moving all the time.'

'I told you, I like walking.'

'You like checking out the talent, that's what. Me, I never go downtown looking for a woman. I'm too recognisable. When I want some fun, I take off for Ottawa. Go on, man, best of luck!' he added, slapping the door with his hand. '*Ciao* till tomorrow.'

'Tears, urine, snot, dirt and semen,' recited Adamsberg.

'Semen, I wish,' said Laliberté frowning, his professional concerns returning. 'If Jules Saint-Croix can make a bit of an effort tonight. He said yes at the start, but I get the feeling he's gone off the idea. Well, we can't force people, for God's sake.'

Adamsberg left Laliberté to his test tube worries and set off for the river.

After listening for a long while to the sound of the Ottawa, he took the portage trail to make his way downtown on foot. If he had read the map right, the path ought to come out by the big bridge across the Chaudière

Falls. From there, it was only a quarter of an hour to the centre. The rocky path was separated from a cycle track by a strip of forest which plunged him into complete darkness. He had borrowed a flashlight from Retancourt, the only member of the mission likely to have thought of bringing one. He made more or less good progress, managing to avoid a small pool the river made at one point and dodging low branches. He no longer felt the cold when he came out near the bridge, a huge metal structure whose crossbars made him think of a triple Eiffel Tower fallen across the Ottawa river.

The Breton pancake house downtown had made an effort to recall the owner's ancestors' native heath, with fishing nets, buoys and dried fish. And, indeed, a trident. Adamsberg froze when he saw the implement with its three points staring him in the face from the wall. A sea-trident, a fishing spear for Neptune, with its three fine blades ending in fish-hooks. Very different in fact from his personal trident, which was a farm-worker's tool, solid and heavy, an earth-trident so to speak. As one might talk of an earthworm or even an earth-toad. But all that was a long way off, murderous tridents, exploding toads, left behind in the mists across the Atlantic.

The waiter brought him an outsize pancake, while chatting about life in general.

Yes, far across the Atlantic: tridents, toads, judges, cathedrals and the locked chamber of Bluebeard's castle.

Left behind, but waiting for his return. All those faces, all those wounds, all those fears, attached to his footsteps by the untiring thread of memory. As for Camille, she had reappeared to him here on the spot, right in the middle of a town lost in the huge wastes of Canada. The idea of the five concerts about to be given, two hundred kilometres from the RCMP post, worried him, as if he would be able to hear the viola from his balcony. He prayed that Danglard would not get to hear of this. The *capitaine* would be quite capable of rushing off full tilt to Montreal and then giving him dirty looks all the next day.

He chose to have a coffee and a glass of wine instead of dessert, and without looking up from the menu, he became aware that someone had sat down at his table uninvited. It was the young woman from the Champlain stone, and she called the waiter back to order another coffee.

'Good day?' she enquired, smiling.

She lit a cigarette and stared at him straight in the eyes.

'Oh shit,' thought Adamsberg and then wondered why. Any other time, he might have jumped at a chance like this. But he felt no desire to take this girl to bed, either because the torments of the past week were still affecting him, or perhaps because he was trying to disprove the intuition of the superintendent.

'I'm bothering you, Jean Baptiste,' she stated. 'You look tired. The pigs have given you a hard time.'

'That's it,' he replied, and realised he had forgotten her name.

'Your jacket's soaked,' she said feeling it. 'Does your car let in the rain? Or did you come on a bike?'

Did she want to know everything about him?

'I walked.'

'You *walked*? Nobody does that here. Hadn't you noticed?'

'Yes. But I came along the portage trail.'

'The whole way? How long did it take you?'

'Just over an hour.'

'Well, you've got some nerve, as my chum would say.'

'Why's that?'

'Because that path at night, it's a homosexual cruising place.'

'So what? What harm would they do me?'

'Well, rapists too. I don't know, it's what people say. But when Noëlla goes there at night, she doesn't go farther than the Champlain stone. That's far enough to look at the river.' Noëlla yawned. 'I've been serving dumb French people all day, I'm worn out. I work at the *Caribou*, did I say? I don't like the French, when they all start shouting in a group, I prefer the Québécois, they're nicer. Except for my boyfriend. I told you about him, didn't I? He chucked me out, the bastard.'

The young woman was launched once more on her story, and Adamsberg couldn't think how to get rid of her.

'See, here's his photo. Good-looker, wouldn't you say? Though you're not bad yourself, of your type. You're unusual-looking, and you're not so young. But you've got a nice nose and eyes. And a nice smile,' she said, running a finger across his eyelids and lips. 'And when you talk, your voice is lovely, did you know that?'

'Hey, Noëlla,' the waiter interrupted, putting the bills on the table. 'You still working up at the *Caribou*?'

'Yeah, gotta save up for the airfare, Michel.'

'Still feeling sore about that boyfriend?'

'Maybe, evenings. Some people get the early morning blues, me it's the evening.'

'Well, forget him. The cops have run him in.'

'You're kidding!' said Noëlla, sitting up straight.

'I kid you not. He was stealing cars and selling them with new plates, that kind of thing.'

'No, I don't believe it,' said Noëlla. 'He's in computers now.'

'Wise up, sweetie. Your pal's a crook. You better believe it, Noëlla, it was in the papers.'

'I didn't know.'

'Black and white in the papers. Son of a bitch went too far one time, he'd had a skinful, the cops caught up with him, and he's in big trouble now. Face it, Noëlla, he was just no good. You need to put that in your pipe and smoke it. I wanted to tell you, so you'd stop fretting over him. Excuse me, folks, I gotta move on to the other tables.'

'I can't believe it,' said Noëlla, wiping the sugar from her cup with a finger. 'Do you mind if I have a drink with you? That's thrown me a bit.'

'OK, ten minutes, then I'm going back.'

'I get it,' said Noëlla as she ordered a drink. 'You're spoken for. But gee, think of that. My boyfriend.'

'What did he mean, about smoking it in your pipe?' asked Adamsberg. 'Did he just mean forget it?'

'No, it means "Stop and have a good think about it". See, my story's even dumber than you thought.' Finishing her glass in a single gulp, Noëlla went on, 'I need a bit of distraction, after that. I'll drive you back to your place.'

Surprised, Adamsberg hesitated to respond.

'I'm in a car, you're on foot,' explained Noëlla impatiently. 'You're surely not going back via the footpath?'

'I was planning on it.'

'It's pouring with rain. Are you scared of me, or what? Does little Noëlla frighten a big forty-year-old. A cop, what's more?'

'No, of course not,' said Adamsberg, smiling.

'Well then. Where are you staying?'

'It's off the rue Prévost.'

'I know it, I'm three blocks away. Come along.'

Adamsberg got up, still not understanding why he felt so reluctant to follow a pretty girl into her car.

Noëlla parked in front of his building and Adamsberg thanked her as he opened his door.

'Not even a little kiss goodbye? You're not very polite, for a Frenchman.'

'I'm sorry, I'm from the mountains. Not civilised at all.'

Adamsberg kissed her on both cheeks with a serious face, and Noëlla frowned, looking offended. He opened the front door with his key, and greeted the janitor, who was always on call after eleven o'clock. After taking a shower, he lay down on the large bed in his room. In Canada, everything is bigger. Except for the memories, which are smaller.

XIX

THE TEMPERATURE HAD DROPPED TO MINUS 4 BY THE MORNING, AND Adamsberg hurried out to see his river. On the path, the edges of the little pools had frozen over, and he enjoyed crunching the ice with his stout shoes, under the vigilant gaze of the squirrels. He was about to go further, when the thought of Noëlla, stationed on her stone, restrained him like a noose. He turned back and sat on a rock to observe the competition going on between a colony of ducks and a gaggle of Canada geese. Wars and territory disputes everywhere. One of the geese was obviously the big boss, and repeatedly returned to the charge, spreading its wings and clacking its beak with despotic obstinacy. Adamsberg disliked this goose – or maybe gander. He distinguished it from the others by a mark on its plumage, with the idea of coming back next day to see whether it would still be running the show, or whether geese practised some kind of democratic pecking order. He left the ducks to their resistance and went up to his car. A squirrel had taken refuge underneath it and he could see its tail near the back wheel. He drove off gently in stops and starts, so as not to squash it.

Superintendent Laliberté was in a good temper once more, having learned that Jules Saint-Croix had performed his civic duty and filled a test tube, which was now inside a big envelope.

'Semen is absolutely fundamental,' Laliberté said loudly to Adamsberg, ripping open the envelope, without any consideration for the Saint-Croix couple, who were huddled in a corner of the room.

'We've got two experiments to conduct, Adamsberg,' Laliberté went on, shaking the test tube in the middle of the sitting room. 'We need a warm sample and a dry one. The warm sample simulates semen taken from the victim's vagina. Dried semen is more problematic. You have to use different ways of collecting it. Depends whether it's on fabric, a road surface, vegetation or on a carpet, for instance. The worst surface of all is grass. You following me? We'll have to distribute four doses in four strategic places: on the drive, in the garden, in the bed, and on the sitting room carpet.'

The Saint-Croix couple disappeared from the room like fugitives, and the morning was spent depositing drops of semen here and there, and surrounding them with chalk-marks so as not to lose sight of them.

'While it's drying, we can move to the toilet and tackle urine. Bring your card and kit.'

The poor Saint-Croix couple spent a difficult day, which filled the superintendent with satisfaction. He had made Linda cry, in order to collect her tears, and made Jules go running in the cold, to collect mucus from his nose. All the samples had been operationally usable, and he returned to the RCMP base a happy man, with all his cards and kits clearly labelled. There had been just one hold-up: the teams had had to be re-organised at the last minute, because two of the volunteers had refused to hand over semen samples to the all-women teams. This had sent Laliberté into a towering rage.

'For Chrissakes, Louisseize,' he yelled down the phone. 'What do they think their semen is? Liquid gold? They're happy enough to spread it around when they're out chasing girls, but to oblige working women, oh no. Go tell him that, your damned volunteer.'

'No I can't, superintendent,' said petite Berthe Louisseize. 'He's as stubborn as a mule. I'll have to swap with Portelance.'

Laliberté had had to give in, but he was still snarling about it at the end of the day.

'People can be as dumb as bison sometimes,' he said to Adamsberg as they returned to HQ. 'Now we've got all the samples, I'm going to give those stupid bastards a piece of my mind. The women in my squad know a damned sight more about their precious semen than that pair of dopes.'

'Let it go, Aurèle,' suggested Adamsberg. 'They're not worth bothering with.'

'I'm taking it real personal, Adamsberg. You go off and find a woman tonight if you want, but I'm going out after supper to give them what for.'

That day, Adamsberg understood that the expansive jovial nature of the superintendent had another side, equally pronounced. The cheery, hail-fellow, tactless buddy could be a determined and ferocious bearer of grudges.

'It wasn't you that set him off, was it?' Sergeant Sanscartier asked Adamsberg anxiously.

Sanscartier was speaking quietly, his whole bearing that of a mild-tempered man.

'No, it was the two idiots who wouldn't hand over their semen samples to the women's teams.'

'Just as well it wasn't you. A word in your ear,' he added, looking at Adamsberg with his big brown eyes. 'He's a good pal, our boss, but when he makes a joke, best to laugh and say nothing. What I mean is, don't provoke him. Because when the boss gets going, he makes the ground shake.'

'Does that happen often?'

'If people cross him, or if he gets out of bed on the wrong side. Have you seen, we're paired up for Monday?'

After a dinner for the whole group at the *Cinq Dimanches* to celebrate the end of the first short week, Adamsberg went back via the forest trail. He knew the way by now, and was able to avoid the potholes and sharp drops, spotting the sparkling of the pools alongside. He made better time than on the way out. He had stopped to retie a shoelace when a flash-light shone out at him.

'Hey, man!' shouted a gruff, threatening voice. 'What are you doing there? Are you after something?'

Holding up his torch in return, Adamsberg found himself facing a burly man, dressed as a logger and wearing a cap with earflaps. He was standing looking at him, legs planted firmly apart.

'What's all this?' Adamsberg asked. 'Don't hikers have the right to use the trail?'

'Ah,' said the man after a pause. 'You're from the old country, I guess. French?'

'Yes.'

'Thought so,' said the man, laughing this time, and coming closer. 'Because you talk like a book. What are you doing here? Looking for a boyfriend?'

'I could ask you the same.'

'Now don't be cheeky, I'm the site watchman. Can't leave the equip-ment unguarded at night, it's worth money.'

'What site?'

'Can't you see?' asked the man, waving his flashlight behind him.

In the section of forest above the path, Adamsberg could just make out through the darkness a pick-up truck, a mobile trailer, and various tools leaning against tree trunks.

'What sort of site is it?' he asked politely. It seemed to be expected in Quebec to make conversation.

'Taking out dead trees and replanting more maples,' the watchman explained. 'I thought you were after the equipment. Sorry to challenge you, buddy, but, hell, it's my job. Make a habit of walking here at night, do you?'

'I just like it.'

'You visiting?'

'I'm a cop. I'm working with the Mounties at Gatineau.'

This admission removed the last suspicions of the watchman.

'Hey, that's fine. Want to come and share a beer in the cab?'

'Thanks all the same, but I've still got work to do. Must get back.'

'Too bad. So long, buddy.'

Adamsberg slowed down as he approached the Champlain tablet. Yes, Noëlla was there on her stone, muffled up in a bulky anorak. He could see the glowing tip of her cigarette. He climbed quietly back into the forest and made a long detour, reaching the path again about thirty metres further along, then hurried towards his residence. Damned girl, after all it wasn't as if she was the devil. The devil suddenly reminded him of Judge Fulgence. You think your thoughts have gone to sleep, but there they are, planted right in the middle of your forehead, three holes in a line. They're just veiled by a transitory Atlantic fog.

XX

VOISENET HAD PLANNED TO SPEND THE WEEKEND OFF IN THE FORESTS
and lakes, with his binoculars and camera. Because of the need to share
cars, he was taking Justin and Retancourt with him. The other four had
chosen the big city, and were leaving for Ottawa and Montreal. Adamsberg
had decided to head off alone for the north. Before leaving in the morning,
he went to check whether the noisy goose of the day before had handed
over to another leader. He was certain it was a gander in fact.

No, the despotic gander had not yielded an inch. The other geese were
following him like sheep, swerving whenever the leader changed direction, and waiting in complete stillness when he went into action, flapping along the surface of the water towards the ducks, wings outspread
and feathers ruffled to make him look even bigger. Adamsberg shouted
an insult at him and shook his fist before going back to the car. Before
moving off, he knelt down to check that no squirrels were underneath.

He headed due north, lunched at Kazabazua, and then drove along an
endless succession of dirt roads. Ten kilometres or so out of town, the
Québécois didn't bother to asphalt the roads, since the frost broke up the
surface every year. If he went on driving in a straight line, he thought,
with immense pleasure, he would end up looking across to Greenland.
That's something you can't say in Paris when you go out after work. Or
in Bordeaux. He allowed himself to wander along, taking side-roads when

they tempted him, finally turning south again before parking at the edge of a forest by Pink Lake. The woods were deserted, the ground strewn with red maple leaves and occasional patches of snow. Here and there, a notice told travellers to watch out for bears and to recognise their claw marks on the trunks of beech trees. 'Warning: black bears climb trees in order to eat beech nuts.' 'Good,' thought Adamsberg, looking up and feeling with his finger the scars left by the claws of bears, peering to see if any beast was overhead. Up till now, he had only seen some beaver dams and some tracks left by deer. Just footprints and traces, but no animals were visible. A bit like Maxime Leclerc in his Haguenau *Schloss*.

Stop thinking about the *Schloss* and go and take a look at this pink lake instead.

Pink Lake was marked on the map as being a small example of the half-million or so lakes in Quebec province, but Adamsberg found it large and beautiful. Because he had taken to reading notices in the days since visiting Strasbourg, he read the information board about Pink Lake. He discovered therefore that he had chanced upon a unique lake.

He recoiled a little. This recent propensity to come across exceptions was unsettling. Waving these thoughts away, with his habitual gesture, he read on. Pink Lake was twenty metres deep and its bed was covered with three metres of mud. So far, so normal perhaps. But because of the great depth, the surface waters did not mix with the lower ones. From fifteen metres down, they did not move, were never disturbed or oxygenated, any more than the mud on the lake bed which enclosed its 10,600 years of history. The lake might look normal, Adamsberg concluded, and indeed it seemed to be reflecting blue and pink colours, but its smooth surface covered a second lake, one that was perpetually stagnant, airless and dead, a fossil. Worst of all, a saltwater fish still lived down there, from the era when the sea had covered it. Adamsberg examined the drawing of the fish, which seemed to be a sort of cross between a carp and a trout, but smaller and with spines. He looked in vain for its name on the notice; it didn't seem to have one.

A living lake lying over a dead one. Harbouring a nameless creature, of which only a sketch or image was available. Adamsberg leaned over the wooden fence to try to glimpse the dead lower waters under the shimmering pink surface. Why did all his thoughts keep leading him back to the Trident? Like the marks of the bears' claws on tree trunks? Like this dead lake, muddy and grey, surviving silently underneath an apparently living surface, and home to a strange creature left over from a bygone era.

Adamsberg hesitated, then got his sketchpad out of his anorak. Warming his hands, he copied as precisely as possible the artist's impression of the damned fish which seemed to swim between heaven and hell. He had intended to spend a long time in the forest, but Pink Lake made him go back. Everywhere he found himself facing the long-dead judge, everywhere he found himself touching the threatening waters of Neptune and the traces of his accursed trident. What would Laliberté have done in the face of this torment that dogged him so continuously? Would he have laughed it off with a wave of his huge hand, opting instead for rigour, rigour and more rigour? Or would he have pounced on his prey and never let it go? Walking away from the lake, Adamsberg had the sensation that the pursuit was the other way round, that the hunter was becoming the hunted, and that the prey was itself sinking its teeth into him. Its spines, claws, and prongs. In that case, Danglard would be right to suspect that he was now becoming obsessive.

He walked slowly back to the car. By his two watches, which he had altered to read local time, while still respecting their five minutes difference, it was twelve and a half minutes past four in the afternoon. He drove along the empty roads, searching for indifference in the uniform immensity of the forests, then decided to turn back towards civilisation. He slowed down as he approached the parking lot of his residence, then gradually speeded up, leaving Hull behind him and heading for Montreal. This was precisely what he had not wanted to do, as he kept telling himself the whole two hundred kilometres of the way. But the car was just taking him there, as if it were radio-controlled, at a speed of ninety kilometres an hour, following the tail-lights of the pick-up trunk in front.

Just as the car knew it was going to Montreal, Adamsberg remembered perfectly the directions from the green brochure, the time and the place. Or perhaps, he thought as he approached the city, he ought to opt for a film or a play, why not? If he could, he ought perhaps to get rid of this damned car and find one that didn't drive him to Pink Lake or to concerts by the Montreal quintet. But at 10.36 that evening, he was slipping into the church, just after the interval. He went to sit on one of the forward pews, behind a white pillar.

XXI

VIVALDI'S MUSIC UNFURLED AROUND HIM, RELEASING SPIRALS OF thought, profuse and confused. The sight of Camille wrestling with her viola affected him more than he would have wished, but this was merely a stolen hour, and an incognito emotion which committed him to nothing. Transferring his professional habits to the music, he heard the thread of the composition stretch as if it were an insoluble enigma, almost reach the point of screaming with impotence, and then resolve itself into an unexpected and fluid harmony, as if it were alternating complexities and resolutions, questions and answers.

It was at one of the moments when the string players had begun a 'resolution' that his thoughts shot back to the hasty departure of the Trident from the Haguenau *Schloss*. He was following the trail, as he watched Camille's bow move. By pursuing the judge, Adamsberg had always forced him to move on, that being the only slight power he had ever acquired over the magistrate. He had arrived in Schiltigheim on the Wednesday, and it was the next day that Trabelmann had exploded with anger at him. There would have been plenty of time for the event to become known and to appear by Friday in the local papers. Which was the very day that Maxime Leclerc had put his house on the market and cleared out. If that was so, both of them were involved now. Adamsberg was once more chasing the dead man, but the dead man knew that his pursuer had reappeared. In that case, Adamsberg had lost his only advantage, and the power of the dead man could block his way at any time.

Forewarned is always forearmed, but the judge's foresight was potent to the power of a hundred. Back in Paris, Adamsberg would have to adapt his strategy to this new threat and escape the alsatians snapping at his legs. 'I'll give you a start, young man. I'll count to four.' Run, Adamsberg, run for your life.

Unless he was totally mistaken. He spared a thought for Vivaldi who was sending him this danger signal across the centuries. A good guy, Vivaldi, a real buddy, and the quintet were doing him proud. It was not for nothing then that his car had driven him here, to steal an hour out of Camille's life, and to receive a precious warning from the composer. Since he was apparently hearing from the dead, he might very well hear a whispered message from Antonio Vivaldi, and he was sure the Venetian musician had been good company. A guy who writes music of such beauty is bound to give you excellent advice.

It was only at the end of the concert that Adamsberg spotted Danglard, whose eyes were fixed on his protégée. The sight immediately destroyed all his pleasure. What the devil was Danglard up to now? Was he going to meet him at every turn? Interfering with his whole life? Obviously he knew all about the concerts and was faithfully at his post, the dependable, loyal and irreproachable Adrien Danglard. Well, shit. Camille didn't belong to him, for God's sake. So what was the *capitaine* planning with this close surveillance? Was he trying to creep into Adamsberg's life? Real anger towards his deputy rose within him. The grey-haired benefactor, slipping in through the door left open by Camille's heartbreak.

The speed with which Danglard then disappeared surprised Adamsberg. The *capitaine* had gone round the back of the church and was waiting at the artists' entrance. To offer congratulations, no doubt. But no, Danglard was loading stuff into a car, and then taking the wheel, and Camille was with him. Adamsberg drove off behind them, anxious to see how far his deputy would take this secret solicitude. After a halt, then a further ten minutes' drive, Danglard parked the car, then opened the door for Camille, who handed him a bundle wrapped in a blanket.

The blanket, and the fact that the bundle made a noise, communicated to Adamsberg, in a spasmodic shock, the extent of the situation.

A child, a baby. And going by the small size of the bundle and the voice, perhaps no more than a month old. Motionless, he watched the door of the house close behind the couple. Danglard, the bastard, the thief in the night.

But Danglard reappeared quickly, gave Camille a friendly wave, and hailed a taxi.

Good God, a child, thought Adamsberg on the long drive back to Hull. Now that Danglard had been absolved from the role of treacherous bastard and had once more become the loyal and dependable friend – which by no means lessened his resentment towards him – his thoughts were concentrated on the young woman. How on earth had Camille ended up with a child? Inevitably, he thought with a pang, that meant some kind of connection with a man. If the baby was a month old, that meant nine plus one, say ten months. So Camille had waited only a few weeks before finding his successor. He trod on the accelerator, suddenly impatient to overtake the damned cars rolling peacefully along at the sacred speed of ninety kilometres an hour. Anyway, that was the situation, and Danglard must have been informed early on, and hadn't breathed a word about it to him. Still, he understood why his deputy had spared him this news, which even now stung him deeply. But why? What had he, Adamsberg, been hoping? That Camille would weep for a thousand years and never forsake her lost love? That she would turn into a statue whom he could bring back to life whenever he wanted to? Like in a fairy story, as Trabelmann would have said. No, she had stumbled, but survived, and then met some other man, it was as simple as that. A harsh reality which he had to digest with difficulty.

No, he thought later, lying on top of his bed, no, he had never really taken on board that he would lose Camille when he lost Camille. It was logical enough after all, but he couldn't handle it. And now there was this bastard of a new father, who was driving him out of the picture. Even Danglard had taken the side of the other man against him. He could easily imagine the *capitaine* walking into the maternity ward and shaking hands with the newcomer, who would be a reliable sort of chap, safe as houses, offering all his uprightness and benevolence in contrast to him, Adamsberg. A man of irreproachable habits and morality, a businessman, with a labrador, no, two labradors, and polished shoes with new laces.

Adamsberg hated him fiercely. That night, he would have massacred the man and his dogs, without hesitation. He, the *flic*, the cop, the pig, would have gladly committed murder. With a trident too, why not?

XXII

WAKING LATE ON THE SUNDAY, ADAMSBERG DECIDED NOT TO GO and look at the boss of the Canada geese, nor to go visiting lakes. He went straight to the portage trail. The young woman wouldn't be working on Sunday, and there was a good chance he would find her sitting on her rock. And indeed, there she was, smoking her cigarette, with an ambiguous smile on her lips, and quite ready to go back to his room with him.

Her enthusiasm offered Adamsberg some partial comfort for the pain he had felt the night before. It was difficult to get rid of her in the early evening, though. Sitting naked on the bed, Noëlla was determined to spend the night there. Out of the question, Adamsberg explained gently, persuading her to get dressed, my colleagues will be back any minute. He had to push her into her jacket, before propelling her through the door.

Once Noëlla had left, his thoughts no longer remained with her, and he called Mordent in Paris. The *commandant* was a night owl and telephoning at quarter past midnight, French time, would not mean waking him up. Mordent combined his taste for rigorous bureaucracy with an old-fashioned liking for the accordion and cabaret songs, and he had just returned from a musical evening which he seemed to have enjoyed.

'To tell you the truth, Mordent,' said Adamsberg, 'I'm not calling to give you any news. The whole thing's going very smoothly, the team's fine, nothing to report.'

'What are the Canadian colleagues like?' Mordent asked.

'Correct, as they say here; pleasant and competent.'

'Do you get evenings off, or is it lights out at ten?'

'We're free, but you're not missing anything. Hull-Gatineau isn't exactly jumping with cabarets and circuses. A bit flat, as Ginette says.'

'But the countryside's beautiful?'

'Yes, very. No problems in the squad back there?'

'Nothing serious. Object of your call, *commissaire*?'

'Can you get hold of a copy of the *Nouvelles d'Alsace* for Friday 10 October. Or any other local paper, it could be.'

'Object of the request?'

'The murder committed in Schiltigheim on the night of Saturday 4 October. Victim, Elisabeth Wind. Handling the investigation, *Commandant* Trabelmann. Chief suspect, one Bernard Vétilleux. What I'm after, Mordent, is an article or just a little news item mentioning the visit by a Parisian detective, and any mention of a serial killer. Something along those lines. Friday 10 October, not any other day.'

'The Parisian detective was you, was it?'

'Correct.'

'Confidential as far as the office is concerned, or is it OK to mention it in the Chat Room?'

'Top secret, Mordent. This business is causing me nothing but grief.'

'Urgent?'

'Yes, top priority. Let me know when you turn something up.'

'And if I don't?'

'That's important too. Just call me either way.'

'Hold on a moment,' said Mordent. 'Can you send me an email every day about your activities with the RCMP? Brézillon's expecting a precise report at the end of the mission and I dare say you'd like me to write it up.'

'What would I do without you, Mordent?'

The report. He had completely neglected to do that. Adamsberg forced himself to write a record of the sampling process of the previous days, while he could still remember the efforts of Jules and Linda Saint-Croix. He was only just in time, since his recent preoccupation with Fulgence, with the new father and then with Noëlla had driven the collection cards, with their samples of sweat and urine, deeper into the past. He would not be sorry tomorrow to be rid of his tough and boisterous companion, and start working with Sanscartier the Good.

Late in the evening, he heard the brakes of a car in the parking lot. Looking down from his balcony, he saw the Montreal group, Danglard in front, bending their heads against a snow shower. He would like to give Danglard a piece of his mind, as the superintendent would have said.

XXIII

STRANGE HOW THREE DAYS ARE ENOUGH TO DISSIPATE FEELINGS OF disorientation, so that one slips readily into a routine, Adamsberg thought, as he parked in front of the RCMP buildings, a few metres from the diligent squirrel who was as usual guarding the doors. The feeling of strangeness was disappearing. Everything was beginning to find its niche in the new territory, shaping it to its own form, as a favourite armchair shapes itself round the body. So the whole group was back in position in the meeting room this Monday, listening to the superintendent. After the fieldwork the laboratory, with extraction of the samples, which were to be placed on paper discs two millimetres in diameter, then inserted into the ninety-six wells of the process plate. All these instructions Adamsberg noted approximately, for his report to Mordent.

Adamsberg let Fernand Sanscartier get out the cards, prepare the discs and switch on the robotic punch. Sitting in front of a white guardrail, they both watched the machine going to and fro. For two days now, Adamsberg had been sleeping badly and the monotonous movement of the synchronised scores of punches mesmerised him.

'It makes you sleepy, doesn't it? Shall I go and get us a regular?'

'Make that a double regular, Sanscartier, as strong as you like.'

The sergeant returned, carrying the plastic cups carefully.

'Watch out, it's scalding hot,' he said, passing one to Adamsberg.

The two men took up their positions, leaning on the rail.

'Time'll come, won't it,' said Sanscartier, 'when a guy won't be able to piss in the snow without setting off a barcode and three helicopters full of cops.'

'Time'll come,' said Adamsberg echoing him, 'when we won't even need to question the guy.'

'Time'll come, when we won't even need to *see* him, hear his voice, wonder whether yes or no he could've done it. We'll just turn up at the crime scene, take a smear of his sweat and the guy'll be picked up at home with a crane, and dropped into a cell just his size.'

'Time'll come, when we'll be totally pissed off.'

'What do you think of the coffee?'

'Not a lot.'

'It's not our specialty.'

'Are you happy in your work, Sanscartier?'

The sergeant thought before answering.

'What I'd really like is to be back out doing hands-on stuff. Where I can use my own eyes, and piss in the snow when I feel like it, if you get my meaning. Specially since my girlfriend lives in Toronto. But don't tell the boss, or I'd get an earful.'

A red light flashed and the two men stayed still for a moment watching the machine come to a stop. Then Sanscartier moved heavily away from the rail.

'Better get a move on. If the boss sees us taking a breather, he'll start bawling at us.'

They emptied the plate and set to work on another set of cartons, discs and wells. Sanscartier activated the robotic process again.

'Do you do a lot of hands-on work in Paris?'

'As much as I can. And I walk a lot too, I just walk round the streets and think.'

'You're lucky. Do you work things out by shovelling clouds?'

'In a way,' said Adamsberg with a smile.

'Got anything good on at the moment?'

Adamsberg pulled a face.

'That's absolutely the wrong word, Sanscartier. I'm shovelling earth with this one.'

'Skull and crossbones, eh?'

'Worse than that. I've come across a whole skeleton. But he's not the victim, he's the murderer. A dead man, an old man who's still going round killing people.'

Adamsberg looked at Sanscartier's brown velvety eyes, almost as round as the ones on children's toys.

'Ah,' said Sanscartier. 'So if he's going round killing people, he can't be entirely dead.'

'Well yes, he is,' Adamsberg insisted. 'He really died, I have to tell you.'

'In that case, he's fighting it then,' said Sanscartier, 'he's struggling like a devil in holy water.'

Adamsberg leant on the rail. At last, someone prepared to stretch out an innocent hand towards him, like Clémentine.

'You're an inspired cop, Sanscartier, you really should be doing hands-on stuff.'

'Think so?'

'I know so.'

'Well, anyway,' said the sergeant, shaking his head, 'time'll come, when you'll get your hand caught in a mangle with this devil. If you'll allow me to give you some advice, you'd be wise to watch out. Some people will say you've completely flipped.'

'Flipped?'

'Lost the plot, making stuff up.'

'Oh, that's already happened, Sanscartier.'

'Then you'd better clam up, and don't try to convince them. But in my book, you've got what it takes, so you should follow your hunches. Keep chasing your damn killer, but until you collar him, lie low.'

Adamsberg remained leaning on the rail, feeling the comfort and relief brought by the words of this warm-hearted colleague.

'Why don't you think I'm crazy, Sanscartier? Everyone else seems to.'

'Because you aren't, that's easy to see. How's about lunch? It's after twelve.'

* * *

The following evening, after another day spent doing automatic DNA extraction, Adamsberg regretfully said goodbye to his kindly colleague.

'Who are you working with tomorrow?' asked Sanscartier, walking over to his car with him.

'Ginette Saint-Preux.'

'She's a good pal. You'll be in safe hands with her.'

'But I'll miss you,' said Adamsberg as they shook hands. 'You've done me a lot of good.'

'How come?'

'You just have, that's all. Who are you working with?'

'The whopper. What's her name?'

'The whopper?'

'Well, er, the big fat one,' said Sanscartier, embarrassed.

'Ah, Violette Retancourt.'

'Forgive me for asking, but when you do catch this dead man walking, even if it's in ten years' time, can you let me know?'

'Are you that interested?'

'Yes. And I've taken a shine to you.'

'I'll let you know. Even if it takes ten years.'

Adamsberg found himself going up in the lift with Danglard. His two days with Sanscartier the Good had calmed him down, and he postponed his decision to pick a bone with his deputy.

'Going out tonight, Danglard?' he asked in a neutral voice.

'No, I'm knackered. I'm going to have a bite to eat, then go to bed.'

'How are the children? Everything OK?'

'Yes, thanks,' replied the *capitaine*, looking a little surprised.

Adamsberg smiled as he went to his room. Danglard wasn't very skilled at subterfuge. The previous night he had heard him start his car at 6.30 p.m. and return at almost two in the morning. Time to drive to Montreal, listen to the concert and do his good deed for the day. So he was short of sleep, as one could tell from the rings round his eyes. Good old

Danglard, so certain that he was undetected, keeping his mouth shut about the secret that was a secret no longer. Tonight was the last concert in the series, which would mean another return trip for the gallant *capitaine*.

Adamsberg watched from his bedroom window, as Danglard made his furtive getaway. Drive safely and enjoy the concert, *capitaine*. He was watching the car's tail-lights, when Mordent called.

'Sorry not to get back to you before, *commissaire*, but we had a crisis on. A guy who was trying to kill his wife and call us at the same time. We had to surround the building.'

'Any damage?'

'No, his first bullet went into the piano and the second into his own foot. A complete loser, luckily.'

'Any news from Alsace?'

'Simplest thing is, I'll read you the article. It was on page eight of the Friday paper. "Doubts about the Schiltigheim murder? Following the investigation by the Schiltigheim *gendarmerie* into the tragic killing of Elisabeth Wind on Saturday 4 October, the authorities have placed in preventive detention the man who was reported to be helping them with their enquiries, Bernard Vétilleux. However, according to information that has reached us, Vétilleux was allegedly questioned by a senior detective from Paris. According to the same source, the murder of this young girl may be linked to a serial killer who has struck elsewhere in France. This theory is however firmly rejected by *Commandant* Trabelmann who is leading the investigation. He dismissed it as an idle rumour, and said that the arrest of Vétilleux was on the basis of cast-iron evidence." Is that what you were after, *commissaire*?'

'Absolutely. Can you hang on to the article for me? I'll just have to pray that Brézillon doesn't read the *Nouvelles d'Alsace*.'

'Would you prefer them not to charge Vétilleux?'

'Yes and no. It's hard to shovel earth.'

'OK,' said Mordent, non-committally. 'Thanks for the emails. It sounds interesting but not exactly fun, all those cards and discs.'

'Well, Justin's in his element, Retancourt can adapt to anything, Voisenet's supernaturally good at it, Froissy is just going through the motions, Noël is getting impatient, Estalère is perpetually amazed, and Danglard is becoming a concertgoer.'

'And what about you, *commissaire*?'

'Me? Oh I'm the shoveller of clouds. But keep that to yourself, Mordent, same as the article.'

From Mordent, Adamsberg went straight into the arms of Noëlla, whose growing passion was certainly a distraction from the irritating discovery in Montreal. A most determined girl, she had quickly resolved the problem of where to meet. He would pick her up at the Champlain stone, then it took them a quarter of an hour to walk along the cycle track to a bicycle-hire shop; one of its sash windows didn't shut properly. Noëlla brought in her rucksack everything they needed, sandwiches, hot drinks and a camping mattress. Adamsberg left her at eleven, returning by the portage trail, which he could now walk blindfold, passing the timber site, waving to the watchman and greeting the Ottawa River before going back to sleep.

Work, river, forest, willing partner. Not so bad after all. Forget about the new father, and as for the Trident, keep repeating Sanscartier's words: 'You've got what it takes, just follow your hunches.' Sanscartier was the one he wanted most to believe, although from various allusions by Portelance and Ladouceur, he was not thought to be the brains of the group.

There had been a slight shadow cast over the scene that evening by Noëlla. A short exchange, which luckily went no further.

'Take me back to Paris with you,' said the young woman, as she lay on the camping mattress.

'Sorry, I can't, I'm married,' said Adamsberg instinctively.

'You're lying.'

He had kissed her then, to put a stop to any further conversation.

XXIV

THE DAYS WORKING WITH GINETTE SAINT-PREUX PASSED PEACEABLY, except for the growing complexity of the course, which obliged Adamsberg to start taking notes from his teammate's dictation. 'Transfer to amplification chamber, production of copies of the sample by the thermal cycler.'

'OK, Ginette, whatever you say.'

But Ginette who was as talkative as she was determined, had spotted Adamsberg's vague expression and was not letting him off the hook.

'Don't switch off, it's not that hard to understand. Imagine a molecular photocopy machine, producing millions of examples of segments. Right?'

'Right,' repeated Adamsberg automatically.

'The products of the amplification carry a fluorescent tag which makes it easy to detect with a laser-scanner. Do you get it now?'

'Yes, Ginette, I get it fine. Just carry on, I'm watching.'

Noëlla was waiting for him on the Thursday evening, perched on her bike, and smiling broadly with a confident air. Once the mattress had been unrolled on the floor of the shop, she leant up on one elbow, and reached out to take something from her rucksack.

'Surprise, surprise,' she said, brandishing an envelope.

She waved it in front of his eyes with a laugh. Adamsberg sat up, apprehensively.

'She's managed to get a seat on the same flight as you, next Tuesday.'

'Are you going back to Paris? Already?'

'I'm going home with you.'

'Noëlla, I've already told you, I'm married. No way.'

'Liar.'

He kissed her again, feeling more worried than before.

XXV

ADAMSBERG LINGERED TO HAVE A CHAT WITH THE SQUIRREL ON DUTY outside the RCMP base, in order to put off for a few minutes the day working with Mitch Portelance. Today, the squirrel had recruited a little girlfriend, who was distracting him somewhat from his guard duty. Quite unlike the humourless Portelance, a high-flying scientist who had taken to genetics like a duck to water, and had dedicated his entire professional fervour to molecules of DNA. Unlike Ginette, the inspector failed to realise that Adamsberg could not follow his explanations, let alone find any enthusiasm for them, and he tended to spit out facts with a machine-gun delivery. Adamsberg took some notes now and then, trying to retain elements of this scientific harangue. 'Deposit of every sample on to a specially-designed membrane sample comb . . . introduction to the sequencer.'

'A membrane comb(?)' Adamsberg was writing. 'Transfer of the DNA into separator gel with the aid of an electric field. Separator gel(?)'

'Now look what's happening!' said Portelance. 'We're witnessing a sort of molecular race, in which the fragments of DNA move through the gel to reach the finishing line.'

'Er . . . really?'

'Which is a detector that picks up the fragments as they emerge from the sequencer, one by one, in increasing order of length.'

'Fascinating,' said Adamsberg, drawing in his notebook a huge queen ant, pursued by about a hundred winged males.

'What's that you're drawing?' asked Portelance, with some irritation in his voice.

'The fragments racing through the gel. It helps me to get a clearer understanding.'

'Now, here's the result,' said Portelance, pointing to the screen. 'The profile made up of 28 bands sorted for us by the sequencer. Beautiful, isn't it?'

'Very.'

'This combination,' Mitch went on, 'which is for Jules Saint-Croix's urine, if you remember, gives us his forensic genetic profile, which is unique in the whole world.'

Adamsberg contemplated the transformation of Jules's urine into 28 bands. So this was Jules: *ecce homo.*

'See, if it was your urine,' Mitch explained, 'it would look completely different.'

'But why 28 strips? And not 142?'

'Where do you get 142 from?'

'Nowhere, I'm just asking why 28?'

'It just is 28, that's what I'm telling you. So if you kill someone, it's not a good idea to piss on the body.'

Mitch Portelance gave a shout of laughter.

'Don't mind me,' he said. 'Just my little joke.'

During the afternoon coffee-break, Adamsberg found Voisenet, drinking a regular, and chatting to Ladouceur. Gesturing to him, he took him aside.

'Voisenet, can you follow all this stuff? The gel, the race, the 28 bands?'

'Yeah, pretty much.'

'Well, I can't. Can you do me a favour and draw up the day's report for Mordent, this stuff's way beyond me.'

'Does Portelance go too fast for you?'

'Well, maybe I go too slowly for him. Tell me something, Voisenet,' said Adamsberg taking out his notebook. 'See this fish, does it mean anything to you?'

Voisenet looked with interest at the sketch of the creature from the bottom of Pink Lake.

'No, never seen one,' he said, intrigued. 'Is the drawing accurate?'

'To the nearest fin.'

'No, not one I know at all,' said the *lieutenant* again, shaking his head, 'and I do know a bit about ichthyofauna.'

'About what?'

'Fish.'

'Can you just call them fish, please? I'm already having enough trouble understanding our Canadian colleagues, don't you start.'

'Where's it from?'

'From a lake that's cursed, *lieutenant*, in fact two lakes, one on top of the other, a living lake on top of a dead lake.'

'Sorry?'

'Twenty metres deep, including three metres worth of ancient mud, ten thousand years old. Nothing stirs at the bottom. But this ancient fish lives down there, left over from when the sea covered the area. A sort of living fossil that oughtn't to be there at all, by rights. Makes you wonder how on earth it survived. Or why. Anyway, there it is, and it's thrashing round in the lake bottom like a devil in holy water.'

'Wow,' said Voisenet, who couldn't take his eyes off the drawing. 'Are you sure this isn't some legend?'

'The notice board looked pretty official. What were you thinking of? The Loch Ness monster?'

'Oh, Nessie's not a fish, she's supposed to be a reptile. Where's the lake, *commissaire*?'

Adamsberg, staring into the distance, did not reply.

'Where is it?' Voisenet repeated.

Adamsberg looked up. He had been wondering what would happen if Nessie was stuffed into the west door of Strasbourg Cathedral. That would have been a sight for sore eyes. But while it might be out of the ordinary, it wouldn't have been too dramatic. Since the Loch Ness Monster didn't breathe out smoke, she would have been unable to blow up the jewel of Gothic architecture.

'Sorry, Voisenet, I was miles away. Pink Lake, it's called, not all that far from here. It's pink and blue, magnificent on the surface. But don't be deceived by appearances. And if you see the fish, grab hold of it for me.'

'Oh no,' Voisenet protested. 'I like fish, I'm not going to harm it.'

'Well, I don't like this one. Come along, I'll show you the lake on the map.'

Adamsberg took care not to risk meeting Noëlla, when he had finished work that evening. He parked in a street some blocks away, went through his building by the back door in the basement, then avoided the portage trail altogether. He cut across through the forest, went past the logging site, and met the watchman just starting his shift.

'Hey man,' said the watchman with a hearty wave. 'Still walking everywhere?'

'Yes, how's yourself?' said Adamsberg with a smile, but without stopping.

He only lit his torch when he was safely two-thirds along the trail, well past Noëlla's stone, and rejoined the path.

Where she was waiting for him, twenty metres further along, leaning against a tree.

'Come on,' she said, grabbing his hand. 'Got something to tell you.'

'Noëlla, I'm supposed to be having dinner with my colleagues tonight, I can't come.'

'This won't take long.'

Adamsberg allowed himself to be dragged to the bicycle-hire shop and sat down prudently a few feet away from the young woman.

'You've fallen in love with me,' she declared. 'I knew it the very first time I saw you on the trail.'

'Noëlla . . .'

'Yes, I knew it,' she interrupted. 'That it was you, and that you would fall in love with me. He told me. That was why I came and sat on the stone every night, not just to take the air.'

'What do you mean, "he"?'

'This old Indian, Shawi. He told me that the other half of Noëlla would appear to me on the stone of the ancient Ottawa Indians.'

'What old Indian are you talking about?'

'In Sainte-Agathe-des-Monts. He's an Algonquin, a descendant of the ancient Ottawa people. He knows. I waited and you came along.'

'Good God, Noëlla, you don't believe that kind of thing?'

'You, and only you,' said Noëlla, pointing at him. 'You love me, as much as I love you. And for as long as the river runs, nothing will separate us now. You are my destiny.'

Nuts, completely nuts.

Laliberté had been right. There was something weird about this girl, all alone at dawn on the portage trail.

'Noëlla,' he said, standing up and walking around. 'Look, you're a beautiful girl, you're fantastic, you're cute, I like you a whole lot – but I am not in love with you. I'm married, and I love my wife. Forgive me, but that's how it is.'

'You're lying. You're not married at all. Shawi told me. And you love me.'

'No, Noëlla. We only met a few days ago. You were sad, because of your boyfriend, I was lonely, away from home, and that was how it happened. But it's over, now. I'm really sorry.'

'It's not over, it's just beginning, for good. Here,' said the young woman pointing to her abdomen.

'What do you mean?'

'Here,' said Noëlla calmly. 'Our baby.'

'Now *you're* lying,' said Adamsberg dully. 'You can't know that so soon.'

'Yes, I can. The tests give a reply in three days. And Shawi told me I would bear your child.'

'That's complete rubbish, Noëlla!'

'No, it's true. And now you can't leave Noëlla, who loves you and who's carrying your child.'

Adamsberg turned instinctively to the sash window. He pushed it up and jumped out.

'See you on Tuesday, at the airport!' cried Noëlla.

Adamsberg reached the cycle track and ran until he was back near the residence. Breathing rapidly, he got into his car and drove off towards the forest, hurtling too fast along dirt roads. He stopped at an isolated bar, and bought a pizza and a glass of beer. He ate hungrily, sitting on a tree stump at the edge of the forest. Trapped, caught like an idiot by that half-crazy girl, who had flung herself round his neck. So unbalanced that he was sure she really would turn up at the airport on Tuesday and insist on coming to his flat in Paris. He ought to have known, or sensed, when he had first seen her sitting on that stone, behaving in such a strange and direct way, that Noëlla was fantasising. He had indeed tried to avoid her for the first few days. But the damned quintet had thrown him, like a brute and a fool, into Noëlla's tentacular arms.

The food and the night cold restored his energy. His panic turned into blind fury. For Christ's sake, no one should have the right to trap a man like that! He'd throw her out of the plane! Or if they got to Paris, he'd throw her in the Seine!

Oh God, he thought as he stood up, the number of people he was ready to massacre was growing daily, with all these blind rages. Favre, the Trident, Danglard, the New Father, and now this girl. As Sanscartier would say, he was losing the plot. And he couldn't make out what was happening to him. Whether with these rages or with the clouds which, for the first time, he had no taste for shovelling. The recurrent images of the dead judge, the trident, the claw marks of the bears, and the evil lake were beginning to weigh heavily on him and it seemed he was losing control of his own clouds. Yes, it was quite possible that he was losing the plot.

He made his way back to his room with a heavy tread, slipping in the back way, like a thief or a man trapped inside himself.

XXVI

VOISENET HAD GONE RUSHING OFF TO PINK LAKE WITH FROISSY AND Retancourt. Another two colleagues had made tracks to the bars of Montreal, dragging the scrupulous Justin with them, and Danglard was catching up on his sleep. Adamsberg meanwhile spent the weekend creeping around surreptitiously. Nature had always been his friend – with the exception of the sinister Pink Lake – and it was better to trust to it than to stay in his room, where Noëlla might turn up at any minute. He slipped out of doors at daybreak, before anyone else was stirring, and drove to Meech Lake.

There he spent long hours, walking across wooden bridges or along the lakeside, plunging his arms up to the elbows in the snow. He thought it wise not to return to Hull overnight, so he slept at an inn in Maniwaki, praying that the dreaded prophetic Shawi would not appear in his bedroom bringing his fervent disciple with him. On the Sunday, he tired himself out hiking all day through the woods, picking up birch bark and redder-than-red maple leaves, and wondering where he would find refuge that night.

Poetry perhaps. Maybe he should go and eat in the poets' pub? The *Quatrain* didn't seem to attract the young, and Noëlla would probably not think of looking for him there. He left the car some distance from the residence again, and went downtown via the big boulevard, not by the wretched trail.

Feeling worn out, and on edge, as well as short of ideas, he swallowed a plateful of French fries, while half listening to the poems being read. Suddenly, Danglard appeared at his side.

'Good weekend?' the *capitaine* asked, trying to be conciliatory.

'What about you, Danglard? Did you get some sleep?' said Adamsberg snappily. 'Treachery can keep you awake sometimes, if your conscience is bothering you.'

'Sorry?'

'Treachery. I'm not speaking Algonquin, as Laliberté might say. Months and months of secrecy and silence, not to mention driving six hundred kilometres or more in the last few days, and all because the *capitaine* likes Vivaldi.'

'Ah!' murmured Danglard, laying his hands on the table.

'As you say, ah! Applauding the concert, fetching and carrying, driving the lady home, opening the door. A proper little knight in shining armour.'

'Well, after all . . .'

'You mean *before* all, Danglard. You've taken his side. The Other One. The one with two labradors and new shoelaces. Against me, Danglard, against me.'

'You've lost me, I'm sorry,' said Danglard, getting to his feet.

'Just a minute,' said Adamsberg, pulling him back by the sleeve. 'I'm talking about the choice you've made. The child, the handshake for the new father, and do come in, welcome to the happy home. That's it, isn't it, *capitaine.*'

Danglard rubbed his fingers across his mouth. Then he leaned towards Adamsberg.

'In my book, *commissaire*, as our colleagues here might say, you're a stupid bastard.'

Adamsberg sat at the table, in shock, letting Danglard walk away. The unexpected insult was echoing round and round his head. Customers trying to listen to the poetry made it clear to him that he and his friend had already disturbed them enough. He left the cafe, looking for the seediest bar he could find downtown, a men-only sort of bar, where crazy Noëlla would not find him. It was a vain hope, since in the clean and tidy streets there were no rundown old bars, whereas in Paris they grew like weeds in the cracks of the pavements. He ended up in a little place called *L'Ecluse*. Danglard's words must have hit a nerve, since he could feel a serious headache coming on, something that happened only about once every ten years.

'*Commissaire*, in my book you're a stupid bastard.'

Nor had he forgotten the words of Trabelmann, Brézillon, Favre, or the imagined new father. Not to mention the scary conversation with Noëlla. Insults, betrayals and threats.

And since the headache was getting worse, the only thing for it was to treat an exception with an exceptional cure, and get well and truly wasted. Adamsberg did not drink much, as a rule, and could hardly remember the last time he had been seriously drunk: it was as a young man, at some village festival, with everything that went with it. But on the whole, from what he had heard, people thought it worked. Drown your sorrows, they said. OK, that's exactly what he needed.

He installed himself at the bar between two Québécois who were already well-launched on beer, and for starters drank three whiskies in a row. The walls didn't seem to be moving around, he felt fine, and the troubled contents of his head were now being transferred to his stomach. Leaning on the counter, he ordered a bottle of wine, having gathered from reliable informants that mixing drinks usually produced fast results. After drinking four glasses, he ordered a cognac to top it all off. Rigour, rigour and yet more rigour, no other way to succeed. Good ol' Laliberté. What a chum, eh.

The barman was beginning to look at him anxiously. Well, you can go fuck yourself, buddy, I'm heading for sweet oblivion. Vivaldi would understand. Oh yeah.

Prudently, Adamsberg had already laid out enough dollars on the counter, in case he fell off his stool. The cognac seemed to put an interesting final touch to his radical loss of bearings, vague feelings of aggression mingled with bursts of laughter, and a sense of immense strength. Come on, I'll fight anyone, a bear, a chum, a dead man, or a fish, anything you like. 'Any nearer and I'll spear ye,' his grandmother had said, brandishing a garden fork against a German soldier, who was advancing on her with rape in mind. That was a laugh, it rhymed. It still made him laugh, that. Good ol' *grand'mère*! From very far away, he heard the barman saying something.

'Don't take this the wrong way, pal, but you'd better call it quits for tonight, and go take the air. You're not making sense.'

'I'm talking to you about my grandma.'

'Grandma, whatever, I don't care, all I know is you've had way too much, and you're gonna fall flat on your face.'

'I'm not goin' anywhere, I'm sitting at this nice bar, on this nice stool.'

'Listen to you, Frenchie. You can't even see straight, you're so smashed. Did your girl let you down, or what? No reason to fall on your ass. C'mon, out with you, I'm not serving you any more.'

'Yes, you are,' said Adamsberg, holding out his glass.

'Shut up, Frenchie. Get out or I'm calling the pigs.'

Adamsberg spluttered. The pigs, eh? What a laugh.

'Any nearer an' I'll spear ye! An' that goes for the pigs as well.'

'Christ Almighty,' said the barman, furiously, 'don't you try any funny business with me, you're really pissing me off. I told you, eff off out of it!'

The man was built like a lumberjack from a story book, and when he came round the bar, he lifted Adamsberg up under the armpits, carried him to the door and dumped him upright on the sidewalk.

'And don't try driving,' he said, handing him his jacket.

The barman was even kind enough to wedge his cap firmly on his head.

'Gonna be cold tonight, 12 below they say,' he explained.

'What time is it? Can't see my watches.'

'Quarter after ten, way past your bedtime. Just walk home. No cars. And don't worry, man, plenty more girls out there.'

The door of the bar slammed shut in Adamsberg's face, and he had difficulty picking up his jacket which had fallen on the ground, and then putting it on the right way round. More girls. No thanks, just what he didn't want.

'Got one girl too many!' he shouted out in the deserted street for the barman's benefit.

His uncertain steps took him automatically towards the portage trail. He had the vague feeling Noëlla might be there waiting for him, in the shadows like a wolf. He found his flashlight and switched it on, sweeping it vaguely in front of him.

'Don't want any more, got enough!' he shouted.

Guy who can beat up a bear, or the cops, he can handle one girl, can't he?

Adamsberg embarked determinedly along the trail. Despite his staggering progress, the memory of the path was implanted in his feet, which carried him along valiantly, even if from time to time he bumped into a tree trunk. He was about half-way home already, he reckoned. You can handle it, my boy, you've sure got what it takes.

Not enough of it, however, to miss a low branch he should have avoided. It hit him full in the forehead, and he felt himself drop to the ground, knees first, then face, without his hands being able to break his fall.

XXVII

WHEN ADAMSBERG REGAINED CONSCIOUSNESS, IT WAS WITH A WAVE OF nausea. His forehead was throbbing so much that he could hardly open his eyes. When he did manage to focus, he could see nothing. The world had gone black.

The black was the night sky, he eventually realised, his teeth chattering. He was no longer on the trail, but on a metalled road, and the air was freezing cold. He raised himself on to one arm, propping up his head. Then he stayed sitting for a while, unable to move further, since the ground seemed to be swaying all over the place. What in heaven's name had he been doing? He recognised the sound of the Ottawa River, not far away. That at least helped him to get his bearings. He was at the edge of the trail, only about fifty metres from the residence block. He must have passed out after hitting his head on the branch, then tottered along for a while, and fallen over again, on reaching the road. Putting his hands on the ground, he pushed himself up, holding on to a tree trunk to counter the dizziness. Just another fifty metres, that was all, and he would be in his room. He moved forward clumsily through the biting cold air, stopping every few steps to regain his balance, then setting off once more. The muscles in his legs seemed to have turned to jelly.

The sight of the well-lit entrance guided him the last few steps. He pushed, and shook the glass door. The key, oh God, where was the damn key? Leaning his elbow on a door-panel, sweat freezing on his face, he managed to locate it in a pocket and pushed it into the lock under the eyes of the night janitor who was looking at him in consternation.

'Jeez, what's happened to you, *commissaire?*'

'I'm not too good,' Adamsberg managed to say.

'Need any help?'

Adamsberg shook his head, accentuating the pain under his skull. He had only one desire, to lie down and not to have to talk.

'It's nothing,' he said feebly. 'Just a bust-up. A gang.'

'Goddamn hoodlums. Going round in gangs looking for trouble. Ought to be locked up.'

Adamsberg nodded agreement and called the lift. Once in his room, he rushed into the bathroom, and expelled a great deal of alcohol. Good grief, what vile concoctions had they served him?

His legs trembling, his arms shaking, he flung himself on the bed, keeping his eyes open, to stop the room from spinning round.

When he woke up, his head felt almost as heavy as before, but he had a sense that the worst was over. He got up and took a few steps. His legs felt a little more solid, but were still inclined to give way under him. He fell back on the bed, then gave a start, when he caught sight of his hands, which were caked with dried blood, even under the nails. He hauled himself to the bathroom and looked in the mirror. Not a pretty sight. The blow on the forehead had made a gash and a large purple bruise. It must have bled a lot, then he must have rubbed his face and got it on his hands. Great, he thought, as he started to sponge his face carefully, a brilliant Sunday night out. Then he froze, and turned off the tap. It was Monday morning. At nine o'clock, he was due at the RCMP building.

His alarm clock was showing a quarter to eleven. Oh Lord, he must have slept more than twelve hours. He took the precaution of sitting down before he called Laliberté.

'What kind of a joke is this?' said the superintendent with a smile in his voice. 'Clock stopped?'

'Forgive me, Aurèle, but I'm not in good shape.'

'What is it?' said Laliberté with concern, his voice changing register. 'You sound terrible.'

'Yeah, I feel terrible. I knocked myself out and took a fall on the trail last night. Blood everywhere, I was sick as a dog and this morning my legs feel weak.'

'Wait a minute, man, you fell over, or you had a skinful? Sounds like those things don't fit together.'

'Both, Aurèle.'

'OK, tell me about it from the beginning. You'd had too much to drink, right?'

'Yes. I don't do that as a rule, so it went straight to my head.'

'You were bingeing with your pals?'

'No, I was on my own in the rue Laval.'

'Why were you drinking on your own? You had the blues?'

'Yeah, right.'

'Homesick? Don't you like it here?'

'I like it fine here, Aurèle, everything's been great. I just had a sudden attack of the blues. Not worth talking about.'

'OK, I won't pry. So then what?'

'I took the portage trail to get home, and God help me, I hit my head on a branch.'

'Christ, where'd it hit you?'

'Bang in the middle of my forehead.'

'You saw stars, right?'

'I just keeled over, knocked right out. After that, I managed to drag myself home to the residence. I'm just waking up now.'

'Did you go to sleep in your clothes? That bad?'

'That bad, yes. This morning, my head's aching and my legs won't carry me. That's why I'm phoning you. I shouldn't drive yet, so I won't be in till two o'clock.'

'Don't be crazy. I'm not a slave driver. Just stay where you are, Jean-Baptiste, relax and take something. Got any pills for the headache?'

'No.'

Laliberté put the phone down and called Ginette. Adamsberg heard his voice echoing through the office. 'Ginette, take some medicine round to the *commissaire*, he's got the mother of all hangovers, can't move.'

'Saint-Preux will bring you some stuff,' the superintendent said into the telephone. 'Don't budge, stay put, OK? See you tomorrow when you feel a bit better.'

Adamsberg took a shower so that Ginette would not see his face and hands covered in dried blood. He brushed underneath his fingernails and, once he was dressed, he looked almost presentable, except for the large purple lump on his forehead.

Ginette gave him various medicaments, for his head, his stomach, his legs. She washed and disinfected the cut on his forehead and applied some ointment. With expert gestures, she looked at his pupils, and checked his reflexes. Adamsberg allowed himself to be dealt with as if he were a stuffed dummy. She was reassured by the examination, and gave him advice for the rest of the day. Take the pills every four hours. Drink a lot, just water of course. Keep the wound clean, and pass plenty of water. Adamsberg agreed, meekly.

Without chatting this time, she left him a few magazines to distract him, if he felt able to read, and some food for the evening. His Canadian colleagues were really very considerate, that had better go into the report.

He left the magazines on the table, and lay down, just as he was. He slept, dreamed, lay looking at the ventilator in the ceiling, got up every four hours to take his pills, had a drink of water, went to the lavatory, and lay down again. By eight in the evening, he was feeling better. The headache had seeped away into the pillow and his legs felt more solid.

Laliberté chose that moment to call and ask how he was, and he was able to get up almost normally to answer the telephone.

'No worse?' asked the superintendent.

'Much better thanks, Aurèle.'

'Not dizzy any more?'

'No.'

'Good. Take your time tomorrow, Jean-Baptiste, someone will drive you to the airport. Do you need any help with your luggage?'

'No, no, I'm feeling almost back to normal.'

'Sleep well then, and I hope you'll be OK for our session tomorrow.'

Adamsberg felt obliged to try and swallow some of the food Ginette had brought him, then decided to risk a short walk as far as the river to see it for the last time. The outside temperature was 10 below.

The janitor stopped him at the door.

'Feeling better?' he asked. 'You were in a helluva state last night. Goddamn gangs. Did you manage to run 'em in?'

'Yeah, the lot. Sorry to have roused you.'

'No harm done, I wasn't asleep. It was nearly two in the morning, but I'm not sleeping well.'

'Nearly two in the morning?' asked Adamsberg turning back. 'Late as that?'

'Yeah, ten to two, to be precise. I didn't get to sleep at all last night.'

Feeling rattled, Adamsberg pushed his fists deep into his pockets as he headed down to the river and turned right. He was certainly not going to sit down in the cold, let alone risk meeting the dreaded Noëlla.

Ten to two in the morning. The *commissaire* paced up and down on the little sandy stretch lining the bank. The geese were there, their commander-in-chief still at it, marshalling his troops for the night, whipping in the stragglers and latecomers. He could hear his imperious cackling behind his back. Well, that was one customer who didn't get depressed and try to drown his sorrows in a bar in the rue Laval, for sure. It made him hate the well-organised bird even more. A Canada gander, who probably checked every morning to see his feathers were in tiptop condition and his shoelaces properly tied. Adamsberg turned up his collar. Never mind the geese, just put your thinking cap on, as Clémentine would say. It isn't rocket science. Follow the advice she and Sanscartier had given him. For the moment they were his only guardian angels: an eccentric old woman and an innocent unpromoted sergeant. Well, everyone has his own guardian angels. Just put your thinking cap on.

Ten to two in the morning. Up to when he had crashed into the branch, he could remember everything. He had asked the barman the time. Quarter after ten, way past your bedtime, man. However much he was swaying about, he could hardly have taken more than forty minutes to reach the place on the path where he had hit the branch. Let's allow three-quarters of an hour maximum, to cover not walking straight. It couldn't have been more, because his legs were working perfectly well then. So he must have hit the tree at about eleven o'clock. Then allow for waking up on the road, and another twenty minutes to make it to the building. He must have regained consciousness at about one-thirty in the morning. Therefore two and a half hours must have passed between hitting the branch and coming to, feeling sick, at the end of the trail. Two and a half hours, for a journey that usually took him little more than half an hour!

What the hell had he been doing in those two and a half hours? His mind was a complete blank. Had he been unconscious all that time? But the temperature was minus 12 degrees. He would surely have frozen to the spot. He must have been walking, moving about. Perhaps he had dragged himself slowly along the trail, falling then getting up again, making erratic progress, interspersed with fainting fits.

Alcohol and mixed drinks. He knew people who could shout all night without having any memory of it next day. Guys in the cells, who had to be told in the morning what they had been up to: beating the wife, chucking the dog out of the window. Black holes of two or three hours, before falling into a deep sleep. In that time, they'd been responsible for actions, words and gestures, plenty of them, but all lost to conscious memory, since their minds were befuddled with drink. It was as if the alcohol diluted any attempt to record a memory, like the ink from a pen writing on sodden paper.

What had he drunk?

Three whiskies, four glasses of wine and one of cognac. And if the barman, who seemed to know his job, judged the time had come to chuck him out, he no doubt had good reason. Barmen can estimate exactly how many degrees of alcohol you have in your blood, as certainly as the Mounties' DNA laboratory. The man had seen his customer go over the line, and refused to serve him another glass, even if it would have meant a few more bucks. They're like that, barmen. They may look like shopkeepers, but they're really chemists, vigilant philanthropists, lifesavers. And indeed he remembered the barman had even taken care to pull his cap firmly on to his head.

Well, that was all there was to it, Adamsberg concluded, turning homewards. He had got monumentally drunk, and then he had hit his head. Pissed out of his mind and knocked unconscious. After that, he had spent two and a half hours crawling along the path, tripping and falling every few steps. So drunk that his sodden memory couldn't register anything. He had gone into the bar in search of forgetfulness, the famous oblivion that lies at the bottom of a glass. Well, he had certainly got more than he'd bargained for.

On his return, he felt well enough to do his packing and clear up the room. A tidy room was what he would have liked to find back home in Paris. He felt overburdened by turbulent clouds, great dark cumulus clouds crashing into each other like swollen toads, not forgetting the thunderbolts as well. What he ought to do was cut up those clouds into little samples, and put them all on collection cards and paper discs. Not mix them all up in a great heavy sack. He would treat obstacles in future as he had learnt to handle them here, methodically taking cloud samples, one by one, in ascending order of length. If he was capable of that. He thought of the next obstacle looming up; the presence of Noëlla tomorrow at the airport, ready for the 20.10 flight to Paris.

XXVIII

HIS HEADACHE HAD LIFTED BY THE MORNING, AND ADAMSBERG ARRIVED punctually at the RCMP base, parking his car under the same maple tree and greeting the usual squirrel, finding a kind of penitential comfort in reconnecting with his briefly-established Quebec routine. All his colleagues asked how he was, but no one made any ironic references to drink. Warmth and discretion. Ginette said approvingly that the swelling on his forehead had gone down and gave him some more of the sticky ointment.

Everyone was in fact so discreet that he realised, with astonishment, that Laliberté could not have thought it necessary to tell the French group about the episode in *L'Ecluse*. The superintendent had stuck to the sober version of events: an accident caused by bumping into a tree branch in the dark. Adamsberg appreciated this considerate omission, since most people enjoy a good story about their superiors hitting the bottle. Danglard would have taken advantage of his drunken fall, and Noël would have made some meaningful jokes. And since one joke led to another, if news of the incident had reached the ears of Brézillon's circle, he would have felt the consequences of it in relation to the Favre affair. Ginette was the only person who knew the full story, so that she could bring him medical help, and she too had not breathed a word to anyone else. This tact and restraint must mean that the Chat Room in Ottawa was of minute proportions, whereas in Paris, it tended to overflow the walls of the building and spill out over the pavement terrace of the *Brasserie des Philosophes*.

Danglard was the only one who did not enquire about his state of health. The imminence of their take-off that evening had once more plunged him into a state of debilitating panic, which he was doing his best to conceal from their Canadian colleagues.

Adamsberg passed the final day as a conscientious student under the tuition of Alphonse Philippe-Auguste, who was as unassuming as his surname was grandiose. At three in the afternoon, the superintendent called a halt to the session and brought the sixteen participants in the course together for a summing-up conference and a farewell drink.

The discreet Sanscartier came up to Adamsberg.

'You had a few too many, the other night, I guess?' he asked.

'Er, you think?' said Adamsberg prudently.

'You're not going to tell me a guy like you just walked into a tree. You've got a feel for nature and you knew the path like the back of your hand by then.'

'So?'

'So in my book, you had an attack of the blues, because of your problem back home, or something. You downed a few drinks, and that's why you walked into that branch.'

Sanscartier was a hands-on policeman, who knew his stuff.

'Does it really matter why I bumped into the branch?' asked Adamsberg.

'Yeah, it does. Because when you've got the blues, that's exactly when you start bumping into branches. And if you're still chasing that devil, you need to keep out of their way. You shouldn't wait for hell to freeze over to get to the other side, if you dig my meaning. Put out more sail, hang on in there, and go for it.'

Adamsberg smiled at him.

'You won't forget me, will you?' said Sanscartier, as they shook hands. 'You promised you're going to let me know when you catch your devil. And could you please send me some almond-scented soap?'

'What was that?'

'I knew this French guy, he had some. I liked the smell.'

'Right, Sanscartier. I'll send you some.'

Happiness is a bar of almond-scented soap. For a few seconds, Adamsberg envied the sergeant his simple desires. Almond-scented soap suited him down to the ground. It could have been invented for him.

In the check-in hall of the airport, Ginette inspected the wound on Adamsberg's forehead one last time, while he looked anxiously around for Noëlla. The moment of their departure was approaching and there was no sign of her so far. He began to breathe more easily.

'If it hurts in the plane because of the pressure, take some of these,' said Ginette, giving him some pills. She put the ointment tube in his bag, and told him to go on applying it for a week.

'Don't forget, now,' she said, distrustingly.

Adamsberg kissed her goodbye, then went over to the superintendent.

'Thanks for everything, Aurèle, and thanks especially for not letting on to the colleagues.'

'Christ, Jean-Baptiste, everyone has too much to drink once in a while. Not a good idea to shout it from the rooftops though, otherwise you won't hear the end of it.'

The sound of the jet engines produced the same disastrous result on Danglard as on the way out. This time, Adamsberg avoided sitting next to him, but he posted Retancourt behind him, with orders to carry out her mission. Which she did twice during the flight, so that when the plane landed next morning at Roissy-Charles-de-Gaulle, everyone was exhausted, except Danglard, who was as fresh as a daisy. Finding himself alive and well and back on Parisian soil opened up new horizons for him, making him feel both indulgent and optimistic. So before getting on the bus, he came over to Adamsberg.

'I'm really sorry about the other night,' he said. 'I apologise sincerely. It wasn't what I meant to say.'

Adamsberg gave a vague nod, then all the members of the Brigade dispersed. It was to be a day of rest and recuperation.

And of getting used to their old existence once more. Compared to the vast expanses of Canada, Paris seemed pinched to Adamsberg, the trees were spindly, the streets crowded with people, and the squirrels like pigeons. Unless, that is, it was he who had shrunk while he had been away. He needed to think, to separate the samples into segments and bands, as he remembered.

As soon as he was home, he made himself some real coffee, sat down at the kitchen table and attempted something unusual for him, organising his thoughts. A cardboard file card, a pencil, a set of test tubes, and samples of the clouds in his head. The results weren't really worthy of the laser sequencer. After an hour of effort, he had managed to make only a few notes.

The dead judge, the trident. Raphaël. Bears' claws on trees, Pink Lake, devil in holy water. Fossil fish. Vivaldi's warning. New father, 2 labradors.

Danglard: 'In my book, you're a stupid bastard.' Sanscartier the Good: 'Look for your damn demon and until you collar him, lie low.'

Drunk. Two and a half hours on the trail.

Noëlla. Seems to be out of the way.

And that was it. All mixed up, what was more. Only one positive thing came out of all this: he was rid of that crazy girl, which was a satisfying point to end on.

While unpacking, he found the ointment left him by Ginette Saint-Preux. Not the best souvenir from a trip abroad, although in the tube there seemed to him to be concentrated all the goodwill of his Québécois colleagues. They were bloody good chums. He must absolutely not forget to send the soap to Sanscartier. That suddenly reminded him that he had brought nothing back for Clémentine, not even a bottle of maple syrup.

XXIX

THE MASS OF PAPERWORK AWAITING HIM AT THE OFFICE THAT THURSDAY morning, arranged in five high piles on his desk, almost sent him fleeing along the banks of the Seine, even if the Paris river seemed humble and narrow compared to the Ottawa River. But a walk was still a more tempting prospect than ploughing his way through mountains of dossiers.

His first move was to pin on his bulletin board a postcard of the Ottawa River Falls, surrounded by red maple leaves. Standing back to judge the effect, he found it so inadequate that he immediately took it down. A picture couldn't convey the glacial wind, the crashing of the water and the furious cackling of the boss of the Canada geese.

He spent the entire day working through the files, checking, signing, sorting out and learning about the cases which had come to the Crime Squad during the two weeks he had been away. One thug had beaten up another on the boulevard Ney and then pissed on him as a finishing touch. 'Not a good idea to piss on the body, man.' So he'd be caught, no problem, thanks to analysis of the piss. Adamsberg countersigned reports by his lieutenants and broke off to visit the coffee machine, and drink a 'regular', Paris-style. Mordent, perched on one of the high stools, like a large grey bird on a chimney-stack, was drinking a cup of chocolate.

'I took the liberty of following that case, the *Nouvelles d'Alsace* one,' he said, wiping his lips. 'Vétilleux's on remand, and he'll go for trial in three months.'

'He's not guilty, Mordent. I tried to convince Trabelmann, but he just won't believe me. Nor will anyone else, come to that.'

'Not enough evidence?'

'Not a scrap. The murderer's someone who melts into thin air and he's been dodging around in the mist for years now.'

He did not intend to inform Mordent that the murderer was dead, and thus start losing credibility with his staff one after another. 'Don't bother trying to convince them,' Sanscartier had said.

'So, how are you going to make any progress then?' asked Mordent.

'I'll have to wait for him to strike again and try to pin him down before he disappears.'

'Not a very cheering prospect,' commented Mordent.

'No. But how do you catch a ghost?'

Curiously enough, Mordent seemed to give serious thought to this question. Adamsberg took a seat alongside him, his legs hanging down from the stool. There were eight of these high stools in the Chat Room and Adamsberg had often thought that if you could get eight people to perch on them, they would look like swallows on the telegraph wires. But so far it hadn't happened.

'Well, how?' he asked.

'By irr-it-ating him,' was Mordent's reply.

The *commandant* always spoke in a very deliberate fashion, detaching each syllable distinctly and sometimes dwelling on one, as if with his finger on a piano key. It was a manner of diction which was both jerky and slow, and it annoyed people in a hurry, but Adamsberg rather liked it.

'And that means?'

'In stories or films, what happens is that a family moves into a haunted house. Until then, the ghost has been quiet, not annoying a-ny-bo-dy.'

Well, well, Trabelmann wasn't the only person who liked stories, Mordent did too. Perhaps everybody did, even Brézillon.

'And then what?' asked Adamsberg, helping himself to a second regular because of his jet-lag, and perching himself back on the stool.

'Then the newcomers start to get on the ghost's nerves. Why? Because they move in and change everything, cleaning cupboards, opening old trunks, emptying the attic. So they flush him out of his regular haunts. His favourite spots are out of bounds. Or perhaps they discover his most in-tim-ate secret.'

'What secret?'

'It's always the same: his or-ig-inal sin, his first murder. Because if he hadn't done something really serious, the character wouldn't have been doomed to haunt the house for three hundred years. Walling up his wife, killing his brother, something like that. The kind of thing that produces ghosts, you know?'

'Very true, Mordent.'

'Then when he's in a corner, with no place to go, the ghost gets cross. That's when things start happening. He starts to appear to people, he takes his revenge, he becomes kind of human. From then on, the struggle can start.'

'The way you talk, anyone would think you believe in ghosts, Mordent. Have you ever come across one?'

Mordent smiled and stroked his bald head.

'You're the one who brought up ghosts. I was just making up a story. For my own amusement. But it's interesting too. Because at the bottom of every story, there's always something monstrous. Thrashing about in the mud.'

Pink Lake immediately flashed into Adamsberg's mind.

'What sort of mud do you mean?' he asked.

'Well, something so traumatic that people daren't speak of it except in terms of a story. In all those fairy-tale castles, with ghosts, magic cloaks that change colour, and geese that lay golden eggs.'

Mordent was getting launched as he threw his plastic cup into the bin.

'The main thing is to solve the riddle correctly, and to guess right whenever you have a choice.'

'So you have to annoy the ghost, close off his exits, and uncover the original sin.'

'Ah, well. Easier said than done! Have you read my report on the Quebec course?'

'Read and signed. Anyone would think you'd been there yourself, it's brilliant. Do you know who guards the main door over there?'

'Yes, a squirrel.'

'Who told you that?'

'Estalère. It made quite an impression on him. Was he a volunteer or recruited?'

'Who? Estalère?'

'No, the squirrel.'

'Oh, a volunteer on principle. But he found a girlfriend and that started to interfere with his work.'

'Estalère?'

'No, the squirrel.'

Adamsberg sat back at his desk, thinking about Mordent's comments. Clear out all the usual hiding places, dislodge, pursue, provoke. Irritate the dead man. Use a laser sword to find out his or-ig-in-al sin. Ride in, sweep across the field, like the hero in a legend. And he hadn't managed to do it in fourteen years. No horse, no sword, no armour.

And no time, either. He attacked the second pile of dossiers. At least this workload meant he had not yet exchanged a word with Danglard. He wondered how he was going to manage this new silence between them. The *capitaine* had certainly offered his apologies, but the ice was still frozen solid. Adamsberg had listened to an international weather forecast that morning, feeling nostalgic for Canada. In Ottawa, the temperature was still about minus 8 in the daytime and minus 12 at night. No thaw in prospect.

While working on the second pile the next day, the *commissaire* felt a slight niggle buzzing inside his head, as if he had an insect trapped inside his body, flying about between his shoulders and his stomach. It was a fairly familiar sensation. Not like the sudden panic attacks that had overcome him when the judge had started to surface in his unconscious. No, just a modest little insect, like an annoying fly that needed swatting. Now and then, he took out the index card, to which he had added Mordent's suggestions for flushing out ghosts. He looked at it, but obviously wasn't seeing straight, as the barman in *L'Ecluse* had kindly informed him.

A slight headache sent him towards the coffee machine at five o'clock. Aha, Adamsberg thought suddenly, rubbing his forehead, I've got that dratted insect. That night of the 26th. What was causing the buzzing wasn't the drink, but the lost two and a half hours. The question had surfaced again with urgency. What the devil had he been up to for all that time on the portage trail? And why was this tiny misplaced fragment of his life, causing him all this worry? He had already filed it away under the heading 'memory loss occasioned by too much alcohol'. But obviously his mind was unhappy with this filing system, and the missing stretch of time had jumped off the shelf to start nagging away at him.

Why? Adamsberg wondered, as he stirred his coffee. Was it the idea of losing a chunk out of his life that was so irritating, as if it had been confiscated without permission? Or was it that the alcohol was not enough of an explanation? Or, more seriously, was he worried about what he might have said or done in the missing hours? But why? That sort of worry seemed as pointless as to worry about talking in one's sleep. What else could he have done, apart from stagger about on the path, fall over, get up again, perhaps even crawling on all fours? Nothing. And yet that insect was still buzzing. Was it just to perplex him or was there some reason?

All he could dredge up about those hours was not an image but a sensation. And, if he tried to formulate it, a sensation of violence. It must have been the branch that hit him. But how could he be angry with a branch that hadn't had a drop of alcohol to drink? A passive, sober enemy. Could he say the branch had done him violence? Or was it the other way around?

Instead of returning to his office, he went to sit on a corner of Danglard's desk and threw his plastic cup with perfect accuracy into the bin.

'Danglard,' he said, 'I've got a bee buzzing round in my bonnet.'

'Really?' said Danglard, cautiously.

'You know the night of Sunday 26 October,' Adamsberg went on slowly. 'The night you told me I was a stupid bastard, you remember.'

The *capitaine* nodded and prepared for a confrontation. Adamsberg was obviously going to let him have it between the eyes, as they would say in the RCMP. But the conversation did not take the turn he was expecting. As usual, the *commissaire* surprised him with something quite different.

'Well, that night, I hit my head on a branch, on the trail by the river. It was a really bad knock, an awful wallop.'

Danglard nodded again. The bruise was still visible, with its covering of yellow antiseptic ointment.

'What you don't know, is that after we spoke, I went straight to that bar, *L'Ecluse*, with the aim of getting well and truly drunk. Which I was doing quite effectively, until the good barman threw me out. I was rabbiting on about my grandmother, and he'd had enough.'

Again Danglard made a discreet sign of understanding, though he had no idea where Adamsberg was heading.

'And when I reached the trail, I just staggered about from tree to tree and that's why I didn't manage to avoid the branch.'

'Yes, I see.'

'But something else you don't know is that when I hit my head, it was about eleven o'clock, no later. And I was almost half way home, probably not far from the logging site. Where they're replanting trees?'

'Er, right,' said Danglard, who had never had the slightest wish to walk along the wild and muddy trail.

'And when I came round, I'd reached the end of the trail. I managed to stagger up to the residence. I told the janitor I'd got into a fight, police versus a gang.'

'Is that what's bugging you? The drinking?'

Adamsberg shook his head slowly.

'What you still don't know, is that between hitting my head and coming to, there was a gap of two and a half hours. The janitor told me the time.

Two and a half hours for a trip that would usually take me about half an hour.'

'Right,' said Danglard again, still maintaining as neutral a tone as possible. 'Well, it was a tricky bit of walking, wasn't it?'

Adamsberg leaned towards him. 'Which I can't remember at all,' he said deliberately. 'Not a thing, not a memory of sight or sound. Two and a half hours on the trail and it's a complete blank. And it was minus 12. I can't have just been unconscious all that time, or I'd have frozen to death.'

'Perhaps it was the shock,' Danglard suggested. 'From the branch.'

'I wasn't concussed, Ginette checked me over.'

'The drink then?'

'Well, obviously. That's why I'm consulting you.'

Danglard sat up, feeling he was on his own ground and relieved to be avoiding a quarrel.

'Can you remember what you had to drink?'

'I can remember everything up to the branch. Three whiskies, four glasses of wine and a generous brandy.'

'Mm, quite a mixture, fair quantity, but I've had worse. Still, your body isn't so used to it, so you have to reckon with that. What symptoms did you have the next day?'

'Cotton-wool legs. Only after the branch. Splitting headache, vomiting, feeling sick, dizzy, all kinds of vertigo.'

Danglard pulled a wry face.

'What's the matter, Danglard?'

'You have to take the bang on the head into account. I've never been sloshed and concussed at the same time. But what with the shock, and then passing out afterwards, I'd say it's just amnesia caused by alcohol. You could have been walking up and down on the path for two hours.'

'Two and a half,' Adamsberg corrected. 'I suppose I must have walked. But when I woke up I was lying on the ground.'

'Walked, fell, staggered. Haven't we seen enough drunks who totter about for a bit and then collapse in our arms?'

'Yes, I know, Danglard. But it's still bugging me.'

'That's understandable. A memory blackout's never nice, even for me, and God knows I've blacked out often enough. I used to ask the guys I'd been drinking with what I'd said or done. But when I was on my own, like you were that night, with nobody to tell you, I used to worry like hell about the missing hours.'

'Really?'

'Oh yes. You think you've fallen down a few steps in your life. You feel robbed, it's sort of like being mugged.'

'Thanks, Danglard, thanks for that bit of help.'

The piles of paperwork were slowly diminishing. If he spent the entire weekend at his desk, Adamsberg hoped, he would be ready by Monday to get back to the field and the Trident. The incident on the path had triggered in him an illogical sense of necessity, an urgent need to deal with his old enemy, whose shadow seemed to be cast over his most trivial actions, over the bears' claw marks, over an inoffensive lake, an old fish and an unremarkable drinking session. The Trident was infiltrating his prongs into all the cracks in the hull.

He raised his head suddenly and went back into Danglard's office.

'Danglard, what if the reason I went out and got drunk, wasn't to forget the judge and the new father?' he asked, carefully omitting to mention Noëlla in his list of torments. 'What if it started when the Trident rose from his tomb? What if I was doing it to *relive* what my brother went through? Drinking, forest path, memory loss? By a sort of imitation? To find a way back to him?'

Adamsberg was speaking in a hoarse and jerky voice.

'Uh-huh. Why not?' replied Danglard evasively. 'Yes, maybe you wanted to feel the same as him, find his tracks, put your feet in his footprints. But that wouldn't change anything about the events that night. If I were you, I'd file it under "went on bender, got bad hangover" and forget it.'

'No, Danglard, it seems to me that it would change everything. Perhaps the river has burst its banks and the boat is taking in water. I need to follow the current, get back in control before it washes me away. And then I have to bail out the water, and stop up the cracks.'

Adamsberg stayed standing for another long couple of minutes, thinking silently, under Danglard's anxious gaze. Then he walked pensively off to his office. If he couldn't get hold of Fulgence in person, at least he knew now where to start.

XXX

BUT ADAMSBERG WAS WOKEN AT ONE IN THE MORNING BY A PHONE CALL from Brézillon.

'Tell me, *commissaire*, is it usual for the Québécois to take no notice of the time difference when they telephone us?'

'What's happened? Something to do with Favre?' asked Adamsberg, who woke up as quickly as he dropped off to sleep, as if for him the border between reality and dreams was not very clear.

'Nothing to do with bloody Favre!' shouted Brézillon. 'What's happened is that you've got to jump on a plane at 4.50 tomorrow afternoon. So get packing!'

'Plane, sir? Where to?' Adamsberg asked politely.

'Where do you think? Montreal, for God's sake. I've just had Superintendent Légalité on the line.'

'Laliberté,' Adamsberg corrected.

'Whatever his name is. They've got some murder case, and they say they need you. Full stop. We're not being offered any choice.'

'Sorry, sir, but I don't get it. We weren't working on homicides with them, we were doing genetic fingerprinting. It's not Laliberté's first murder case.'

'Well it's the first time he needs you to solve it, for crying out loud.'

'Since when does the Paris Serious Crime Squad have to take on murders in Quebec?'

'Since they got a letter – anonymous if you please – saying you were the man for the situation. Their victim is French, and connected to some bloody file or other you've been handling over here. There's a connection anyway, and they're screaming for you.'

'Oh, for Christ's sake,' said Adamsberg, who was getting rattled in turn, 'they can send me a report and I can send them any information they need from here. I can't spend my life flying across the Atlantic and back.'

'That's what I said to him of course. But he insisted. He said they need your eyes. He won't give up. He wants you to view the body.'

'No, nothing doing. I'm up to my eyes in work here. The superintendent can send me the file.'

'Listen, Adamsberg, to what I'm telling you. You don't have a choice, I don't have a choice. The Ministry had to lean on them very hard to get them to cooperate over the DNA stuff. They weren't too keen at first. So we owe them one. Can't wriggle out of it. Now do you get it? We just agree politely, and you take the plane tomorrow. But I've told Légalité I can't let you go alone. You're taking Retancourt along as assistant.'

'I don't need a guide, thanks, what's the point?'

'I dare say. But you'll be accompanied, and that's the end of it.'

'What do you mean? Under escort?'

'Why not? I've been told you're chasing a dead man, *commissaire*.'

'Ah,' said Adamsberg, dropping his eyes.

'Ah, yes indeed. I have a friend in Strasbourg who told me what you've been up to. I thought I told you to keep a low profile for a bit, remember?'

'Yes, I do remember. So Retancourt has to keep an eye on me, does she? I'm going under orders and under supervision is that it?'

Brézillon's voice softened.

'Under protection is more like it.'

'With what in mind exactly?'

'It's just that I don't let any of my men go off unaccompanied.'

'Well, give me someone else, Danglard for instance.'

'No, Danglard will have to take over while you're away.'

'Well, Voisenet then. Retancourt doesn't like me. Our relations are correct but cold.'

'That'll do. Retancourt it is. She's a many-talented officer and can channel her energy in any direction.'

'Yes, you don't have to tell me. It's practically become a myth round here in less than a year.'

'I'm not going to hang about arguing, I want to get some sleep. You're on a mission and you'll do it. Your papers and tickets will be at the office by one o'clock. *Bon voyage*, get this thing sorted out, and get right back.'

Adamsberg sat on his bed, holding the receiver, still feeling dazed. So what, if the victim was French? It was still a matter for the Mounties. What was Laliberté playing at? Getting him to fly back across the Atlantic to see the corpse with his own eyes? If they wanted him to help with the identification, they could send him photos by email. What was Aurèle's game – did he suppose he could act like the boss of the Canada geese?

He woke both Danglard and Retancourt to tell them they had to be on duty the next morning, Saturday, by orders of the *divisionnaire*.

'What the hell's he playing at?' he said to Danglard next morning. 'Does he think he's top goose in Canada? Does he think I've nothing better to do than keep flying between Paris and Montreal?'

'Honestly, you've got all my sympathy,' said Danglard with genuine fellow-feeling. He would have been quite incapable of facing another flight.

'What's it all about? Any ideas, *capitaine*?'

'Absolutely not.'

'My eyes? What's so special about my eyes?'

Danglard said nothing. It was true that Adamsberg had unusual eyes. They reminded you of brown seaweed and could sometimes, like seaweed, sparkle in certain lights.

'And with Retancourt what's more,' Adamsberg added.

'Maybe that's not such a bad idea. I'm beginning to think Retancourt's an exceptional woman. She can channel her energy in any . . .'

'Yes, Danglard, I know.'

Adamsberg sighed and sat down. 'Since I've got no choice, as Brézillon shouted down the line at me, you're going to have to do a bit of urgent research for me.'

'OK, fire away.'

'I don't want to trouble my mother with this, you have to understand. She's already got enough problems.'

Danglard screwed up his eyes, chewing the end of a pencil. He was well used to the non sequiturs of his *commissaire*'s conversations, but the current number of oddities and sudden leaps in subject were alarming him more and more every day.

'So you'll have to do it, Danglard. It's right up your street.'

'Do what?'

'Find my brother.'

Danglard bit off a large splinter of the pencil which stuck between his teeth. He could do with a glass of white wine right now, at nine o'clock in the morning. *Find his brother.*

'Er, where?' he asked delicately.

'I've no idea.'

'Cemeteries?' murmured Danglard, spitting out the bit of wood.

'What do you mean?' said Adamsberg, startled.

'What I mean is, you're already looking for a murderer, who's been dead for sixteen years, and I don't buy it.'

Adamsberg looked down, disappointed.

'You're deserting me, Danglard. You're not with me any more.'

'Well, where am I expected to go with you?' Danglard said, raising his voice. 'Digging up graves?'

Adamsberg shook his head.

'You're not with me, Danglard. You're turning your back on me, whatever I say. Because you've decided you're on his side. The other guy.'

'It's nothing to do with any "other guy".'

'Well, what is it then?'

'I'm fed up chasing after the dead.'

Adamsberg shrugged wearily.

'Too bad, Danglard. If you won't help me, I'll have to do it myself. I've got to see him and talk to him.'

'And just how will you do that?' asked Danglard through clenched teeth. 'By table-turning?'

'*Table*-turning? What do you mean?'

The *capitaine* looked at the astonished expression on Adamsberg's face.

'But your brother's dead!' he shouted. 'Dead! How are you going to fix up an interview?'

Adamsberg seemed to freeze on the spot and the light went out of his eyes.

'Dead?' he repeated in a low voice. 'How do you know?'

'Christ Almighty, because you told me! You said you'd lost your brother. That he committed suicide after the trial.'

Adamsberg leaned back in his chair and took a deep breath.

'Aaah, you really scared me, *mon vieux*! I thought you'd had news of him . . . Yes, I did say I lost my brother, thirty years ago. I meant he went away, and I've never seen him since. But goddamnit, he's still alive as far as I know, and I have to see him. No tables to turn, Danglard, just some hard disks to spin. You're sure to be able to find him on the internet: Mexico, the US, Cuba, somewhere. He went travelling, different cities, different jobs, at least at the beginning.'

The *commissaire* was moving his finger in vague curves over the table, tracing the wanderings of his brother. Speaking with difficulty, he went on:

'Twenty-five years ago, he was a pedlar in Chihuahua province, near the US border. He sold coffee, china, linen, mescal, brushes. And he used to do portraits in the street. He was always pretty good at drawing.'

'Sincerely, *commissaire*, I beg your pardon,' said Danglard. 'I'd completely misunderstood. You spoke of him as if he were no longer here.'

'Well, he is no longer here.'

'Do you have any more precise information, anything more recent?'

'We avoid the subject at home, my mother and I. But when I was in the village about four years ago, I found a postcard he'd sent her from Puerto Rico. Love and kisses. Last known sighting.'

Danglard noted this on a sheet of paper.

'What's his full name?'

'Raphaël Félix Franck Adamsberg.'

'Date of birth, place, parents' names, schooling, what does he like doing?'

Adamsberg gave him the necessary information.

'Will you do it, Danglard? Will you look for him?'

'Yes, all right,' muttered Danglard, still feeling guilty at having buried Raphaël before his time. 'At least I'll try, but with all this backlog of paperwork, it's not a priority.'

'It's getting urgent. The river's burst its banks, I told you.'

'Well there are other urgent things to do as well,' said Danglard grudgingly. 'And it's a Saturday.'

The *commissaire* found Violette Retancourt dealing in her usual manner with the photocopier, which had jammed again. He told her about their mission and the time of the flight. Brézillon's order forced an unaccustomed look of surprise on her face. She undid her short ponytail and did it up again, with automatic gestures. Her way of taking time to think. So it was possible, after all, to catch her unawares.

'I don't get it,' she said. 'What's going on?'

'I don't know either, Retancourt, but we've got to go back there. They say they need my eyes. I'm really sorry, but the *divisionnaire* says you've got to come too. It's meant to be protection, according to him.'

Adamsberg was in the departure lounge half an hour before take-off, sitting silently alongside his large blonde *lieutenant*, when he saw Danglard arrive, flanked by two airport security guards. The *capitaine* looked tired and was out of breath. He'd evidently been running. Adamsberg would never have believed that possible.

'These guys nearly drove me mad,' he puffed, pointing to the guards. 'They didn't want to let me through. Here you are,' he said, handing Adamsberg an envelope. 'Good luck.'

Adamsberg had no time to thank him properly, because the guards were already escorting his *capitaine* back to the public zone. He looked down at the brown envelope in his hand.

'Aren't you going to open it?' asked Retancourt. 'It seemed to be urgent.'

'It is. But I'm hesitating.'

With trembling fingers, he opened the envelope. Danglard had provided an address, in Detroit, USA, and a job: taxidriver. He had also put in a photograph from the internet, taken from a website of illustrators. Adamsberg looked at the face he had not seen for thirty years.

'Is that you?' asked Retancourt.

'My brother,' said Adamsberg quietly.

Who still looked like him. An address, a job, a photo. Danglard was extremely skilled at finding missing persons, but even so he must have been hard at it to come up with the results and get them to him in a few hours. He closed the envelope with a shiver.

XXXI

DESPITE THE FORMAL CORDIALITY OF THEIR WELCOME AT MONTREAL airport, where Portelance and Philippe-Auguste had come to meet them, Adamsberg had the sensation of being taken in charge. Their destination was the Ottawa mortuary, in spite of the fact that for the French visitors the time was past midnight. During the journey, Adamsberg tried to extract some information from his ex-colleagues, but they remained vague as if they were anonymous drivers. No doubt they had been told not to prejudice the inquiry, so it was not worth insisting. He indicated to Retancourt that he was giving up and took advantage of the time to sleep. When they were woken up at Ottawa, it was past two in the morning, French time.

The superintendent gave them a warmer welcome, shaking hands energetically and thanking Adamsberg for agreeing to make the trip.

'No choice!' said Adamsberg. 'Aurèle, we're on our knees. Can't this wait until the morning?'

'Sorry, we'll have you driven straight to a hotel afterwards. But the family is pressing us to repatriate the body. The sooner you can take a look, the better.'

Adamsberg saw the superintendent's eyes shift under the pressure of lying. Was Laliberté intending to exploit his fatigue in some way? It was an old police trick, but he used it himself only with certain suspects and never with colleagues.

'OK, but can you get me a regular, please, then. Nice and strong.'

* * *

Adamsberg and Retancourt, huge polystyrene cups in their hands, followed the superintendent into the cold room, where the duty doctor was nodding off.

'Don't keep us waiting, Reynald,' Laliberté ordered. 'These people are tired.'

Reynald started to lift the blue sheet covering the victim's feet.

'Stop!' Laliberté ordered, when the fabric had been moved up as far as the shoulders. 'That'll do. Come and have a look, Adamsberg.'

Adamsberg leaned over the body which was that of a young woman and winced.

'Oh, shit!' he breathed.

'Something surprising?' asked Laliberté with a fixed smile.

Adamsberg was suddenly back in the mortuary in the Strasbourg suburbs, looking at the body of Elisabeth Wind. Three wounds in a straight line had perforated the abdomen of the young female victim. Here, ten thousand kilometres from the Trident's territory.

'Aurèle, have you got a ruler?' he asked, holding out his hand, 'and a tape measure. Centimetres if possible.'

Laliberté looked stunned. He stopped smiling and sent the doctor off to fetch the measuring aids. Adamsberg took his measurements silently, checking three times. Exactly as he had three weeks earlier, for the Schiltigheim victim.

'17.2 centimetres long, 0.8 centimetres wide,' he muttered, writing the figures in his notebook.

He checked the pattern of wounds one more time: they were in a perfect straight line, not a millimetre out.

'17.2 centimetres,' he repeated to himself, underlining it. Three millimetres longer than the maximum he was used to. Even so.

'How deep were the wounds, Laliberté?'

'About six inches.'

'What's that in centimetres?'

The superintendent frowned as he tried to convert the figure.

'About 15.2,' the doctor said.

'The same for all three wounds?'

'Yes, identical.'

'Any earth in the wounds? Dirt?'Adamsberg asked the doctor. 'Or was it a clean, new weapon?'

'No, there were elements of humus, leaves and tiny stones deep inside the wounds.'

'Ah, really?'

He gave the ruler and tape measure back to Laliberté and surprised an expression of discomfiture on the superintendent's face. As if he had been expecting something completely different from this minute examination.

'What is it, Aurèle? Wasn't that what you wanted me here for? To see this?'

'Er, yeah, yeah, sure,' said Laliberté with some hesitation. 'But what's with all this measuring stuff?'

'Do you have the murder weapon?'

'No, it's vanished, much as you might expect. But the technicians tell me it was probably a big screwdriver.'

'Your technicians are better at molecules than at weaponry. No screwdriver did that. It was a trident.'

'How do you know?'

'You try to plunge a screwdriver into somebody three times, and get both a straight line and identical depth of all three wounds. You could try for twenty years. That was done with a trident, or at least a three-pronged fork of some kind.'

'Christ, is that what you were checking?'

'Yes, that and something else, much deeper. As deep as the mud in Pink Lake.'

The superintendent still seemed thrown off balance, his arms hanging down against his large frame. He had had them driven here at almost provocative speed, but the measurements had disconcerted him. Adamsberg wondered what Laliberté had really been hoping for.

'Is there a bruise on the head?' he asked the doctor.

'Yes, a serious blow, back of the cranium, must have knocked the victim unconscious but not enough to kill her.'

'How did you know about the bang on the head?' asked Laliberté.

Adamsberg folded his arms as he turned towards the superintendent.

'You called me over because you knew I had a file on all this, right?'

'Er, yeah,' the superintendent replied, still hesitating.

'Yes or no, Aurèle? You've brought me across the Atlantic to haul me off at two in the morning, French time, to look at a murder victim, but what do you want from me? Do you want me to tell you you've got a dead woman here? If you took all this trouble to get me here, you must surely have known that I've got something on this. That's what they said in Paris. And yes, I do, but you don't seem satisfied. It's not what you were after?'

'Don't take it personal. I'm surprised, that's all.'

'You haven't heard it all yet, there's more that would surprise you.'

'Pull the sheet right up,' Laliberté ordered the doctor. Reynald carefully rolled up the sheet, just as Menard had in Strasbourg. Adamsberg stiffened as he caught sight of four small moles in a diamond shape at the base of the throat. He had just time to prevent himself from jumping, and blessed the meticulous slowness of the pathologist.

It was indeed Noëlla, lying in the mortuary drawer. Adamsberg tried to control his breathing and examined the dead woman without flinching, he hoped. Laliberté had not taken his eyes off him.

'Can I see the bruise?' he asked.

The doctor lifted the head to expose the back of the skull.

'A blow from a blunt instrument,' Reynald explained. 'That's all we can say. Probably made of wood.'

'The handle of the trident,' Adamsberg stated. 'He always does that.'

'Who's this "he"?' asked Laliberté.

'The murderer.'

'You know who it is?'

'Yes, I think so. But what I don't know is who told you about him.'

'And this woman, do you know her?'

'Come on, Aurèle, think I know the names of the sixty million French people in the world?'

'If you know the murderer, you might know the victim.'

'I'm not a clairvoyant, as you would say yourself.'

'Never seen her?'

'Where, in France? Paris?'

'Anywhere.'

'No, never,' said Adamsberg with a shrug.

'She was called Noëlla Corderon. Ring any bells?'

Adamsberg turned away from the body and moved closer to the super-intendent.

'Why do you keep insisting that I ought to know something about her?'

'She'd been living in Hull for six months. You could have met her.'

'So could you. What was she doing here? Married? Student?'

'She'd followed a boyfriend over, but he chucked her out. She worked in a bar in Ottawa, called the *Caribou*. Mean anything to you?'

'Never set foot in it. Aurèle, you're keeping something back. I don't know what this famous anonymous letter said, but you're being evasive.'

'And you're not?'

'No. I'll tell you all I know about this case tomorrow. Or at least anything that might be of help to you. But I'd like to get to bed now, I'm asleep on my feet and so's my *lieutenant*.'

Retancourt, sitting massively at the back of the room, was in fact in perfect shape.

'We've got to have a word or two first,' said Laliberté, with a slight smile. 'Let's go to my office.'

'For crying out loud, Aurèle. It's past three in the morning for us.'

'It's only nine o'clock local time. I won't keep you long. We can let your *lieutenant* go if you like.'

'No,' said Adamsberg suddenly. 'She stays with me.'

Laliberté had placed himself in his official chair, which was vaguely imposing, and was flanked by his two inspectors, both standing along-side. Adamsberg was familiar with this triangular scenario, intended to impress suspects. He had not had time to take in the atrocious knowledge that Noëlla had been murdered with a trident in Quebec. He was concentrating on Laliberté's ambiguous behaviour, which might indicate that he suspected Adamsberg's links with the girl. But nothing seemed certain. The game was a difficult one to play, and he would have to weigh every word from the superintendent. The fact that he had slept with Noëlla had nothing to do with her murder, so he must absolutely forget it for now. And prepare himself to meet every possibility, drawing on the power of his passive forces, the safest defences of his private citadel.

'Ask your men to sit down, Aurèle. I know the system, and it's disagreeable. Anyone would think you've forgotten I'm a policeman myself.'

Laliberté waved Portelance and Philippe-Auguste to the side. They both took out notebooks, preparing to make notes.

'Is this an interrogation?' Adamsberg asked, pointing to them. 'Or am I just helping you with your enquiries?'

'Don't bite my head off, Adamsberg. They're just taking notes for the record that's all.'

'Don't bite mine off either, Aurèle. I've been up twenty-two hours and you know it. That letter,' he added. 'Let's see the letter.'

'I'll read it to you,' said Laliberté, opening a thick green file. 'Corderon murder. See *Commissaire* J.-B. Adamsberg, Paris Crime Squad. Has taken a personal interest in it.'

'Tendentious,' Adamsberg commented. 'Is that why you're acting like a cop? You told them in Paris that it was a case I'd been working on. Here, you seem to think I took an interest in this woman.'

'Don't put words in my mouth.'

'Well don't take me for an idiot either. Let me see the letter.'

'You want to check what it says?'

'Precisely.'

There was not a word more on the sheet of paper, which seemed to have come from an ordinary printer.

'You took fingerprints, of course.'

'It was clean.'

'When did you get it?'

'When the body surfaced.'

'Surfaced from where?'

'From the water. It was frozen into the ice. Remember the cold spell last week? The body must have stayed put till it thawed. She was found Wednesday. We got the letter next day at midday.'

'So she must have been killed before the freeze, if the murderer could throw her in the water.'

'No, the murderer had broken the ice, pushed her under, and weighted her down with stones. The ice froze over again in the night like a lid.'

'How can you tell that?'

'The victim had bought herself a new belt that day. She was wearing it. We know where she ate her supper and what she ate. See, with the cold, the stomach contents stayed quite fresh. Now we know the date and time of the murder. No need to ask me more questions on that kind of stuff, we're specialists here.'

'Isn't that a bit suspicious, an anonymous letter turning up next day? The moment the murder was announced in the press?'

'No, why should it be? We get lots of anonymous letters. People don't like contacting the cops directly.'

'I can understand them.'

Laliberté's expression changed slightly. He was a skilled player but Adamsberg was able to read changes in a look more quickly than the RCMP laser detector. Laliberté was moving on to the attack and Adamsberg increased his air of nonchalance, folding his arms and leaning back in the chair.

'Noëlla Corderon died on the evening of 26 October,' the superintendent said simply. 'Some time between 22.30 and 23.30.'

Perfect, if that was the right choice of word. The last time he had seen Noëlla alive was when he had jumped out of the sash window on Friday 24 October. He had been afraid that Laliberté was going to bring that sash down on his neck by saying she had been killed on the 24th.

'Can you be any more precise about the time?'

'No, she had supper about seven-thirty, and digestion was quite advanced.'

'Which lake did you find her in? Was it far from here?'

Pink Lake, it has to be, Adamsberg thought. Where else?

'Look, we'll leave this till tomorrow,' announced Laliberté suddenly, standing up. 'Otherwise you're going to go round saying the Québécois cops are bastards. I just wanted to tell you about it, that's all. We've reserved you two rooms in the Hotel Brébeuf in Gatineau Park, OK?'

'Brébeuf's the name of someone?'

'Yeah, a Frenchie, stubborn as a mule, who got eaten by the Iroquois because he preached them a pack of lies. We'll pick you up about 2 p.m. so you can get over the jet-lag.'

Looking amiable once more, the superintendent held out his hand.

'Then you can tell me all about this trident.'

'If you'll listen, Aurèle.'

In spite of all his resolutions, Adamsberg could not think calmly about the ghastly connection which had brought him face to face with the Trident half way across the world. The dead can travel fast, like lightning. He had felt the danger in the little church in Montreal, when Vivaldi had whispered to him that Fulgence knew he was on his trail and he'd better watch out. Vivaldi, the judge, the quintet, that was all he had time to think about before he fell asleep.

Retancourt knocked at his door towards midday, local time. His hair was still wet, he had just finished dressing and the prospect of starting the day by a conversation with his steely *lieutenant* did not cheer him up. He would have preferred to lie down and think, that is, wander through the million particles of his mind, which were now completely mixed up in the damned process wells. But Retancourt sat down calmly on the bed, placing on the low table a thermos of real coffee – how had she managed that? – two cups and some fresh rolls.

'I went downstairs to get these,' she explained. 'Then if those two guys turn up early, we can talk in private here. Mitch Portelance's face would ruin my appetite.'

XXXII

RETANCOURT SWALLOWED HER FIRST CUP OF COFFEE AND A ROLL, without saying a word. Adamsberg made no attempt to engage her in conversation, but his silence did not seem to bother her.

'I'd like to understand something,' said Retancourt, after finishing her first roll. 'This murderer with the trident, we've never heard anything about him back in Paris. It's a long-standing business, I suppose. And going by your expression when you saw the body, there's some personal connection, am I right?'

'Retancourt, you've been sent out here because Brézillon won't let any of his staff go abroad alone. But you haven't been asked to explore my private affairs. I don't have to take you into my confidence.'

'Forgive me,' objected the *lieutenant*, 'but I'm here to protect you, that's what you told me. And if I don't know anything, I'm not going to be able to provide any defence.'

'But I don't need any. Today, I'll give Laliberté the information I have, and that's it.'

'What information?'

'You'll hear it the same time he does. He may accept it or not, that's up to him. And tomorrow we're out of here.'

'Oh really? You think so?'

'Why not, Retancourt?'

'*Commissaire*, you're a sensitive man. Don't pretend you haven't noticed anything.'

Adamsberg looked at her questioningly.

'Laliberté isn't the same man any more,' she continued. 'Nor are Portelance and Philippe-Auguste. The superintendent was taken aback when you took those measurements. He was expecting something else.'

'Yes, I noticed that.'

'He was expecting you to crack. When you saw the wounds, and again when you saw the face of the victim, which he took good care to uncover in two stages. But it didn't happen, and that shook him. It shook him, but it didn't deflect him. The inspectors are in on it too. I watched them the whole time.'

'You didn't seem to be taking any notice, just sitting in a corner, looking bored.'

'That was an act.' said Retancourt, pouring out two more cups of coffee. 'Men pay no attention to a fat, plain woman.'

'That's not at all what I meant, *lieutenant*.'

'But it's exactly what I mean, sir,' she said waving away the objection. 'They don't bother looking at her, she's just part of the furniture, and they actually forget she's there. I depend on that. Add a bored expression and hunched shoulders, and you're sure to be able to see everything without being seen. Not everyone can get away with it, and it's served me well in the past.'

'You channelled your energy?' said Adamsberg with a smile.

'Into being invisible,' said Retancourt, quite seriously. 'I could watch Mitch and Philippe-Auguste quite easily. During the first two acts, when they showed you the wounds, then the face, they were sending each other signals. Same thing when we got to Act Three at headquarters.'

'When was that?'

'When Laliberté told you the date of the crime. Your failure to react disappointed them again. I wasn't fooled. You're very good at looking phlegmatic, *commissaire*, and it seemed authentic, while at the same time it had a bit of play-acting about it. But I need to know more, if I'm going to work for you.'

'You're accompanying me, Retancourt. Your mission is simply that.'

'I belong to the squad and I'm doing what I'm supposed to do. I think I know what they're after, but I need your version. You ought to trust me, sir.'

'But why, *lieutenant*? You don't really like me, do you?'

This impromptu accusation did not upset Retancourt.

'Not much,' she confirmed. 'But that really doesn't matter. You're my boss and I'm doing my job. Laliberté is trying to trap you; he's sure you knew that girl.'

'Not true.'

'You have to trust me,' Retancourt repeated coolly. 'You're relying entirely on yourself. That's your usual way, but today it would be a bad mistake. Unless, that is, you have a cast-iron alibi for the night of the 26th after ten-thirty.'

'That bad?'

'I really think so.'

'They *suspect me* of killing the girl? You're imagining things, Retancourt.'

'Just tell me, yes or no, did you know her?'

Adamsberg remained silent.

'Come on, tell me, *commissaire*. The bullfighter who doesn't know his beast is certain to get gored.'

Adamsberg looked at his *lieutenant*'s round, intelligent and determined face.

'OK, *lieutenant*, yes, I did know her.'

'Shhhit!'

'She was waiting for me on the portage trail, from the very first day we were there. I won't tell you why I ended up taking her back to my apartment on the first Sunday, it has nothing to do with the story. But that's what I did. More's the pity, because she turned out to be completely nuts. A few days later, she told me she was pregnant, and started to talk about blackmail.'

'Uh-oh. Not nice,' said Retancourt helping herself to another roll.

'She was determined to catch the same flight as us, follow me to Paris and move in, despite anything I could say. She claimed that some old Indian at Sainte-Agathe had told her I was predestined to be her soulmate. She'd sunk her teeth into me.'

'This kind of thing hasn't ever happened to me, but I can imagine it's no fun. So what did you do?'

'I argued, I said it wasn't on, I told her it was over. In the end I just ran away. I jumped out of the window, and ran away into the woods like a squirrel.'

Retancourt nodded, her mouth full.

'And I never saw her again,' Adamsberg insisted. 'I took great pains to avoid her until we'd left the country.'

'Was that why you were looking jumpy at the airport?'

'She'd said she'd be there. It's only now that I know why she didn't make it.'

'She'd been dead for two days.'

'If Laliberté had known about this shortlived fling, he'd have let me have it from the start, surely. So Noëlla didn't tell anyone, or at least didn't tell anyone my name. The superintendent can't be sure. He's on a fishing expedition.'

'He must have something else that's allowing him to grill you: Act Three, I would guess, the night of the 26th.'

Adamsberg stared at Retancourt. The night of the 26th? He hadn't thought about it, because he was so relieved that the murder hadn't been committed on the Friday night, after their quarrel.

'You know what happened that night?'

'I don't know anything, except that you came in with a bad bruise in the morning. But since Laliberté was holding this card until last, I presume it must mean something important.'

It was almost time for the RCMP inspectors to pick them up. Adamsberg filled his *lieutenant* in rapidly about his evening's drinking and the two and a half hours' memory loss.

'Oh shit again,' said Retancourt. 'That doesn't help, but what I don't know is what he's got to link a girl he'd never heard of before and a man who'd had too much to drink walking home on the portage trail. He's got something else up his sleeve that he's not letting on about. Laliberté operates like a stalker. He takes a certain pleasure in the chase. He may drag it out.'

'Careful, Retancourt, he doesn't know anything about my lost two hours. Danglard is the only person besides you who knows.'

'But he's sure to have looked into it since. You left *L'Ecluse* at ten-fifteen and you arrived back at the residence at ten to two. That's a long time for a man with nothing on his mind.'

'Don't worry. Don't forget, I know who the real murderer is.'

'Right,' said Retancourt. 'Let's hope that settles it.'

'There's just one snag. It's a detail compared to what this murderer can do, but I'm afraid it won't go down well.'

'You're not sure about it?'

'Yes, I'm sure. But the man I'm thinking of has been dead for sixteen years.'

XXXIII

FERNAND SANSCARTIER AND GINETTE SAINT-PREUX WERE THE ACCOM-
panying officers this time. Adamsberg imagined that they might perhaps
have volunteered to come to work on Sunday to give him some moral
support. But his two former allies both seemed embarrassed and
constrained. Only the squirrel, still on duty outside the door, with his
girlfriend in tow, greeted him by wrinkling its muzzle. A faithful little
buddy.

'Right, Adamsberg, it's your turn,' Laliberté greeted him with a cordial
expression. 'Tell me all about it, what you've found out, what you know.
OK?'

The approach friendly. Laliberté was using all the old techniques.
Alternating between hostility and affability. It destabilises the suspect,
first reassuring him, then scaring him again, and he becomes disoriented.
Adamsberg stiffened his resolve. The superintendent was not going to
make him run off course like a frightened animal, still less with Retancourt
sitting behind him. He had an odd feeling that she was propping him
up.

'We're friends today, are we?' asked Adamsberg with a smile.

'Today, I'm listening. Just tell me what's on your mind.'

'I warn you, Aurèle, it's a long story.'

'OK, man, but try not to drag it out too much.'

Adamsberg took his time in describing the judge's bloody itinerary,
from the 1949 murder to the reappearance at Schiltigheim. He omitted

no details about the assassin's technique, the scapegoats he set up, the measurements of the trident, the changing of the blades. Nor did he conceal his own inability to catch the judge, who was protected by the high walls of his power, his network of contacts and his ability to move around the country. The superintendent took notes, but with a degree of impatience.

'Call me picky, but I see three flaws in the story,' he said at the end, holding up three fingers.

'Rigour, rigour and yet more rigour,' thought Adamsberg to himself.

'First, you want me to believe that this murderer's been running round France for fifty years?'

'Without getting caught, you mean? I told you about his influence and the way he changes the blades. Nobody has ever thought of challenging the judge's reputation, nor has anyone ever linked these murders together, except me. Nine, counting Schiltigheim, ten counting Noëlla Corderon.'

'What I mean is that this guy can't be a spring chicken.'

'Well, suppose he started when he was twenty. He'd still only be about seventy.'

'Second of all,' said Laliberté, putting a cross against his notes. 'You went on at length about this trident thing and its crossbar. But the idea of the altered blades is just your own hypothesis. You've got no evidence.'

'Yes I have, the measurements in all directions.'

'Exactly. But this time, your maniac killer broke his usual practice. As you saw, the line of wounds is longer than your crossbar, 17.2 centimetres, not 16.9. So all of a sudden, the murderer changes his routine. Seventy isn't the kind of age when a serial killer starts changing a ritual, so how do you explain that?'

'I thought about that, and I can only come up with one explanation. The airport controls. He couldn't have brought the original trident, he'd never have been allowed through security. He must have had to buy another over here.'

'It wasn't bought, Adamsberg, it was borrowed. It had traces of soil on it. It wasn't brand new.'

'That's true.'

'So now we've got some departures from routine, and not minor ones, for this so-called ritualistic murderer. Add to that that we didn't find anyone roaming about dead drunk beside the victim, with a murder weapon in his hands. No fall guy. That makes a helluva lot of differences, if you ask my opinion.'

'Changes of circumstance. Like all super-intelligent people, the judge is adaptable. He had to deal with the ice, since the victim was frozen in for three days before being found. And he had to deal with a foreign country.'

'I was coming to that,' said Laliberté, making another cross against his notes. 'Isn't there enough room for him back in the old country, your judge? Until now, he's only been killing people in France, according to you.'

'I wouldn't know. I only told you about the French murders because those were the only ones where I could get hold of records. If he's been off killing people in Sweden or Japan, I don't know about it.'

'Christ Almighty, you're an obstinate bastard. You've got an answer for everything, haven't you?'

'Isn't that what you wanted? You wanted me to give you a lead to the murderer, didn't you? Do you know many people who kill with a trident? Because what I say makes sense for the weapon, doesn't it?'

'Yeah, right, it was some kind of fork that killed her. But as for who was on the other end, that's something else again.'

'Judge Honoré Guillaume Fulgence. Guaranteed to use a trident. A man I'm going to get my hands on, I promise you.'

'Well, I'd like to see your files then,' said Laliberté tipping back his chair. 'Your nine files.'

'I'll have them copied and sent over to you when I get back.'

'No. I want them now. Can't you ask one of your men to send them to me by fax or email?'

No choice, thought Adamsberg, as he followed Laliberté and his men into the computer room. He was thinking about Fulgence's death. Sooner or later Laliberté was going to find out about it, as Trabelmann had. The most worrying aspect though, for the moment, was the file on his brother.

It contained a sketch of the screwdriver which he had thrown into the Torque, and notes about his false alibi during the trial, which were strictly confidential items. Danglard was the only person who could help him out – if he realised that he should weed the files before sending them. But how was he going to tell him that while he was under the superintendent's eagle eye? He would have liked an hour or so to think it through, but he was going to have to be quicker than that.

'I just want to fetch something from my coat,' he said, going out again.

In the superintendent's now empty office, Retancourt was sitting looking half asleep, slumped in a chair. He took a little time to take a few bags out of his bulging coat pockets, and ambled back in a casual manner, to see the three officers.

'Here,' he said to Sanscartier, holding out the bags, with an unobtrusive wink, 'there are six packs. Share them with Ginette if she likes it. If you need more, give me a call.'

'What are you giving them?' grumbled Laliberté. 'French booze?'

'Almond-scented soap. I'm not corrupting any public servants, it's just balm for the soul.'

'Christ, Adamsberg, less of the bullshit. We're here on serious business.'

'It's after ten at night now in Paris. Danglard is the only one who can find the files. I'd better send him a fax to his home address. He'll get it when he wakes up and you'll gain a bit of time that way.'

'OK, man, go ahead, write something for the big slouch.'

This concession enabled Adamsberg to send Danglard a handwritten message. The only idea he had come up with during the brief soap-fetching sortie was a schoolboy trick, but it might work. He would deform his handwriting, which Danglard knew by heart, by enlarging all the D's and R's, the beginning and end of DangeR. That was quite possible in a short message with the words Danglard, Dossier, Address, Adamsberg and Trident. He hoped that Danglard would be wide awake and understand it, or at any rate smell a rat before he scanned the papers in the files.

The fax went off, having been checked by the superintendent, carrying Adamsberg's hopes with it along the sub-Atlantic cable. He now had to place his faith in the alert mind of his second-in-command. He thought of Danglard's angel with the sword and for once prayed that in the morning his deputy would be in full possession of his logical faculties.

'He'll get it tomorrow. I can't do any more for now,' said Adamsberg. 'I've told you all I know.'

'I'm not through yet,' said Laliberté, raising another finger. 'There's a fourth point that intrigues me.'

Rigour and yet more rigour. Adamsberg sat down again by the fax machine. Laliberté remained standing. Another old police trick. Adamsberg tried to catch the eye of Sanscartier, who was standing still, clutching his bag of soap. And in those eyes which seemed still to beam out one and the same expression, that of goodness, he seemed to read something else. Trap ahead. Watch your step.

'Didn't you say you started chasing this guy when you were only eighteen?' Laliberté asked.

'Yes.'

'Thirty years on the trail, doesn't that seem a bit long?'

'No more than fifty years killing people. We've each got our job. He keeps on going; I keep on going after him.'

'Do you people ever have cases in France that you have to give up on?'

'Yes.'

'Have you ever personally had any files you've had to close, without finding the killer?'

'Not many.'

'Still, you have had some?'

'Yes.'

'So why didn't you give up on this one?'

'I told you, because of my brother.'

Laliberté smiled as if he had scored a point. Adamsberg glanced towards Sanscartier, and got the same signal.

'So you were really that fond of your brother?'

'Yes.'

'You wanted to avenge him?'

'No, not to avenge him, Aurèle, to clear his name.'

'Don't mess with words, Adamsberg, it comes to the same thing. Do you know what this makes me think of, this inquiry of yours? That you've been carrying on for thirty years?'

Adamsberg did not reply. Sanscartier was looking at his boss, without any kindness in his eyes. Ginette was looking at the floor.

'A pathological obsession,' Laliberté declared.

'In your book maybe, Aurèle, not in mine.'

Laliberté changed his position and line of attack.

'OK, I'm speaking to you as one cop to another. Your travelling murderer, don't you think it's odd that he's struck over here, at the very time when the guy tailing him is in Quebec? I mean you. The obsessive cop who's been after him for thirty years. Don't you think that's a bit of a coincidence?'

'More than a bit. Perhaps it's not one at all. As I told you, since Schiltigheim, Fulgence knows I'm after him again.'

'Jeez! Do you think he'd come all this way, just to bug you? If he had any sense at all, he'd wait till you were back home. A man who kills every four or five years can wait a fortnight, can't he?'

'I'm not inside his head.'

'I'm beginning to wonder about that.'

'What's that meant to mean, Aurèle?'

'I think you're dreaming in technicolour. You're seeing him everywhere, this Trident of yours.'

'I don't give a toss what you think, Aurèle. I've told you what I know and what I believe. If it's no use to you, too bad. You do your investigation, and I'll do mine.'

'Well, see you tomorrow at nine,' said the superintendent, smiling once more and holding out his hand. 'We've still got a lot of work ahead. We'll look through the dossiers together.'

'No, *you* look at them,' said Adamsberg, getting up. 'You'll need all day, and I know them by heart. I'm going to visit my brother. I'll see you on Tuesday morning.'

Laliberté frowned.

'I suppose I *am* free to come and go? Yes or no?' asked Adamsberg.

'Cool it, Adamsberg, of course you are.'

'OK. So I'm going to visit my brother.'

'Where is he?'

'In Detroit. Can I borrow a pool car?'

'I guess so.'

Adamsberg set off to find Retancourt, who had remained sitting slumped in the superintendent's office.

'I know you've got your orders,' Laliberté said with a grin. 'But, don't take this personally, I don't know what good she's going to be to you, your fatso *lieutenant*. She doesn't look as if she could rub two sticks together. Wouldn't want her in my squad.'

XXXIV

BACK IN HIS HOTEL ROOM, ADAMSBERG WONDERED IF HE SHOULD CALL Danglard, and warn him to pull out the papers connected with his brother's case. But perhaps his line was bugged. And once Laliberté learned that Fulgence was dead, things would heat up, in any case. Well, so what? The superintendent didn't know about his liaison with Noëlla, and if it hadn't been for the anonymous letter, he wouldn't have thought about him at all. On Tuesday, they would have to say goodbye and agree to differ, as with Trabelmann, and then each go their separate ways.

He packed quickly and closed his overnight bag. He was intending to drive through the night, snatching a couple of hours' sleep on the way, and to arrive at Detroit at dawn, so as to be sure to catch his brother. It was such a long time since he had seen Raphaël that he could feel no emotion, so unreal did the situation seem. He was changing his T-shirt when Retancourt walked in.

'Christ, Retancourt, you might knock.'

'Sorry, but I was afraid you might already have gone. When do we leave?'

'I'm going on my own. Private trip.'

'I've got my orders,' the *lieutenant* repeated obstinately. 'I'm supposed to accompany you. Everywhere.'

'Look, I appreciate your sympathy and help, Retancourt, but this is my brother, and I haven't seen him for thirty years. Just leave me alone.'

'Sorry, sir, but I'm coming. I'll leave you alone with him, don't worry.'

'*Lieutenant*, will you please just leave me alone, full stop.'

'OK, but I've got the car keys. You won't get far on foot.'

Adamsberg took a step towards her.

'You may be strong, *commissaire*, but you won't get these keys off me. I suggest we stop messing about like kids. We go together, and we can take it in turns to drive.'

Adamsberg gave up. Fighting it out with Retancourt might take at least an hour of his time.

'Very well,' he said resignedly. 'Since I'm stuck with you, get your things. You've got three minutes.'

'All done. I'll see you at the car.'

Adamsberg finished getting dressed and met her in the car park. His blonde bodyguard had channelled her energy into sticking to him like glue for his personal protection.

'I'll drive first,' said Retancourt. 'You've been arguing all afternoon with the superintendent, while I was taking a nap. I'm perfectly fresh.'

She pushed back the driving seat to accommodate her legs, and took off on the highway to Detroit. Adamsberg had to remind her of the ninety kilometre speed limit and she slowed down. In fact, Adamsberg was not reluctant to let someone else do the driving. He stretched out his legs, and put his hands on his thighs.

'You didn't tell them he's dead, did you?' said Retancourt after a few kilometres.

'They'll find that out soon enough tomorrow. But you're worrying unnecessarily. Laliberté hasn't any evidence against me. It's just that anonymous letter that's bugging him. I'll finish my business with him Tuesday, and we're out of here Wednesday.'

'If you finish your business with them on Tuesday, we certainly won't get away on Wednesday.'

'Why not?'

'Because if you set foot there on Tuesday, they're not going to have any more friendly chats. They're going to charge you.'

'You certainly like to dramatise, Retancourt.'

'I'm simply observing. There was a car outside the hotel. They've been following us since Gatineau. They're following *you* to be precise. Philibert Lafrance and Rhéal Ladouceur.'

'Putting a tail on someone isn't the same as arresting him. You're channelling your energy into exaggerating things.'

'You know that anonymous letter that Laliberté didn't want you to see? There were two faint black lines on it, five centimetres from the top of the page, one centimetre from the bottom.'

'A photocopy, you mean?'

'Yep. With the heading and bottom of the page covered up. A hasty DIY job. The paper, the typeface and layout were all just like the paper we used on the course. I had to put together the dossier in Paris if you remember. And the formula "Has taken a personal interest in it" sounded a bit official to me. The RCMP fabricated that letter.'

'What on earth for?'

'To provide a credible motive to get your bosses to send you back over. If Laliberté had revealed why he really wanted you, Brézillon would never have allowed him to extradite you.'

'*Extradite* me? What are you driving at, *lieutenant*? Laliberté will want to know what I was doing on the night of the 26th, yes, OK. I wonder the same thing myself. And he may well wonder what I was up to with Noëlla. I wonder about that myself too. But good grief, Retancourt, I'm not a suspect for her murder!'

'This afternoon, you all went off to send faxes, forgetting fat old Retancourt on her chair, yes? Remember?'

'Sorry, you could perfectly well have come along.'

'Absolutely not. The whole point was that I was already invisible, none of them realised they'd left me there on my own. Alone, sitting next to the big green dossier. I had time to get away with it.'

'Get away with what?'

'Photocopying it. I've got the essentials in my bag.'

Adamsberg looked at his *lieutenant* in the dark. The car was going well over the speed limit.

'Do you do that back home? Photocopy dossiers whenever you feel like it?'

'When we're back home, I'm not on a mission to protect.'

'Slow down. It's not the moment to get caught by those inspectors with a timebomb in your bag.'

'You're right,' said Retancourt, taking her foot off the gas. 'It's these damned automatics, I can't seem to go slowly.'

'That's not the only risk you've taken. The shit would really have hit the fan if one of those cops had caught you at the photocopier.'

'The shit would have hit all right if I hadn't made the copies. It was Sunday and there was no one else around. I could hear everything you were saying echoing down the corridor. At the least scrape of a chair, I would have been able to get back in position. I know what I'm doing.'

'I wonder.'

'They've done their homework on you. A lot of it. They know you were sleeping with the girl.'

'How? From the friends she was staying with?'

'No. But Noëlla had a pregnancy test in her handbag, a urine sample.'

'And was she? Pregnant?'

'Can't have been. There aren't any tests that would give a result in a few days, but men wouldn't know that.'

'So why did she have the test in that case? Her old boyfriend?'

'Just to get you hooked. Find the report, it's in my bag. Blue file, round about page 10.'

Adamsberg opened Retancourt's capacious bag which seemed to contain an entire survival kit: pliers, rope, pitons, make-up, knife, flashlight, various plastic bags. Putting on the overhead light, he looked up page 10, analysis of Noëlla Corderon's urine, evidence item RRT 3067. 'Residual traces of semen,' he read. 'Comparison with sample STG 6712, taken from the bedding in the apartment of Adamsberg, Jean-Baptiste. DNA comparison positive. Formal identification of sexual partner.'

Underneath the text were two diagrams showing the DNA sequences in 28 strips, one taken from the test tube, one from his own sheets. Exactly the same. Adamsberg put away the file and turned off the light. Although he would not have been over-intimidated by talking about semen to his *lieutenant*, he was grateful to her for letting him read this stuff in silence.

'Why didn't Laliberté say anything about this before?' he asked quietly.

'He likes the chase. He's having fun. He's watching you get deeper in and he likes that. The more lies you feed him, the bigger his pile of false statements.'

'Even so,' sighed Adamsberg. 'Even if he knows I slept with Noëlla, he surely can't link that to her murder. It must be a coincidence.'

'You don't believe in coincidence, do you?'

'No.'

'Neither does he. Where do you think the girl was found? On your portage trail.'

Adamsberg froze.

'Oh no, impossible, Retancourt,' he gasped.

'Yes. In a little pool near the bank,' she said gently. 'Let's stop and have something to eat.'

'I couldn't eat anything,' said Adamsberg in an exhausted voice.

'Well, I'm going to, otherwise I can't carry on, and it would do you good too.'

Retancourt pulled into the next lay-by, and got out some sandwiches and apples. Adamsberg chewed a few mouthfuls mechanically, staring into the distance.

'Even so,' he repeated. 'What does that prove? She was always on that damned path, morning and evening. She said herself it was dangerous. I wasn't the only person to use it.'

'In the evening there wasn't anyone else much. Maybe the odd homosexual who wasn't interested in Noëlla Corderon. The cops know a lot. They know that you were on that trail for a long time, from half past ten till half past one.'

'Well, I didn't see anything, Retancourt. I was drunk, as I told you. I must have been going up and down. When I fell, I lost my torch. Your torch, I should say.'

Retancourt took out a bottle of wine.

'Don't know what this is like,' she said. 'But have a little.'

'I'm never going to drink again.'

'Just a few mouthfuls. Please.'

Adamsberg obeyed, feeling shattered. Retancourt took back the bottle and corked it carefully.

'They questioned the barman at *L'Ecluse*: apparently you said to him: "Any nearer and I'll spear ye".'

'I was talking about my grandmother. She was a tough old bird who said it to the Germans.'

'Tough old bird or not, they didn't like the sound of that at all.'

'Is that all, Retancourt?'

'No. They also know you can't remember anything about that night.'

There was a long silence. Adamsberg leaned back in his seat, looking at the roof, in a state of shock.

'The only person,' he said, 'the *only* person I told that to was Danglard.'

'Well, anyway, they know.'

'I was always on the path, every day,' he went on in the same dull voice. 'But where's any motive, or evidence?'

'Well, there is a motive, isn't there? The pregnancy test, blackmail.'

'Unthinkable, Retancourt. A conspiracy, a devilish conspiracy.'

'By the judge?'

'Why not?'

'He's dead, *commissaire*.'

'I don't care. And they haven't got any evidence.'

'Well, yes. The girl was wearing a belt, bought that very day, a leather belt.'

'So he said. What about it?'

'They found it lying in leaves near the pool.'

'And?'

'I'm sorry, *commissaire*, but it's got your fingerprints on it. They compared them with prints from your apartment.'

Adamsberg could no longer move. He was stupefied, powerless under the waves that were crashing one after another over his head.

'I've never seen any belt. I couldn't have touched it. I hadn't seen her since the Friday night.'

'I know,' murmured Retancourt. 'But the only suspect you can come up with is an old man who's dead. Your only alibi is loss of memory. They'll say you were obsessed with the judge, that your brother had already killed someone, that you were out of control. Placed in the same circumstances as your brother, drunk, in the woods, faced with a girl who said she was pregnant, you did the same as Raphaël.'

'The trap's closed on me,' said Adamsberg, shutting his eyes.

'I'm sorry to give you all this straight, but you needed to know. They're going to charge you on Tuesday. The warrant's all ready.'

Retancourt threw her apple core out of the window and drove off again. She didn't suggest that Adamsberg take the wheel and he did not offer.

'Retancourt, I did not do this.'

'It won't be any good telling Laliberté that. He won't give a damn, deny it all you like.'

'Retancourt, Noëlla was killed with a trident. Where on earth would I have got hold of one? Did it appear on the path, by magic?'

Suddenly, he stopped and slumped back in the seat.

'What were you going to say, *commissaire*?'

'Oh, my God, the logging site.'

'Where's that?'

'Half way along. There's a site with a pick-up, and plenty of tools for guys who come and take out dead trees and plant new ones. I'd seen it, I'd been past it. I could have gone past, seen Noëlla, seen the weapon and used it. Yes, they could say that. Because there was earth in the wounds. Because it wasn't the same trident as the judge's.'

'Yes, they could say that,' Retancourt agreed, her voice serious. 'What you told them about the judge doesn't help you. On the contrary. They think it's a crazy story, improbable and obsessive. They'll use that to charge you. They have the surface motive, you've provided them with the deeper motive.'

'An obsessive man, who's had too much to drink, who's lost his memory, and who's being driven nuts by that girl. Me, reliving my brother's life. Reliving the judge's career. Crazy, off balance. I'm finished, Retancourt. Fulgence has got me. He's got inside my skin.'

For a quarter of an hour, Retancourt drove in silence. Adamsberg's state of collapse needed, she thought, the respite of silence. Probably days of it, driving all the way to Greenland, but she didn't have time for that.

'What are you thinking about?' she asked after a while.

'My mother.'

'I understand. But it's not the moment.'

'You think about your mother when you've come to the end of the road. And I've come to the end of the road.'

'No, you haven't. You can still make a break for it.'

'If I make a break for it, I've really had it. Proof of guilt.'

'Well, you've certainly had it if you turn up at the Mounties' head-quarters on Tuesday morning. You'll sit rotting here until the trial, and there won't be any way of getting out to try and investigate what happened. You'll be stuck in a Canadian prison, then eventually they'll transfer you to Paris. Twenty years minimum. No, in my view, the only thing for it is to cut and run.'

'Do you realise what you're saying? Do you realise that you'd be making yourself an accomplice in my escape?'

'Yes, perfectly.'

Adamsberg turned to his *lieutenant*. 'But what if I *did* kill her, Retancourt?' he forced himself to say.

'You've got to run,' she said, evading the question.

'Retancourt, what if I did kill her?' repeated Adamsberg insisting.

'Well, if you have any doubts on that score, we've both had it.'

He leaned over to examine her face.

'And *you* haven't any doubts?' he asked.

'No.'

'Why not? You don't like me, and there's a mountain of evidence stacked up against me. But you don't think I did it?'

'No. You're not the sort of man who would kill anyone.'

'How do you know?'

Retancourt pursed her lips slightly, seeming to hesitate.

'Well, let's just say that it wouldn't interest you enough.'

'Are you sure of that?'

'As sure as I can be. Your best course is to trust me, or yes, you've had it. You're not defending yourself, you're getting yourself deeper in it.'

Into the mud of the dead lake, thought Adamsberg.

'I just can't remember anything about that night,' he repeated, mechanically. 'I had my face and hands covered in blood.'

'Yes, I know. The janitor told them that.'

'Perhaps it wasn't my own blood?'

'You see? You're getting yourself in deeper and deeper. You're accepting it. The idea's wriggling into your mind like a worm, and you're allowing it to.'

'Maybe the idea's always been in my mind, since the Trident came back to life. Maybe something went off in my head when I saw the fork.'

'You're going down into his grave,' Retancourt insisted. 'You're putting your head on the block.'

'I realise that.'

'*Commissaire*, think quickly. Who are you going to choose to trust? You or me?'

'You,' Adamsberg replied instinctively.

'OK. Run for it.'

'Can't be done. They're not stupid.'

'Neither are we.'

'But they're already right behind us.'

'Well, we certainly can't run in Detroit. The arrest warrant has been issued to cover Michigan. We're going to return to the Hotel Brébeuf on Tuesday morning as arranged.'

'And sneak out via the basement? But when they see I haven't turned up at the right time, they'll look everywhere. In my room, everywhere in the building. They'll see the car's gone, put a watch on the airports. I'd never have time to get a flight, or even leave the hotel. They'll eat me alive, like they did Brébeuf.'

'But they're not going to be chasing us, *commissaire*. We're going to lead them where we want them.'

'Where?'

'Into *my* room.'

'But your room's as small as mine. Where are you going to hide me? On the roof? They'll go up there.'

'Of course.'

'Under the bed, in the wardrobe?'

Adamsberg hunched his shoulders in a gesture of despair.

'No, on me.'

The *commissaire* turned to the *lieutenant*.

'I'm sorry,' she said, 'but it'll only take two or three minutes. There's no other way.'

'Retancourt, I'm not a hairpin. What are you going to turn me into?'

'Nothing, I'm going to turn myself into something. A pylon.'

XXXV

RETANCOURT HAD STOPPED FOR TWO HOURS TO SLEEP AND THEY entered Detroit at seven in the morning. The city was as mournful as an old duchess, in the ruins of her estate, still wearing the ragged remains of her robes. Dirt and poverty had replaced the former wealth of old Detroit.

'Here's the block,' said Adamsberg, consulting his street plan.

He looked up at the building, which was soot-blackened but otherwise in good condition, with a cafe on the ground floor, as if he were examining a historic monument. And in a sense he was, since behind these walls Raphaël lived, moved and slept.

'The Mounties are parking twenty metres behind us,' Retancourt remarked. 'Very clever. What can they be thinking of? Do they really imagine we haven't noticed they've been behind us all the way from Gatineau?'

Adamsberg was leaning forward, his arms folded tightly against his stomach.

'You go in on your own, *commissaire*,' she said. 'I'll go and sit in the cafe.'

'I can't,' said Adamsberg in a whisper. 'And what's the use anyway? I'm on the run like he is.'

'Exactly, so you're quits. He won't be alone any more, nor will you. Go on, it's the best thing to do, *commissaire*.'

'You don't understand, Retancourt. I just can't. My legs won't move. They feel as if they've turned to iron bars.'

'Shall I have a go?' asked the *lieutenant*, turning sideways and putting her hands on his shoulder blades.

He nodded. After about ten minutes of the massage, he felt as if a kind of warm oil was flowing down through his thighs, making it possible to move again.

'Is that what you did to Danglard in the plane?'

'No, Danglard was just afraid of dying.'

'So what am I afraid of?'

'Exactly the opposite.'

Adamsberg nodded and got out of the car. Retancourt was about to leave him and go into the cafe when he put a hand on her arm.

'He's in there,' he said. 'With his back to us, at that table, I'm sure it's him.'

The *lieutenant* looked at the silhouette of the man Adamsberg pointed to. That back could indeed only belong to his brother. Adamsberg's grip tightened on her arm.

'Go in on your own,' she said. 'I'll go back to the car. But I'd like to see him.'

'Raphaël?'

'Yes, Raphaël.'

Adamsberg pushed the glass door, his legs still feeling stiff. He went over to Raphaël and put his hands on his shoulders. The man with his back turned didn't jump. He looked at the brown hands one after the other.

'So you found me?' he said

'Yes.'

'I'm glad.'

From the other side of the narrow street, Retancourt watched as Raphaël got up, and the two brothers embraced, looking at each other with their arms intertwined, holding each other tightly. She took a small pair of binoculars from her bag and focussed on Raphaël Adamsberg, whose forehead was now touching his brother's. Same

219

body, same face. But whereas Adamsberg's elusive beauty was a miraculous combination emerging from his chaotic features, his brother's was altogether more regular and obvious. They were like twins who had grown from the same root, one into a shapely plant, the other into an engaging disorder. Retancourt refocussed on Adamsberg whose three-quarters profile was towards her. But she quickly dropped the binoculars, mortified at having trespassed too far on to another's emotion. Once they had sat down, the two Adamsbergs still did not let go of each other's arms, but clasped them, forming a closed circle. Retancourt sat down in the car again with a slight shiver. She put the binoculars away and closed her eyes.

By ten o'clock, Raphaël had found them something to eat and settled them on a sofa in his flat, with some coffee, Adamsberg having fetched his *lieutenant* in from the car by rapping on the window. The two brothers did not move more than a few inches away from each other, Retancourt noted.

'Will Jean-Baptiste be found guilty? Are you sure?' Raphaël asked her.

'Sure as I can be,' Retancourt stated. 'The only way out is to make a run for it.'

'With about a dozen cops watching the hotel,' added Adamsberg.

'It's do-able,' Retancourt said.

'So what's your plan, Violette?' asked Raphaël.

Raphaël had argued that since he was neither a *flic* nor a soldier he was not going to call the *lieutenant* by her surname.

'We go back to Gatineau tonight,' she explained. 'We get to the Hotel Brébeuf in the morning at about seven, and walk in quite openly, for them to see us. You, Raphaël, will follow us three and a half hours later. Can you do that?'

Raphaël nodded.

'You get to the hotel at about ten-thirty. What do the cops see? Just another guest arriving at the hotel. They're not bothered about you, they're looking for someone leaving, and there's plenty of toing and froing at about that time. The two who followed us last night won't be on duty again in the morning, so none of the police on duty will recognise you. You check in under your own name and go to your room.'

'OK.'

'Have you got a suit? A smart business suit with shirt and tie?'

'Three, two grey, one blue.'

'Perfect. Wear one and bring the other, both the grey ones. And bring two coats and two ties.'

'Retancourt, don't get my brother in the shit over this,' pleaded Adamsberg.

'No, it's just the Gatineau cops who will be. You, *commissaire*, as soon as we arrive, clear your room with signs of haste, as if you were going to make a break for it. We'll get rid of your stuff. You haven't got much, so that's handy.'

'What do we do, cut it up and eat it?'

'No, just dump it in the waste bin on the landing.'

'Everything, clothes, books, razor?'

'Yes, everything, including your service revolver. We chuck your clothes, and we save your skin. Keep your wallet and keys.'

'The holdall won't go in the bin.'

'We'll leave it in my wardrobe, empty, as if it was mine. Women have lots of luggage as a rule.'

'Can I keep my watches?'

'Yes.'

The brothers were both looking intently at Retancourt, one with a mild and gentle expression, the other mobile and alert. Raphaël Adamsberg had the same peaceful suppleness as his brother, but his movements were more lively, his reactions sharper.

'The cops will be expecting us at the RCMP headquarters at nine,' Retancourt went on, looking from one to the other. 'When we still haven't turned up after about twenty minutes, no longer, I guess, Laliberté will try to phone the *commissaire* at the hotel. No reply. Alarm raised. The cops downstairs will rush up to your room. Empty, the bird has flown.

That's the impression we have to give. That their suspect has disappeared, he's already slipped between their fingers. At about nine twenty-five, they'll come to my room, in case I'm hiding you.'

'Where could you have hidden me?' Adamsberg asked anxiously.

Retancourt raised her hand.

'The Québécois are more prudish than the French,' she said, 'they don't have naked women all over their magazine covers or hanging about on the lake shores. We're going to bank on this shyness. On the other hand,' she said, turning towards Adamsberg, 'you and I are going to have to abandon any embarrassment, because this is not the moment for it. And if it bothers you, just remember that it really is a matter of life and death.'

'I'll remember.'

'Well, this is how we do it. When the cops burst in, I'll be in my bathroom and in fact in the bath, with the door open. We haven't much choice.'

'And Jean-Baptiste?' asked Raphaël.

'Will be hidden behind the open door. When the cops catch sight of me, they'll retreat into the bedroom. I'll start shouting and tearing them off a strip for walking into my room like that. They'll call out their apologies from the bedroom, they'll be embarrassed and say they were looking for the *commissaire*. I say what's all this about, I don't know where he is, he just told me to wait at the hotel, while he went to headquarters. They want to search my room. OK, but can you please just allow me to put something on? Yes, of course, they retreat further, and allow me to get out of the bath and close the door. You with me so far?'

'Yes,' said Raphaël.

'I put on a bathrobe, a very big one, down to the ground. Raphaël will have to go out and buy me one, I'll give you the size.'

'Any particular colour?' asked Raphaël.

This considerate question interrupted Retancourt's strategic briefing and she thought a moment.

'Cream-coloured, if you can find one.'

'OK, cream-coloured. What next?'

'Now, we're in the bathroom, both of us and the door's shut. The cops are in the bedroom. You see where we are, *commissaire*?'

'No, I'm lost now. Because in the hotel bathrooms there's just a cabinet with a mirror, a towel cupboard and nothing else. Where are you going to put me, in a Hollywood-style bubble-bath?'

'No, on me, like I said. Or rather behind me. We'll be one person standing up. I allow them in once I've got the robe on and stand looking shocked, in the corner, with my back to the wall. They aren't stupid, so they'll look over the bathroom thoroughly, including behind the door, and they'll feel under the water in the bath. I'll make them even more embarrassed by letting the robe gape open a bit. They won't dare look hard at me, they won't want to be taken for peeping toms. They're predictable that way, and that's our one advantage. OK, nothing in the bathroom, they go out and let me get dressed, with the door closed again. While they're still searching the bedroom, I come out, fully dressed by now and naturally, I leave the bathroom door open. You're back behind the door by then.'

'*Lieutenant*, I haven't grasped exactly what you mean by "we will be one person".'

'Have you ever done close combat training? When someone jumps you from behind?'

'No.'

'I'll show you how it's done,' said Retancourt, getting up. 'Let's be as impersonal as we can. You have one person standing. Me. Big fat person, luckily for you. And we have another individual, who's lighter and smaller. You. You are hidden under the bathrobe. Head and shoulders buried in my back, arms tight round my waist, invisible under the robe. To hide your legs, you'll have to have your feet off the ground and twined round my calves, again shielded by the robe. I'll stand in the corner, arms folded, feet apart, to maintain my centre of gravity. Do you follow?'

'Christ Almighty, Retancourt, you want me to flatten myself to your back like a monkey?'

'Or like a flatfish even. Flatten is the right word. It will last only a few minutes, two maximum, I'd say. It's a tiny bathroom, they won't take long to check it out. They won't be looking at me, I won't be moving. Nor will you.'

'They'll see me, Retancourt, it's too awkward.'

'No they won't. I'm a big woman. I'll be wrapped up in my bulky robe, wedged into the corner, looking out. My skin will be wet, so I'll put a belt on underneath for you to hold on to, then you won't slip. You can fix your wallet on it too.'

'I'll be too heavy,' said Adamsberg shaking his head. 'I weigh 72 kilos, you know. It's madness. It'll never work.'

'It will work, *commissaire*, because I've done it before. Twice. For my brother, when the cops were after him for one thing or another. When he was nineteen, he was about your size, and he weighed 79 kilos. I put on my father's dressing gown, and he clung on to my back. We managed four minutes. If that helps to reassure you.'

'Well, if Violette thinks it will work . . .' said Raphaël looking slightly panicky.

'If she says so,' Adamsberg said.

'We have to agree on one thing. If this is going to work, we can't cheat, and risk getting discovered. Total realism is our best bet. I really will be naked in the bath, naturally. So I really will be naked under the bathrobe. And you really will be clinging to my back. You can wear undershorts, but nothing else. Clothes make it more likely you would slip, and also they'd stop the robe looking natural.'

'The folds would look awkward, you mean?' said Raphaël.

'Precisely. We can't take that risk. I realise it's embarrassing, but I really don't think this is the moment to be prudish. We must be agreed on that before we start.'

'It won't bother me,' said Adamsberg, 'as long as it doesn't bother you.'

'I brought up my four brothers, and in extreme circumstances I think embarrassment is a luxury. These are extreme circumstances.'

'But damnit, Retancourt, even if they leave you and your room without finding anything, they're not going to give up the search. They'll go through the Hotel Brébeuf with a toothcomb.'

'Yes, of course.'

'So even after this vanishing trick, I won't be able to leave the hotel.'

'No, Raphaël will leave,' said Retancourt, pointing to his brother. 'Or in other words, you will leave, as him. You leave the hotel at eleven o'clock, wearing his suit, shirt and tie, and shoes. I'll cut your hair in advance, to look like his. It'll work because from a distance, you're very alike. But they'll be looking for you, dressed in your usual scruffy style. They've seen a smart businessman in a suit enter the hotel at ten-thirty. If he goes out again at eleven, they won't bother about him. The businessman, that's you *commissaire*, will just go to his car.'

Both Adamsbergs, sitting side by side were listening attentively to the *lieutenant*, almost subjugated. Adamsberg was beginning to take in her plan, based on two elements which were usually in contradiction: audacity and finesse. Together they made up an unpredictable force, like a battering ram with the delicacy of a needle.

'What then?' he asked, as the plan began to revive him.

'You take Raphaël's car, you drive to Ottawa, and park it at the corner of North Street and Laurier Boulevard. You take the eleven-forty bus to Montreal. The real Raphaël will leave much later, in the evening, or even next morning, depending when the cops give up watching the hotel. He'll pick up his car from Ottawa and go back to Detroit.'

'But why not do it more simply?' asked Adamsberg. 'If Raphaël were to arrive *before* Laliberté's phone call, I could take his suit and car, and get away before they raise the alarm. He could leave straight away by bus. Then we don't do all the close combat stuff in the bathroom. When they turn up, we'll both have gone.'

'Except that his name will be on the register, or if he has just come as a visitor, his brief visit will be noticed. We're not complicating things for fun, *commissaire*, but so as not to drop Raphaël in the shit. If he arrived before the alarm, he'd certainly be traced. The cops will ask the receptionist and hear either that Raphaël Adamsberg came in, but left immediately, or else that a "visitor" asked for you. Either way it'll alert them. They'll quickly realise about the substitution and pick Raphaël up in Detroit, and arrest him for helping you escape. But if he arrives *after* the rooms have been searched and you've been reported missing, he won't be noticed among the arrivals, and can't be held responsible for anything. In the worst-case scenario, if the cops check and find his name later, all they can accuse him of is coming on a return visit to see his brother, and to his surprise finding he's missed him, which isn't a crime.'

Adamsberg looked at Retancourt.

'Of course, you're right,' he said. 'Raphaël must come later, I should have thought of that. I'm a cop myself, so why can't I think clearly any more?'

'You can't think like a cop for now,' Retancourt replied gently. 'You're reacting like a criminal on the run, who tends to panic, not like a policeman. You've changed your territory, you're on the wrong side, and the sun's in your eyes. You'll revert to form once you're back in Paris.'

Yes, thought Adamsberg, a wanted criminal whose reflexes just tell him to run, without being able to see the big picture or follow through on details.

'But what about you? When will you get away?'

'When they've finished searching the area and realise they've lost you. They'll stop searching and put out an alert to the roads and airports. I'll join you in Montreal as soon as they're off the premises.'

'Where in Montreal?'

'With a pal of mine. I'm afraid I don't have holiday romances, but I do try to have a friend in every port, because I like it and because you never know when you might need a little help from your friends. Basile will provide us with a safe house.'

'Perfect,' murmured Raphaël, 'absolutely perfect.'

Adamsberg nodded silently.

'Raphaël,' said Retancourt, getting up. 'Can you find me somewhere to sleep? I'd like to rest, we'll be driving all night again.'

'You'd better get some sleep too,' Raphaël told his brother. 'I'll go out and buy this bathrobe.'

Retancourt wrote down her measurements.

'I don't think the two cops will follow you,' she said. 'They're more likely to stay on watch outside the building. But come back with some food bags, bread, vegetables and so on, it'll look more convincing.'

Lying on his brother's bed, Adamsberg found he was unable to sleep. His night of 26 October was jabbing into him like a physical pain. Drunk, on the path, furious with Noëlla and with the rest of the world too. Furious with Danglard, Camille, the new father, Fulgence, a great ball of hate which he could no longer control, and which had been inside him for some time already. Then coming across a forester's fork. What better implement for digging up saplings? He could have seen one when he was talking to the watchman or when he was walking through the forest. He knew it was there. Walking around at night, out of his mind with drink, obsessed with the judge and the need to find his brother. Then glimpsing Noëlla, who must have been watching out for him on the path. The ball of hate explodes, the path to his brother opens, the judge gets inside his skin. He rushes away and grabs the fork. Who else could there be on the deserted path? He creeps back, hits the girl on the head and she falls unconscious. He takes off the belt which stops him getting at her stomach, and throws it away. He kills her with the trident. He breaks the ice on the pool, pushes the dead woman in and throws stones in on top of her. Exactly as he had done with the screwdriver for Raphaël thirty years earlier. The same gestures. He throws the trident into the Ottawa River, which carries it off over the falls on the way to the St Lawrence. Then he wanders about, bangs his head and passes out into willed oblivion. When he wakes up, the whole thing has been buried in the inaccessible depths of his memory.

Adamsberg felt cold suddenly and pulled the quilt over him. Running away, close combat, clinging on, naked, to that woman's body. Extreme circumstances. Escaping and living like a murderer wanted by the police. Maybe even being one.

Change your perspective for a moment, start thinking like a policeman again. There was one question he had asked Retancourt, but had then forgotten, as the catastrophic contents of the green file had swept over him. Now it came back into his mind. How had Laliberté found out that he had no memory of the night of the 26th? Someone must have told him. But only Danglard knew about it. And who had suggested to the superintendent the obsessive nature of his quest? Danglard was the only person who knew how the judge had taken over his life. Danglard, who had been angry with him for a year, over the business with Camille. Danglard who had chosen the side he was on in this split, who had spat out an insult at him. Adamsberg closed his eyes, groaned, and put his arm across his face. Adrien Danglard, his incorruptible second-in-command. His noble and faithful deputy.

At six in the evening, Raphaël came into the room. He watched his brother sleeping for a while, observing the face in which all his childhood was summed up. Sitting on the bed, he gently shook Adamsberg awake.

The *commissaire* sat up.

'Time to go, Jean-Baptiste.'

'Time to run for it,' said Adamsberg, looking for his shoes in the dark.

'It's all my fault,' said Raphaël, after a silence. 'I've ruined your life.'

'Don't say things like that. You didn't ruin anything at all.'

'I did, I ruined everything for you.'

'No.'

'Yes. And now you're down in the mud of the Torque with me.'

Adamsberg was slowly putting his shoes on.

'Do you really think it's possible?' he asked. 'Do you think I could have killed her?'

'What about me? Do you think *I* could have killed *her*?'

Adamsberg looked at his brother.

'Like I told you, you could never have struck three blows in a straight line.'

'Remember how pretty Lise was. She was as light and lovely as the wind.'

'But I wasn't in love with Noëlla, and there was also a fork lying around. I could have done it.'

'Just possibly.'

'Possibly or very possibly? Very possible or very true, Raphaël?'

Raphaël put his chin in his hands. 'My answer is your answer.'

Adamsberg put his other shoe on.

'Remember once when you had a mosquito in your ear for two hours?'

'Do I?' Raphaël grimaced. 'I nearly went mad, with the buzzing.'

'We were afraid you really would go mad before it died. So what we did was make the house quite dark and hold a lighted candle near your ear. It was the priest's idea, Father Grégoire: "We'll exorcise it with bell, book and candle," he said. Typical priest talk. Remember? And the mosquito crawled out your ear towards the flame, then it burnt its wings with a little hiss. Remember that little hiss?'

'Yes, Father Grégoire said, "the devil's roasting in hell now". Typical priest.'

Adamsberg pulled on his sweater and reached for his jacket.

'Do you think it's possible or very possible?' He went on, 'to tempt our devil out of the tunnel with a little light?'

'If he's in your ear.'

'He is, Raphaël.'

'I know it. I hear him at night too.'

Adamsberg put on the jacket and sat down by his brother. 'Think we can get him out?'

'If he exists, Jean-Baptiste. If we're not the devils ourselves.'

'Only two other people believe this devil exists. A sergeant that everyone else thinks is stupid, and an old woman who's a bit crazy.'

'And Violette.'

'I don't know whether Retancourt is doing all this out of duty or conviction.'

'It doesn't matter. Just do what she says. What a magnificent woman!'

'What do you mean? You think she's beautiful?' asked Adamsberg, astonished.

'Well, that too, of course.'

'Do you think her plan can work?'

As he whispered this last sentence, it was as if he and his brother were boys back in the village, plotting some adventure from their mountain den. Who would be able to dive deepest into the Torque, or play a trick on the grocer, or scratch horns on the judge's gate, slipping out at night without waking anyone?

Raphaël hesitated.

'So long as Violette is strong enough to take your weight.'

The two brothers shook hands, thumbs entwined, as they had when they were small boys, before they dived into the river.

XXXVI

ADAMSBERG AND RETANCOURT TOOK IT IN TURNS TO DRIVE ON THE return journey, with Lafrance and Ladouceur tailing them. The *commissaire* woke Retancourt as Gatineau came into sight. He had let her sleep as long as possible, so worried was he that she would be unable to take his weight.

'This Basile,' he said, 'are you sure he'll take me in? I'll be arriving on my own before you.'

'I'll give you a note for him. You just explain you're my boss and that I've sent you. Then we'll call Danglard to get some false papers as soon as possible.'

'Not Danglard. Don't call him. Not under any circumstances.'

'Why ever not?'

'Nobody else knew about my memory loss.'

'But Danglard is the most loyal person in the world,' said Retancourt, shocked. 'He's devoted to you, he'd never give you away to Laliberté.'

'Yes, he might, Retancourt. He's been angry with me for a whole year. I'm not sure how far it goes.'

'You mean because of the business with Camille?'

'How do you know?'

'Oh, nothing much gets past the Chat Room. It's a gossip factory, everyone's love life gets talked about. You can pick up some good ideas too. But Danglard never says anything there, he's totally loyal.' She frowned.

'I'm not sure of course,' said Adamsberg. 'But don't call him all the same.'

By seven forty-five, Adamsberg's room had been cleared, and the *commissaire*, clad only in his boxer shorts and two watches, was having his hair cut by Retancourt. She carefully flushed the clippings down the lavatory, so as to leave no traces.

'Where did you learn to cut hair?'

'In a hairdresser's, before I took up massage.'

Retancourt had probably lived several lives, Adamsberg thought. He allowed her to move his head about, soothed by the light touches and the regular sound of the scissors. At ten past eight she took him over to look in the mirror.

'Pretty good, eh?' she said with the pride of a little girl passing a test.

Yes, it was exactly like Raphaël's. Raphaël's hair was shorter than Jean-Baptiste's, and neatly layered at the back. Adamsberg thought he looked different now, more severe and conventional. Yes, when he was wearing a suit and tie, for the few yards' walk across the parking lot, his appearance ought not to alert the police. By eleven o'clock in any case, they'd be certain he had long since fled the hotel.

'It was easy,' said Retancourt, still smiling. The immediate operational future did not seem to be worrying her.

By ten past nine, the *lieutenant* was sitting in her bath, while Adamsberg was behind the door, both in complete silence.

Adamsberg raised his arm slightly to look at his watches: nine twenty-four and a half. Three minutes later, the police burst into the room. Retancourt had told him to breathe slowly and he was doing his best to comply.

The Mounties' fast retreat, on seeing the bathroom door open, and Retancourt's furious reaction all happened as planned. She banged the door in their faces and less than twenty seconds later, the close contact position, body against body, had been assumed. In a voice indicating contained anger, Retancourt gave the Mounties permission to come in and get on with it, for God's sake. Adamsberg clung on tight to her waist and belt, his feet off the ground, his cheek pressed into her wet back. He had been sure his *lieutenant* would stagger when he took his feet off the ground, but nothing of the kind happened. Retancourt, as she had said, had turned herself into a pylon. He felt as if he were clinging to a maple tree. She didn't even wobble or lean against the wall. She stood up straight, arms folded in the ample bathrobe, without a tremor. The sensation of total solidity stupefied Adamsberg and left him strangely calm all at once. He felt he could have stayed there for an hour quite safely. But by the time he had absorbed this feeling of stability, the cop had completed his quick check of the bathroom and gone out, shutting the door behind him. Retancourt quickly dressed and went back into the bedroom, where she continued to yell at the three Mounties for walking into her room like that and surprising her in her bath.

'We did knock first, ma'am,' said the voice of one he didn't recognise.

'Well, I didn't hear you!' Retancourt retorted. 'And stop messing up my stuff. I've already told you, the *commissaire* told me to stay here. He wanted to see the super on his own this morning.'

'When did he say that?'

'When we parked in front of the hotel, seven o'clock this morning. He must be over in Laliberté's office by now.'

'Nope, no way. He's not over in the RCMP base, he's not in his room. Your boss has done a runner!'

From behind the door, Adamsberg understood that Retancourt was reacting with a shocked silence.

'No, no, he was due there at nine,' she said firmly. 'He's sure to be over there. Don't try and tell me any different.'

'Christ, woman, don't you understand? He's fooled us and gone AWOL.'

'No, that can't be right. He won't have gone without me, we're supposed to work together, we're a team. Something must have happened to him.'

'Wake up, *lieutenant*! Your fucking boss is the devil on skates, and he's fooled you too.'

'I don't get it,' Retancourt muttered obstinately. 'He wouldn't do that.'

The voice of another cop – it sounded like Philippe-Auguste, Adamsberg thought – broke in.

'Nothing in here.'

'Nope, nothing,' came the dry voice of Portelance.

'Don't worry,' said the first voice. 'When we catch him, he can do his explaining to you, if you're his "team-mate". Come on, we've got to search the rest of the hotel.'

He shut the door, apologising again for bursting in rudely.

At eleven, wearing a grey suit, white shirt and tie, Adamsberg walked calmly over to his brother's car. There were police all over the place, but he didn't glance at them. At eleven-forty, his bus left for Montreal. Retancourt had told him to get off one stop before the terminus. All he had in his pockets was Basile's address and a note from Retancourt.

As he watched the trees go past the bus window, he thought he had never been sheltered so solidly and securely as against Retancourt's gleaming white body. Better than the mountain crannies where his great-uncle had taken refuge. How on earth had she managed it? It was a complete mystery. One that all Voisenet's chemistry would never be able to explain.

XXXVII

LOUISSEIZE AND SANSCARTIER APPROACHED LALIBERTÉ'S OFFICE, WITH-
out enthusiasm, to present their report.

'The boss is about to go ape,' said Louisseize in a whisper.

'Yeah, he's been cursing like crazy since this morning,' said Sanscartier
with a smile.

'You think that's funny?'

'What's really funny, Berthe, is that Adamsberg has given us all the slip.
He's rattled Laliberté's cage all right.'

'Well, laugh if you like, but we're the ones who are going to pick up
the tab.'

'It's not our fault, Berthe, we did our best. Want me to do the talking?
He doesn't scare me.'

Standing at his desk, Laliberté was completing the orders he was now
issuing by telephone: photographs of the suspect to be circulated, roadblocks, police checks at all the airports.

'Well?' he yelled, hanging up. 'Where did you look?'

'We searched the whole park, superintendent,' Sanscartier replied.
'Nothing. He might have gone for a walk and had an accident. Met a
bear?'

The superintendent wheeled round and turned on his sergeant. 'Have
you completely lost it, Sanscartier? Don't you get it? He's cut and run.'

'We don't know that for sure. He meant to come back. After all, he kept his promise about sending us all those files on the judge.'

Laliberté thumped the table with his fist.

'His story's a load of bullshit! Take a look at that,' he said, holding out a sheet. 'His precious judge died sixteen years ago! So put that in your pipe and smoke it.'

Sanscartier registered the judge's date of death without showing surprise and nodded.

'Maybe there's a copycat at work,' he suggested. 'After all, the trident story seemed to fit.'

'His story's ancient history. We've been taken for a ride and that's all there is to it.'

'I didn't think he was lying.'

'If he wasn't lying, it's even worse. It means he's completely cuckoo and living in a world of his own.'

'He didn't seem crazy to me.'

'Don't make me laugh, Sanscartier. His story was strictly for the birds.'

'But he didn't invent those other murders, did he?'

'Look, sergeant,' said Laliberté, motioning to Sanscartier to sit down, 'you've been off message for a few days now, and my patience is running out. So listen hard, and get thinking. That night, Adamsberg was in a black mood, right? He'd had so much to drink he couldn't see straight, right? When he was chucked out of *L'Ecluse*, he was all over the place, talking rubbish. The barman told us that, right?'

'Right.'

'And aggressive with it. "Come any nearer and I'll spear ye." *Spear ye*, Sanscartier, does that by any chance ring a bell? About the choice of weapon?'

Sanscartier agreed.

'He was having a fling with that girl. And the girl often used the path, right?'

'Right.'

'Maybe she gave him the brush-off, maybe he was jealous and got mad at her. Possible, yes or no?'

236

'Yes,' said Sanscartier.

'Or else, and this is what I think, she told him some stuff and nonsense about being pregnant. Maybe she wanted to get him to marry her. And it turned into a fight. He didn't get beaten up by a branch, Sanscartier, he got beaten up because he was beating *her* up.'

'We don't even know for sure he met her.'

'Are you listening or what?'

'I only said, we don't have any evidence.'

'I've had it up to here with your lip, Sanscartier. We've got bucketsful of evidence. Fingerprints on the belt?'

'Maybe he left them there earlier? He knew her after all.'

'I'm beginning to wonder if you're off your trolley as well, sergeant. I'll spell it out. She bought the belt *that day*. Look, the girl turns up on the path. He sees red, goes bananas, and kills her. Full stop.'

'I do understand what you're saying, superintendent, it's just that I find it hard to believe. I can't make it fit together, Adamsberg and murder.'

'Give up, won't you! You met him a couple of weeks ago. What do you know about the guy? Nothing! He's a phoney bastard. He killed her all right. And what proves he's got a screw loose is he can't remember what happened that night. He's wiped it from his memory. Right?'

'Right,' said Sanscartier.

'So *you* are going to nail this guy for me. Get the hell outta here and you're on overtime till he's under lock and key.'

XXXVIII

BASILE RAISED NO OBJECTION TO TAKING IN AN EXHAUSTED INDIVIDUAL with no luggage, since the man brought a recommendation from Violette, which was as good as an official pass.

'Will this be OK?' he asked, showing him into a small room.

'Yes, fine, Thanks a million, Basile.'

'Have something to eat before you go for a nap. Violette's some woman, eh?'

'An earth goddess, I'd say.'

'And she fooled all the cops in Gatineau?' Basile asked, highly amused.

So he knew roughly what had happened. Basile was small and pink-cheeked, his eyes magnified by red-framed spectacles.

'Can you tell me how she did it?'

Adamsberg summed it up quickly.

'Oh no, that's too much!' said Basile, fetching some sandwiches. 'Sit down and give me the whole story, from the beginning.'

So Adamsberg told him the Retancourt epic, starting with her invisibility at HQ and ending with the imitation of a pylon. What for Adamsberg was an appalling situation amused Basile a great deal.

'What beats me,' Adamsberg ended, 'is how she didn't lose her balance. I weigh 72 kilos, you know.'

'Well what you gotta understand is that Violette knows the score. She can channel her energy in any direction.'

'I know that. She's on my staff.'

Or was, he thought as he went to his room. Since even if they managed to cross the Atlantic, he wouldn't be able to go and sit in his office any more, with his feet on his desk. He was a wanted man, a criminal on the run. Later, he thought. Later, he would slice up all the elements into slivers and put them through the test.

Retancourt arrived at about nine that evening. Basile, entering into the spirit of things, had already made up her room, got some food in, and obeyed her requests. He had bought enough overnight equipment, clothes and razors for Adamsberg to last him a week.

'Piece of cake,' Retancourt told Adamsberg, munching her way through Basile's pancakes and maple syrup.

It reminded Adamsberg that he had still not managed to get any maple syrup for Clémentine. A sort of mission impossible.

'The Mounties came back at about three. I was on my bed, reading a book, but terribly worried, and convinced you'd met with an accident. A *lieutenant*, distraught about her superior officer. Poor Ginette, I almost made her cry. Sanscartier was with them.'

'How did he seem?' asked Adamsberg eagerly.

'He looked devastated. I got the impression he liked you.'

'It's mutual,' said Adamsberg, imagining how gut-wrenching it would be for the sergeant to find that his new friend had killed a girl with a trident.

'Devastated, but not convinced,' Retancourt went on.

'In the RCMP, some of them think he's dumb. Portelance says he's a wool-gatherer.'

'Ah well, he's wrong there.'

'And Sanscartier didn't agree with their line?'

'Looked like he didn't. He was doing the minimum, as if he was trying not to get his hands dirty. Not taking part in the hunt. He smelled of almond soap.'

Adamsberg refused any more pancakes. The thought that Sanscartier the Good was using the almond soap, and had not yet given up on him, cheered him up.

'From what I heard in the corridor, Laliberté was fit to be tied. A couple of hours later, they completely abandoned the search and went away. I left without any problem. Raphaël's car was back in the hotel parking lot. He must have slipped the net too. Good looker, your brother.'

'Yes.'

'We can talk in front of Basile,' said Retancourt, helping herself to wine. 'For the new ID papers, you don't want to go to Danglard. OK. But do you have a tame forger anywhere in Paris?'

'I know a few from the old days, but no one I could trust.'

'I only know one, but he's safe as houses. No problems there. Only if we use him, you'll have to promise me that he won't get into any trouble. You'll never ask me any questions and you won't give my name, even if Brézillon calls you in for a grilling.'

'Sure, of course.'

'And he's given it up now. He used to be in the business but he'll only do it now if I ask him.'

'Your brother?' asked Adamsberg. 'The one under the dressing gown?'

Retancourt put down her glass. 'How did you know?'

'You seem concerned. That was a lot of precautions you mentioned just now.'

'You're thinking like a *flic* again, *commissaire*.'

'Maybe. How long would it take him?'

'Couple of days. Tomorrow, we'll have to change our appearance and get some new ID photos. We'll scan them to him by email. The earliest he could get passports for us would be Thursday. So if they send them express, we could have them by next Tuesday and leave at once. Basile will have to get our tickets. On separate flights, Basile.'

'Yeah, good thinking,' Basile said. 'By then they'll be looking for a couple. Makes sense to split up.'

'We'll reimburse you from Paris. You're going to have to look after us till then, like the brigand's mother in the story.'

'Yeah, right, no way you can go out for now,' said Basile, 'and you can't go paying with your credit cards. The *commissaire*'s photo is sure to be in *Le Devoir* by tomorrow – and yours too, is my guess, Violette.

You left the hotel without saying goodbye, so you're not much better off than he is.'

'Seven days confined to barracks then,' Adamsberg said.

'It's no big deal,' said Basile. 'You've got all you need here. We can read the papers. They'll all be talking about us, it'll be a laugh.'

Basile didn't seem to take anything seriously, even sheltering a potential murderer in his flat. Violette's word appeared to be good enough for him.

'I like to walk,' said Adamsberg with a wry smile.

'There's a long corridor in the flat. You'll just have to use it for exercise. Violette, I think we'd better turn you into a desperate housewife, OK? I'll get you a smart suit and a necklace and we'll dye your hair darker.'

'OK. For the *commissaire*, I thought we should shave his head about three quarters, make him look bald.'

'Good idea,' said Basile. 'It would really change the way he looks. Tweed suit, beige check I think, receding hairline, and a bit of a pot-belly.'

'We'll whiten the rest of his hair,' said Retancourt. 'Get some foundation too, I think we ought to make his complexion paler. And some lemon juice. It needs to be professional quality make-up.'

'I gotta colleague does the cinema column, he'll know where to get studio make-up. I'll fetch some stuff tomorrow and develop the photos in our lab.'

'Basile is a photographer,' Retancourt explained. 'For *Le Devoir*.'

'A journalist?'

'Yup,' said Basile with a friendly pat on his shoulder. 'And here's a godalmighty scoop sitting at my table. You're in a hornets' nest now. Scarey, eh?'

'It's a risk,' said Adamsberg, smiling faintly.

Basile burst out laughing.

'It's OK, *commissaire*, I know when to keep my mouth shut. And I'm less dangerous than you.'

XXXIX

ADAMSBERG MUST HAVE COVERED SOMETHING LIKE TEN KILOMETRES over the week, pacing up and down in Basile's corridor. After being cooped up for seven days, he was almost able to take pleasure in walking freely in the Montreal airport terminal. But the place was crawling with cops, which took away his appetite for relaxation.

He glanced at himself sideways in a glass door, to check if he passed muster as a salesman aged about sixty. Retancourt had done a fantastic job, and he had let her manipulate him like a puppet. The transformation had tickled Basile. 'Make him look depressed,' he had advised Violette, so that was what they had done. His expression was much altered, under eyebrows which had been whitened and plucked. Retancourt had taken the trouble even to dye his eyelashes and half an hour before they left the house, she put a drop of lemon juice in the corner of each eye. His bloodshot gaze and pale complexion made him look tired and unhealthy. His nose, lips and ears remained unchangeable however, and seemed to him to betray his identity at every turn.

He felt for his new ID papers in his pocket, checking now and then to make sure they were there. Jean-Pierre Emile Roger Feuillet was the name Violette's brother had provided for him, in an impeccably forged passport. It included stamps from Roissy and Montreal attesting to his voyage out. Professional stuff. If the brother was as capable as the sister, the Retancourts were a family of experts.

His real papers had been left with Basile, in case his bags were examined. What a pal Basile had been. He had fetched the Canadian news-papers every day. The virulent articles about the runaway murderer and his accomplice had delighted him. And he was considerate too. So that Adamsberg should not feel too lonely, he had often walked up and down the corridor with him. He liked going on outdoor hikes himself and understood that the prisoner felt cooped up. They would chat as they walked, and after a week Adamsberg had heard all about Basile's various girlfriends, as well as the geography of Canada from Vancouver to the Gaspé peninsula. Still, Basile had never heard about the fish in Pink Lake and promised he'd go and take a look. You should see Strasbourg Cathedral too, if ever you come to little old France, Adamsberg had told him.

He went through security, trying to empty his mind of worries, as Jean-Pierre Emile Roger Feuillet would have, if he were on his way back to France to interest his company in placing orders for maple syrup. But strangely, the faculty of emptying his mind, which normally came to him quite naturally and spontaneously, seemed very hard to achieve that day. He, who could usually daydream at any moment and miss whole chunks of other people's conversations, who was forever shovelling clouds, now found himself breathing rapidly and processing a thousand jumbled thoughts in his head as he went through the routine baggage checks.

But the officials showed no interest in Jean-Pierre Emile Roger Feuillet and once he was in the departure lounge, Adamsberg forced himself to relax and buy a bottle of maple syrup. A very typical gesture on the part of Feuillet, taking a present for his mother. The sound of jet engines starting up and then taxi-ing to take-off produced in him a relief that Danglard would never have been able to conceive. He watched the Canadian landscape disappear beneath them, imagining that there were hundreds of Mounties down there, engaged in their fruitless search.

Now all he had to do was get through immigration at Roissy. And of course Retancourt still had to make her getaway, after an interval of two and a half hours. Adamsberg was worried for her. Her new persona as a rich suburban housewife was unsettling – and had given Basile plenty of fun – but Adamsberg was afraid that her figure would give her away. The image of her naked body flashed in front of his eyes. Impressive, yes, but well-proportioned. Raphaël was right, Retancourt was indeed a beautiful woman, and he reproached himself for not having seen this before, preoccupied as he was with her vigour and determination. Raphaël had always been more sensitive than he.

Seven hours later, the plane touched down on French soil at Roissy-Charles-de-Gaulle airport. He went through customs and passport control and for a moment felt ridiculously free. It was a mistake. The nightmare was going to continue now in another country. In front of him, the future was as empty and white as an icefield. Retancourt could at least go back to the office, arguing that she had been afraid that the Mounties would arrest her for complicity. But for him a journey to nowhere was about to begin. Accompanied only by the aching doubt about his forgotten actions. He would almost rather have been guilty and killed someone, than have to carry around the terrible vagueness about what had happened on the night of October 26.

Jean-Pierre Emile Roger Feuillet went through all the checks at Roissy, but Adamsberg could not bring himself to leave the airport until he knew whether Retancourt had arrived safely. He wandered about for a couple of hours in the terminal buildings, trying to make himself inconspicuous, and imitating Retancourt's invisibility at RCMP headquarters. But he need not have bothered, since Jean-Pierre was obviously of no interest to anyone, just as in Montreal. He kept checking the arrivals boards, to see when the jumbo jets were arriving on long-haul flights. His own jumbo jet, he thought: Retancourt. Without whom he would now be rotting in a Canadian jail, and completely without hope. Retancourt, his escape route on a 747.

The inconspicuous Jean-Pierre therefore stationed himself without too much panic about twenty metres from the arrivals gate. Retancourt must have channelled all her energy into becoming Henriette Emma Marie Parillon. He clenched his fists, as the passengers started pouring into the hall, but couldn't see her anywhere. Had she been picked up at the airport? Taken back to headquarters? Grilled all night? And what if she had cracked? Mentioned Raphaël's name? Or her brother's? Adamsberg grew irritated at all the strangers as they walked past him looking relieved that their flight was over, clutching their bags full of maple syrup and fluffy caribou. He was angry that they were not Retancourt. A hand caught his arm and drew him further into the hall. It was Henriette Emma Marie Parillon.

'You must be nuts!' whispered Retancourt, while maintaining the haughty expression of Henriette.

They travelled together as far as Châtelet metro station, where Adamsberg suggested to his *lieutenant* that they profit from his last hours of freedom under the incognito of Jean-Pierre Emile, to go and have lunch in a cafe, like normal people. Retancourt hesitated, then accepted, feeling relieved that their escape had proceeded so incredibly successfully, as well as by seeing the hordes of people in the streets.

'We'll pretend everything's OK,' said Adamsberg, once he was sitting bolt upright as Jean-Pierre would, in front of his plate. 'We'll pretend I'm not him. That I never did anything.'

'The episode is over,' said Retancourt sternly which made Henriette Emma's expression look suddenly different. 'It's over, and you didn't do it. We're in Paris, on your own territory and you're a policeman. I can't go on believing for both of us. We may have got away with close combat, but I can't do close thinking. You'll have to get your brain back.'

'Why do you believe in me so firmly, Retancourt?'

'We've already discussed that.'

'But why?' Adamsberg insisted. 'Since you don't really like me?'

Retancourt gave an impatient sigh.

'What does it matter?'

'It's important to me. I need to understand. Really.'

'I don't know if it's relevant now. Or later, even.'

'Because of my trouble in Quebec?'

'Among other things. I don't know.'

'Even so, Retancourt, I need to know.'

Retancourt thought a moment, twisting her empty coffee cup.

'Look,' Adamsberg said, 'we may never see one another again. These are extreme circumstances. Rank doesn't matter. I will always regret not having understood.'

'OK, extreme circumstances. What the others in the squad all thought was so marvellous about you got up my nose. The casual way you wandered in and solved cases like a lone ranger, or a Zen archer who went straight to the target. It was certainly impressive, but I could see something else, the way you were so calmly confident of your own internal certainty. You were always right. Yes, you were an independent thinker, but you were royally indifferent to what anyone else might have to contribute.'

She stopped, hesitating.

'Go on,' said Adamsberg.

'I admired your flair of course, everyone did, but not the air of detachment it seemed to give you, the way you disregarded anything your deputies said, since you only half listened to them anyway. I didn't like your isolation, your high-handed indifference. Perhaps I'm not expressing myself well. The sand dunes are smooth and the desert feels soft, but for someone obliged to cross it, it's arid. You can cross a desert, but you can't live there. It isn't very generous, it won't support you.'

Adamsberg was listening attentively. Trabelmann's harsh words came back to him, and the resemblance to what he was hearing formed a great shadow which passed over his brow with the flapping of dark wings. Following his own inclination, leaving other people aside, not bothering to distinguish between them, discarding them as distant interchangeable figures, whose names he couldn't even remember. And yet he was sure the *commandant* of gendarmes had been wrong about him.

'Makes me sound a miserable bastard, doesn't it,' he said without looking up.

'Yes, I suppose so. But perhaps you were really always somewhere else, far away, with Raphaël, just in a twosome with him. I thought about it in the plane. When you were in the cafe where you met him, you formed a circle, an exclusive circle.'

She drew a circle on the table with her finger and Adamsberg knotted his thin, newly-white brows.

'You were with your brother,' she explained. 'You didn't want to abandon him, you were with him, wherever he'd gone. In the desert with him.'

'In the mud of the Torque,' said Adamsberg, drawing another circle.

'If you like.'

'What else do you see in your analysis of me?'

'Well, for the same reasons, you ought to listen when I say you didn't murder anyone. To kill, you need to be emotionally involved with other people, you need to get drawn into their troubles and even be obsessed by what they represent. Killing means interfering with some kind of bond, an excessive reaction, a sort of mingling with someone else. So that the other person doesn't exist as themselves, but as something that belongs to you, that you can treat as a victim. I don't think you're remotely capable of that. A man like you, who wanders through the world without any meaningful contact with other people, doesn't kill. He's not close enough to them, he can't be bothered to sacrifice them to an act of passion. I don't say you *can't* love anyone, but you certainly didn't love Noëlla. You'd never have taken the trouble to kill her.'

'Go on,' said Adamsberg, resting his cheek on his hand.

'Watch out, you're messing up your make-up, I told you not to touch it!'

'Sorry. Carry on.'

'Well, that's all really. Someone who has a meaningless affair is not involved enough to kill.'

'Retancourt,' said Adamsberg forcefully.

'Shh, Henriette,' his *lieutenant* corrected him. 'Be careful, someone might hear you.'

'Henriette, I hope one day I will deserve the help you've given me. But for now, please go on believing in me about that night I can't remember. Please believe I didn't kill, channel all your energy into that. Be a pylon, be a mountain of belief. Then I'll be able to as well.'

'Well, use your own brain,' Retancourt insisted. 'I told you. Your inner confidence. Now is the time to count on it.'

'I hear what you're saying,' said Adamsberg, holding her arm, 'but your energy will be a lever. Just keep it there for me, for a while.'

'I've no reason to change my mind.'

Adamsberg released her arm with reluctance, as if he were jumping down from a tree, and left.

XL

THE COMMISSAIRE, HAVING CHECKED IN A GLASS DOOR THAT HIS MAKE-up was still intact, stationed himself from six that evening on the home-ward route of Adrien Danglard. He spotted from a distance Danglard's large shambling figure, but the *capitaine* gave no sign of recognition as he walked past Jean-Pierre Emile Roger Feuillet. Adamsberg caught him by the arm.

'Don't say anything, Danglard, just keep walking.'

'Good God, who are you? What do you want?' said Danglard trying to pull free.

'It's me, Adamsberg, got up like a salesman.'

'Shit,' Danglard gasped, staring at the face in front of him and trying to make it fit Adamsberg's features behind the pale skin, red-rimmed eyes and balding hairline.

'OK now, Danglard?'

'I've got to talk to you,' said the *capitaine*, looking around.

'Me too. Let's turn here and go to your place. No funny business.'

'No, not my place,' said Danglard in a low, firm voice. 'Pretend you were asking me the way and leave me. I'll see you in five minutes, in my son's school, second street right. Tell the janitor you've come to see me, and I'll be in the games room.'

Danglard pulled away his arm and the *commissaire* watched as he went down the street and turned a corner.

*   *   *

In the school, he found his deputy sitting on a child's blue plastic chair, surrounded by a confusion of balls, books, cubes and little tables. Perched thirty centimetres above the floor, Danglard looked ridiculous. But Adamsberg had no choice but to take another chair, a red one, and sit down beside him.

'Surprised to see I've got away from the Mounties?'

'Yes, I have to say.'

'Disappointed? Anxious?'

Danglard looked at him without a word. This pale-faced balding creature, with Adamsberg's voice coming from his mouth, fascinated him. His youngest child was looking by turns at his father and at the funny man in a beige tweed suit.

'I'm going to tell you another story now, Danglard, but ask your little boy to go away. It's unsuitable for children.'

Danglard whispered to the child and sent him off across the room, still looking at Adamsberg.

'It's like a cops and robbers movie, Danglard. With a chase. But perhaps you've heard it?'

'I've read the papers,' said Danglard prudently, watchful of his boss's fixed gaze. 'I saw the charges that they'd brought against you, and that you'd escaped police surveillance.'

'So you don't know any more than the man in the street?'

'If you like.'

'Well, I'll fill you in on the detail,' said Adamsberg, pulling his chair closer.

During the entire time he was telling his tale, omitting nothing, from his first meeting with Laliberté to the stay at Basile's flat, Adamsberg examined the expressions on the *capitaine*'s face. But Danglard's face reflected nothing but concern, scrupulous attention and at times astonishment.

'I told you she was an exceptional woman,' he said when Adamsberg had finished.

'I didn't come here to talk about Retancourt. Let's talk about Laliberté. Pretty quick off the mark, wasn't he? All that stuff he'd been able to collect on me in such a short time. Including the fact that I had no memory at all of the two and a half hours on the trail. That amnesia was the fatal piece of evidence in his file.'

'Obviously.'

'But who knew about it? Nobody at the Mounties knew, nor anyone in our squad.'

'Perhaps he was guessing? Perhaps he just assumed it?'

Adamsberg smiled.

'No, it was down in the file as a certainty. When I said, "nor anyone in our squad", there was of course an exception. You knew about it, Danglard.'

Danglard nodded slowly.

'So you think I might have told him?' he said calmly.

'Exactly.'

'It's logical enough,' Danglard agreed.

'For once when I try to be logical, you should be glad.'

'No, this time, you shouldn't have tried it.'

'I'm in hell, Danglard, I have to try everything. Including the damned logic you keep trying to teach me.'

'Fair enough. But what does your intuition tell you? Your dreams, your imagination? What do they say about me?'

'You're asking me to do it my way?'

'For once, yes.'

His deputy's calm demeanour and steady gaze shook Adamsberg. He knew by heart Danglard's washed-out blue eyes, which were unable to conceal any of his emotions. You could read anything in them: fear, disapproval, pleasure, distrust, as easily as fish swimming in a fountain. But he could see nothing there indicating the least hint of withdrawal. Curiosity and wonder were the only fish swimming in Danglard's eyes at the moment. And possibly a discreet relief at seeing him again.

'My dreams tell me you don't know anything about it. But those are just dreams. My imagination tells me you'd never do anything like that, or not in that way.'

'And your intuition?'

'Tells me the judge is behind it all.'

'Pretty stubborn, your intuition, isn't it?'

'Well, you asked. And you know you don't like my answers. Sanscartier told me to keep on sailing and hang on in there. So that's what I'm doing.'

'Can I say something?' asked Danglard.

Meanwhile, the little boy, tired of reading, had come back to them and was sitting on Adamsberg's knee, having finally managed to identify him.

'You smell sweaty,' he said, interrupting the conversation.

'I expect so,' said Adamsberg. 'I've been travelling a long time.'

'Why are you in disguise?'

'I was playing games in the plane.'

'What sort of games?'

'Cops and robbers.'

'You were the robber?' the child said.

'Yes, that's right.'

Adamsberg patted the boy's hair to indicate the end of the exchange and looked up at Danglard.

'Someone's been searching your flat,' Danglard said. 'Though I can't be sure.'

Adamsberg motioned him to go on.

'It was over a week ago, Monday morning. I found your fax asking me to send the files to the Mounties. With the D's and R's written in big letters. I thought it was just for "Danglard" at first. Like a warning. Meaning, Danglard, look out, be careful. Then I thought of "DangeR".'

'Well spotted, *capitaine*.'

'So you didn't suspect me when you sent it?'

'No, the gift of logic only descended on me the day after that.'

'Pity,' muttered Danglard.

'Go on. The files?'

'Well, so I was a bit wary. I went to fetch your spare house key where it usually is, in your top drawer, in the box of paper clips.'

Adamsberg nodded.

'The key was there all right, but it was outside the box. Maybe you had been in a hurry when you left. But I was suspicious. Because of the D's and R's.'

'You were right. I always put the key in the box, because the drawer's got a crack in it.'

Danglard shot a glance at his pale-faced boss. Adamsberg's face had almost regained its usual mild expression, and curiously enough the *capitaine* did not resent the suspicion of treachery. He might have gone through the same thought process himself.

'When I got to your flat, I looked at everything carefully. Remember I put away the files myself for you, and the box they were in?'

'Yes, because my arm was in a sling.'

'It seemed to me that I would have put them back more carefully than that. I'm sure I pushed the box to the back of the cupboard. But that morning it wasn't right up against the back. Maybe you got them out again, for Trabelmann?'

'No, I didn't touch the box.'

'Good heavens! How did you do that?'

'Do what?'

Danglard pointed to his youngest child who had dropped off to sleep on Adamsberg's knee, with the *commissaire*'s hand still resting on his head.

'Well you know, Danglard, I do send people to sleep. It works for kids too.'

Danglard looked at him enviously. Vincent was a hard child to get to sleep.

'Well,' he went on, 'everyone in the office knows where you keep the key.'

'You think there's a mole in the squad, Danglard?'

Danglard hesitated and gave a gentle kick to a ball, sending it across the room.

'Possibly,' he said.

'But looking for what? My files on the judge?'

'That's what I can't fathom. What would be the motive? I took prints from the key – just my own. Either I covered up the previous handler's, or else the visitor wiped the key before putting it back in the drawer.'

Adamsberg half closed his eyes. Who on earth would have been interested in the Trident case? It was not as if he had ever made a mystery of it. The tension of travelling and a day without sleep were beginning to weigh on his shoulders. But knowing that Danglard was unlikely to have betrayed him was a relief. Not that he had any proof of his deputy's innocence, apart from the transparency of his expression.

'You didn't think of any other way the "DangeR" might have been interpreted?'

'Well, I thought some elements of the 1973 murder would be better held back from the RCMP. But the visitor had been there before me.'

'Shit,' said Adamsberg, with a start, interrupting the child's sleep.

'And had put everything back.'

Danglard brought out three folded sheets of paper from his inside pocket.

'I've kept these on me ever since,' he said handing them to Adamsberg.

The *commissaire* glanced over them. Yes, those were the documents he had been hoping that Danglard would spot. And the *capitaine* had been carrying them round on him ever since, for eleven days. That must be proof that he had not betrayed him to Laliberté. Unless he had sent copies.

'This time,' Adamsberg said, handing them back, 'you understood what I meant when I was thousands of kilometres away, and on the strength of an inconspicuous signal. So why is it that sometimes we can't communicate when we're only a metre apart?'

Danglard threw another ball up in the air.

'A matter of what it's about, I dare say,' he said with his thin smile.

'Why are you keeping the papers on you?' Adamsberg asked after a pause.

'Because since your escape, I've been under constant surveillance. They're watching my building, because they're hoping that if you slip through their fingers, you'll try to see me. Which is what you were about to do, just now. That's why we're sitting in this school.'

'Brézillon?'

'Of course. His men went into your flat officially, as soon as the RCMP sounded the alarm. Brézillon has his orders and they've turned everything upside down. One of their own *commissaires* a murderer and on the run. The Minister has agreed with the Canadian authorities to arrest you the minute you set foot in France. The entire French police force is on alert. So you can't go home. Or to Camille's studio. Your usual haunts are all watched.'

Adamsberg stroked the child's head automatically. It seemed to make the little boy sleep more soundly. If Danglard had betrayed him, he wouldn't have taken him to the school to help him avoid the police.

'My apologies for my suspicions, *capitaine*.'

'Logic isn't your strong point, that's all. In future, don't count on it.'

'That's what I've been telling you for years.'

'No, not logic in general, just *your* logic. Where can you find a safe house? That make-up won't protect you for ever.'

'I thought of going to Clémentine's.'

'Yes, good idea,' said Danglard approvingly. 'They won't think of that, and you won't be disturbed there.'

'But cooped up there for the rest of my days.'

'I know. That's what I've been thinking of for the last week.'

'Are you sure, Danglard, that my lock wasn't forced?'

'Certain. The visitor used the key. It must be someone from the office.'

'A year ago, I didn't know anyone there except you.'

'Well, perhaps one of them knew you. You've put plenty of people behind bars, after all. That can spark off hate, thirst for vengeance. Perhaps a family member who wants to make you pay? Someone who's trying to get back at you, using this old business of the judge.'

'But who would have known about the Trident case?'

'Everyone saw you go off to Strasbourg.'

Adamsberg shook his head.

'Nobody else could have known the link between Schiltigheim and the judge. Unless I'd told them. There's only one person who would make the connection. Himself.'

'Do you really think your walking corpse went to the office? Took your keys, searched your files, to find out what you thought you were on to at Schiltigheim? Anyway the living dead don't need keys, they just walk through walls.'

'Very true.'

'Look, can we agree just one thing about the Trident? You can call him the Judge, or Fulgence if you like, but let me call him the Disciple. A real live person who for some reason is trying to carry on the judge's work. I'm willing to grant you that much and it'll avoid a lot of tension.'

Danglard threw another ball up into the air and caught it.

'Sanscartier,' he said, changing the subject abruptly. 'You said he wasn't that convinced?'

'According to Retancourt. Does it matter?'

'I liked the guy. A bit slow of speech, yes, but I liked him. His reaction on the spot is interesting. And what about Retancourt? What did you think of her?'

'Exceptional.'

'I'd have liked to do a bit of close combat with her,' said Danglard with a sigh which seemed to contain genuine regret.

'I don't think it would work with someone your size. It was a remarkable experience, Danglard, but it's not worth committing murder just to give it a try.'

Adamsberg's voice had become gruff. The two men walked slowly to the back of the room, since Danglard had decided Adamsberg had better leave by the garage exit. Adamsberg was still carrying the sleeping child in his arms. He knew the endless tunnel he was about to enter, and so did Danglard.

'Don't use the metro or bus,' Danglard advised him. 'Go there on foot.'

'Danglard, who else could possibly have known I had no memory of 26 October? Apart from you.'

The *capitaine* thought for a moment, rattling his coins in his pocket.

'Just one other person,' he concluded. 'The one who helped you lose it.'

'Logical.'

'Yes, my sort of logic.'

'But who, Danglard?'

'Someone who was there with us, among the eight people? Take out you, me and Retancourt, that leaves five, Justin, Voisenet, Froissy, Estalère, Noël. Someone who could look in your files.'

'And the Disciple, what do you make of him?'

'Nothing much. I'm concentrating on more concrete elements.'

'Such as?'

'Such as your symptoms that night of the 26th. Now that's something that really bothers me. The wobbly legs for instance.'

'I'd had a hell of a lot to drink, as you know.'

'Yes. Were you taking any pills? Tranquillisers?'

'No, Danglard, I don't think I'm the kind of person who normally needs a tranquilliser.'

'True. But your legs wouldn't carry you, that's what it felt like, wasn't it?'

'Yes,' said Adamsberg in surprise. 'They just wouldn't hold me up.'

'But only after you hit the branch. That's what you told me. Sure of that?'

'Yes, but what of it?'

'It just bothers me. And the next day, no bruises, no pain?'

'My forehead was hurting, I had a headache, and I felt sick, I told you. What's bothering you about the legs?'

'Let's just say it's a missing link in my logic. Forget it for now.'

'*Capitaine*, can you give me your pass-key?'

Danglard hesitated, then opened his bag and took it out, slipping it into Adamsberg's pocket.

'Don't go taking risks. And you'd better have this,' he said passing him some banknotes. 'You can't go near a cash machine.'

'Thanks, Danglard.'

'Do you mind giving me back my kid before you go?'

'Sorry,' said Adamsberg passing the child across.

Neither man said 'au revoir'. An indecent expression, if you don't know whether you will ever meet again. An ordinary everyday expression, Adamsberg thought, as he went off into the night, but which he would not now be able to use.

XLI

CLÉMENTINE HAD TAKEN IN THE EXHAUSTED COMMISSAIRE WITHOUT showing the least surprise. She had settled him in front of the fire and forced him to eat up some pasta and ham.

'This time, Clémentine, I haven't just come for supper,' Adamsberg said. 'I need a safe house. I've got every *flic* in France after me.'

'It happens,' said Clémentine calmly, passing him a pot of yoghurt with a spoon planted in it. 'The police don't always think the same way we do, it's their job. Is that why your face is all made up?'

'Yes, I had to escape from Canada.'

'That's a smart suit you're wearing.'

'And I'm a *flic* too,' said Adamsberg, going on with his idea. 'So I'm chasing myself. I've been so stupid, you can't imagine, Clémentine.'

'How was that?'

'By doing something very, very stupid. In Quebec, I got roaring drunk, met a girl and killed her with a trident.'

'I've got an idea,' said Clémentine. 'We'll pull out the sofa and put it near the fire with two nice quilts, you'll sleep like a prince. I've already got Josette sleeping in the little office, so that's all I can offer you.'

'Perfect, Clémentine. Your friend Josette – can we can count on her keeping her mouth shut?'

'Josette's seen better days. When she was young, she was a real lady, rich, you can't imagine. Not like now. She won't talk about you, any more than you will about her. And that's enough of your nonsense

258

about tridents, m'dear, it sounds to me like your monster's been at it again.'

'I just don't know, Clémentine. It's between him and me now.'

'That's good, a real fight,' said Clémentine approvingly, as she fetched the quilts. 'That'll buck you up.'

'I hadn't looked at it that way.'

'Of course it will, or else you'd get bored. You can't spend all day sitting here eating pasta. But do you perhaps have some idea whether it was him or you?'

'Trouble is,' said Adamsberg as he helped pull the sofa over, 'I'd drunk so much that I can't remember a thing about it.'

'Something like that happened to me when I was expecting my daughter. I tripped on the pavement and afterwards I couldn't remember anything at all.'

'Were your legs too wobbly to carry you?'

'Oh no. Apparently I went running all over the place afterwards like a rabbit. What was I running after? Goodness knows.'

'Goodness knows,' repeated Adamsberg.

'Well, what's it matter, m'dear? We never know what we're running after in this life. So if you run a bit more or a bit less, makes no difference.'

'Are you sure it's all right for me to stay, Clémentine? I won't be in your way?'

'Ah no, m'dear, not at all, I'm going to fatten you up. You'll need your strength to run.'

Adamsberg opened his bag and gave her the bottle of maple syrup.

'I brought it from Quebec for you. You can eat it with yoghurt or bread or pancakes. It would go well with your cookies too.'

'Now, that's really kind of you. With all your troubles, that touches my old heart. It's pretty, that bottle. They get it from trees, I do hear.'

'Yes. Actually the bottle is the most difficult thing to make. For the syrup, they just cut the tree trunks and out it comes.'

'Now that's practical, if you like. If only pork chops grew on trees.'

'Yes. Or truth.'

'Oh truth, you won't find that so easily. Truth now, it hides away like mushrooms, and no one knows why.'

'How do you get at it then, Clémentine?'

'It's the same as mushrooms. You have to lift up the leaves, one by one, in dark places. It can take a long time.'

For the first time in his life, Adamsberg slept until midday. Clémentine had re-lit the fire and was tiptoeing around to do her cooking.

'I need to make an important visit, Clémentine,' said Adamsberg as he drank his coffee. 'Can you help me get the make-up right? I can shave my head, but I don't know how to put this foundation stuff on my hands.'

The shower had left his complexion streaky, as his own dark skin showed through.

'Not my department, dear,' said Clémentine. 'You'd do better to ask Josette. She's got lots of make-up. She takes an hour in the morning doing her face.'

Josette, with somewhat trembling hands, set about applying the light-coloured foundation to the *commissaire*'s hands and then touched up his face and neck. She helped him replace the cushion round his waist, which made him look portly.

'What do you do all day on your computer, Josette?' asked Adamsberg as the old woman carefully arranged his bleached hair.

'Oh, I transfer stuff, I balance it up, I share it out.'

Adamsberg did not try to explore this enigmatic answer. Any other time, Josette's activities might have interested him, but not in extreme circumstances. He was chatting with her out of politeness, and because he had taken in what Retancourt said about him. Josette's quavery voice was delicately modulated, and Adamsberg recognised the remnants of her upper-class intonations.

'Have you been in computers a long time?'

'I started when I was sixty-five.'

'Not so easy to get the hang of it then, I suppose?'

'Oh, I manage,' said the old woman, in her fragile voice.

XLII

DIVISIONNAIRE BRÉZILLON HAD SUMPTUOUS QUARTERS ON THE AVENUE de Breteuil, and was never home before six or seven o'clock. Furthermore, it was known in the Chat Room that his wife had gone to spend autumn in the mists and mellow fruitfulness of England. If there was one place in France where the *flics* would not go looking for a fugitive, it was the avenue de Breteuil.

Using his pass-key, Adamsberg entered the apartment quietly at five-thirty that afternoon. He sat down in an opulent reception room, with bookshelves full of works on law, administration, policing and poetry. Four topics, all carefully separated from each other. There were six shelves full of poetry – much more than the parish priest had, back in his village. Adamsberg took down a volume of Victor Hugo, taking care not to get his make-up on the precious bindings. He was looking for the golden sickle in the field of stars. A field he currently supposed to be located over Detroit, but he had not yet been able to release his sickle. At the same time, he rehearsed the speech he had prepared for the *division-naire*: it was a version in which he hardly, if at all, believed himself, but it was the only one that might convince his boss. He repeated whole sentences from this speech over to himself, trying to conceal the great gulfs of doubt that lurked underneath it, and to inject into his voice a note of total sincerity.

* * *

Less than an hour later, the key turned in the lock and Adamsberg lowered the book to his knee. Brézillon gave a genuine start, and was on the point of crying out, when he saw this unknown Jean-Pierre Emile Roger Feuillet sitting peacefully in an armchair. Adamsberg put his finger on his lips and going towards Brézillon, took him gently by the arm, guiding him to a chair opposite his own. The *divisionnaire* was more astonished than afraid, no doubt because Jean-Pierre Emile did not look a very threatening person. And the surprise also prevented him finding his tongue for a moment or two.

'Hush, *Monsieur le divisionnaire*. Please don't make a noise. It would only get you into trouble.'

'Adamsberg!' said Brézillon, recognising his voice.

'I've come a long way for the pleasure of this interview.'

'Not so fast, *commissaire*,' said Brézillon, once more in control of himself. 'See that bell? If I press it, there'll be a couple of dozen *flics* in here in two minutes.'

'Please let me have the two minutes before you press it. I know you've been a lawyer, you should hear evidence from both sides.'

'Two minutes with a murderer? That's asking a lot, Adamsberg.'

'I didn't kill that girl.'

'They all say that — as you and I know full well.'

'But they don't all have a mole in their team. Somebody got into my flat, before your men went in, using the spare key left at headquarters. Someone consulted my dossiers on the judge, and was already looking at them, even before my first trip to Canada.'

Hanging on to his shaky story, Adamsberg was speaking rapidly, knowing that Brézillon wouldn't give him much time, and that he must take him by surprise as fast as possible. He wasn't used to talking quickly, and stumbled over words like a runner hitting stones on the path.

'Somebody knew I used the portage trail. Somebody knew I'd met this girl over there. Somebody killed her, using the same methods as the judge, and put my prints on her belt. And dropped the belt on the path, not in the frozen water. That makes too many coincidences, *Monsieur le divisionnaire*. The file's too clear, no loose ends in it. Have you seen anything like that?'

'Or perhaps it's the regrettable truth, Adamsberg. Your girlfriend, your prints, your evening out drinking. Your usual route back and your obsession with the judge.'

'It's not an obsession, it's a police matter.'

'So you say. But how do I know you're not sick, Adamsberg? Do I have to remind you about the Favre affair? Worst of all, and it could be a sign of major disturbance, you've wiped the night of the murder from your memory.'

'And how did they know that?' Adamsberg asked leaning forward. 'Danglard was the only person who knew about that, and he didn't tell anyone. So how did they know?'

Brézillon frowned and loosened his tie.

'Only one other person could possibly have known I'd lost my memory,' Adamsberg went on, using Danglard's words. 'And that's the person who managed to make me lose it. It's evidence that I wasn't alone on that path, or in the whole affair.'

Brézillon lumbered to his feet, fetched himself a cigarette from the bookshelf and sat down again. It was a tiny sign of interest, a momentary distraction from the alarm bell.

'My brother lost his memory too, and so did all the other men arrested after the judge's murders. You've seen the files, haven't you?'

The *divisionnaire* nodded, lighting his coarse untipped cigarette, much the same kind as Clémentine smoked.

'So where's your proof?'

'I don't have any.'

'The only defence you can put up is this judge, who died about sixteen years ago.'

'The judge, or a follower.'

'Phantoms, Adamsberg.'

'But phantoms are worth some consideration. Like poems,' Adamsberg risked.

He was approaching his man from another direction. Would a poet hit the panic button without hesitating?

Brézillon leaned back in the chair, expelled a puff of smoke and pulled a face.

'The RCMP, now,' he said. 'What I didn't like, Adamsberg, was the way they did this. They hauled you back over there to help in the investigation, and I believed it. I don't like being lied to, or having one of my men trapped like that. It's absolutely against all the rules. Légalité deceived me with false explanations. It was a premature extradition and a legal sleight of hand.'

Brézillon's pride and professional integrity had been offended by the superintendent's trick. Adamsberg had not anticipated this favourable element.

'Of course, now Légalité tells me he only discovered the evidence against you after you'd arrived.'

'Quite untrue. He'd already put his file together.'

'That was dishonest,' said Brézillon with a contemptuous grimace. 'On the other hand, you're a refugee from Canadian justice, and I do not expect that kind of behaviour from one of my *commissaires*.'

'I didn't run from Canadian justice, because no one had said anything about an arrest at that stage. There were no charges, nobody had cautioned me, I still had my freedom of movement.'

'I suppose that's technically correct.'

'I was free to have had enough, to smell a rat, and to leave.'

'In disguise and with false papers, *commissaire*.'

'Well, shall we say that was the necessary path to take. A sort of game,' said Adamsberg, improvising.

'And you often play games with Retancourt?'

Adamsberg paused, as the image of the close-combat incident flashed into his mind.

'All she was doing was fulfilling her mission, which was to protect me. She was strictly obeying your orders.'

Brézillon stubbed out his cigarette end with his thumb. His father was probably a roofer and his mother a laundress, like Danglard's parents, Adamsberg thought. Origins which he did not trouble to conceal when sitting on a velvet armchair, a sort of noble lineage one assumes proudly, and honours by the choice of cigarettes and a way of putting them out.

'So what do you want from me, Adamsberg,' said the *divisionnaire*, rubbing his finger. 'You want me to take your word for it? There's too much evidence stacked up against you. The fact that someone searched your flat is a slight point in your favour. As is Légalité's previous knowledge of your memory loss. Two points, but they're both very slender.'

'If you hand me over, the credibility of your whole squad goes down with me. I think I could avert the scandal, if I was allowed some freedom.'

'You want me to go to war with the Ministry and the Mounties, both?'

'No, just to stand down the police surveillance.'

'Oh, that's all, is it? I've given my word about it.'

'But you could get round that. By certifying that I am known to be abroad. I'll stay in a safe house of course.'

'Is it really safe?'

'Yes.'

'Anything else?

'A gun. A police badge, in a new name. A little money to survive on. And for Retancourt, her return to the squad, no questions asked.'

'What were you reading?' asked Brézillon, pointing to the small leather-covered volume in Adamsberg's hands.

'I was looking for the poem *Boaz asleep*.'

'Why?'

'For a couple of lines.'

'Which ones?'

'What god, what harvester of eternal summertime,

Had, as he strolled away, carelessly thrown down

That golden sickle in the field of stars?'

'Golden sickle? And what's that meant to signify?'

'My brother, thrown away like a tool that had served its purpose.'

'Or yourself, right now. The sickle isn't just the new moon. It can cut. It can cut off a head, pierce a stomach, it can be sweet or cruel. Let me ask you a question, Adamsberg. Do you ever have any doubts about what you're doing?'

The way that Brézillon was leaning forward, Adamsberg sensed that this unassuming question was decisive. His answer might mean the difference between extradition or freedom of movement. He hesitated. Logically, Brézillon would like a solid assurance, which would keep him out of trouble. But Adamsberg suspected he was expecting a more philosophical answer.

'I doubt myself every minute of the day,' he replied.

'That's the best guarantee that you're on the level,' said Brézillon curtly, leaning back once more. 'Right, from tonight you're free, armed and invisible. But not for all eternity, Adamsberg. For six weeks. After that, you come back here, and sit down in that chair. And next time, ring the bell before you come in.'

XLIII

JEAN-PIERRE EMILE ROGER FEUILLET'S FINAL MISSION WAS TO GET HOLD of a new mobile phone. Then Adamsberg abandoned his assumed identity under Clémentine's shower, with some relief. With a touch of regret as well. Not that he was particularly attached to this rather uptight character, but it seemed a little uncaring, he thought, to let a stream of foundation-tinted water carry away the Jean-Pierre who had given such impeccable service. So he mentally saluted his alter ego, before returning to his usual dark hair, slim figure, and brown complexion. Only the receding hairline remained, and he would have to cover that up until it had grown back.

Six weeks' reprieve, a huge extension of his freedom allowed by Brézillon, but a very tight deadline for tracking down the devil or his own demons.

What he needed to do, according to Mordent, was dislodge the phantom from his usual haunts: sweep out the attics, close up his bolt-holes, and padlock the old trunks and creaking wardrobes he frequented. In other words, fill in the gaps in his records between the judge's death and the Schiltigheim murder. It might not help to find out where he was now, but who knew whether the judge might from time to time return to his old haunts?

He raised the question while dining with Clémentine and Josette in front of the fire. He was not expecting Clémentine to come up with any technical suggestions, but to have her listen to him was relaxing, and perhaps by some kind of osmosis, encouraging.

267

'Is it important?' Josette asked in her quavery little voice. 'The places he used to live. Old addresses?'

'Sure and certain it is,' Clémentine answered for Adamsberg. 'Wherever that monster lived, he's got to find out. Mushrooms now, they always grow back the same place, so that's where you've got to look, stands to reason.'

'But is it really important? For the *commissaire*?' Josette insisted.

'He's not a *commissaire* any longer, m'dear,' Clémentine pointed out. 'That's why he's here, he's just telling us about it.'

'It's a matter of life and death,' Adamsberg said with a wry smile, to Josette. 'It's his skin or mine.'

'*Mon dieu*, as serious as that?'

'Yes, Josette. As serious as that. And I can't just go out and about to search the country for him.'

Clémentine helped everybody to a rice and raisin pudding with a compulsory double helping for Adamsberg.

'And you can't send some of your men out to do it, if I have understood correctly, monsieur,' asked Josette timidly.

'Haven't I told you, Josette, he's got no men to order about now. He's on his own,' said Clémentine.

'Well, I do have two unofficial agents. But I can't put them on to it, because my movements are blocked.'

Josette seemed to consider for a moment, as she built a little house out of her pudding.

'Now c'mon, Josette,' said Clémentine. 'If you've got an idea in that little head of yours, you just come out with it. Poor boy's got no more than six weeks.'

'This wouldn't go any further?' queried Josette.

'Josette, he's eating at our table. And you ask something like that!'

'Well, the thing is,' Josette said, still building her tottery pudding castle, 'there are ways and means of going out and about, if you see what I mean. If Monsieur Adamsberg can't go out himself, and if it's a question of life and death . . .'

She paused.

268

'You have to humour Josette,' Clémentine explained. 'There's no getting round it, it was the way she was brought up. Rich people, it's always the same with them. Look round corners. Worry about everything. Well you're poor now, Josette, so spit it out.'

'What I mean is,' Josette went on, 'you don't always have to use your legs. That was what I meant. And you can go faster and farther this other way.'

'What do you mean?' asked Adamsberg.

'With a computer. If you want to find out an address for instance, you can go on to the internet.'

'I do know about the internet, Josette,' Adamsberg said politely. 'But the addresses I'm looking for are not publicly available. They're hidden, secret ones, underground if you like.'

'Ye-es,' said Josette hesitantly. 'But that's what I meant. The under-ground web. The secret internet.'

Adamsberg said nothing, not sure what to make of her words. Clémentine took advantage of the pause to pour him a glass of wine.

'Stop, Clémentine. Since that ghastly night, I'm not touching a drop of anything.'

'Come on, m'dear, you're not going to tell me it disagrees with you. One glass with the meal is the rule here.'

Clémentine went on pouring. Josette tapped on the walls of her pudding castle to make the raisins into windows.

'The secret internet, Josette?' said Adamsberg gently. 'Is that the way you get about?'

'Oh, Josette goes wherever she likes in her secret underground,' Clémentine declared. 'She's in Hamburg one day, New York the next.'

'Are you a computer pirate?' asked Adamsberg, in astonishment. 'A hacker?'

'She's a hackeress,' Clémentine declared proudly. 'Josette takes from the rich and gives to the poor. Underground. Pour me a glass please, my little Adamsberg.'

'Is that what you meant by "transfers and distribution"?' Adamsberg asked.

'Yes,' she said, briefly meeting his eyes. 'I equalise things.'

Josette was now putting a raisin on top of the castle as a chimney.

'Where do you put the money you take?'

'Into an association, and it pays my wage.'

'Where do you take it from?'

'All over the place. Wherever the fat cats are hiding it. I go into their numbered bank accounts and take a percentage.'

'You never get caught?'

'I've only had one scare in the ten years I've been doing it, and that was three months ago, because I was rushing things. I've had to cover my tracks and I've nearly finished.'

'You should never rush things,' Clémentine opined. 'But for him it's special, he's only got six weeks. Mustn't forget that.'

Adamsberg contemplated in amazement this internet pirate, the little hacker sitting alongside him: a tiny frail old woman whose fingers trembled. With the old-fashioned name of Josette.

'Where did you learn to do it?'

'You can teach yourself if you've got the touch. Clémentine told me you were in trouble. And for Clémentine's sake, perhaps I can help you.'

'Josette,' interrupted Adamsberg. 'Would you be able to get inside a solicitor's files for instance? His client's business?'

'It's a database like any other,' the little voice replied. 'The files would have to be computerised of course.'

'Could you unlock their access codes and get through their passwords? Have you got some kind of way through?'

'Yes,' replied Josette modestly.

'Like a ghost,' Adamsberg concluded.

'Just as well,' said Clémentine. 'Because what the *commissaire*'s got on his back is a real ghost. And he's got his claws in your neck, hasn't he? Josette, I've asked you before not to play with your food. It's not so much that I mind, but I was brought up not to do it.'

Sitting on the old chintz sofa in his tweed suit, with bare feet, Adamsberg got out his new phone to call Danglard.

'Excuse me,' said Josette, 'but are you telephoning somebody you can trust? Is the line safe?'

'It's a new line, Josette. And I'm using a new mobile.'

'Well, it's true that that makes it harder for them, but if you're going to be more than eight to ten minutes, you'd do well to change the frequency. I'll lend you mine, it's already fixed up. Watch the time, and change frequency: you press this button. I'll fix yours up for you tomorrow.'

Impressed, Adamsberg accepted Josette's hi-tech mobile.

'Danglard, I've got six weeks. I managed to get on the right side of Brézillon.'

Danglard whistled his astonishment.

'I thought he had two wrong sides.'

'No, there was a pathway through and I used my ice-axe. I've got a gun, a new badge and partial and unofficial lifting of the wanted status. I can't tell whether there are phone taps, and I can't move about freely. If I get caught, Brézillon will go down with me, he's taking that risk. He's allowing me a bit of line on this short-term basis. And anyway, he puts out his fag with his thumb without burning himself. Good guy. So I can't compromise him, I can't just breeze in to check the files.'

'I take it you want me to do that then?'

'And past records. We need to check the period between the judge's death and Schiltigheim. That is find out whether there were any murders with some kind of trident during the last sixteen years. Think you could do that?'

'Look for the disciple, all right.'

'Send the results by email, *capitaine*. Wait a minute.'

Adamsberg pressed the frequency button.

'What's that buzzing?' asked Danglard.

'I just changed frequency.'

'Sophisticated, huh,' said Danglard. 'Who's supplying your phones, the Mafia?'

'I've had to change addresses and keep different company now, *capitaine*. I'm merging into the background.'

*   *   *

Late in the night, under the rather light quilts, Adamsberg gazed into the embers of the fire through the darkness, evaluating the immense possibilities opened up by having an aged electronic wizard in the house. He tried to remember the name of the solicitor who had arranged the sale of the manor in the Pyrenees. He used to know it in the old days. Fulgence's lawyer must have been sworn to total secrecy. Someone who had committed some youthful indiscretion which Fulgence had covered up for him. And who had then fallen through the trapdoor and become a vassal of the judge for life. What the devil was his name? He could see the brass plate shining on the façade of a solid stone-built house, when he had gone to ask the solicitor the date when the Manor had been bought. He remembered a youngish man at the time, about thirty. With any luck he was still practising.

The brass plaque mingled with the glowing ashes in the grate. He thought it was a sort of unpleasant name, a bit like 'deceiving' or 'disservice'. He ran through the alphabet and came up with it. Desseveaux, *Maître* Jérôme Desseveaux, solicitor, conveyancer, house purchases. With his balls held tight in the iron grip of Judge Fulgence.

XLIV

FASCINATED BY JOSETTE'S UNSUSPECTED DEXTERITY AND EXPERTISE, Adamsberg sat alongside her and watched her operate the computer, her tiny wrinkled hands trembling over the keyboard. On the screen, an endless series of numbers and letters flashed up in quick succession, and Josette responded with equally hermetic contributions of her own. To Adamsberg, the computer now seemed no longer an everyday tool, but a sort of gigantic Aladdin's lamp, from which a genie might emerge at any time and offer him three wishes. But one had to know the secrets of operating it, whereas in the old stories, any ignorant boy could come along with a rag and shine up the lamp. Things were certainly more complicated these days, if you wanted to make a wish.

'Your man is very protected,' Josette commented, in her quavery voice, which had however lost its timidity once she was on her own ground. 'All these extra codes and passwords seem excessive for a country solicitor's office.'

'It's no ordinary solicitor's office. A ghost's got him by the balls.'

'Ah, in that case.'

'Can you get in, Josette?'

'There are four levels of protection. It's going to take some time.'

Like her hands, the old woman's head was shaky, and Adamsberg wondered whether these effects of age hampered her reading of the screen. Clémentine, who was still intent on fattening up the *commissaire*, had come in with a plate of cookies and maple syrup. Adamsberg looked at

Josette's clothes: an elegant beige ensemble, combined with an old pair of tennis shoes.

'Why do you wear those shoes? So as not to make any noise when you tiptoe into secret passages?'

Josette smiled. Maybe. A burglar's equipment, flexible and practical.

'She just likes to be comfortable, that's all,' said Clémentine.

'In the old days,' said Josette, 'when I was married to my shipbuilder, I wore court shoes. With twin-sets and pearls. Real ones.'

'Very chic,' commented Clémentine approvingly.

'He was rich?' asked Adamsberg.

'So rich, he didn't know what to do with it. But he kept control of it all himself. I used to lift small sums now and then, from his account, to help out my friends. That was how it started. I wasn't very good at it in those days, and he caught me at it.'

'And that led to a bust-up?'

'The bust-up, as you call it, was messy. There was a lot of publicity. After the divorce, I started to explore his bank accounts more systematically, but I said to myself, Josette, if you're going to be any good at this, you have to learn about finance and think big. And it just grew from there. By the time I was sixty-five, with computers around, I was ready for the big time.'

'Where did you meet Clémentine?'

'In the fleamarket, oh, thirty-five years ago. I used to run a little antique shop my husband had set up for me.'

'He wanted her to have something to occupy her,' Clémentine said, as she stood over Adamsberg seeing that he was eating up as instructed. 'Only the best stuff, mind, nothing tatty. We had fun in those days, didn't we, Josette, m'dear?'

'Here's our solicitor,' said Josette, pointing to the screen.

'About time too,' said Clémentine, who had never touched a keyboard in her life.

'This is the right name, yes? *Maître* Jérôme Desseveaux and Partners, Boulevard Suchet in Paris.'

'You've got into his files?' said Adamsberg, fascinated, pulling his chair closer.

'Yes, it's as if we were walking round the room. He's got a very big practice now, seventeen partners and thousands of files. Put your tennis shoes on, *commissaire*, we're going hunting. What was the name again?'

'Fulgence, Honoré Guillaume.'

'Several files here for that name,' said Josette after a few moments. 'But nothing dated later than 1987.'

'That's when he died. He must have changed his name.'

'Do you have to do that if you die?'

'Depends on what work you have on hand, I guess. Try Maxime Leclerc, who might have bought a property in 1999.'

'Yes, here he is,' said Josette. 'He bought a property called *Das Schloss* in the Bas-Rhin *département*. That's the only file in that name.'

Fifteen minutes later, Josette had provided Adamsberg with a list of all the properties bought by the Trident between 1949 and 1987, the Desseveaux office having taken over the earlier files. So the same vassal had been taking charge of the judge's affairs not only up to his death, but also in his afterlife, since he had handled the recent purchase of *Das Schloss*.

Adamsberg was in the kitchen, stirring a bechamel sauce with a wooden spoon, under Clémentine's orders. That is to say, he had to keep stirring at constant speed, making figures of eight in the pan. Those were her express instructions, to prevent lumps from forming. The location and names of the properties bought by the judge confirmed strikingly what he already knew about Fulgence's past. They each corresponded to one of the murders with three stab wounds which he had collected during his long inquiry. For ten years, the judge had been on circuit in Loire-Atlantique, in north-west France, living at a house called *Le Castelet-les-Ormes*. In 1949, he had killed his first victim, about thirty kilometres away, a 28-year-old man, Jean-Pierre Espir. Four years later, in 1953, in the same sector, a young girl, Annie Lefebure, had been murdered in circumstances very like those of Elisabeth Wind. The judge had struck again six years later, in 1959, and this time his victim was a young man,

Dominique Ventou. At which point he had prudently decided to sell *Le Castelet*. And Fulgence had moved to his second circuit, in Indre-et-Loire, also in the west. The lawyer's files recorded the purchase of a small seventeenth-century chateau, *Les Tourelles*. In this area, he had killed two men, 47-year-old Julien Soubise and, four years later, an older man, Roger Lentretien. In 1967, he had left the region and moved to *Le Manoir*, in Adamsberg's native village in the Pyrenees. He had waited six years before killing Lise Autan. This time, the threat from the vengeful young Adamsberg had obliged him to move on at once, and he had relocated to the Dordogne, living in a large farm called *Le Pigeonnier*. Adamsberg actually knew this aristocratic property, since he had located it and turned up there, but too late, as in Schiltigheim. The judge had already left before he traced him, following the murder of 35-year-old Daniel Mestre.

Adamsberg had then followed his trail to the Charente, still in the west, after the case of the murder of Jeanne Lessard, aged 56, in 1983. He had been quick off the mark, and had confronted Fulgence in his new address, *La Tour-Maufourt*. It was the first time that he had seen the man in ten years, and his haughty imperiousness had not changed. The judge had laughed at the accusations of the young policeman, and threatened him with every kind of harassment and the destruction of his career if he went on pestering him. He had another two dogs by then, dobermans, who could be heard barking in their kennel. Adamsberg had been intimidated by the judge, who was no easier to confront now than when he had been a teenager back at the *Manoir*. He had however listed the eight murders of which he was accusing him, from Jean-Pierre Espir to Jeanne Lessard. Fulgence had pressed the end of his cane into Adamsberg's chest, and shoved him backwards pronouncing a few final words, calmly and courteously as if he were wishing him farewell.

'Do not touch me, do not attempt to come near me. I can bring a thunderbolt down on your head whenever I please.'

Then putting down the cane, he had taken out the keys to the kennel, and repeated the exact formula he had used ten years earlier.

'I'll give you a start, young man. I will count to four.'

And as in the past, Adamsberg had had to run for it, followed by the frantic barking of the dobermans. In the train, as he recovered, he had done his best to react with disdain to the judge's high and mighty airs. He was not going to allow himself to be reduced to ashes by the pressure of a cane on his chest from this would-be aristocrat. He had carried on with his enquiries, but the sudden departure of Fulgence from *La Tour-Maufourt* had taken him by surprise. It was only when the judge's death was reported, four years later, that Adamsberg had discovered the name of his final retreat, a town house in Richelieu, Indre-et-Loire.

Adamsberg carried on stirring his figures of eight in the bechamel. In a way this activity helped him to keep going, and not to visualise himself in the demoniacal skin of the Trident, attacking Noëlla on the portage trail as Fulgence would have done.

While manipulating his wooden spoon and listening to its comfortable sound, he planned the next sortie into the underground internet he would have to make with Josette. He had had doubts about her expertise, imagining that she was exaggerating her powers: the fantasy life of an old woman in her final years. But no, he really did have access to a bold and practised hacker, in the shape of this former high-society lady. He was simply filled with admiration. He took the pan off the fire, as the sauce reached the desired consistency. At least he had managed not to ruin the bechamel sauce.

He picked up Josette's Mafia-style mobile to call Danglard.

'Nothing to report yet,' came the reply. 'It's going to take a long time.'

'I've found a short cut, *capitaine*.'

'What do you mean, a way through the ice?'

'I've got some solid information. The same lawyer acted for Fulgence, buying all his properties up to the date of his death. but he's also handled the house purchases of . . . er, the disciple.' Adamsberg was prudent enough to add, 'Or at any rate the Haguenau *Schloss*.'

'Where are you, *commissaire*?'

'I'm in a solicitor's office on the Boulevard Suchet. I can get into it easily. I'm wearing tennis shoes, so as not to make a noise. Deep-pile carpets, modern filing cabinets, ventilator fans. Very chic.'

'Ah.'

'But since his death, the properties have all been bought under other names, like Maxime Leclerc. So I might be able to trace them over the last sixteen years, but I'd need to imagine the kind of names Fulgence might choose.'

'Yes, I suppose that's right,' Danglard agreed, doubtfully.

'But I can't do that. I don't know much about etymology and names. Can you give me a list of names that might suggest thunder, lightning, light, or power, like in the case of Maxime Leclerc? Just write down anything you can think of.'

'No need for a list, *commissaire*, I can tell you straight off. Do you have a pen?'

'Go ahead, *capitaine*,' said Adamsberg, as usual admiring his deputy's intellectual powers.

'There wouldn't be a lot of possibilities. If you take light as the starting point, from the Latin *lux*, that would give you surnames like Luce, Lucien, Lucenet, or alternatively Flamme, Flambard. He might go for derivatives of *clarus*, meaning bright: Clair, Clar, Claret, Clairet. For power, well we already know about Maxime, but there are other versions like Mesme, Mesmin, Maximin, Maximilien. Try Legrand, Mestraud, or Major, because they come from Latin words for superior and excellent. Primat would be a possibility or Primaud, it means "first". And for forenames, you might try the names of emperors or ancient Romans: Alexandre, Auguste, César, Napoléon even, though that might be a bit too obvious.'

Adamsberg took his list to Josette.

'What we need to do now is try out some of these combinations on the solicitor's files, to identify buyers of property in the years between the judge's death and the date when Maxime Leclerc moved to Alsace. They would have to be big properties, country houses, manors, small chateaux, that kind of thing, in isolated rural areas.'

'I see,' said Josette. 'We're on the trail of the ghost, are we?'

Adamsberg sat with fists clenching and unclenching as he waited for the old lady to work her keyboard.

'I've got three possibles,' she reported. 'There's a Napoléon Grandin too, but since he bought a little flat in La Courneuve, which is a working-class suburb, I don't think he's your man, if I've understood you. But here for instance is an Alexandre Clar, who bought a manor in the Vendée in 1988, in the village of Saint-Fulgent, incidentally. Sold it again in 1993. A Lucien Legrand bought a property in the Puy-de-Dôme, at Pionsat, in 1993, and sold it in 1997; and an Auguste Primat bought a very grand house up by the English Channel, a place called Solesmes in 1997. He sold it again in 1999. Then you have your Maxime Leclerc, who bought his chateau in 1999. The dates all tally, *commissaire*. I'll run you off a printed version of all that. But first give me some time to wipe out our footsteps on the lawyer's carpet.'

'I've got him, Danglard,' said Adamsberg , still breathless from this voyage into the underworld. 'I've got some names you need to check against the registration records: Alexandre Clar, born 1935; Lucien Legrand, born 1939, and Auguste Primat, born 1931. And for the crimes, try a sweep of a radius of between five and sixty kilometres around the communes of Saint-Fulgent in the Vendée, Pionsat in the Puy-de-Dôme, and Solesmes in the Nord. OK?'

'That'll speed things up. What dates for the murders?'

'The first one's between 1988 and 1993. The second between 1993 and 1997. The third between 1997 and 1999. Don't forget that the last crimes probably took place not long before the properties were sold again. That would give us spring 1993, winter 1997 and autumn 1999. Try those dates first.'

'Always an odd number in the year,' Danglard commented.

'Yes, he seems to like odd numbers. Like the number three and a trident.'

'You know, the idea of a disciple might have something in it after all. It's beginning to take shape.'

The idea of the phantom, you mean, Adamsberg thought, as he hung up. A spectre which was rapidly gaining in consistency as Josette unearthed its haunts. He waited impatiently for Danglard to call back, pacing round the little house with the list in his hand. Clémentine had congratulated him on his bechamel. He'd got something right, at least.

'I've got some bad news,' announced Danglard. 'The *divisionnaire* got in touch with Légalité, I mean Laliberté, he keeps calling him the wrong name, to call him to account. Brézillon tells me that one of the two points in your favour is null and void. Laliberté said he found out about your memory loss through the night janitor. You had told him some yarn about a fight between a gang and the police. But the next day, the janitor said, you'd seemed very surprised when he told you how late it was when you got in. And in any case the story about the fight was untrue, and your hands were covered in blood. That's how Laliberté decided you must have had a memory blackout for some of the time, because you'd assumed it was earlier, and made up a story for the porter. So there was no anonymous phone call, no traitor, nothing. That whole scenario falls to bits.'

'And Brézillon's going to call me in?' said Adamsberg, stunned.

'He didn't say so.'

'What about the murders. Anything to report?'

'All I can tell you for now is that your Alexandre Clar never existed, nor did Lucien Legrand or Auguste Primat. They're all false names. I haven't had time to do any more, because of this business with the *divisionnaire*. And we've got a homicide, rue du Château. Some political connection. I don't know when I'll be able to get back on to the disciple. Sorry, *commissaire*.'

Adamsberg hung up, overcome by a wave of despair. Just because the janitor couldn't sleep. And Laliberté's conclusions were perfectly logical.

The thin thread of hope to which he had been clinging had snapped. His confidence had collapsed with it. There was no traitor, no conspiracy. Nobody had told the superintendent about his memory loss. So logically, nobody could have taken it from him. There was no third man, plotting away in the dark against him. He had been alone on the trail, with the trident in easy reach, and Noëlla threatening him with all kinds of things. And he had had that murderous folly in his mind. Like his brother. Or in his brother's footsteps perhaps.

Clémentine came to sit by him, without speaking, bringing him a glass of port.

'What is it, m'dear?'

Adamsberg told her in a dead voice, staring at the floor.

'Now that's the *flics*' way of looking at things,' she said gently. 'Your ideas are different.'

'But it means I was the only one there, Clémentine.'

'How do you know that, m'dear, since you can't remember anything? You've got this ghost cornered, you and Josette now, haven't you?'

'What does that change though, Clémentine? I was on my own.'

'You're just tormenting yourself, and that's the long and short of it,' said Clémentine, putting the glass in his hand, 'and it's no good twisting the knife in the wound, m'dear. You'd do better to go back to our Josette and her computer stuff, and drink up this port for me.'

Josette had been standing by the fire, without saying anything. She seemed about to speak, then hesitated.

'Come on, Josette, out with it,' said Clémentine, shifting the cigarette in her mouth. 'You know you shouldn't keep it to yourself.'

'Well, I'm not sure if I should say,' Josette explained.

'M'dear, we're long past the point of being shy here, can't you see?'

'Well, what I thought was that if Monsieur Danglard – that's his name, isn't it? – if he can't look for the murders, we could have a try ourselves. The trouble is, it means, er, going into the records of the *gendarmerie*.'

'And what would be wrong with that?'

'Monsieur here is a *commissaire*.'

'Josette, how many times do I have to tell you? He's no policeman any more. And what's more, m'dear, the police and the *gendarmes*, they're two different systems.'

Adamsberg, looking distracted, glanced up at the little old woman.

'Could you really do that, Josette?'

'I did get into the FBI archives once, just for fun,' she admitted shyly.

'No need to look so shy, Josette. It's no sin to do good for other folks.'

Adamsberg looked in even greater astonishment at this frail old woman, one-third society lady, one-third shy little creature, and one-third seasoned hacker.

*　*　*

After dinner, which Clémentine had forced Adamsberg to eat, Josette tried the crime files. She had noted on a piece of paper spring 1993, winter 1997 and autumn 1999. From time to time, Adamsberg went over to see how she was getting on. In the evenings, she changed from her tennis shoes into huge velvety grey slippers, which made her feet look like those of a baby elephant.

'Very well protected, I guess,' he said.

'Firewalls everywhere, but you'd expect that. If they had a dossier on me, I wouldn't like it to be available to the first old lady who comes along.'

Clémentine had gone to bed, and Adamsberg stood by the chimney, twisting his hands and staring into the embers. He did not hear Josette come up behind him in her big slippers. With her hacker's silent footsteps.

'Here you are, *commissaire*,' she said, handing him a sheet of paper with the modesty of one who has done a good job of work, and does not realise how talented she is, as if she had simply been stirring a bechamel sauce. In March 1993, thirty-three kilometres from Saint-Fulgent, a 40-year-old woman, Ghislaine Matère, had been killed in her house, stabbed three times. She lived alone, out in the country. In February 1997, twenty-four kilometres from Pionsat, a girl had been killed with three blows to the stomach. Sylviane Brasillier had been waiting at a bus stop late on a Sunday evening. In September 1999, 66-year-old Joseph Fevre had been murdered, thirty kilometres from Solesmes. With three stab wounds.

'And was anyone charged?' asked Adamsberg, looking at the sheet.

'Here we are. In the first case, a woman, who lived in a forest hut. She was generally regarded as a witch in the neighbourhood, and was certainly a bit touched, and given to drink. In the second case, they arrested an unemployed man who was always round the bars in Saint-Eloy-les-Mines. For the Fevre murder, they found a gamekeeper, out for the count on a bench in a suburb of Cambrai, dead drunk and with the knife in his pocket.'

'Memory loss?'

'All three.'

'New weapons?'

'All three.'

'Brilliant, Josette! We've got a trail as clear as daylight now, from *Le Castelet-les-Ormes* in 1949 to Schiltigheim. Twelve murders. Twelve, Josette! Good God!'

'Thirteen, with the one in Quebec.'

'I was alone there though, Josette.'

'You and your colleague were talking about a disciple. If he did four murders after the judge died, why mightn't he have been able to kill someone in Quebec?'

'For a very simple reason, Josette. If he bothered to come all the way to Quebec, it would be in order to trap me, like the other scapegoats. And if a disciple had taken over Fulgence's mission, it would be out of veneration for the judge and a wish to complete his wishes. But whoever it was, even a fanatical follower of his couldn't have the same thought processes as Fulgence himself. The judge hated me personally. He wanted me out of the way. But a disciple couldn't have hated me as much, he wouldn't know me. Finishing some kind of series is one thing, but killing someone to do a favour for a dead man doesn't make sense. I don't buy that. That's why I tell you, I was alone on that path.'

'Clémentine says that's depression talking.'

'Maybe, but it's got something real behind it. And if there is a disciple, he can't be very old. Veneration is a youthful emotion. He might be, say, thirty to forty years old. Men of that generation don't smoke pipes, or hardly ever. The man who lived in the *Schloss* smoked a pipe, and his hair was white. Josette, I have to tell you, I don't believe in a disciple. I've reached a dead end.'

Josette twitched her grey slipper up and down on the ancient brick floor.

'Unless,' she said after a minute or two, 'you believe in people coming back from the dead.'

'Unless, as you say.'

They both fell silent for some time. Josette poked the fire.

'Are you tired, Josette, my dear?' asked Adamsberg, surprised to find himself falling into Clémentine's way of speaking.

'I'm often up all night.'

'Take this man, Maxime Leclerc, Auguste Primat, whatever he calls himself. Since the judge's death, he's been invisible. Either the disciple wants to prolong the image of Fulgence in some way, or our back-from-the-dead person doesn't want anyone to see his face.'

'Because he's dead.'

'Yes. In four years, nobody clapped eyes on Maxime Leclerc. Not the estate agents, not the cleaning lady, not the gardener, not the postman. Every contact outside the house was through the cleaning lady. The owner of the house communicated with her by notes, occasionally by phone. So it *is* possible to avoid being seen, because he managed it successfully. But you see, Josette, I don't think it's possible for someone to stay totally invisible. Maybe for two years, but surely not for five, let alone sixteen. It could work, but only if nothing unexpected ever happened, none of the little accidents of everyday life. In sixteen years, something like that has got to have happened. If we go back over the sixteen years, we ought to be able to find something.'

Josette was listening, in conscientious hacker mode, for more precise instructions, her head and her grey slippers making little movements.

'I'm thinking maybe a doctor, Josette. Let's suppose our man has some health problem, a fall for instance, or an injury. If something serious happens, you have to make an emergency call. But our man wouldn't call the local doctor. He'd call one of those telephone services, SOS-Médecins or something, where you get a stranger, a mobile team. You see them once, and then they forget all about you.'

'I see. But they probably don't keep much in the way of records, certainly not more than a few years.'

'Well, that means concentrating on Maxime Leclerc. So if we tried a search for the emergency services of the Bas-Rhin *département*, we might unearth a doctor's visit to the *Schloss*.'

Josette put the poker down, adjusted her earrings and pushed up the sleeves of her cashmere sweater. It was one in the morning when she switched the computer back on. Adamsberg stayed by the fire, piling on a couple more logs, as tense as an expectant father. His new superstition was to keep away from Josette while she operated her magic lamp. If he stood over her, he was afraid of witnessing the expressions of disappointment on her face. He sat motionless, still plunged into the hell of the portage trail. His only hope was the tiny glimmer resulting from these painstaking explorations by the old lady. Which he was carefully gathering, and putting into the process wells of his mind. Hoping that the protective devices would all crumble, as his little hacker went about her work with her magic lantern. He had noted the various terms she used to describe the levels of resistance in ascending order of difficulty: password protected, locked, key-chained, firewalled, barbed wire, concrete. And she had tunnelled under the defences of the FBI. He raised his head as he heard the shuffle of slippers in the narrow corridor.

'Here you are,' said Josette. 'It was locked, but not impregnable.'

'Tell me quickly, what did you get?' said Adamsberg, his heart pounding.

'Maxime Leclerc called the emergency services two years ago, on 17 August at 14.40. He had seven wasp stings, which had made his neck and jaw swell up. Seven, that's a lot. The doctor arrived very fast. He came back again at eight o'clock, and gave him another anti-histamine injection. I've got the name of the doctor, Vincent Courtin. I took the liberty of finding out his address and telephone number.'

Adamsberg put his hands on Josette's shoulders. He could feel her slender bones.

'These last few days, my life has been in the hands of magical women. They've been tossing me from one to another, and every time they save me from falling into the abyss.'

'Is that a problem?' asked Josette, seriously.

He woke his deputy up at two in the morning.

'Stay where you are, Danglard. I just want to give you a message.'

'I'm still sleeping. Fire away.'

'When the judge died, there must have been some press photos. Can you get me four, two in profile, one full-face, and one three-quarters, if they exist, and get the lab to age the face for me.'

'There are plenty of drawings of skull types in any good dictionary.'

'Danglard, this is serious, and it's urgent. Can you get a fifth picture, full face, and have them augment it with swellings, as if the man had been stung by wasps.'

'If it amuses you,' said Danglard, resignedly.

'Can you get them to me as quickly as possible? Don't bother about the missing murders. I've got them, all three, and I'll send you the names of the new victims. For now, go back to sleep, *capitaine*.'

'I already have.'

XLV

FOR HIS FALSE POLICE BADGE, BRÉZILLON HAD GIVEN HIM A NAME HE found hard to remember. Adamsberg repeated it to himself under his breath, before he called the doctor. He took out his mobile carefully. Since his hacker had 'improved' his phone, it had six bits of red and green wire sticking out of it like an insect's legs, and two little switches, to change frequency, which looked like eyes on each side. Adamsberg handled it as if it was a mysterious scarab beetle. When he called, on Saturday at ten in the morning, he found Dr Courtin at home.

'*Commissaire* Denis Lamproie,' Adamsberg announced, 'Paris Serious Crime Squad.'

Doctors, from long experience of being called on in connection with autopsies and burials, generally react calmly to a call from the police.

'How can I help you?' Dr Courtin said, without enthusiasm.

'Two years ago, on 17 August, you treated an emergency patient about twenty kilometres from Schiltigheim, in a property called *Das Schloss*.'

'I'll stop you right there, *commissaire*. I can't recall the names of my emergency patients. I sometimes do up to twenty calls a day and I hardly ever see those people again.'

'I realise that, but this man had seven wasp stings. He had an allergic reaction and needed two injections, one in the afternoon and again in the evening.'

'Ah, yes, I do remember that one, because you don't usually get a lot of wasp stings all at once. Tell you the truth, I was quite anxious about the old guy. He lived alone. He was as stubborn as hell, and didn't want me to see him again after the first injection. But I called back at the end of the day, and he had to let me in, because he was still having difficulty breathing.'

'Could you describe him, doctor?'

'Oh, I don't know about that. I see hundreds of faces. He was elderly, tall, white hair, rather offhand in manner I seem to recall. I couldn't say more, because of course his face was all swollen with the stings.'

'I have some photos.'

'Frankly, *commissaire*, you'd be wasting your time. I can't remember much about him, it's just that the wasp stings did stick in my mind.'

By early afternoon, Adamsberg was on his way to the Gare de l'Est, with his photographs of the judge, artificially aged. Off to Strasbourg again. In order to keep his face and his bald patch hidden, he had put on a Canadian lumberman's cap with earflaps which Basile had bought him in Montreal. It was too warm for the milder temperatures which had returned to France. The doctor would probably think it odd if he kept it on. Courtin did not appreciate having this forced consultation, and Adamsberg had the impression he was spoiling his weekend.

The two men sat down at a table covered with papers. Courtin was quite young, though already putting on weight, and his normal expression seemed to be grumpy. The old man and the wasps did not inspire him with any curiosity, and he did not ask the reason for the enquiries. Adamsberg spread out the photographs of the judge. 'The ageing and the swelling are artificial,' he explained. 'Does he look familiar?'

'*Commissaire*,' the doctor asked, 'don't you want to take off your hat?'

'Yes, I do, actually,' said Adamsberg who was dripping with sweat under the Arctic headgear. 'To tell you the truth, I caught fleas from a prisoner in a cell, and half of my hair has been shaved off.'

'Funny way of dealing with it,' said the doctor, after Adamsberg had taken off the cap. 'Why didn't they shave the whole head?'

'A friend did it for me, an ex-monk.'

288

'Oh,' said the doctor with a shrug. He shook himself and turned back to the photographs.

'This one,' he said, pointing to a photograph of the judge in left profile. 'That's the fellow with the wasps.'

'I thought you only had a vague memory of him.'

'Him yes, but his ear I remember very well. Doctors tend to remember abnormalities. And I certainly remember his left ear.'

'What's the matter with it?' asked Adamsberg.

'Look at the way it's lying. He must have had protruding ears in his youth. In those days, the operation was a bit dodgy. The scar has turned into a lump and the outer surface of the ear is deformed.'

The press photographs dated from the time when the judge was still in post. He had had short hair in those days, and his ears were clearly visible. Adamsberg had known him only when he had retired, and his hair was longer.

'He had long hair, but I had to lift it up to see how far the swelling went,' the doctor explained, 'so I noticed the malformation. As for the rest of the face, well it could be him, I suppose, same type.'

'Are you absolutely sure, doctor?'

'I'm sure that that ear has been operated on, and that the scar didn't heal properly. And I'm also sure that the right ear wasn't the same way, as you can see in the photos. I remember looking at the left one with some curiosity. But he wouldn't be the only man in France with a misshapen left ear. See what I mean? Still, it's not all that common. Normally, both ears would have been left looking the same shape after the operation. You don't often get a bad reaction on one side and not the other. So all I can say is that this corresponds to my memory of your Maxime Leclerc.'

'Two years ago, he would have been about ninety-seven. Very old indeed. Does that correspond too?'

At this, the doctor shook his head in disbelief.

'Good Lord, no! He couldn't have been over, oh say, eighty-five.' The doctor looked incredulous. 'Never in his nineties.'

'Are you sure?' asked Adamsberg in surprise.

'Absolutely. If he'd been ninety-seven, I'd never have left him on his own with seven wasp stings. I'd have hospitalised him right away.'

'But Maxime Leclerc was born in 1904,' Adamsberg insisted. 'He'd been retired about thirty years.'

'No, no,' said the doctor. 'No doubt whatsoever in my mind. Take off about fifteen years.'

Adamsberg avoided the cathedral, for fear of seeing Nessie in the doorway, along with the dragon or the fish from Pink Lake swimming out of a window.

He stopped and rubbed his eyes. Lift leaf after leaf in the dark hidden places, Clémentine had said, to find the mushrooms of truth. For now he had to follow up the malformed ear. It was rather like a mushroom in fact. He would have to remain alert, and not let the dark clouds of his thoughts obscure the narrow trail he had to follow. But the categorical affirmation by the doctor about Maxime Leclerc's age had unsettled him. Same ear, different age. But still, Dr Courtin judged the age of human beings, not ghosts.

Rigour, rigour *and* yet more rigour. Adamsberg clenched his fists in memory of the Québécois superintendent and climbed into the train. When he reached the Gare de l'Est, he knew exactly whom he had to contact in pursuit of the judge's ear.

XLVI

THE PARISH PRIEST IN HIS VILLAGE ROSE IN THE MORNING WITH THE farmyard fowls, as Adamsberg's mother had always said, hoping to make her children follow his example. Adamsberg waited until half-past eight on his two watches to call the priest, since he calculated that he must now be over eighty. He had always seemed rather like a large dog hunting truffles, and Adamsberg hoped that he hadn't changed. Father Grégoire had spent a lifetime absorbing masses of useless details, since he was delighted with the diversity that the Good Lord had included in the natural world. Adamsberg introduced himself by his surname.

'Which Adamsberg is this?'

'The one who used to look at your old books.

What god, what harvester of eternal summertime,

Had, as he strolled away, carelessly thrown down

That golden sickle . . .'

'Abandoned, Jean-Baptiste, abandoned, you mean,' said the priest, without appearing surprised at being telephoned.

'Thrown down.'

'Abandoned.'

'It doesn't matter, Father. I need to ask you something. I hope I didn't wake you up.'

'Oh, I get up when the chickens do, you know. And the older I get . . . Wait a minute, I have to check. You've sown a doubt in my mind.'

Adamsberg sat with the phone in his hand, anxiously. Didn't

Grégoire understand these days when something was urgent? He was known in the village for being able to spot the slightest worry on the part of one of his parishioners. Nothing could be concealed from Father Grégoire.

'Thrown down. You were right, Jean-Baptiste,' said the priest, disappointed. 'I must be getting old.'

'Father, do you remember the judge? The one we called the Lord and Master?'

'Still fretting about him, are you,' said Grégoire, with reproach in his voice.

'He's come back from the dead. I'll get the old devil by the horns or lose my soul in the attempt.'

'Jean-Baptiste, don't talk like that!' ordered the priest sharply, as if he were still talking to a child. 'What if God could hear you?'

'Father, can you remember what his ears looked like?'

'Do you mean his left ear?'

'Yes,' said Adamsberg quickly, picking up a pencil. 'Tell me about it.'

'One shouldn't speak ill of the dead, but that ear was deformed. Not by God, but by doctors.'

'God sent him into the world with ears sticking out.'

'But He had also given him great beauty. God shares things out in this world, Jean-Baptiste.'

Adamsberg thought that God was not currently doing his work very well, and that it was a good thing there were Josettes in the world to help sort out the mess.

'Tell me about the ear,' he said, hoping Grégoire would not launch into a sermon about God's mysterious ways.

'It was big and deformed, with a long lobe. The entrance to the ear was very narrow, and the rim was scarred. Remember the time we got that mosquito out of Raphaël's ear? We managed it in the end with a lamp, like when you go fishing at night.'

'I remember very well. It hissed in the flame with a funny little sound, remember?'

'Yes, I remember, I made a joke about it.'

'Yes, indeed. But tell me more about the judge. You're sure his ear was out of shape?'

'Oh yes. And let me see, he had a wart on his chin, on the right, which must have given him some trouble shaving,' said Grégoire, who was now launched into instant recall. 'The right nostril was larger than the left, and his hair grew low down on his cheeks.'

'How on earth do you do it?'

'I can describe you as well, if you like.'

'No thanks, Father. I've got enough problems as it is.'

'The judge is dead, my son, don't forget. Don't get into trouble.'

'I'm doing my best, Father.'

Adamsberg thought about the old priest, sitting at his greasy old wooden table, then returned to the photos with a magnifying glass. Yes, the wart on the chin was visible, as was the irregularity of the nostrils. The old priest's memory was as efficient as ever, a real telephoto lens into the past. Apart from the problem of the age difference insisted upon by the doctor, it was as if Fulgence had stepped out of the grave. Or had been pulled out by his ear. It was true, he thought, as he looked at the photographs of Fulgence taken at the time of his retirement, that the judge had never looked his age. He had always had much greater strength than one would anticipate and Courtin couldn't be expected to know that. Maxime Leclerc was no ordinary patient, and by the same token he was no ordinary ghost.

Adamsberg made some more coffee and waited impatiently for Clémentine and Josette to come back from shopping. Now that he had had to leave the sheltering tree trunk of Retancourt, he felt the need of their support and an urge to tell them of any little progress he made.

'We've got him by the tips of his ears, Clémentine,' he announced as he helped her empty her shopping basket.

'Aha, it's like a ball of wool, once you find the end, you just have to pull it.'

'Shall we try a new line, *commissaire*?' Josette asked.

'I keep telling you, Josette. He isn't a policeman any more. It's a funny old world.'

'Let's try the town of Richelieu, Josette. Can you find the name of the doctor who signed the death certificate, sixteen years ago?'

'Child's play,' she said, dismissively.

It took her only twenty minutes to find the GP, Colette Choisel, the judge's doctor ever since he had come to live in Richelieu. She had examined the body, diagnosed a heart attack, and signed the certificate for the burial.

'And her address, Josette?'

'She closed the practice, four months after the judge died.'

'Retired?'

'Hardly. She was only forty-eight.'

'Perfect. Let's check her out.'

'That might not be so easy. She has a common enough name. But if she's sixty-four, she might still be in practice, and then she'd be on the medical register.'

'And take a look at court records too, to see if her name crops up.'

'If she had a record, she wouldn't be able to practise.'

'Exactly. We're looking for an acquittal.'

Adamsberg left Josette to her Aladdin's lamp and went to give a hand to Clémentine who was peeling vegetables for their lunch.

'She slips in there like an eel under a rock,' he said, sitting down.

'Well, that's her work, you know,' replied Clémentine who was unaware of the complexity involved in Josette's hacking activities.

'It's like spuds,' she went on. 'Now mind you peel them properly for me, Adamsberg.'

'I know how to peel potatoes, Clémentine.'

'No, you don't. You leave the eyes in. Got to take them out, they're poisonous.'

Clémentine showed him, with the practised movements of a professional, how to dig the end of the peeler into the eye and dig out the little black cones.

'They're only poisonous when they're raw, Clémentine.'

'Never mind. I want those eyes out, please.'

'OK. I'll be careful.'

The potatoes, checked over by Clémentine, were cooked and on the table by the time Josette returned with her results.

'Any luck?' asked Clémentine as she served up.

'I think so, yes,' said Josette putting a sheet of paper on the table.

'I don't really like people working when they're eating. Not that it upsets me, you understand, but my old father wouldn't have let us do that. But seeing as you've only got six weeks.'

'Colette Choisel has been in practice in Rennes for the last sixteen years,' Josette said. 'When she was very young, twenty-seven, she was involved in a court case. One of her patients died, an elderly woman. She'd been giving her morphine injections for pain. But the death was from a serious overdose. It could have cost her her career.'

'I should think so!' said Clémentine.

'And where was that, Josette?'

'In Tours, that was on the judge's second circuit.'

'Acquitted?'

'Yes. The defence lawyer argued that she had a blameless record. And he pointed out that the patient, who was a retired vet, could have got hold of the morphine and dosed herself.'

'The lawyer must have been one of Fulgence's men.'

'The jury decided it was suicide. Choisel got off without anything on her record.'

'But in hock to the judge for life. Josette,' said Adamsberg, putting his hand on the old lady's arm, 'your tunnellings are going to bring us up into the air now. Or rather, they're taking us back under the earth.'

'About time too,' said Clémentine.

Adamsberg sat for a long time thinking, in the chimney corner, with his dessert plate balanced on his knees. The road ahead was not going to be easy. Danglard, despite having apparently calmed down, would tell him to take a running jump. Retancourt would listen to him more objectively. He took the scarab with red and green legs out of his pocket and dialled her number on its shiny back. He felt a little surge of well-being and relaxation on hearing the serious voice of his maple-tree *lieutenant*.

'Don't worry, Retancourt, I change frequency every five minutes.'

'Danglard told me you'd been able to buy some time.'

'Not long, *lieutenant*, and I have to act quickly. I believe the judge survived his own death.'

'Meaning?'

'All I've got for the moment is a tip of his ear. But that ear was alive and well two years ago, twenty kilometres from Schiltigheim.'

He had a vision of that lone velvety ear, fluttering like a huge malevolent moth through the attics at the *Schloss*.

'Anything attached to the ear?' asked Retancourt.

'Yes, a dodgy death certificate. The doctor who signed it was one of Fulgence's blackmail victims. Retancourt, I think the judge went to Richelieu in the first place because that doctor was in practice there.'

'He programmed his own death, you mean?'

'That's what I think. Can you pass this on to Danglard?'

'Why don't you call him yourself?'

'He'd bite my head off, *lieutenant*.'

Less than ten minutes later, Danglard called back. His voice was unsympathetic.

'If I've got this right, *commissaire*, you've managed to bring your judge back to life. Simple as that, eh?'

'I think I have, Danglard. We're not chasing a dead man now.'

'But we are chasing an old man of about ninety-nine years old. *Commissaire*, he's practically a *hundred*!'

'I realise that.'

'It's just as improbable. Not a lot of people live to ninety-nine.'

'There was one in my village.'

'And was he in good shape?'

'Well, no, not really,' Adamsberg admitted.

'Listen,' Danglard went on patiently, 'if you think an old guy of a hundred can attack a young woman, kill her with a trident and then drag her and her bicycle across the fields, you're raving mad. Only in fairy stories.'

'Well, stories are like that, I can't help it. The judge had superhuman strength.'

'*Had* is the operative word. But nobody has superhuman strength when they're that old. A murderer who's a hundred years old just doesn't exist, he wouldn't be able to do it.'

'The devil doesn't give a damn how old he is. I want to request an exhumation.'

'Jesus Christ, are you going that far?'

'Yes.'

'Well, don't count on me. You're going way beyond anywhere I'm prepared to follow.'

'I understand.'

'I was ready to believe in a disciple, let me remind you. But not a dead man walking. Or a hundred-year-old murderer.'

'Well, in that case, I'll have to try making the request myself. But if it gets through to the squad, will you please attend? You, Retancourt and Mordent?'

'Uh-oh. Not me, *commissaire*.'

'Whatever is in that grave, Danglard, I want you to see it. You'll come.'

'I know what's in a coffin. I don't need to leave my desk for that.'

'Danglard, the new name Brézillon gave me was "Lamproie". Does that mean anything to you?'

'Yes, it's a primitive type of fish, a lamprey,' said the *capitaine*, and Adamsberg could hear him smiling. 'Well not exactly a fish, a cyclostome. It's long and thin like an eel.'

'Ah,' said Adamsberg, disappointed and slightly disgusted, as he remembered the prehistoric creature in Pink Lake. 'Does it have any special features?'

'The lamprey has no hinged jaws. It hangs on by suction, like a leech, if you like.'

Adamsberg wondered as he hung up, why the *divisionnaire* had given him this odd name. Perhaps it meant he lacked polish? Or maybe it was a reference to the six weeks' grace he had managed to snatch out of him? Perhaps this creature was a sort of sucker, pulling contrary wills towards it?

Trying to convince Brézillon to order the exhumation of Judge Fulgence looked an unpromising enterprise. Adamsberg concentrated on being a lamprey and tried to pull the *divisionnaire*'s will towards him, as he telephoned. Brézillon had quickly and volubly refused to give any credence to the ear living in Alsace after the death of the judge. As for the suspect death certificate, it looked a very flimsy bit of evidence to him.

'What day is it today?' he asked suddenly.

'Sunday.'

'Tuesday 2 p.m. then,' he announced in one of those sudden about-turns which had given Adamsberg his brief freedom.

'Retancourt, Mordent and Danglard in attendance, please,' Adamsberg just had time to ask.

He put his mobile away carefully, so as not to damage its antennae. Possibly Brézillon had felt under some constraint, since he had taken the responsibility of letting 'his man' go free, to follow through with the logic and let it take its course. Or perhaps the lamprey had managed to draw him into its orbit. But the force would work the other way, once Adamsberg had to go back, a defeated man, and sit in that chair in Brézillon's apartment. He remembered Brézillon's thumb and couldn't stop himself wondering what would happen if you put a cigarette in the mouth of a lamprey. No, of course, you couldn't, it lived under water. Another creature to join the strange assortment which was blocking up the door of Strasbourg Cathedral. Add to that the ghastly moth haunting the *Schloss*, half-ear, half-mushroom.

Well, never mind what had gone through the *divisionnaire*'s mind, he had authorised the exhumation. Adamsberg felt torn between febrile excitement and genuine fear. Not that it was the first time he had ordered an exhumation. But opening the magistrate's coffin suddenly seemed a blasphemous undertaking, full of menace. 'You're going way beyond anywhere I'm prepared to follow you,' Danglard had said. But where? Profanation, desecration, horror. A journey underground in the company of the judge who might carry him off into the underworld. He looked at his watches. In precisely forty-six hours.

XLVII

WITH THE CANADIAN CAP PULLED DOWN OVER HIS EARS AND HIS COLLAR turned up, Adamsberg was watching from a distance the sacrilegious operations taking place under the freezing rain which had blackened the tree trunks in the cemetery at Richelieu. The police had put red and white plastic tapes round the judge's grave, as if it were a danger zone.

Brézillon had turned up in person, surprisingly for a man who had long since risen above ordinary police work. He was standing erect near the grave, in a grey overcoat with a black velvet collar. Apart from the lamprey effect, which might have drawn him to Richelieu, Adamsberg suspected that he was secretly curious about the terrifying career of the Trident. Danglard had come, of course, but was standing some way from the grave, as if to disclaim all responsibility. Alongside Brézillon, Mordent was shifting from one foot to another under a battered umbrella. He was the one who had suggested irritating the ghost in order to join battle, but perhaps he was now regretting his rash advice. Retancourt was standing, apparently placidly, without an umbrella. She was the only person to have spotted Adamsberg lurking in the depths of the cemetery, and had made him a discreet sign of greeting. The group was silent and concentrated. Four local *gendarmes* had moved the gravestone. Which, Adamsberg noted, seemed not to have suffered the ravages of time but was still shining in the rain, as if the tomb, like the judge, had defied the last sixteen years.

A mound of soil was gradually rising, as the *gendarmes* dug into the soft damp earth. The police officers blew on their hands or shuffled their

300

feet to keep warm. Adamsberg felt tense all over, and glanced at Retancourt, imagining himself clasping her back tightly, breathing along with her and watching through her eyes.

The shovels struck wood. Clémentine's voice seemed to reach him in the cemetery. You have to lift up leaves, one after another, in dark places. You have to lift the lid of the coffin. And if the judge's body was inside it, Adamsberg knew that he would be plunged into the earth alongside him.

The *gendarmes* had finished placing their ropes and were now hauling up the oak coffin, which came awkwardly to the surface, also looking in quite good condition. The men had started to work with screwdrivers when Brézillon appeared to ask them with a gesture to force the lid up instead. Adamsberg moved closer by degrees, from one tree to another, taking advantage of the fact that all eyes were on the scene in front of them. He followed the metal crowbars as they worked on the wooden lid. It yielded and slid on to the ground. He looked at the silent faces. Brézillon squatted down and put his hand into the coffin. He borrowed a knife from Retancourt and seemed to be cutting into a shroud, then stood up, letting fall from his gloved hand a trickle of shining white sand. Harder than cement, as sharp as glass, fluid and mobile, like Fulgence himself. Adamsberg tiptoed away.

An hour later, Retancourt knocked at the door of his hotel room. Adamsberg opened it happily, greeting his *lieutenant* with a pat on the shoulder. She sat on the bed, making it sag in the middle, like the bed in the Hotel Brébeuf in Gatineau. And as in the Brébeuf, she opened a thermos of coffee and put two cups on the bedside table.

'Sand,' he said with a smile.

'A long bag of it, weighing 83 kilos.'

'Put in the coffin after the death certificate had been signed, and sealed down before the undertaker arrived. What did they make of it, *lieutenant*?'

'Danglard was genuinely surprised, and Mordent was greatly relieved. He hates this kind of thing. Brézillon was secretly relieved as well. Maybe rather pleased with himself – it's hard to tell with him. What about you?'

'Hmm. I'm free of the dead man, but now I've got the living one after me.'

Retancourt undid and redid her pony tail.

'Are you in danger?' she asked, handing him a cup.

'Now I am, yes.'

'I think you're right.'

'Sixteen years ago, I had got quite close and the judge was seriously threatened. I think that's the reason he decided to fake his death.'

'He could have tried to kill you instead.'

'No, I don't think so. Too many people in the force knew about it, he could have come under suspicion. All he wanted was a clear road ahead, and he got it. After his so-called death, I gave up looking and Fulgence could get on with his crimes without anyone chasing him. He would have carried on if the Schiltigheim murder hadn't alerted me by chance. I would have done better not to open the paper that Monday morning. It's brought me to this, being a murderer on the run, hiding in safe houses.'

'One good thing about the newspaper,' said Retancourt, 'was that you found Raphaël.'

'Yes, but I haven't cleared his name. Nor mine. All I've managed to do is alert the judge all over again. He knows I got back on his trail once he had left the *Schloss*. Vivaldi told me.'

Adamsberg sipped his coffee while Retancourt looked at him seriously.

'Excellent,' he said.

'Vivaldi?'

'The coffee. But Vivaldi too. A good pal. But now, Retancourt, the Trident is probably aware that I've found out about his fake death. Or he soon will be. I'm in his way again, but I've no chance of catching him, or of saving Raphaël, who's still out there in the field of the stars, orbiting without being able to return to earth. And so am I. Fulgence is still at the helm, in charge, still and for ever.'

'What if he came out after us to Quebec?'

'A man who's a hundred years old?'

'I said "what if?". A man a hundred years old is at least better than a dead man. Anyway, he didn't get you, did he?'

'You think so? I'm still in his trap up to my neck, and I've only got five weeks left.'

'It could be enough. You're not in jail, you've got your freedom. He's in charge, yes, he's at the helm, but there's a storm brewing.'

'If I were him, Retancourt, I'd want to get rid of this damned policeman, once and for all.'

'I agree. I'd prefer to know you're wearing a bullet-proof vest.'

'He kills with a trident though.'

'For you it might be different.'

Adamsberg thought for a moment.

'You mean he might shoot me without any ceremony. As if I was a sort of extra who didn't count?'

'Yes, that's exactly it, an extra. Do you think this adds up to a series? Not just a succession of psychopathic murders?'

'I've thought a lot about it, and I still can't make up my mind. Psychopathic, compulsive murderers usually operate at shorter intervals than the judge's. His crimes are separated by years of silence. And with a psychopath, it tends to speed up, the murderous impulses get closer and closer together. The Trident's different. His murders are regular, programmed, spaced out. It's as if it were a lifetime's occupation, without needing to hurry.'

'Or perhaps he's dragging it out, if his life is governed by the sequence. Schiltigheim might have been the last act. Or the murder in Hull.'

Adamsberg's face fell. A shaft of despair pierced him, as it did every time he thought about the crime by the Ottawa River, and his hands with blood all over them, even under his nails. He put down his cup and sat on the bed, cross-legged.

'What's against me,' he said, looking at his hands, 'is this hundred-year-old man's presumed journey all the way to Quebec. After Schiltigheim, he had plenty of time to work out a way of catching me.

He didn't have to rush it in a few days, did he? There was no need to dash across the Atlantic.'

'On the contrary, it could be the ideal opportunity,' Retancourt objected. 'The judge's technique doesn't work so well in town. Killing a victim, placing them somewhere, then fetching or luring some poor befuddled scapegoat to the spot, none of that would really work in Paris. He always strikes in the countryside. Canada offered him an unusual chance.'

'I suppose that's possible,' said Adamsberg still looking at his hands.

'There's something else as well. Getting you on to new territory.'

Adamsberg looked at his *lieutenant.*

'Well, let's say removing you from your home ground. All the landmarks, routines, reflexes and structures are changed. In Paris, it would be virtually impossible to get people to believe that a *commissaire* of police would walk out of his office one fine day and have an attack of homicidal mania in the street.'

'New place, unknown territory, different acts,' Adamsberg agreed, sadly.

'In Paris, nobody could possibly believe you capable of murder. But over there, well . . . The judge took his chance and it worked. You saw what they said about you in that RCMP dossier: "Unblocking of repressed drives". It would be the ideal set-up, if he could manage to get you alone in the forest.'

'He must have been aware of my habits, since he'd known me for several years, from when I was a boy until I was eighteen. He knew that I like to go walking alone at night. Well, it's all possible, I suppose, but there's nothing to prove it. He would have had to know all about our trip. But I've stopped believing that there was a mole in the department.'

Retancourt examined her nails as if she was consulting a notebook.

'It's true, I can't work it out either,' she admitted, with a frown. 'I've talked to everyone. I've made myself invisible and listened in all the rooms. But nobody there seems to believe you could possibly have killed Noëlla. The atmosphere is very tense and everyone's talking in whispers, as if they're in a state of suspended animation. Luckily Danglard is in charge and he's keeping people calm. I take it you don't suspect him any more?'

'No, on the contrary.'

'Well, I'll leave you now, *commissaire*,' said Retancourt, putting the top back on the thermos. 'The car leaves at six. I'll get that vest for you.'

'I don't need it.'

'I'll get it to you all the same.'

XLVIII

'CAN YOU BEAT THAT?' BRÉZILLON WAS SAYING, IN THE CAR TAKING THE others back to Paris: he was somewhat excited by this ghoulish excursion. 'Eighty kilos of sand. He was right then, damnit.'

'He very often is,' commented Mordent.

'It changes everything,' Brézillon went on. 'Adamsberg's accusation is a lot more solid. Anyone who fakes his death is no choirboy. That old man is still around, after committing twelve murders.'

'Of which the last three were committed when he was ninety-three, ninety-five and ninety-nine years old,' Danglard pointed out. 'Does that really seem possible, sir? A man of a hundred years old dragging a girl and her bicycle off the road?'

'That's a problem, I grant you. But Adamsberg was right about Fulgence's death, we can't deny that. Are you telling me you don't go along with him, *capitaine*?'

'I'm simply pointing out facts and probabilities.'

Danglard shrank into himself in the back of the car and said no more, letting his colleagues, who were quite worked up, talk about the resurrection of the old judge. Yes, Adamsberg had been right. And that made things even more difficult.

Once he was home, he waited until the children were asleep before he called Quebec. It was only six in the evening there.

'How are things going?' he asked his Québécois colleague.

He listened with impatience to the explanations he received from the other end.

'We have to work faster,' Danglard interrupted the other speaker. 'Things are moving here. The exhumation was this afternoon. No body, just a bag of sand . . . Yes . . . absolutely . . . And the *divisionnaire* seems to think it's on the level. But there's still no evidence. Hurry up, do the best you can. He might get away with it.'

Adamsberg had dined alone in a little restaurant in Richelieu, in that comfortable, slightly melancholy atmosphere you get in provincial hotels in the off-season. Not like the *Liffey Water* pub in Paris. By nine o'clock, there was nothing doing in Cardinal Richelieu's town. Adamsberg had returned to his hotel room and was lying on his back on the pink bedcover, hands clasped behind his head. He tried not to let his thoughts wander, but on the contrary tried to separate them into tiny slices of DNA material ready for analysis. The trickle of sand through which the judge had disappeared from the land of the living. The three-pronged threat hanging over him. The choice of Quebec as the territory for his execution.

But Danglard's objections were extremely persuasive. How on earth could such an old man have dragged the body of Elisabeth Wind through the fields? She was a healthy eighteen-year-old, and no will o' the wisp, even if her name suggested the lightness of the wind. Adamsberg blinked. That was what Raphaël had said about his girlfriend, Lise. That she was as light and lively as the wind. And she even had the name of a wind too, the warm south-easterly wind, the Autan. Odd, two names for wind, Wind and Autan. He raised himself on one elbow, trying to recall the names of the other victims, in a whisper, in chronological order: Espir, Lefebure, Ventou, Soubise, Lentretien, Mestre, Lessard, Matère, Brasillier, Fevre.

Ventou and Soubise immediately jumped out at him. Vent = 'wind' in French; and the Bise is the French name of a north wind. That made four winds. Adamsberg put on the overhead light, sat at his little table and wrote down a list of all twelve victims, trying to see if there were any connections between their names. But apart from the four names reminiscent of winds, he could find no obvious links.

Wind equals air. One of the four elements with water, fire and earth. Perhaps the judge had some cosmogonic fantasy about making himself master of the four elements. That would make him a god, like Neptune with his trident, or Jupiter with his thunderbolts. Frowning, he looked at the list again. Only Brasillier was a bit like the word 'brazier', suggesting fire. None of the others seemed to relate to flames or water or earth. Tired, he pushed the paper away. An elusive old man, hellbent on an incomprehensible career of serial killing. He thought again about the old man in the village, Hubert, who had lived to a hundred, but was scarcely able to move about by the end. He lived at the top of the village and yelled at the boys in the evenings when they were up to their tricks with the toads. Ten or fifteen years earlier, he would have been down there, giving them a thrashing. 'Take off about fifteen years.'

Now Adamsberg sat up again, putting his hands on the table. Listen to other people, Retancourt had said. And the doctor in Alsace, Courtin, had been quite sure about it. Don't disregard his opinion, his professionalism, just because it doesn't fit what you know. 'Take off about fifteen years.' The judge was ninety-nine years old, because he had been born in 1904. But what was a birth certificate to a devil?

For a while Adamsberg paced round his room, then he picked up his coat and went out into the night. He walked along the rectilinear streets of the small town, and found himself in a park where a statue of Cardinal Richelieu himself loomed up out of the shadows. A cunning politician, the old Cardinal, and not afraid of bending the rules if he had to. Adamsberg sat down near the statue, chin in hand. 'Take off about fifteen years.' OK, let's try that. Born not in 1904 but in 1919. He would have been only fifty, not sixty-five when he retired from his circuit. And today he would be eighty-four, not ninety-nine. When he was eighty-four, Hubert had still been able to climb his trees to prune them. Yes, the judge had always looked younger than his age, even when his hair was white.

Aged twenty at the start of the Second World War, not thirty-five, he calculated. Twenty-five in 1944, not forty. Why 1944? Adamsberg looked up at Richelieu's bronze features as if expecting them to offer an answer. You know quite well why, young man, the Cardinal seemed to say. And yes, of course, the young man did know.

1944, a murder committed with three blows in a straight line. He had come across it in the records, but had ruled it out, because the undisputed killer had been a young man of twenty-five or so, when Fulgence was supposedly forty. He lowered his head to his knees, trying to concentrate. The fine rain formed a mist and seeped into his clothes, as he sat at the wily cardinal's feet. He waited patiently for the ancient information to come up out of the mist. Or for the fish to swim up out of the depths of Pink Lake. A woman, it had been. Killed with three puncture wounds. And someone had drowned too. When was that? Before the murder? After? Where, in a lake, a pond? In the Landes? No, in the marshes of the Sologne, where people went duck-shooting. The man had drowned, that was it, in a marsh. A father. And after his burial, the woman, his wife, had been killed. He could vaguely picture some photographs in an old press cutting. Probably the father and mother under a headline. A double death, enough to merit a large spread, at a time when news of the war and anticipation of the Allied landings had pushed most small news items off the front pages. Adamsberg clenched his fists and tried to recall what the headline had said.

'Tragic matricide in the Sologne.' That was it. True to his habit, Adamsberg sat stock still trying not to breathe. Whenever a fragmentary thought flashed across his mind he tried not to move, afraid of scaring it away, like an angler handling a bite. He wouldn't pounce on it until it was safely landed in the conscious brain. After the father's funeral, the couple's son, aged twenty-five, had killed his mother and fled. There was a witness, a domestic servant, who had been pushed aside by the son in his frantic flight. Had he been caught? Or had he vanished in the turmoil of the Allied Landings and the Liberation? Adamsberg did not know the answer, since he had not pursued the case. It had not seemed to fit the pattern and, in any case, the man was too young to be Fulgence. 'Take off about fifteen years.' So perhaps it could have been Fulgence after all. A man who'd killed his own mother. With a trident. Mordent's words came back to him, in a flash: 'The o-ri-gin-al sin, the first murder. The kind of thing that produces ghosts.'

Adamsberg looked up into the rain and bit his lip. He had blocked all the spectre's bolt-holes, he had forced the phantom to come back to life, and now he had put his finger on the original crime. He dialled Josette's number, sheltering the phone and hoping the rain wouldn't affect its little antennae.

On hearing her voice, he felt as if he was calling up a super-efficient colleague in the most natural way in the world. An elderly little old police inspectress, shuffling along in her earrings and slippers in the secret underworld of the internet. Which earrings would she be wearing tonight, the pearls or the gold clover-leaves?

'Josette, did I disturb you?'

'Not at all, I'm having fun in a Swiss bank account.'

'Josette, the coffin was full of sand. I think I've forced our man into the open.'

'Wait a minute, *commissaire*, I'll get a pen.'

Adamsberg heard Clémentine's loud voice in the corridor:

'How many times do I have to tell you, Josette, he's not a *commissaire* now.'

He heard Josette explaining about the sand.

'Ah, about time too,' said Clémentine.

'Very well, I'm ready,' said Josette.

'Can you locate the case of a mother, murdered by her son in 1944. It was some time before the Allied Landings, in March or April. It was in the Sologne region, just after the father's funeral.'

'Three puncture wounds, like the others?'

'Yes. The killer, the son, was young, about twenty-five. I can't recall what the name of the family was or the exact place.'

'It's very old, it will only be in some very remote place if it's on computer at all. But I'll give it a try, *commissaire*.'

'How many times do I have to tell you,' the distant voice of Clémentine began.

'Josette, call me back any time if you find anything.'

Adamsberg put away the mobile and walked slowly back to the hotel. Everyone in this story had contributed something, just the right words at the right time. Sanscartier, Mordent, Danglard, Retancourt, Raphaël, Clémentine, and of course Vivaldi. And then Dr Courtin, Father Grégoire and Josette. Now he had to add Cardinal Richelieu. And perhaps even Trabelmann with his damned cathedral.

Josette called back at two in the morning.

'Well, now,' she began as usual. 'I had to try the National Archives, and the police records. Very well protected, as I said.'

'Sorry, Josette.'

'No, it wasn't too difficult, I enjoyed the chase. Clémentine got me a bowl of coffee with some Armagnac and warm rolls. She looked after me as if I was a submarine captain, getting the torpedoes ready. Anyway. 12 March 1944. A village called Collery in the Loiret. The day of the funeral of Gérard Guillaumond, who had died aged 61.'

'Drowned?'

'Yes. It was either an accident or suicide, they never found out which. His boat had sprung a leak and it sank in a marshy lake. And after the funeral, when everyone had gone home, the son, Roland Guillaumond, killed his own mother, Marie Guillaumond.'

'There was a witness, I seem to remember, Josette?'

'Yes, the cook. She heard screams from upstairs. She went up and the son of the family pushed past her on the stairs, as he rushed out of his mother's bedroom. The cook found her mistress lying dead. There wasn't anyone else there, so there was never any doubt at all who had killed her.'

'And did they catch him?' Adamsberg asked anxiously.

'No, never. The police appeared to think he had gone to earth in the local maquis, and perhaps had been killed in the fighting afterwards.'

'Were there any photos of him in the press?'

'No. It was wartime, remember. The cook is dead now, I checked the registration records. So, *commissaire*, do you really think he's our judge? I thought he was born in 1904, so he'd have been forty in 1944.'

'Take off about fifteen years, Josette.'

XLIX

CURTAINS TWITCHED DISCREETLY AS THE STRANGER WENT BY. Adamsberg was walking through the narrow streets of Collery, wondering where to begin. The murder had taken place almost sixty years earlier, and he wanted to find someone who could remember it. The little village smelt of wet leaves and the wind carried the slightly vegetal smell from the green weed-covered pools of the Sologne. It was quite unlike the majestic order of Richelieu's purpose-built town. Just a little village, with houses higgledy-piggledy and huddled together.

A child pointed out the mayor's house on the main square. Adamsberg presented himself, with his badge in the name of Denis Lamproie, asking to be directed to the former house of the Guillaumond family. The mayor was too young to have known the family, but of course everybody in the village had heard about the famous Collery murder.

In Sologne, as in other rural areas, it was not easy to extract a quick answer to a question on the doorstep. Parisian abruptness was not the style. Adamsberg found himself with his elbows on the oilcloth-covered kitchen table, facing a little glass of eau-de-vie at five in the afternoon. In these parts, wearing a Canadian lumberman's cap did not appear to surprise anyone: the mayor kept his cloth cap on and his wife her headscarf.

'Normally,' the chubby and inquisitive mayor explained, 'we wouldn't open the bottle before seven o'clock. But since it isn't every day a *commissaire* comes down from Paris, it's allowed, isn't it, Ghislaine?' turning to his wife for approval.

Ghislaine, who was peeling potatoes on the corner of the table, nodded, as if she were used to it. She had to lift a finger to keep her glasses on which were patched up with sticking plaster. There wasn't a great deal of money in Collery. Adamsberg peered across to see whether she took the eyes out like Clémentine. Yes, she did. Had to get rid of the poison.

'Ah, the Guillaumond affair,' said the mayor, banging the cork back in the bottle with the palm of his hand. 'That caused a stir all right. I was only five, but I heard all about it.'

'Children shouldn't be exposed to things like that,' Ghislaine said.

'The house was left empty. Nobody would move in. People said it was haunted. Rubbish of course.'

'Of course,' murmured Adamsberg.

'In the end they knocked it down. What people said was that Roland Guillaumond was off his head. I don't know if he was. But to impale his own mother like that, something must have been wrong.'

'He impaled her?'

'Well, when someone takes a garden fork to do it, I call it impaling. Is that the word? Isn't that right, Ghislaine? If someone lets off a shotgun or bashes their neighbour over the head with a shovel, well, I'm not excusing them, but you know it happens sometimes, if people are having a go at each other. But to take a garden fork and stick it in your mother's guts, begging your pardon, *commissaire*, I call that barbaric.'

'His own mother too,' Ghislaine added. 'What are you looking into that old story for?'

'I'm looking for Roland Guillaumond.'

'You don't give up in Paris, do you? But surely after all this time, he couldn't be arrested even if he was alive?'

'No, of course not. But the Guillaumond father was a relation of one of my colleagues. He's distressed about it. So there's a personal side to the investigation if you like.'

'Oh, if it's a personal matter, that's different,' said the mayor, raising up his calloused hands, rather as Trabelmann had surrendered to the claims of childhood memory. 'Nobody wants a murderer in the family.

314

But you won't find Roland now. Everyone says he died in the maquis. There was a lot of fighting round here in '44.'

'What did the father do for a living?'

'He was a metalworker. Salt of the earth, they used to say. He'd married well, you know, a girl from a good family in La Ferté-Saint-Aubin. And to think it ended in a bloodbath, bad business, eh, Ghislaine?'

'Would there be anyone still in Collery who knew the family? Who might be willing to talk to me?'

'Well, you could try André,' said the mayor, after thinking. 'He must be about eighty-four. He used to work with the father long ago.'

He looked at the clock.

'You'd better go round before he starts his supper.'

The mayor's eau-de-vie was still burning his stomach when Adamsberg knocked at the door of André Barlut. The old man, wearing a thick corduroy jacket and a cloth cap, looked suspiciously at the badge. Then he took it in his gnarled fingers, and twisted it this way and that, looking at both sides in curiosity. He had a three-day beard and sharp dark eyes.

'Let's just say it's something personal, Monsieur Barlut.'

Two minutes later, sitting in front of another glass of spirits, Adamsberg was asking his questions again.

'As a rule, I don't open the bottle before the Angelus,' the old man said, without answering the questions. 'But when I have visitors . . .'

'I'm told you're the memory of the village, monsieur.'

André winked. 'Ah, if I told you everything that's in here,' he said tapping his head, 'it'd make a book. A book about what folks get up to, commissaire. How do you like this then? Not too fruity? Helps to think, is what I say.'

'It's excellent,' Adamsberg agreed.

'Makes it myself,' said André. 'Drop of this won't hurt you.'

Sixty degrees of alcohol, Adamsberg estimated silently. It set his teeth on edge.

'Now old Guillaumond, you want to know about him, oh, he were almost too good to be true. Took me on as his apprentice and we were a good team. You can call me André, monsieur.'

'You were a metalworker too, André?'

'Ah, no. I'm talking now about when he were a gardener. The metal-working, that stopped after his accident. Lost his fingers in the grinder,' André explained, demonstrating with his own hand.

'How did he do that?'

'Like I said. Got his hand caught. His thumb and little finger. So his right hand, he just had the three middle fingers left,' said André holding out his hand with three fingers up. 'After that of course, he couldn't do metalworking. But his hand didn't stop him working as a gardener. Garden tools, he could use them all right.'

Adamsberg looked in fascination at the wrinkled old hand. Three fingers. The father's mutilated hand, like a fork or a trident. Three fingers, three claws.

'Why did you say he was "almost too good to be true", André?'

'Well, so he was. Good as gold, always help you out, always had a joke and a kind word. Mind you, I wouldn't say the same for his wife. And I got my own ideas about that.'

'About what?'

'About him drowning. She wore him out, that woman. She ground him down. And in the end, mebbe he couldn't be bothered patching up the boat, and it got a leak in the winter, or mebbe he just let himself drown. It's my opinion, she's the reason he ended up in the water.'

'You didn't like her, then?'

'No, weren't nobody liked her. Now her, she were the daughter of the big pharmacy in La Ferté-Saint-Aubin. Plenty of money there. But she took it into her head to marry Gérard. In those days, he were a fine figure of a man, see. But it all went bad. She had to be a fine lady, she looked down on him. Living in Collery with a metalworker, that weren't good enough for her, oh no. She thought she'd married beneath her. And it got worse after his accident. She were ashamed of him, and she didn't mind who knew it. She were no good at all, that woman.'

* * *

André had known the family well. As a small boy, he had played with Roland, an only child like himself, the same age and living opposite. He used to go to the house after school and in the evening. Every night after supper they did the same thing: they had to play Mah Jong. Because that was what they did at the pharmacy in La Ferté, and the mother insisted on keeping it up. But it gave her plenty of chances, which she never missed, to humiliate Gérard. Because in Mah Jong, the rules say you can't dilute. What does that mean, asked Adamsberg who didn't know anything about the game. It means mixing different suits to try and win more quickly, like mixing hearts and clubs at cards, for instance. That wasn't supposed to happen if you were playing properly. Only coarse people did that. André and Roland didn't do it, because they dared not disobey her. They would rather lose than dilute. But Gérard, Roland's father, couldn't care less. He picked tiles with his three-fingered hand and made jokes. And Marie Guillaumond would be saying 'Oh for heaven's sake, Gérard, the day you get a Hand of Honours, hens will have teeth.' It was just another way of putting him down. The Hand of Honours was a sort of especially good hand, like a fistful of aces. André had heard her say this more times than he could remember, always with that sarcastic tone, *commissaire*. But Gérard just laughed, and he never got one. Nor did she neither, come to that. She always wore white, his wife, so she could see the least little speck of dirt on her clothes. As if it mattered in Collery. The cook and maid called her 'the white dragon' behind her back. Yes, that woman had really worn Gérard down.

'What about Roland?' Adamsberg asked.

'She brainwashed him, *commissaire*, no other word for it. She wanted him to be a gentleman, make a lot of himself, go to the city. It was "Roland, my pet, you won't be a failure like your father", "You won't be a lazy so-and-so." So then of course, he got to thinking he were too good for the likes of us boys in the village. Got very stuck up. But really, I think it was the white dragon as didn't want him to play with us. We weren't good enough, she said. So in the end, Roland, he turned out different from his dad. Proud and stuck-up, you couldn't say anything to him. Bite your head off, he would.'

'Did he fight other boys?'

'Threatened to. Tell you what we used to do, when we were oh, fourteen, fifteen, we used to catch frogs and make 'em blow up with cigarettes. Not a nice thing, you might think, monsieur, but there wasn't a lot to do in Collery.'

'Frogs, did you say, or toads?'

'Frogs, now. Green ones. If you put a cigarette in their mouth they puffs it and they just blows up, like that, ploff! Gotta see it to understand.'

'I think I can imagine,' said Adamsberg.

'So now Roland, he'd turn up with a knife, and splat, just cut the heads off the frogs. Blood all over. I suppose it came to the same for the poor old froggy, he were dead, just the same. But we didn't like that, us others, no. Then he'd wipe the blood off on the grass, and march off. Just showing us he could do what he wanted.'

André helped himself to another glass. Adamsberg did his best to drink as slowly as possible.

'Still must've been more than that to him,' André went on. 'Cause Roland, he really did worship his pa. He didn't like the way the dragon treated the old man. Didn't say so, but I'd see how he'd clench his fists like this when she were tearing strips off his old pa.'

'Was Roland good-looking as a lad?'

'Oh, like a film star. All the girls were after him, the rest of us wasn't anywhere. But Roland didn't go with girls, tell you the truth, monsieur, I think he wasn't quite normal, that way. Anyway, off he went one fine day to the city to do studying, and be a gentleman. Ambitious, see.'

'Law school?'

'That's right. And then what happened, well it was bound to happen. Couldn't anything good come out of a house like that, with all the bad feelings. At poor old Gérard's funeral, the mother, she didn't shed a tear. Not a one. I always thought what happened was when they got back home, she must have said summat.'

'Such as?'

'Well the kind of thing she *would* say. "Good riddance to bad rubbish" or summat of that. She'd a sharp tongue on her, that woman. And then,

Roland, he'd have seen red, because the funeral would have shaken him up a lot. I'm not defending him, mind, but that's what I think. So he just up and at her. Grabbed his dad's fork and chased her up the stairs. And that's how it fell out, if you ask me. Killed the old white dragon.'

'With a trident?'

'That's what the police thought, because it looked that way and the fork had disappeared. That fork, it was a bit special. Gérard, he were always messing about with it, sharpening the points in the fire. He looked after his tools, that man. Once when he was digging, he broke a point off. Think he'd throw it away? Oh no, soldered it back on. Knew what he was about in metalwork, of course. And carved stuff on the handle and all. She didn't like that either, the wife. Thought it was stupid. I don't say it were art, but it were pretty enough, the handle.'

'What kind of thing did he carve?'

'Like in school. Stars, suns, flowers. Nothing too fancy, I s'pose, but Gérard that's how he was. Liked to make things nice. Same thing with his spade, his pick, his shovel. You couldn't mistake his tools for anyone else's. I've still got the spade, kept it as a souvenir when he died. Oh, salt of the earth, Gérard was.'

The old man went out and fetched a spade, polished by years of use. Adamsberg examined the glossy handle, with its hundreds of tiny patterns carved into the wood, covered now with the patina of age.

'Yes, it is pretty,' he said sincerely, running his fingers over the handle. 'I can see why you keep it, André.'

'Makes me sad to think of him. Always a kindly word, or a joke. But not her. No, nobody missed her. I always wonder whether she didn't do it. And whether Roland knew about it.'

'Do what, André?'

'Split the boards in the boat,' the old man muttered, taking back his spade.

The mayor had driven Adamsberg in his van to Orleans station. As he sat in the freezing cold waiting-room, he chewed mechanically on some

319

bread to mop up the eau-de-vie which was burning his guts, much as André's words were burning in his brain. A humiliated father with a mutilated hand, and an ambitious and scornful mother. The future judge growing up caught between them, having a twisted boyhood, making him eager to wipe out his father's weakness, to transform it into strength. Killing her with the trident, which echoed the father's deformed hand, now turned into an instrument of total power. Fulgence seemed to have inherited from his mother the urge to dominate others and from his father the unbearable frustrations of a weak man. Every blow dealt with the trident restored the strength and courage of Gérard Guillaumond, who had been defeated and then swallowed up in the mud of the marsh. The last laugh.

So of course the killer would not want to abandon the decorated handle of the weapon. It was the hand of the father. But why then had he not gone on attacking mother-figures? If he hated his mother, one would have expected him to target women in middle age, bossy, maternal figures. But in the list of those killed, there were as many men as women, and they were all ages, from teenagers to old people. Even among the women, there were young girls, quite unlike Marie Guillaumond. Was he trying to extend his power to the whole human race, by striking at random? Adamsberg chewed some more brown bread, shaking his head. This rage to destroy must have some other logic. It wasn't just wiping out the humiliation, it was amplifying the judge's power, like his choice of name. It was building a kind of rampart, a defence against any decline. But how could stabbing an old man to death with a fork bring Fulgence that kind of sensation?

Adamsberg suddenly felt the need to call Trabelmann and tell him that after tracking down the ear, he had extracted the judge's whole body from the dead, and was now moving inside his head. A head he had promised to bring him on the end of a trident, in order to save poor old Vétilleux in his cell. When he remembered the aggressive behaviour of the *commandant* of *gendarmes*, Adamsberg felt an urge to stuff him into one of the windows of Strasbourg Cathedral as well. Just one third of him, up to the waist. Then he'd be face to face with the dragons of fairy stories, the Loch Ness monster, the fish from Pink Lake, the toads, the lamprey, and all the other creatures which Adamsberg was using to turn the jewel of Gothic architecture into a menagerie.

But that would not wipe out the *commandant*'s words. If it could, everyone would use this handy way of dealing with annoyances and there wouldn't be a single free church window in the country, even in the tiniest chapel. No, he couldn't wipe out that memory so easily. No doubt because Trabelmann was not so very far off the truth. A truth which he was skirting round gingerly, thanks to the extra impetus from Retancourt in the cafe on the Place du Châtelet. And when his blonde *lieutenant* gave you a push, it went through your brain like a drill. But Trabelmann had been talking about the wrong ego. Because there's self and self, he thought as he walked along the platform. Self and brother. Was it perhaps true that the absolute protection he felt he ought to have given Raphaël had kept him in orbit, far from earth, far from other people in any case, in a kind of weightless existence? And the same went for his relations with women too, of course. To allow himself to get carried away would have been to abandon Raphaël to die alone in his cave. And that was impossible. So it might explain why he had always fled from love, and even destroyed it? Had he really gone that far?

He watched as the train came into the station. That was a deep and dark question that took him straight back to the horrors of the portage trail. Where there was no evidence that the Trident had ever set foot.

As he turned into Clémentine's little sidestreet, he snapped his fingers. He must tell Danglard about the frogs in Collery. He would certainly be glad to hear it worked with frogs as well. Ploff, bang! A slightly different sound.

L

BUT IT WASN'T THE MOMENT TO TALK ABOUT FROGS. ALMOST AS SOON as he got in, a call from Retancourt informed him that Michel Sartonna, the young man in charge of cleaning the departmental office, had been found murdered. He normally came in to work between five and nine in the evening. When he had not been seen for two days, someone was sent round to his flat. He had been shot dead, with two bullets in the chest from a handgun with a silencer, some time between Monday night and Tuesday morning.

'Could it have been a gangland killing, *lieutenant*? I had the feeling Michel was into drug dealing.'

'If so, he wasn't rich. Except for a large sum of money deposited in his bank on 13 October, four days after the news item appeared in the *Nouvelles d'Alsace*. And there was a brand new laptop in his flat. I should also say that he'd put in for two weeks' leave, without warning, which exactly tallies with the dates we were in Quebec.'

'You're thinking he was the mole, Retancourt? But I thought we'd established there wasn't one.'

'Well, we might have to think again. Michel could have been contacted after Schiltigheim, and been paid to do some spying, and perhaps follow us out to Quebec. And it might have been him who got into your flat.'

'And then killed Noëlla on the path?'

'Why not?'

'I can't believe that, Retancourt. Even if we suppose there was someone else there, the judge would hardly have left it to someone like Michel to carry out such a refined kind of vengeance. And certainly not with the trident.'

'Danglard doesn't think so either, actually.'

'As for murder with a gun, that doesn't sound like the judge.'

'I've told you what I think about that. A gun is OK for outsiders, murders that don't fit the scheme. No need to use the trident on Michel. My guess is that the stupid boy misjudged his contact, asked for too much money or maybe even threatened blackmail. Or perhaps the judge just wanted to get him out of the way.'

'If it was the judge.'

'We took a look at Michel's laptop. The hard disk's empty, or rather it's been wiped. Our computer people are coming tomorrow to see if they can resurrect anything.'

'What about his dog?' Adamsberg asked, surprising himself by his concern for the large dog that went everywhere with Michel.

'Shot as well.'

'Retancourt, since you're going to send me the bullet-proof vest, can you send over the laptop? I've got a Grade A hacker here.'

'Mm-hm, how'm I going to do that? You're not a *commissaire* at the moment.'

'Yes, I do realise that,' said Adamsberg, seeming to hear Clémentine's voice reminding him of it. 'Ask Danglard, convince him, you're good at that. Since the exhumation, Brézillon's more favourably inclined to me, and Danglard knows it.'

'All right, I'll try, but he's the boss for now.'

LI

JOSETTE TOOK POSSESSION OF MICHEL SARTONNA'S LAPTOP WITH HUGE
delight. Adamsberg felt that he could hardly have made her happier than
with this suspect machine, a real gift for a hacker. It had not arrived at
Clignancourt until the late afternoon, and Adamsberg suspected that
Danglard had had it checked out by his own computer people first. That
was perfectly logical and normal, since he was the acting head of the
department. The courier who delivered it also brought a note from
Retancourt, saying that as far as they could see the hard disk was as clean
as a whistle. This had only spurred Josette on to greater efforts.

She spent a long time trying to penetrate the lost memory of the
computer, and confirmed that someone else had already had a try.

'Your men didn't bother to wipe out their footsteps. That's fair enough,
they weren't doing anything illegal.'

The last defence came down only with Michel's dog's name spelt backwards: *ograc.* He had often brought the dog into the office, a huge but
harmless beast, as unthreatening as a snail, hence its name, Escargot,
shortened to Cargo. It liked eating any papers it found lying around, and
could transform a report into a wet soggy ball in no time. So it was
perhaps a good code name for the mysterious transmutations that took
place inside computers.

But once inside, Josette came up against the same blank wall as the
police had.

'Nothing at all, wiped clean, scraped with wire wool,' she said.

324

Well, that figured. If the police specialists hadn't been able to find anything, there was no reason to think Josette would fare any better. But she kept tapping doggedly with her shaky little hands on the keyboard.

'I'll keep trying,' she said obstinately.

'Don't bother, Josette, they've obviously tried everything in the lab.'

It was time for their ritual glass of port, and Clémentine summoned Adamsberg to come and have his aperitif, as if he was a teenager being called to do his homework. She added an egg yolk, beating it up in the sweet wine. Egg-flip with port was supposed to give him strength.

'Josette's still at it,' he explained as he accepted the glass filled with the opaque mixture to which he was becoming accustomed.

'To look at her, you'd think you could knock her over with a feather, wouldn't you,' said Clémentine clinking her glass against Adamsberg's.

'But you can't.'

'No. Not like that,' Clémentine interrupted him to stop him putting the glass to his lips. 'When you clink glasses, you have to look at the other person. I told you that already. Then drink it off without putting the glass down. Elsewise it won't work.'

'What won't work?'

She shook her head as if that was a supremely silly question.

'Start again,' she said sternly. 'Now what was I saying?'

'We were saying Josette couldn't be knocked over with a feather.'

'Right. Now then. Inside my little Josette there's a compass, and it's fixed on the north. She's taken thousands and thousands from those fat cats. So she won't just give up on it.'

Adamsberg took a glass of the health-giving mixture into the computer room. Josette clinked glasses properly, with a smile.

'I found the fragments of one line,' she said in her quavery voice. 'It's the ruins of a message that's broken up. Your men didn't find this,' she said rather proudly. 'There are always a few corners people don't manage to go through with a toothcomb.'

'Like the space between the wall and the washbasin.'

'Yes, that's right. I always clean things thoroughly, and my husband thought I was fussy. Come and have a look.'

Adamsberg came over to the screen and read a meaningless series of letters, all that had survived the crash: *dam ea ezv ort la ero*.

'Is that all?' he asked in disappointment.

'That's all, but it's better than nothing,' said Josette, who was still elated. '*ezv* could only be from "rendezvous", for instance.'

'I'm sure Michel was involved with drugs, I often thought so,' Adamsberg said. 'So *dam* is most likely from Amsterdam or Rotterdam. Classic drugs centres.'

'And the *ea* could be from "deal" or "dealer"?'

'Yes, Josette, it looks like a message about dealing to me. From what's left.'

Josette noted down the letters on a piece of paper and looked at it in silence.

'I suppose you could make it something like: "Amsterdam – dealer – rendezvous – port – heroin", for instance,' she suggested reluctantly.

'I don't see how it can have anything to do with the Trident,' said Adamsberg in a defeated voice. 'It looks as if Michel simply got involved in something too heavy for him. We should probably pass it over to the drugs squad, Josette.'

Josette sipped her port-flip delicately, but her little face expressed frustration.

Retancourt must be wrong about the mole, Adamsberg thought, as he stirred the fire. The two women had gone to bed and he was alone by the hearth, unable to sleep. He would never succeed in identifying the mole, who had probably never existed. It was after all the janitor who had given Laliberté the key information. And as for believing someone had searched his flat, well that was based on the flimsiest evidence. A key in the wrong place, perhaps, and a box file not quite in the same position, when Danglard thought he had put it away more tidily. Not much to go on. He would never find the unlikely second man on the portage trail. Even if he traced all Fulgence's crimes, he would be forever alone on that sinister path. Adamsberg felt all the threads snapping one after another, cutting him off from the world, as if he were a ferocious bear on an ice floe, floating away from land. He was isolated here with Clémentine's egg-flips and Josette's grey slippers.

He put on his coat and his Arctic cap, and slipped out into the night. The shabby streets of Clignancourt were dark and empty, and the street-lamps gave only fitful light. He took Josette's old moped, which was painted in two shades of blue, and twenty-five minutes later, he braked to a halt outside Camille's windows. What was driving him was an urge to find a different refuge, and the desire to breathe, if only from outside the building, a little of the clear and healthy air that came to him from Camille, or rather that formed when he and Camille were together. It takes two windows to make a draught, as Clémentine would have put it. He had a shock on looking up to the seventh floor. The lights were on. She must have come back from Montreal. Unless she had let the flat. Or maybe the new father was up there, acting as if he owned the place, with his two labradors, one of them drooling under the sink and the other by Camille's synthesiser. Adamsberg looked up at the provocative square of light, watching for the new father's shadow. The idea of someone else taking possession went through him like a drill, conjuring up the vision of a muscular man, walking about in the nude with his firm buttocks and flat stomach, an image that burned itself into his brain.

From the little cafe at street level came welcoming smells, and the hum of people drinking. Just like *L'Ecluse*. Perfect, thought Adamsberg nervously, as he locked up the moped. A good glass of cognac, that would drown the image of the naked he-man allowing his dogs to drool all over Camille's studio floor. He would use the same technique as the late lamented Cargo: he'd transform the intruder into a sticky wad of blotting paper.

This was the second time in his life he had deliberately got drunk, or at least since he was a teenager, thought Adamsberg, pushing open the steamed-up cafe door. Perhaps he would not try mixing his drinks tonight. Or again, perhaps he should. After all, in another five weeks he would be sitting in Brézillon's armchair, having lost his memory, his job, his brother, his girl from the north, and his freedom. It was hardly the moment to be scared of mixing his drinks. Bloody labradors, he thought, downing his first cognac, and he decided to stuff them into some of the windows on the cathedral façade, with their back legs kicking in the air. When he had succeeded in filling all the orifices of the jewel of Gothic architecture with his imaginary menagerie, what would happen to the monument? Perhaps it would choke for lack of air and fall down. Or perhaps puff, puff, it would explode. Would it just collapse inwards, he wondered, ordering his second cognac, And what would they do with the ruins, not to speak of all the creatures lying beneath the masonry? Big problem for the canons of Strasbourg.

How about stuffing the windows of the Mounties' headquarters with surplus animals while he was at it? Starving the atmosphere of oxygen and filling it with the stinking breath of the beasts. Laliberté would drop dead. He would have to save Sanscartier the Good of course, and the kindly Ginette. But would there be enough animals? It was a serious question, since you needed really big creatures. Moths and snails wouldn't do. Good big creatures, preferably spitting smoke like dragons. But you couldn't easily locate a dragon, they hide away sneakily in caves.

Well, of course he knew where to find some dragons, in a Mah Jong set, he thought, hitting the counter with his fist. All he knew about the Chinese game was that there were dragons in it, of various colours. He would just have to find some, like old Guillaumond with his three fingers, and push the reptiles in randomly, into all the doors and windows. Red ones for Strasbourg, green ones for Ottawa.

Adamsberg was unable to finish his fourth glass and staggered out to the moped. He couldn't undo the lock, so instead he pushed open the door of Camille's block of flats, and climbed up the seven storeys, clinging on to the bannister. He'd have a word with the new father, give him a piece of his mind, that's what he'd do, and see him off. Might keep his labradors though, and add them to the judge's dobermans. They'd do very well for some of the cathedral windows. But not Cargo, he was a good dog, and on Adamsberg's side in all this, as was his little beetle-mobile phone. A foolproof plan, he thought as he leaned on Camille's door. But a thought stopped him as he was about to ring the bell. A pang of memory. Look out. Last time you were drunk, you killed Noëlla. Don't go in. You don't know who you are, you don't know what you're capable of. Yes, but he really needed those labradors.

Camille opened the door, and was amazed to find him on the landing.

'Are you alone?' he asked.

She nodded.

'No dogs?'

He was having difficulty forming his words. Do not go in, roared the waters of the Ottawa River. Do not go in.

'What dogs?' asked Camille. 'Jean-Baptiste, you're drunk. You turn up out of the blue at midnight, and you start babbling about dogs.'

'I'm talking about Mah Jong. Let me in.'

Unable to react quickly enough to stop him, Camille stood aside. He sat down clumsily on a stool at the bar in the kitchen, where the remains of her supper were still lying. He fiddled with the glass, the water jug, the fork, feeling its points. Camille, looking perplexed, had gone to sit crosslegged on her piano stool in the middle of the room.

'I know your grandmother had a Mah Jong set,' Adamsberg began again stumbling over the words. 'I bet she didn't let you dilute, did she? Dilute an' I'll shoot you!'

Ah, grandmothers, always good for a laugh, eh?

LII

JOSETTE SLEPT BADLY AND WAS WOKEN AT ONE IN THE MORNING BY A nightmare: out of her printer, pages of paper, all of them bright red, were spilling all over the room. Nothing could be read on them, because of their glossy red surface.

She got up quietly and tiptoed into the kitchen, where she helped herself to some cookies and maple syrup. Clémentine came to join her, wrapped up in a huge dressing gown, like a nightwatchwoman.

'I didn't want to wake you,' Josette pleaded.

'Something going on in that little head, isn't there,' declared Clémentine.

'It's just that I couldn't sleep. Nothing really, Clemmie.'

'Not your machine giving you headaches?'

'Yes, I suppose it is. In my dream, I couldn't read anything it printed.'

'You'll manage it, Josette, m'dear. I'm sure you can.'

But manage what, Josette wondered.

'Clemmie, I thought I was dreaming about blood. All the paper was red.'

'Was the machine leaking red ink?'

'No, just the sheets of paper.'

'Well then, it couldn't be blood.'

'Has he gone out?' asked Josette, realising that Adamsberg was not sleeping on the couch.

'Suppose so. He must be worrying about something. He's fretting away too. Eat up and drink this too, m'dear, it'll help you sleep,' she said, offering Josette a bowl of warm milk.

After putting away the biscuit tin, Josette was still wondering what, if anything, she was going to manage. She put a sweater on over her pyjamas and sat brooding over the computer, without switching it on. Michel's laptop was alongside, a useless but irritating ruin. She would have to get to the real answer, Josette thought, the one she was trying to chase unsuccessfully in her dream. The unreadable pages were a sign that she had not decoded Michel's scraps of message properly. A big mistake crossed out in red.

Well, that must be it, she thought, going back to her version of the fractured sentence. It was silly to think people would put in those details if they were really talking about a drugs deal. You wouldn't put the town, the kind of drug and so on. A dealer surely wouldn't put out an email message like that. He might as well have put his name and address on the internet. She had set off completely along the wrong track, and her book had been corrected in red.

Josette patiently took up the succession of letters and tried various combinations without success: *dam ea ezv ort la ero*. Her failure irritated her. Clémentine came and looked over her shoulder, holding a bowl of milk. 'That's what's bothering you?'

'I must have gone wrong, and I'm trying to understand why.'

'Do you know what I think?'

'Tell me.'

'Well it looks like double Dutch to me. In some other language from some other country. Would you like some more hot milk?'

'No thanks, Clemmie, I need to concentrate.'

Clémentine tiptoed away quietly. One shouldn't bother Josette when she was working.

Josette looked back at the letters again. Another country. Yes. And what other country was involved in this case? Canada. She suddenly had a thought. What if this referred to the events in Canada? What was the name of the place where Adamsberg had stayed? Gatineau? That gave an 'ea'. A slight chance of course. Then she suddenly had the feeling that 'dam' was simply part of Adamsberg's name, nothing to do with

Amsterdam or Rotterdam. How odd it is, she thought, that you can be up against something and not see it. But she had seen it, in her sleep she had seen red leaves, red sheets of paper. Not blood, Clémentine was right, but the red maple leaves of Canada, falling on the portage trail in autumn. So 'ort' could be portage, 'ero' could be Corderon, Noëlla's name. Rendezvous would still be the only possibility for 'ezv'. Biting her lips, Josette tried to see where an alternative reading could lead her. She had the sudden warm feeling of a hacker breaking through a stubborn obstacle.

A few minutes later, exhausted and now at last ready for sleep, she was looking at another sentence: *dam ea ezv ort la ero.* 'Adamsberg – Gatineau – rendezvous – portage trail – Noëlla Corderon.'

She put the sheet of paper on her knee.

Adamsberg must have been followed out to Quebec by Michel Sartonna. It didn't prove anything about the murder, but what it did show was that the young man was watching Adamsberg's movements and reporting on his meetings on the portage trail, sending word of them to somebody else. Josette stuck the paper on the keyboard and went back to snuggle under her blankets. So it hadn't been a hacking mistake, just a matter of straightforward code-breaking.

LIII

'YOUR MAH JONG SET,' ADAMSBERG WAS REPEATING.

Camille hesitated, then joined him in the kitchen. In drink, Adamsberg's voice had lost all its charm, becoming harsher and less strong. She dissolved two tablets in a glass of water and handed it to him.

'Drink this,' she said.

'I need dragons, you see, very, very big dragons,' Adamsberg explained, before draining the glass.

'Shh. Don't talk so loudly. What do you want dragons for?'

'I need them to stuff into some windows.'

'Mmm,' said Camille. 'All right, you do that.'

'And that guy's labradors as well.'

'Yes, OK. Please don't talk so loudly.'

'Why?'

Camille did not reply but Adamsberg followed her glance. At the back of the studio he could vaguely make out a little cot.

'Aha! Yes, of course,' he declared, raising one finger. 'Mustn't wake the baby. Oh no! Or its father, the one with the dogs.'

'You know then?' said Camille in a neutral voice.

'I'm a cop. I know everything. Montreal, the baby, the new father and his bloody dogs.'

'Right. How did you get here? Did you walk?'

'On someone's moped.'

Shit, thought Camille. She couldn't let him go out on the road in this state. She got out her grandmother's old Mah Jong set.

'Here you are, play if you like,' she said, putting the box on the bar. 'You have fun with the tiles, I'm going to read.'

'Don't leave me. I'm lost and I've killed a woman. Explain this Mah Jong to me, I need some dragons.'

Camille looked sharply at Jean-Baptiste. The best thing to do at present, it seemed to her, was to get his attention firmly fixed on the tiles. Until the pills started working and he could be sent away. She'd make some strong coffee too, to stop him going to sleep on the bar.

'Where are the dragons?'

'There are three suits,' Camille explained, soothingly, with the prudence of all women who are approached in the street by a man in an aggressive state. Humour him, distract him, and get away as soon as you can. Get him interested in your grandmother's Mah Jong tiles. She poured him some coffee.

'This suit is the Circles, this one the Characters, this one the Bamboos. They go from 1 to 9, see?'

'What's all that for?'

'To play with. And these are the honours: East, West, North and South, and your dragons.'

'Ah,' said Adamsberg satisfied.

'Four green dragons,' said Camille putting them together for him to see, 'four red ones and four virgins. That makes twelve dragons all together, OK? Is that enough?'

'What's that one?' he asked, pointing a wavering finger at a tile covered with decorations.

'That's a Flower. There are eight of them. They don't count except as extras, like ornaments.'

'And what do you do with all this stuff?'

'You play the game,' Camille went on patiently. 'You have to try and make up a special hand, or a sequence of three tiles, depending on what you pick up. The special hands carry the most points. Are you still interested?'

Adamsberg nodded vaguely and sipped the coffee.

'What you have to do is keep picking up tiles till you get a full hand. Without diluting if possible. Then you go Mah Jong.'

'Aha, "dilute, and I'll shoot you". Like my grandmother. "Any nearer and I'll spear ye."'

'OK. Now you know how to play. If you like it so much, you can have the rule book.'

Camille went to sit at the far end of the room with a book. She would wait until it had passed. Adamsberg was building little columns of tiles until they fell over, then he rebuilt them, muttering to himself, wiping his eyes from time to time as if the collapses caused him deep sorrow. Alcohol brought out various emotions and outbursts from him, to which Camille replied by reassuring signs. After more than an hour, she closed her book.

'If you're feeling better now,' she said.

'I want to see the guy with the dogs first,' said Adamsberg, jumping to his feet.

'How do you think you're going to do that?'

'I'll get him out of his hole. This fellow who's hiding, and daren't look me in the face.'

'Perhaps you're right.'

Adamsberg walked all over the studio, with uncertain steps and prepared to go up to the bedroom on the mezzanine floor.

'He's not up there,' said Camille, as she cleared away the tiles. 'You can take my word for it.'

'Where is he then?'

She shrugged, in a gesture of powerlessness.

'Not there,' she said.

'Not there?'

'No. Not there.'

'He's gone out?'

'He went away.'

'He left you?' cried Adamsberg.

'Yes. Hush, don't shout, and stop trying to look for him.'

Adamsberg sat on the arm of a chair, already sobering up from the remedies and the shock.

'Good God! He left you? With the child?'

'It happens.'

Camille finished putting the tiles in the box.

'Well, shit,' said Adamsberg heavily. 'You really know how to pick them, don't you.'

She shrugged again.

'I shouldn't have gone away,' he declared, shaking his head. 'I would have protected you, I would have put a wall round you,' he said opening his arms, and was suddenly reminded of the Canada goose.

'Can you walk now, do you think?' said Camille gently, looking up at him.

'Of course I can.'

'Right, well, off you go now, Jean-Baptiste.'

LIV

ADAMSBERG RETURNED TO CLIGNANCOURT THROUGH THE DARKNESS, surprised to find that he was able to steer the bike fairly well. Camille's treatment had given a shock to the system and cleared his head, so that he was neither feeling sleepy nor suffering from a headache. He went into the dark house, put a log on the fire and watched it flare up. Seeing Camille again had unsettled him. He had left her on an impulse, then found her again in an impossible situation: she had been abandoned by that rat who had tiptoed away with his smart tie and polished shoes, taking his dogs with him. She had thrown herself into the arms of the first smooth talker who had come along, someone who had promised her eternal affection, no doubt. And there was the result. Goddamnit, he had not even thought of asking the child's name, or even what sex it was. He hadn't thought about it at all. He had just sat there piling up tiles. He had talked about dragons and Mah Jong. Why had he been so obsessed with dragons? Ah yes, to stuff them into the cathedral windows.

He shook his head. Going on benders obviously didn't suit him. He had not seen Camille for a year, and he had just turned up on her doorstep, roaring drunk, had insisted on her getting out the Mah Jong, and then clamoured to see the new father. Exactly like the boss of the Canada geese. Well that damned bird could certainly be thrust without any pity right into the cathedral, and could honk as much as he liked from the top of the spire.

* * *

He pulled the rules of the game out of his pocket and flipped through it sadly. It was an old set of rules, on yellowing paper from the days of the old grandmothers. Circles, bamboos, characters, winds and dragons, he could remember it all now. He looked through the pages slowly, searching for the famous Hand of Honours that Madame Guillaumond always mocked her husband for never getting. He stopped at Special Hands, the ones that were hard to get. The Green Snake for instance was a complete set of bamboos along with a trio of green dragons. He went on down the list and found it: 'Hand of Honours', made up of combinations of dragons and winds. Example: three west winds, three south winds, three red dragons, three white dragons and a pair of north winds. It was the ultimate hand, almost impossible to acquire. Old man Guillaumond had been absolutely right not to give a damn about it. Just as he, Jean-Baptiste, didn't give a damn about the piece of paper he was holding. It wasn't the paper he wanted to hold, it was Camille, one of the best things in his life. And he had messed everything up. Just as he had messed everything up on that Canadian path, and messed up his pursuit of the judge, which had come to a dead end in Collery, the home of the maternal white dragon.

He froze. The white dragon. Camille hadn't told him about that. He picked up the rules again and looked at them. Honours were red dragons, green dragons and white dragons. Camille had called them 'virgins'. And the four winds: North, South, East and West. He gripped the fragile paper tightly. Four winds: Soubise, Ventou, Autan and Wind. And Brasillier had to be a red dragon. On the back of the rules, he quickly scribbled the twelve names of the judge's victims, adding the mother, which made thirteen. The mother, the original White Dragon. Grasping his pencil tightly, he tried to relate the list to the Mah Jong tiles, to see if he could make up the Hand of Honours. The one that the judge's father had never got, but that Fulgence was furiously assembling, in order to give him back his dignity. With a trident, like his father's mutilated three-fingered hand, pulling out the tiles. Fulgence pulled out his victims with iron fingers. How many tiles would it take to make up a hand?

With moist palms, he went back to the very beginning of the rules: you had to assemble fourteen tiles. There was just one left to make up the number.

Adamsberg read and re-read the names of the victims, trying to find the missing piece. Ghislaine Matère: that must be related to 'maternal', the mother, so it could count as a white dragon. Jeanne Lessard, a green dragon, perhaps, since her name sounded like 'lizard'. The other names were a puzzle. They didn't seem to be either dragons or winds. He didn't know what to do with Lentretien, Mestre or Lefebure. But he did have four winds and three dragons, seven out of thirteen, surely too many for coincidence. And, he realised with a start, that if he was right, if the judge really was trying to accomplish his fourteen tiles, Raphaël could not possibly have killed Lise. The choice of the young Mademoiselle Autan had been because of her *name*, which pointed to the Trident, thus clearing his brother. But not in his own case. The name of Noëlla Corderon, did not seem to be linked to anything. Flowers? thought Adamsberg. Camille had said something about flowers. He looked at the rules again. Flowers were supernumerary honours, you could hold them but they didn't count in making up a hand. Ornaments, asides in some sense. Supplementary victims, allowed by the rules, but who did not have to be stabbed with the trident.

By eight in the morning, Adamsberg was waiting in a cafe for the local library to open, looking at his two watches and learning the rules of Mah Jong, as well as checking over the victims' names. He could of course have called on Danglard's help, but his deputy would surely have sent him off with a flea in his ear at this new fantasy. Adamsberg had already put him through a dead man walking, a hundred-year-old murderer, and now he would be inflicting a Chinese game on him. But the Chinese game had been very popular in Fulgence's childhood, even in the countryside, as in Camille's grandmother's house.

Now he realised why, in his drunken condition, he had asked Camille for the game. He had been thinking about the four winds in the Richelieu hotel room. He had been in the company of dragons. He had discovered the game that in the judge's boyhood home had been played every night, with pitiless references to the Hand of Honours, as opposed to the mutilated hand of the father.

When the library doors opened, he hurried inside, and a few minutes later received at his table a large etymological dictionary of French surnames. With the same fervent prayer as a gambler rolling the dice, hoping for a treble six, he unfolded his list of names. He had already had three cups of coffee to neutralise his sleepless night, and his hands were shaking as badly as Josette's.

First of all, he checked to see if he was right about Brasillier: yes, it derived from 'brazier'; fire, a red dragon. Next he looked for Lessard: 'name of a place, Essart Essard, or can mean lizard.' OK, green dragon. Then he looked under Espir, hoping it could be counted as a wind, since it seemed to contain the letters of 'respiration'. Yes, Old French for 'breath'. That made five winds, eight tiles out of thirteen. Adamsberg passed his hand across his face, with the feeling that he was only just clearing the jumps, his horse's belly just brushing the bars.

The other names were harder to fit in. The least promising was Fevre. Perhaps this was going to bring him to a juddering halt, in his fantasy of shovelling clouds. Fevre, he discovered, to his chagrin, came from the Latin *faber*, a blacksmith. Adamsberg shut his eyes and leaned back. Think about the blacksmith, with a hammer. Forging the points of the trident perhaps? He opened his eyes. From the old school book in which weeks ago he had found the picture of Neptune, he remembered now the opposite page had shown Vulcan, the god of fire, represented as a toiler in front of a blazing furnace. A smith, the master of fire. Taking a deep breath, he wrote red dragon, the second, opposite Fevre. When he tried Lefebure, he was referred back to Lefevre or Fevre. So that meant the same thing. The third red dragon. A trio. Ten out of thirteen.

Adamsberg let his hands fall and shut his eyes for a while before embarking on the last names, Lentretien and Mestre. Lentretien turned out, amazingly to be a deformation of *lattelin*, meaning an obscure kind of lizard. Must be a green dragon then, he thought, his handwriting becoming a scrawl by now as his hands contracted with anguish. He flexed his fingers before trying Mestre.

340

'Mestre: old Occitan term, southern form of Master. Diminutive forms Mestrel or Mestral, variants of Mistral. Refers to the north side of a hill exposed to the Mistral, the master wind from the north.'

'The master wind,' he wrote. He put down the pen and breathed deeply, trying to take in a lungful of the cold master wind from the north, which would close the list and cool his burning cheeks. He quickly sorted the suits. A trio of red dragons: Lefebure, Fevre and Brasillier; two trios of winds, Soubise, Ventou, Autan, Espire, Mestre and Wind. A pair of green dragons, Lessard and Lentretien. A pair of white dragons with Matère and the matricide. Thirteen, seven women and six men.

So one more tile would close the Hand of Honours. It would have to be either a white dragon or a green dragon. It would be a man no doubt, to get a balance between the sexes, father and mother. Aching and sweating, Adamsberg returned the precious dictionary to the librarian. Now he had found the open sesame, the key, the little golden key that opened the door to the room full of corpses in Bluebeard's castle.

He returned to Clémentine's house exhausted and anxious to send the key across the Atlantic to his brother, to tell him his personal nightmare was over. But Josette did not give him time to do anything, as she pushed before his eyes the decoded message she had worked on. 'Adamsberg – Gatineau – rendezvous – portage trail – Noëlla Corderon.'

'Josette, I haven't slept a wink, I'm in no state to understand this stuff.'

'These are the letters from Michel's computer. I was quite wrong, I should have realised. Look what it could mean.'

Adamsberg concentrated on the words.

'Portage trail,' he murmured.

'Michel must surely have been passing this to someone. You weren't alone on the path. Someone else knew you'd been there.'

'It's just one interpretation, Josette.'

'There aren't thousands of words with these combinations. I'm sure this is right.'

'It's remarkable, Josette, congratulations. But I'm afraid nobody will believe in an interpretation, it's not the same thing as evidence for the police, you see. I've rescued my brother from the abyss, but I'm still there myself, buried under piles of rocks.'

'Locks, you mean,' said Josette. 'Big strong locks. And where there are locks there are keys.'

LV

RAPHAËL ADAMSBERG FOUND THE MESSAGE ON THE FRIDAY MORNING. His brother had given it the name 'Land!' which must refer, Raphaël thought, to the cry of sailors when they first see the faint outline of a landmass on the horizon. He had to read the email several times before he dared believe he had understood the meaning of this confusing mixture of dragons and winds, written down in great haste and in a state of exhaustion: the judge's ear, sand, matricide, Fulgence's real age, his father's mutilated hand, the village of Collery, the trident, Mah Jong, the Hand of Honours. Jean-Baptiste had typed so fast that he had missed out letters and even entire words. Raphaël could sense the trembling of his hands, a sensation that came directly from brother to brother, from shore to shore, carried through the waves and ending up in his Detroit bolt-hole, ripping devastatingly through the shadowy network in which he had been living his furtive life. He had not killed Lise. He stayed lying back in his chair, letting his body float along the shore, unable to guess what strange leaps Jean-Baptiste had made in order to exhume the judge's murderous itinerary. As children once, they had wandered so far into the mountains that they were unable to find the way back to the village or even a path. Jean-Baptiste had climbed on Raphaël's shoulders. 'Don't cry,' he had said. 'We'll try and find the way people went in the olden days.' Every five hundred metres, Jean-Baptiste would climb up on his back. 'This way,' he would say as he jumped down.

So that's what Jean-Baptiste must have done. Climbed up and seen where the Trident had passed by, following his blood-stained trail. Like a dog, like a god, thought Raphaël. For the second time, Jean-Baptiste was bringing him home to the village.

LVI

THAT EVENING, JOSETTE WAS LOOKING AFTER THE FIRE. ADAMSBERG HAD telephoned Danglard and Retancourt, then slept all the afternoon. In the evening, still feeling dazed, he had taken his seat by the fire and was watching the little hacker stir the flames, then playing with a burning twig. She was drawing incandescent circles and figures of eight in the twilight. The orange tip of the twig shook as it turned, and Adamsberg wondered whether, like the wooden spoon in the sauce, the twig had the power of dispersing lumps, all the lumps that surrounded him. Josette was wearing some tennis shoes he had never seen before, blue with a gold stripe. Like the golden sickle in the field of stars, he thought.

'Can you lend me the magic wand?' he asked.

He pushed its tip into the coals then waved it in the air.

'Pretty, isn't it?' said Josette.

'Yes.'

'You can't draw squares in the air, only circles.'

'Doesn't matter, I don't like squares much.'

'Raphaël's crime was a big square lock,' suggested Josette.

'Yes.'

'And now that lock has been exploded.'

'Yes, Josette.'

Puff, puff, bang, he thought.

'But there's another,' he went on. 'And we can't get any further with that one.'

'There's no end to the underground tunnels, *commissaire*. They're designed for that, to get you from one place to another. Path to path, door to door.'

'Not always, Josette. We have the biggest, firmest lock of all ahead of us now.'

'Which one?'

'My stagnant memory, dead at the bottom of a lake. My memory is blocked by a rock fall, and my own trap, my fall on the path. There's no hacker can break through to that.'

'Lock by lock, one after another, one thing at a time, that's the way a hacker moves,' said Josette, pushing the coals closer together. 'You can't get through lock number nine until you have unlocked number eight. Understand?'

'Yes, Josette, of course I do,' said Adamsberg gently.

She went on moving the coals into the centre.

'Before the lock of the lost memory,' she said, carefully picking up a coal in the tongs, 'there's the one that made you go out to get drunk in Hull, and then again last night.'

'That's blocked too, with a high barrier.'

Josette shook her head, obstinately.

'Josette,' sighed Adamsberg. 'I know you've broken into the files of the FBI. But you can't break into the files of life like you can into computers.'

'They're not so different really,' replied Josette.

He stretched out his feet towards the fire, still turning the stick and letting the warmth of the flames warm him through his shoes. His brother's innocence was coming back to him now in a slow boomerang movement, distancing him from his usual landmarks and habits, displacing his point of view, opening up forbidden places where the world seemed to be discreetly changing texture. What the texture was exactly, he didn't know. What he did know was that in other times, and even as recently as yesterday, he would never have confided the story of Camille, the girl from the north, to a fragile little hacker wearing blue and gold tennis shoes. But that is what he did, from the beginning down to his drunken conversation of the previous night.

346

'So you see,' he concluded, 'there's no way through.'

'Can you give me the stick?' Josette asked timidly.

He gave her the twig. She rekindled the point in the fire and began her wavery circles in the air again.

'Why are you trying to get through there, when you were the one that blocked it off, yourself?'

'I don't know. Because that's where the air comes from, perhaps, and without air we choke or explode. Like Strasbourg Cathedral with all its windows blocked.'

'What?' said Josette in surprise, stopping her hand moving. 'Has someone blocked up the cathedral? What on earth for?'

'I don't know,' said Adamsberg with a vague wave of his hand. 'But it's blocked. With dragons, lampreys, dogs, toads, and one third of a *gendarme*.'

'Hmm,' said Josette.

She dropped the twig and disappeared into the kitchen. She brought back two glasses and put them shakily on the mantelpiece.

'Do you know the name?' she asked, pouring in the port and spilling some alongside the glasses.

'Trabelmann. One third of Trabelmann.'

'No, I meant the name of Camille's baby.'

'Ah. No. I didn't ask. And I was drunk.'

'Here we are,' she said handing him the port. 'It's yours.'

'Thank you,' said Adamsberg, taking the glass.

'I wasn't talking about the drink,' said Josette. She drew a few more incandescent circles, drank the wine, and passed the stick to Adamsberg.

'Here you are,' she said. 'I'll leave you now. It was only a little lock, but maybe it'll let in some air, a bit too much perhaps.'

LVII

DANGLARD WAS TAKING NOTES QUICKLY, AS HE LISTENED TO HIS Québécois colleague.

'Get it as fast as you can,' he said. 'Adamsberg has unravelled the judge's career. Yes, and it all hangs together now, it looks pretty solid. All except the murder on the portage trail, which still doesn't seem to fit. So don't give up looking. No . . . Well, see what you can do. Sartonna's message won't cut any ice, it's just a reconstitution. The prosecution would wipe the floor with it. Yes. Sure. He may still get away with it, so keep at it.'

Danglard exchanged a few more words with his interlocutor, then hung up. He had the sickening feeling everything would hang by a thread. It would stand or fall by very little. He only had a short time left and not much thread.

LVIII

ADAMSBERG AND BRÉZILLON HAD ARRANGED TO MEET AT A DISCREET cafe in the 7th *arrondissement* at the quiet time of mid-afternoon. The *commissaire* was making his way there, head down and muffled in his lumberjack's cap. The previous evening he had sat up long after Josette had left him, drawing circles in the fire. Since he had casually picked up that newspaper in the office, he seemed to have been travelling for five weeks and five days now, through endless tumult, buffeted by storms, on a raft tossed by the winds of Neptune. Josette, like a perfect hacker, had homed in straight to the target, and he was amazed at himself for not realising the truth earlier. The child had been conceived in Lisbon and was his. This stupefying truth had calmed one storm, only to provoke a wind of anxiety which was now puffing and blowing on the near horizon.

'You really are a stupid bastard, *commissaire*.' Because he had understood nothing. Danglard had been sitting, like a sad heavy weight, on his secret. Meanwhile he and Camille had each retreated into a stiff silence, and he had fled so far away. As far as Raphaël in his exile.

Raphaël might be able to relax now, but Jean-Baptiste would have to keep running. Lock after lock, according to Josette in her celestial running shoes. The lock on the path still seemed impregnable. But the one relating to Fulgence was now within reach. Adamsberg pushed the revolving door of an upmarket cafe on the corner of the avenue Bosquet. A few ladies were taking tea, one was drinking *pastis*. He spotted the *divisionnaire,* sitting like a grey monument on a red velvet bench, his glass of beer placed before him on the polished wooden table.

'Take that hat off,' Brézillon said at once. 'Makes you look like a lumberjack.'

'It's my camouflage,' Adamsberg explained, putting it on a chair. 'Arctic technology, covers eyes, ears, cheeks and chin.'

'Get on with it, Adamsberg. I'm already doing you a favour by agreeing to meet you.'

'I asked Danglard to tell you about what's happened since the exhumation. The judge's false age, the Guillaumond family, the matricide, the Mah Jong stuff.'

'Yes, he told me all that.'

'And your view of it, *Monsieur le divisionnaire?*'

Brézillon lit one of his coarse cigarettes.

'Favourable, but two points bother me. Why did the judge make himself out to be fifteen years older? I can see why he'd change his name after killing his mother. And in the maquis, it must have been quite easy. But why his age?'

'I think it's because he values power, rather than youth. As a recent law graduate of twenty-five, what could he hope for after the war? Just the slow career path of a small-town lawyer, gradually moving up through the ranks. He wanted better than that. With his acute intelligence and a few fake references, he could quickly aspire to better posts. On condition he was the right age. Maturity was necessary to feed his ambition. Five years after he disappeared, he was already a judge in Nantes.'

'All right, granted. Second point. Noëlla Corderon doesn't seem to fit the profile of the fourteenth victim. The name doesn't mean anything in Mah Jong terms, so I'm still talking to a murderer on the run. All this doesn't get you off the hook, Adamsberg.'

'There have been some other supplementary victims, on the way. Michel Sartonna for instance.'

'We don't know that for sure.'

'No, but it's a reasonable assumption. and it's an assumption too for Noëlla Corderon. And it's an assumption we could make for me as well.'

'Meaning?'

'If the judge did try to trap me in Quebec, the mechanism hasn't worked properly. I got away from the RCMP, and the exhumation has smoked him out of his safe hiding-place. If I manage to persuade other people, he'll lose everything, reputation and honour. He won't want to take that risk. He's going to react pretty soon.'

'By taking you out?'

'Yes. I should therefore try to make things easy for him. I mean, go back to my own flat quite openly. And he'll come. That's what I've come to ask you, to let me take a few days and do that.'

'Adamsberg, you're crazy. You're going to do a stakeout for the lion, with yourself as the goat? With a madman who's already committed thirteen murders?'

Or maybe the old trick of the mosquito in the ear, thought Adamsberg, or the fish in the muddy bottom of a lake, being tempted up by a lamp. Fishing by night with lanterns. Only this time the fish was holding the trident, not the fisherman.

'There isn't any other way to get him to break cover.'

'That's simply self-sacrifice, Adamsberg, and it won't get you cleared of the crime in Hull. That's if the judge doesn't manage to kill you first.'

'It's a risk.'

'If you're found in your own flat, dead or alive, the RCMP will accuse me of incompetence or complicity.'

'You'll say you lifted the surveillance to trick me into coming back.'

'Which would oblige me to extradite you right away,' said Brézillon, putting out his cigarette with his thumb.

'Well, you'll have to do that anyway, in four and a half weeks.'

'I don't like sending my men over the top.'

'Just let's say I'm no longer one of your men, just an independent fugitive.'

'Agreed then,' sighed Brézillon.

Drawn in by the lamprey effect, Adamsberg thought. He got up and put his camouflage cap back on. For the first time Brézillon put out his hand to shake. An admission, no doubt, that he was not sure of seeing him alive again.

LIX

BACK IN CLIGNANCOURT, ADAMSBERG PUT ON HIS BULLET-PROOF VEST, holstered his gun and kissed the two old women goodbye.

'Just a little expedition,' he said. 'I'll be back.'

Not so sure about that, he thought as he went out into the alleyway. What was the point of this unequal high noon confrontation? Was it his last throw, or was he taking a chance to anticipate death, exposing himself to Fulgence's trident rather than sink into the shadows of the portage trail without ever knowing whether or not he had stabbed Noëlla? He saw, as if through frosted glass, the young woman's body trapped under the ice. He could hear her plaintive voice. 'And you know what he did, my buddy? Poor Noëlla, all washed up? Has Noëlla ever told you that before? About the cop from Paris?'

Adamsberg quickened his pace, head down. He couldn't involve anyone else in his old mosquito trap. The weight of guilt round his neck ever since the Hull murder made him incapable of it. Fulgence might surround himself with henchmen and unleash a bloodbath, killing Danglard, Retancourt, Justin, the whole department. The blood spread before his eyes, carrying off the red robes of Cardinal Richelieu. You're on your own, young man.

The sex and the name. The idea of dying without ever knowing that seemed crazy, or neglectful. He pulled out the mobile by one of its red feet and called Danglard.

'Any news?' the *capitaine* asked.

'Might be,' said Adamsberg prudently. 'But that aside, I should tell you I have worked out the name of the new father. He's an unreliable character, whose shoes are not polished.'

'No? Who is he then?'

'Just this guy.'

'Glad you've got the answer.'

'Yes. There's just one thing I want to know first.'

'First, before what?'

'I just want to know the baby's sex and first name.'

Adamsberg stopped in order to take in the information properly. It wouldn't stick in his memory if he went on walking.

'Thanks, Danglard. One last thing. Did you know it works with frogs as well as toads? The cigarette thing.'

As he walked down to the Marais district, a gloomy fog surrounded him. He came to as he saw his block of flats, and looked carefully around. Brézillon appeared to have kept his word, there were no watchers around; the way was clear out of the shadows into the light.

He looked quickly round the flat, then wrote five letters: one each for Raphaël, for his family, for Danglard, for Camille and for Retancourt. On an impulse he wrote a quick note for Sanscartier as well. Then he placed the sombre packet in a hiding-place known only to Danglard. 'To be read in the event of my death.' After eating a snack, standing up, he tidied the rooms, sorted the linen and destroyed his private letters. You're preparing for this as if you'd lost already, he said to himself, as he put the bin out in the hall. You're a dead man.

Everything seemed ready. The judge would not need to break in. He would certainly have obtained a spare key through Michel Sartonna. Fulgence was a man who left nothing to chance. And to find the *commissaire* waiting for him with a gun would not surprise him. He knew he would be armed, just as he knew he would be alone.

354

By the time the judge learnt he had returned, he would have to plan his arrival either for tomorrow or the next day in the evening. Adamsberg could anticipate only one point of detail: the time. The judge was obsessed with symbolism. It would probably please him to try to dispose of Adamsberg at the same time of day as his brother thirty years ago. Between eleven and midnight. So there was the slight advantage of not being surprised by the time of day. He could therefore strike at Fulgence's pride, where he thought he was untouchable. Adamsberg had bought a Mah Jong set on his way home. He set some of the tiles out on the coffee table and arranged the judge's Hand of Honours on a rack. He added two flowers, one for Noëlla, one for Michel. The sight of his secret exposed to the light might provoke Fulgence to talk before he attacked. And that might give Adamsberg a few seconds' start.

LX

ON SUNDAY EVENING AT TEN-THIRTY, ADAMSBERG PUT ON HIS THICK bullet-proof vest and holster again. He switched on all the lights to indicate he was at home, so that the great insect in its cave would crawl up into the light.

At eleven-fifteen, the front door clicked open, signalling the arrival of the Trident. The judge slammed the door casually behind him. It was exactly like him, Adamsberg thought. He was at home, anywhere and everywhere he pleased. 'I can bring down a thunderbolt on your head whenever I wish.'

Adamsberg raised his gun, as the old man moved into his field of vision.

'What a barbaric welcome, young man,' said Fulgence in his gravel-toned voice.

Taking no notice of the muzzle pointing at him, the judge took off his long cape and threw it on a chair. For all Adamsberg's anticipation of this moment, he had tensed at the sight of the tall old figure. He had aged in the face since their last meeting, but still held himself erect, with his haughty air and the same arrogant gestures Adamsberg remembered from his boyhood. The deep lines etched on the judge's face enhanced even further that devilish beauty which the village women had admired and done penance for. The judge sat down and, crossing his legs, examined the game laid out on the table.

'Sit down,' he ordered. 'We have a few things to talk about.'

Adamsberg stayed where he was, adjusting his range, watching both his enemy's eyes and his hands. Fulgence smiled and leaned back in the chair, perfectly at his ease. The judge's dazzling smile, which was an element of his beauty, was unusual in that it stretched back to the first molars. This feature had accentuated over time, giving his lean jaws a macabre air.

'You're not in my league, young man, and you never have been. Do you know why? Because when I kill, I kill. But you're just a small-time cop. A banal and messy murder on a footpath changes you into a miserable creature. Yes, a very little man.'

Adamsberg walked slowly round behind Fulgence, holding the barrel of the gun a few inches from his neck.

'Nervous too,' went on the judge. 'Just what I would expect from a little man.'

He pointed to the dragons and winds.

'Quite correct,' he said. 'But it took you some time.'

Adamsberg followed the movements of that feared hand, a white hand with long fingers, and well-kept nails, its joints now enlarged with age, but moving at the end of its wrist with that strange, slightly dislocated grace that one sees in paintings by old masters.

'The fourteenth tile is missing,' he said, 'and it will be a man.'

'But not you Adamsberg,' said Fulgence, 'you'd dilute the hand, being of the wrong suit.'

'A green dragon or a white one?'

'What does it matter to you? Even in prison or in the grave, the last tile will not escape me.'

The judge pointed to the two flowers which Adamsberg had placed alongside the Hand of Honours.

'I take it this represents Michel Sartonna, and this one Noëlla Corderon,' he remarked.

'Yes.'

'Permit me to make a correction.'

Fulgence put on a glove and picked up the tile corresponding to Noëlla, which he threw back into the pile.

'I don't care for mistakes,' he said coldly. 'You may be sure I would never have troubled to follow you to Quebec. I don't follow people, Adamsberg, I go ahead of them. I have never been to Quebec.'

'Sartonna kept you informed about the portage trail.'

'Yes, I was watching your movements after Schiltigheim, as you know. The murder on the footpath afforded me much amusement. A crime committed by a drunken man, with neither grace nor premeditation. How vulgar, Adamsberg.'

The judge turned round looking directly at the gun.

'I'm sorry, little man, that's your very own crime, and I'm leaving it to you.'

A fleeting smile from the judge and Adamsberg broke out into a sweat all over his body.

'Don't worry,' Fulgence went on. 'You'll find it's easier to live with than you might think.'

'Why did you kill Sartonna?'

'He knew too much,' the judge said, turning back to the game. 'It's the kind of risk I don't take. You ought to know as well,' he said, picking up another flower and placing it on the rack, 'that Dr Colette Choisel is no longer with us. An unfortunate car accident. And former *Commissaire* Adamsberg will shortly be following her into the underworld,' he went on, picking up a third flower. 'Overwhelmed by his crime, too weak to face a lifetime in prison, he killed himself, if you please. What can you expect from a little man?'

'That's what you think you're going to do?'

'It's quite simple. Sit down, young man, your nervousness is annoying me.'

Adamsberg sat down opposite the judge, still pointing the gun at him.

'You should be grateful to me,' smiled Fulgence. 'This brief formality will release you from an intolerable existence, since the memory of your crime will leave you no peace.'

'My death won't save you, though. There's a complete dossier on you now.'

'Others have been found guilty of these crimes. Nothing will be proved without my confession.'

'The sand in the coffin points to you.'

358

'True, and that is the only point at issue. That is why Dr Choisel has disappeared. And that is why I am here to have this little chat, before your suicide. It is tasteless, young man, to dig up people's graves. A very serious lapse in taste.'

Fulgence's face had lost its disdainful smile. He was now looking at Adamsberg with all the harshness of a former judge.

'Which you are going to correct. By signing a little confession, quite usual in suicide cases. Indicating that you arranged the fake coffin yourself. You re-buried my body in the woods near Richelieu. Driven by your obsession, of course, and because you were determined to go to any lengths to blame the footpath murder on me. Do you understand?'

'I won't sign anything that helps you, Fulgence.'

'Yes, you will, little man. Because if you refuse, we can find two more flowers for the set. Your friend Camille, and her child. Whom I will have executed immediately after your death, believe me. Seventh floor, left.'

Fulgence handed Adamsberg a sheet of paper and a pen, which he first wiped carefully. Adamsberg put his gun under his left arm, and began to write under the judge's dictation, enlarging the letters D and R.

'No, no, no,' said the judge, taking away the paper. 'Your normal writing, if you please. Begin again,' he said, passing over another sheet.

Adamsberg finished writing and put the paper on the table.

'Perfect,' said Fulgence. 'Now please put the game away.'

'And how do you propose to suicide me?' asked Adamsberg, using his free hand to put the tiles in the box. 'Since I'm armed.'

'But, you are also ridiculously human. So I count on your complete cooperation. You will allow it to happen. You will put your own gun to your head and fire. Should you choose to shoot me instead, which is of course open to you, two of my men have orders to take care of your girlfriend and your child. Am I making myself clear enough?'

Adamsberg let fall the revolver under the judge's dazzling smile. He was so sure of himself that he had arrived without any apparent firearm himself. He would leave behind him a perfect suicide and a confession which would exonerate him.

Adamsberg examined his Magnum, of pathetically little use to him now, then looked up and stiffened. Danglard was standing a couple of feet behind the judge, moving with the silence of a cat. His pompom on his head, a tear-gas canister in his right hand, and his Beretta in his left. Adamsberg raised the revolver to his forehead.

'Give me a moment or two,' he said. 'Just to gather my thoughts.'

Fulgence looked scornful.

'A cowardly little man. I will count to four.'

On the count of two, Danglard threw the gas, moving his Beretta to his right hand. Fulgence leapt up, with a cry, to face Danglard. The *capitaine*, seeing the face of the judge for the first time, had a second's hesitation, in which Fulgence's fist hit his chin. Danglard crashed violently into the wall and his shot missed the judge who was already at the door. Adamsberg ran into the stairwell, following the old man in his headlong escape. The retreating judge was in his line of fire for a moment. Danglard joined him, as he let his gun drop to his side.

'Listen,' said Adamsberg. 'That must be his car.'

Danglard ran down the last few stairs and into the street with his gun at the ready. Too far, he couldn't even hit the tyres. The car must have had the engine running.

'Christ Almighty, why didn't you shoot him?' he shouted as he came back up.

Adamsberg was sitting on the stairs, his Magnum by his side, his head bent, and his hands hanging between his knees.

'Target seen from behind, running away,' he said. 'Not self-defence. I've done enough killing as it is, *capitaine*.'

Danglard led the *commissaire* back into the apartment. With a policeman's flair, he found the bottle of gin and poured two glasses. Adamsberg lifted his hand.

'Look how I'm shaking, Danglard. Like a maple leaf.'

You know what he did to me? That Paris cop? Did I tell you about that?

Danglard downed his first glass swiftly. Then he picked up the telephone, while helping himself to a second.

'Mordent? Danglard here. Top-level protection, immediately, Camille Forestier, 23 rue des Templiers, 4th arrondissement, 7th floor, left. Two men day and night for two months. Tell them I gave the order.'

Adamsberg drank the gin, with chattering teeth.

'Danglard, how the hell did you get here?'

'Just doing my job.'

'How?'

'Go to sleep first,' said Danglard, who could see Adamsberg's drained features.

'To sleep, perchance to dream, *capitaine*. He said I killed Noëlla.'

She was all washed up, poor Noëlla. Did I tell you about that? My chum?

'I know, I got it all on tape.'

The *capitaine* felt in his trouser pocket and took out a handful of pills. He looked them over expertly, and chose a greyish capsule.

'Take this and go to bed. I'll call for you at seven in the morning.'

'What for?'

'Taking you to see a policeman.'

LXI

DANGLARD HAD DRIVEN OUT OF PARIS AND WAS NOW CAREFULLY NEGO-
tiating the three-lane highway through patches of thick fog. He was talking
to himself, cursing himself for not having been able to clap hands on the
judge. No ID on the car, no possibility of roadblocks. At his side,
Adamsberg seemed indifferent to their failure to thwart the judge's
getaway: he was alone still on the portage trail. In the space of a night,
the certainty of having committed the crime had wrapped itself round
him like the bands of a mummy.

'Don't blame yourself, Danglard,' he said at last in a flat voice. 'Nobody
can catch the judge, I already told you.'

'I had him in arm's reach, for God's sake.'

'I know. It's happened to me too.'

'I'm a cop, I was armed.'

'Me too. Doesn't alter anything. He runs away like sand.'

'He's heading for his fourteenth murder.'

'How did you come to be there, Danglard?'

'*You* read things in people's eyes, in their voices, in their movements.
I go by the logic of the word.'

'I didn't tell you anything.'

'On the contrary, you had the excellent intuition to send me a warning.'

'No, I didn't.'

'You called me about the child. You said "There's something I want to
know first." First before what? Going to see Camille? No, you'd already

paid her a visit when you were drunk. I phoned Clémentine. I got a quavery little voice on the other end – is that your hacker?'

'Yes, Josette.'

'She told me you'd gone out with your bullet-proof vest and your gun, and said you'd be back, before you kissed them goodbye. Gun, kisses and reassurance all pointed to your being uncertain. About what? About a fight to the death. It had to be with the judge of course. And the only way to do that was to expose yourself to him on your own territory. The old stakeout technique, with yourself as the goat.'

'Well, the technique was for a mosquito, in fact.'

'A goat surely?'

'Whatever you say, Danglard.'

'Well the goat generally gets eaten. Crunch, gone. As you knew.'

'Yes.'

'But you didn't really want that to happen, because you warned me. So from Saturday I kept watch from the basement in the house opposite. I had a good view from the basement window, across to your main door. I thought the judge would strike at night, probably after eleven. He's a symbolist.'

'Why were you alone?'

'Same reason as you. Didn't want anyone else to get hurt. I was wrong, I took on too much. We could have cornered him.'

'No, six men wouldn't have caught him.'

'Retancourt would have blocked him.'

'Yes, she'd have stood in his way, and he'd have killed her.'

'He wasn't armed.'

'Yes, he was. His walking stick – it's a sword-stick, a third of a trident. He'd have stabbed her.'

'I suppose it's possible,' said Danglard rubbing his chin. Adamsberg had given him some of Ginette's yellow ointment to treat it.

'No, he really would have. Don't blame yourself.'

'I left the lookout during the day and came back in the evening. He appeared soon after eleven. Looking very relaxed, and so tall, so old, that I couldn't mistake him. I came up behind him and waited at your door. I got his confession on tape.'

363

'And you heard him deny that he committed the crime on the path.'

'Yes, that too. He raised his voice when he said, "I don't follow people, Adamsberg, I go ahead of them." I took advantage of that to open the door.'

'Well, you saved the goat anyway. Thanks, Danglard.'

'You'd called me. It was my duty.'

'And it's your duty now to hand me over to Canadian justice. We're on our way to the airport, aren't we?'

'Yes.'

'Where a fucking cop from the RCMP is waiting for me, right?'

'Yes.'

Adamsberg leaned back and shut his eyes. 'Don't drive too fast in this fog, *capitaine*.'

LXII

DANGLARD TOOK ADAMSBERG TO ONE OF THE CAFES IN THE TERMINAL building and chose a table off to one side. Adamsberg sat down. His body felt as if it didn't belong to him, and his eyes were fixed on the silly pompom on Danglard's cap, a mocking and ridiculous ornament. Retancourt would have grabbed him, and got him over the border, she would have helped him escape. It was still possible. Danglard had been discreet and avoided handcuffs. He could still jump up and run for it, because his *capitaine* wouldn't be able to keep up with him. But the image of himself stabbing Noëlla paralysed his capacity to move. What was the point of running, if he couldn't even walk? Frozen with fear in case he was capable of striking again, finding himself staggering over a corpse on the ground. He might just as well end it here, with Danglard who was morosely sipping a coffee laced with cognac. Hundreds of travellers went past, departing or arriving, with their consciences as spotless as fresh linen. While his own conscience felt repulsive to him, a shred of cloth, stiff with dried blood.

Danglard suddenly waved to someone. Adamsberg made no attempt to look round. The triumphant face of the superintendent was the last thing he wanted to see.

Two large hands landed on his shoulders.

'I told you we'd catch the sonofabitch,' he heard someone say.

Adamsberg turned to find himself looking into the face of Fernand Sanscartier. He jumped up and instinctively grabbed his arms. Oh God, why had they done this? Sent Sanscartier to take delivery of the culprit?

365

'They gave you this mission?' he asked, in despair.

'Just doing what I was told,' said Sanscartier without losing his benign smile. 'And we've got a lot to talk about,' he went on, sitting down opposite them.

He shook hands warmly with Danglard.

'A good job well done, *capitaine*. Greetings. Jeez, it sure is warm over here,' he said taking off his padded jacket. 'Here's your copy of the file, and the sample.'

He shook a little box in front of Danglard, who nodded approval.

'We've already analysed it. The comparison ought to clinch it.'

'A sample of what?' Adamsberg asked.

Sanscartier plucked a hair from Adamsberg's head.

'Hair,' he said. 'Giveaway stuff, hair. It falls like autumn leaves. But we had to shift six cubic metres of leafmould to find it. Think of that. Just to find a few hairs. Like looking for a needle in a haystack.'

'You didn't need it. You already had my prints on the belt.'

'Yeah, but not his.'

'What do you mean, not his?'

Sanscartier turned towards Danglard, with a frown in the big kind eyes.

'Haven't you told him yet?' he asked. 'Have you left him stewing in his own juice all this time?'

'I couldn't tell him until we were certain. I don't like to raise false hopes.'

'Sure, but last night, damnit? You could have told him then?'

'Last night we had a bit of a to-do on.'

'This morning then?'

'Yes, OK, I did leave him in the dark. For eight hours.'

'Some pal, you are,' said Sanscartier in disapproval. 'Why didn't you tell him?'

'So that he would really know what it was like for Raphaël. Being afraid of your own shadow, being in exile, unable to face the world. It was necessary. Just eight hours, Sanscartier, not a life sentence, so that he'd be able to catch up with his brother.'

Sanscartier turned to Adamsberg, and banged his box on the table.

'Some hairs from the head of your devil,' he said. 'Which had to be found in six cubic metres of rotten leaves.'

Adamsberg understood at that moment that Sanscartier was engaged in hauling him to the surface, to the fresh air of the atmosphere, from the mud at the bottom of Pink Lake. That he had been working for Danglard, not for Laliberté.

'It wasn't easy either,' Sanscartier went on. 'Because I had to do it all outside office hours. In the evenings, or early in the morning. Without the boss catching me. Your *capitaine* here was the one who pushed me. He couldn't believe the business of your cotton-wool legs after hitting the branch. I went down the path and tried to find the place where you fell. I walked from *L'Ecluse*, at the time you said. I went a hundred yards. I found a lot of newly broken twigs and overturned stones just by the timber site. The men had struck camp but there were new maple saplings there.'

'I said it was near the site,' said Adamsberg, breathing fast. He had folded his arms, clutching his sleeves in his fingers, hanging on to the sergeant's words.

'But there were no low branches round there, chum. Whatever you hit, it couldn't have been a branch. So your *capitaine* asked me to find the nightwatchman. He was the only possible witness after all.'

'I see, but did you find him?' asked Adamsberg, through lips stiff with anguish, hardly able to speak.

Danglard stopped a waiter and ordered water, more coffee, beer and croissants.

'Jeez, that was the worst bit. I had to take a sickie to get off work and first of all I asked at the town hall. But no, it was a federal camp. So second of all, I had to go to Montreal to find the name of the lumber outfit. Laliberté was getting fed up with my sick leaves, I can tell you. And your *capitaine* was on at me the whole time by phone. I got the watchman's name. He was up the Ottawa River somewhere by then, so I had to take more leave to go there. Thought the super was going to burst a blood vessel.'

'And you found him?' asked Adamsberg swallowing a glass of water in a single gulp.

'Don't worry, I nabbed him in his pick-up. But getting him to say anything was another matter. He spun me yarn after yarn. Finally I threatened him with the cells if he didn't come clean. Withholding information, hiding vital evidence. I'm a bit embarrassed to tell you what he said. Adrien, can you go on?'

'The watchman, Jean-Gilles Boisvenu, saw a man crouching by the path that Sunday night,' said Danglard. 'He took out his binoculars and had a good look.'

'A good look?'

'Boisvenu was sure that he was waiting for another homosexual,' Sanscartier explained. 'You know the portage trail was supposed to be a gay pick-up place after dark?'

'Yes, he asked me if that was why I was there.'

'He was interested, sort of a voyeur,' Danglard explained, 'so he was glued to his windscreen. A very good witness, because he was paying close attention. He was delighted when he heard someone else coming, he could see quite well. But it didn't work out as he was hoping.'

'How did he know it was the Sunday night, the 26th?'

'Because he was on duty when he should have been off, and furious with the weekend watchman who had called in sick. He saw the first man, who was tall with white hair, hit the other guy on the head with a sawn-off branch. The other one, that's you, *commissaire*, fell to the ground. Boisvenu crouched down in the truck. The big guy looked mean and he didn't want to get involved in a lover's tiff, if that's what it was. But he went on looking.'

'Rooted to the spot.'

'Yes, he was thinking, well hoping, in fact, that it might turn into a rape of the victim.'

'Understand now?' said Sanscartier, his cheeks bright red.

'Well, the big guy started to take the scarf off the other one and undo his jacket. Boisvenu went on looking. And what he saw was that the big guy took your hands and pressed them on something like a strap.'

'The belt,' said Sanscartier.

'Exactly, the belt. But he didn't do anything else to your clothing. He injected something into your neck. Boisvenu is absolutely certain about that. He saw him take a syringe out of his pocket and test the pressure.'

'Cotton-wool legs,' said Adamsberg.

'I told you I couldn't get my head round that,' said Danglard. 'Until the branch, even if you were drunk, you were walking normally. But when you woke up, your legs could hardly carry you. And they were still not normal in the morning. On alcohol, I'm an expert, I know what it can do. Amnesia's not a regular effect, and as for the legs, I just thought that was very odd. I needed to see if something else was involved.'

'That was his hunch,' Sanscartier explained.

'Some drug,' Danglard explained, 'something which would give you memory loss, like all the other people who'd been arrested.'

'Anyway,' Sanscartier went on, 'the old guy got up, and left you where you were. At that point, Boisvenu thought he'd better do something, after seeing the syringe. He's tough, not a nightwatchman for nothing, but he couldn't get out of his truck right away. Can you tell him why, please, Adrien?'

'Well his legs were caught in his pants,' Danglard explained. 'He'd got himself all ready for a peepshow, and he'd pulled his dungarees down to his ankles.'

'Boisvenu was embarrassed to tell me that,' Sanscartier went on. 'By the time he was decent, the old man had gone. The watchman found you lying there, out for the count and covered in blood. He dragged you over to his truck and put you inside with a blanket over you. And he waited.'

'Why did he wait. Why didn't he call the police?'

'He didn't want people asking him why he hadn't done anything. He didn't want to say what he was doing. If he said he was scared, or hadn't seen the attack because he was asleep, it might have cost him his job. They don't recruit nightwatchmen to panic or go to sleep. He preferred to keep mum and put you in the truck.'

'He could have just left me there and washed his hands of me.'

'Well yes, theoretically. But he couldn't square that with God and his conscience, leaving someone to die, and he wanted to retrieve himself.

With the temperature that night, you would have frozen to death. He decided to see if you were coming to after the knock on the head and the injection. He didn't know whether it was just a tranquilliser or a poison. If it looked bad, he'd call the cops and invent something. He watched you for two hours, and since you were sleeping with a regular pulse, he decided you'd be OK. When you seemed to be waking up, he drove off up the cycle track and put you down on the road. He knew you'd come from there, he recognised you.'

'Why did he drive me back?'

'He thought you wouldn't be in a fit state to get back along the path under your own steam, you might fall in the river.'

'A good egg in the end then,' said Adamsberg.

'There was still a tiny drop of dried blood in the back of his pick-up truck. I took a sample, well, you know our methods. The guy wasn't lying, it was your DNA, OK. I compared it with . . .' Sanscartier hesitated.

'Your semen,' Danglard completed the sentence. 'So between eleven and one-thirty in the morning, you weren't on the path, you were in Boisvenu's pick-up truck.'

'But before that?' asked Adamsberg, rubbing his cold lips. 'Between ten-thirty and eleven?'

'You left *L'Ecluse* at ten-fifteen. By half-past, you had started down the path. You couldn't have reached the work site and picked up any trident before eleven, which is when Boisvenu saw you coming. And you didn't take a fork from the site. Nothing was missing. The judge had his weapon already.'

'Brand new, bought on the spot?'

'Yes, we traced it. Sartonna was sent to buy it.'

'But there was earth in the wounds.'

'You're not very quick this morning, Jean-Baptiste,' said Sanscartier with a grin. 'That's because you don't dare believe it. Your devil, you see, he'd knocked the girl unconscious up by the Champlain stone. He'd sent her a message, supposedly from you, to meet her there, and he was waiting for her. He hit her from behind, then dragged her along to the little pool. Before he stabbed her, he'd already had to break the ice on the pool, and the pool was full of mud and leaves. That's why the prongs had earth on them.'

'And he killed Noëlla,' whispered Adamsberg.

'It must have been before eleven, and well before, ten-thirty maybe. He knew the time you usually came back along the path. He took the belt, he pushed the girl's body under the ice. Then he came back to surprise you.'

'Why not wait till I got nearer the body?'

'There was a greater risk of meeting someone. The site was a good place to wait, plenty of big trees in case anyone else came by. He bashed you on the head, drugged you, and then took the belt back and left it by the body. It was the *capitaine* who thought of looking for some of his hairs. Because of course nothing so far proved it was the judge, you see. Danglard hoped he might have lost a few hairs between the Champlain stone and the pool, when he was dragging the body over. He could have stopped for breath, put his hand to his head, something like that. So we took up the surface about an inch and a half down. It had frozen over again, which meant the hairs might still be there. So that's why I found myself with six cubic metres of leafmould and twigs to comb. And the contents of that box,' said Sanscartier, pointing to it. 'Apparently you've got some of the judge's hairs over here.'

'From the *Schloss*! Shit, Danglard, what about Michel? He could have taken them from my flat, they were in the kitchen cupboard with the bottles.'

'I took the sachet the same time I weeded the files of documents about Raphaël. Michel didn't know anything about the hairs.'

'So how come you looked in the cupboard?'

'I was looking for a little something to help me think about the papers.'

Adamsberg nodded, thinking how fortunate it was his *capitaine* knew where to find the gin.

'And anyway, he left his cape in your flat last night,' said Danglard. 'So I got two more hairs from the collar while you were asleep.'

'What's happened to the cape? Have you still got it?'

'Why? Do you want it?'

'Might do, I don't know.'

'I'd rather have caught the devil than his coat.'

'Danglard, why did he want to pin the murder on me?'

'To make you suffer, but above all to get you to agree to shoot yourself.'

Adamsberg nodded. It was truly diabolical wickedness at work. He turned to the sergeant.

'Sanscartier, surely you didn't search that pile of leaves on your own?'

'No, at that stage I had to tell Laliberté. I already had the statement from the watchman and the DNA of your blood. Christ, though, he went up the wall when I told him what I'd been doing on the so-called sick leaves. I won't tell you what he said. He even accused me of having been your accomplice from the start and helping you escape. He went ballistic. Sure, I'd been way out of line. But in the end I got him to calm down and see reason. Because with our boss, you know, it's rigour, rigour always that counts for him. So he cooled off and he had to admit there was more to the case than met the eye. After that, he moved heaven and earth and authorised us to do the search. And he lifted the warrant that was out for you.'

Adamsberg looked at them in turn. Danglard and Sanscartier. Two men who had not abandoned him for a second.

'Don't try to say anything,' said Sanscartier. 'It's too much to take in right now.'

The car was moving slowly through the traffic jams on the outskirts of Paris. Adamsberg was in the back, leaning his head against the window, his eyes half shut, watching the familiar landmarks go by and glancing at the two men in front who had rescued him. The end of Raphaël's exile. And the end of his own purgatory. The novelty and the relief were so great that they created in him an immense fatigue.

'Hey, pretty good work, all that stuff about the Mah Jong,' said Sanscartier. 'Laliberté was stunned, he said it was a fantastic bit of detection. He'll tell you so tomorrow.'

'He's coming over?'

'I guess you might not want to see him, but he's coming for your *capitaine*'s promotion the next day. Have you forgotten? Your big boss Brézillon asked him over, because they've got a few bones to pick and need to make it up.'

Adamsberg found it hard to take it in that now he could just walk into the office if he liked. Without his lumberjack hat, he could just open the door and say hullo, shake people's hands. Go and buy a loaf of bread. Sit by the banks of the Seine.

'I'm trying to think how to thank you, Sanscartier, but I can't find the words.'

'Don't worry, it's all sorted. I'm going to a Toronto posting. Laliberté has promoted me to inspector. And all because you got drunk that night.'

'But the judge has got away with it,' said Danglard gloomily.

'He'll be found guilty in absentia,' said Adamsberg. 'And Vétilleux and those other people will be released. That's what matters most, after all.'

'No,' said Danglard, shaking his head. 'There's still the fourteenth victim to think about.'

Adamsberg sat up and leaned forward. Sanscartier smelled of almond soap.

'I've worked out who the fourteenth victim is,' he said, smiling.

Danglard glanced in the mirror. It was the first time in six weeks that he had seen Adamsberg smile.

'The last tile is the major element. Until you have that one, the game isn't over and nothing makes sense. It closes the Hand of Honours, and gives its shape to the whole thing.'

'OK, that's logical,' said Danglard.

'And that major piece has to be a white dragon. But a dragon that's white because it's perfect, honour through excellence. Lightning, white light. It's himself, Danglard. The Trident will join his father and mother, in a perfect run of white dragons, three tiles, once the whole thing is finished.'

'He's going to stab himself with a trident?' frowned Danglard.

'No. His natural death will complete the hand. It's on what you taped, Danglard. "Even in prison, even in the grave, the last one won't escape me."'

'But he always kills everyone with the damn trident,' Danglard objected.

'Well, not the last one. The judge *is* the Trident.'

Adamsberg leaned back in his seat and fell fast asleep. Sanscartier looked round in surprise.

'Does he often go off to sleep like that?'

'When he's bored, or in shock,' Danglard explained.

LXIII

ADAMSBERG GREETED THE TWO POLICEMEN, UNKNOWN TO HIM, WHO were on duty on Camille's landing, and showed them his badge – still in the name of Denis Lamproie.

He rang the bell. He had spent the previous day coming back to life in solitude and in a daze, finding great difficulty in getting back in touch with himself again. After these seven weeks buffeted by winds from all four quarters, he found himself thrown up on the sandy shore, soaked and calmed, with the wounds inflicted by the Trident all healed. And at the same time, stunned and surprised. He knew at least that it was imperative that he tell Camille that he had not killed anyone. At least he must do that. And if he could manage it, he would tell her that he had expelled the image of the new father with the dogs from his mind. He felt ill at ease, with his uniform cap under his arm, his sharply-creased trousers, his jacket with its gold epaulettes and his medal in the button hole. The cap would at least have covered the remains of his tonsure.

Camille opened the door and signalled to the two officers that she knew her visitor.

'There are two policemen on the landing the whole time,' she said, 'and I don't seem to be able to reach Adrien.'

'Danglard's at the Prefecture. He's putting the finishing touches to a massive file. The uniforms will be guarding you for two months.'

* * *

Pacing up and down the studio, Adamsberg managed to tell his story, more or less. Trying not to say too much about Noëlla. and mixing up various elements. He interrupted himself half-way through.

'And you know,' he said, 'I've sorted out that business about the man with the dogs.'

'Ah,' said Camille slowly. 'So what do you think of him now?'

'He's much the same as his predecessor.'

'Glad you like him.'

'It's easier this way. We can shake hands.'

'For instance.'

'Exchange a few words, like human beings.'

'Yes . . .'

Adamsberg nodded, and went on with the story: Raphaël, exile, dragons. He gave her back the rules of Mah Jong, and left, closing the door quietly behind him. The quiet click shocked him. Each of them on one side of the wooden barrier, living on separate levels. Separated by his own actions. At least the two watches were not separate, but locked together in a a discreet coupling on his left wrist.

LXIV

EVERYONE WAS IN DRESS UNIFORM AT THE SQUAD HEADQUARTERS.
Danglard looked around contentedly at the hundred or so people in the
Council Chamber. At one end, a dais had been prepared for the official
speech by the *divisionnaire*, who would recount Danglard's merits in the
service, compliment him and pin on his new stripes. Then he would have
to make an acceptance speech, crack a few jokes and convey some emotion.
After that, his colleagues would congratulate him, everyone would relax,
and there would be booze, canapés and chatter. He was watching the door
to see whether Adamsberg turned up. It was possible the *commissaire* might
not want to return to the squad on such a formal occasion. Clémentine
was there however, in her best flowered dress, accompanied by Josette who
wore a smart suit and tennis shoes. Clémentine was quite at ease, a cigarette in her mouth, and happily reunited with *Brigadier* Gardon, who had
once, long ago, lent her a pack of cards, as she had not forgotten. The
fragile hacker, the indispensable lawbreaker, afloat in a sea of police, stuck
close to Clémentine's side, holding her glass in both hands. Danglard had
seen to it that the best quality champagne had been ordered, and had laid
in plenty of it, as if wishing to make this evening as dense as possible, to
impregnate it with fine bubbles which would run through it like molecules. For him the ceremony was less about his promotion than about
the end of Adamsberg's long agony.

* * *

The *commissaire* appeared discreetly at the door and for a moment, Danglard was vexed to see that he had not even put on his uniform. Then he realised who he was, as the man advanced hesitantly through the crowd. This man, with a handsome dark face with high cheekbones was not Jean-Baptiste but Raphaël Adamsberg. The *capitaine* understood how Retancourt's plan had been able to work, if he was glimpsed across a car park in Gatineau. He pointed him out to Sanscartier.

'That's him, the brother,' he said. 'The one talking to Violette Retancourt.'

'I can see how he fooled my colleagues,' said Sanscartier with a grin.

The *commissaire* had followed his brother in soon afterwards, his uniform cap covering his tonsure. Clémentine looked at him, openly appraising him.

'That's three kilos he's put on with us, Josette,' she said proudly surveying her work. 'It suits him well, his blue uniform.'

'Now he has no more locked doors, we won't be hunting in the underground any more,' said Josette with regret.

'Don't worry. *Flics* pick up trouble non-stop, it's their job. He hasn't finished with his troubles, you can be sure, m'dear.'

Adamsberg gripped his brother's arm and looked around. In the end it was probably a good thing to re-enter the office like this, seeing all the officers and other staff at once. In a couple of hours it would all be over, his return, the questions and answers, emotions and thanks. Much more simple than going round to see people one by one, office after office, in confidential conversations. He let Raphaël's arm go, made a friendly sign to Danglard and joined the official top brass, Brézillon and Laliberté.

'Hey man,' said Laliberté, slapping him on the back, 'I got you royally wrong, I was way out of line. Will you accept my apologies? I tracked you like a damned murderer.'

'You had every reason to think it,' said Adamsberg with a wry smile.

'I was talking about the profiling with your boss. Your lab worked overtime to get it done by tonight. They're the same hairs, goddamnit, they belong to your infernal judge. I wouldn't have credited it, but you were right. A great piece of work.'

Unsettled by Laliberté's familiarity, Brézillon had stiffened into a very unbending French manner, and shook Adamsberg's hand formally.

'But say, you made me look a real dummy, slipping out under my nose like that,' Laliberté interrupted, giving Adamsberg a vigorous shake. 'I'll tell you straight, I was fit to be tied.'

'I bet you were, Aurèle. You don't do things by halves.'

'Don't worry, I'm not mad at you now. Right? It was the only thing for you to do. You've got your head screwed on right, for someone who shovels clouds.'

'*Commissaire*,' Brézillon broke in, 'Favre has been posted to St Etienne under observation. There are no further consequences as far as you're concerned. I condoned your action as a mere show of strength in the face of insubordination. But that's not what I think it was. The judge had already got under your skin. Am I right?'

'Yes, sir.'

'In future, please be on your guard.'

Laliberté took Brézillon by the shoulder.

'Don't worry, pal,' he said. 'A hellhound like that isn't going to turn up again in a hurry.'

Embarrassed, the *divisionnaire* extracted himself from the superintendent's large hand and made his excuses. The platform was waiting.

'Bit uptight, your boss, isn't he?' commented Laliberté. 'Talks like a book, walks like he could shit logs. He always like that?'

'No, he puts out his cigarette with his thumb.'

Trabelmann was advancing on them.

'So that's your childhood memory wrapped up then,' he said, shaking Adamsberg's hand. 'Prince Charming can spit fire after all.'

'The black prince.'

'The black prince, yeah.'

'Thanks for coming, Trabelmann.'

'Sorry about what I said about Strasbourg Cathedral. Shouldn't have said that.'

'Don't be sorry, on the contrary. It's been keeping me company all through this.'

Adamsberg realised, as they spoke of the cathedral, that the menagerie had melted away from its apertures. The spire, windows and doors were all open and unencumbered. The beasts had returned to their usual haunts. Nessie was back in her loch, the dragons in their fairy tales, the labradors in fantasy land, the fish in its pink lake, the general of the Canada geese in the Ottawa River, the one-third of the *commandant* of *gendarmes* back in place. The cathedral had returned to being a jewel of Gothic architecture and was soaring high among the clouds, much higher than him.

'A hundred and forty-two metres,' said Trabelmann, picking up a glass of champagne from a passing tray. 'None of us is that big, not you or me.'

And he burst out laughing.

'Except in fairy tales,' said Adamsberg.

'How right you are, *commissaire*.'

Once the speeches were over and Danglard had had his medal pinned on his chest, the Council Chamber was full of chatter, discussion and cries, all made louder by the champagne. Adamsberg went to greet the twenty-six agents of the squad who, during his absence, had been waiting with bated breath for twenty days, without one of them believing the charges against him. He heard the voice of Clémentine, around whom a little group had gathered, consisting of Gardon, Josette, Retancourt, who was followed everywhere by Estalère, and Danglard, who was watching the level of champagne in the glasses and topping them up relentlessly.

'When I said the phantom was a real devil, I was right, wasn't I?' she was saying. 'And it was you, my little one,' she went on, turning to Retancourt, 'who hid him in your skirts, under the noses of the Mounties. How many of them were there?'

'Three, in a room six metres square.'

'Well, there you are. He was as light as a feather, easy to lift, before I fattened him up. I always say the simplest ideas are the best.'

* * *

Adamsberg smiled, as Sanscartier moved over to him.

'Gee, it's great to see them all in this full dress stuff. You look a treat in your ceremonial gear. What are those leaves on the epaulette?'

'Not maple leaves: oak and olive.'

'They meant to mean something?'

'Wisdom and peace.'

'Don't take this the wrong way, but I'd say that's not quite your style, Jean-Baptiste. Inspiration is more like it, and I'm not saying that to make you big-headed. Only there aren't any leaves that mean that.'

Sanscartier's kind face contorted into a thoughtful frown as he tried to think of a symbol for Inspiration.

'What about grass, just ordinary meadow grass?' suggested Adamsberg.

'Sunflowers perhaps? But they'd look silly on your shoulders.'

'My intuitions, or inspirations as you call them, are sometimes a damned nuisance. Get me into big trouble. More like couch-grass.'

'That so?'

"Yes, and sometimes I put my foot right in it. Sanscartier, listen to this, I have a son who's five months old, and I only realised it three days ago.'

'Christ, you missed out on that?'

'Completely.'

'Had she given you your marching orders?'

'No, it was my fault.'

'You didn't love her any more?'

'Yes. No. I don't know.'

'But you played the field.'

'Yes.'

'So you gave her the runaround and she was unhappy?'

'Yes.'

'Then one fine day you broke all your promises and walked out, just like that.'

'You couldn't put it better.'

'Was that why you got drunk that night at *L'Ecluse*?'

'Among other things.'

Sanscartier gulped down his champagne.

'Don't take this the wrong way, but if it's hurting you now, it could mean you made a mistake. You follow me?'

'Only too well.'

'I'm not a clairvoyant, but I'd say take your logic in both hands and switch on your lights.'

Adamsberg shook his head.

'She looks at me from a long way off, as if I'm a huge threat.'

'Well, if you want to get her to trust you again, you can always try.'

'How?'

'Like on the timber site. They pull up old tree trunks and plant maples.'

'How?'

'Like I said. They pull up old trunks and plant new maples.'

Sanscartier drew a circle on his temples, indicating that the operation required a little reflection.

'Should I put that in my pipe and smoke it? Or as Clémentine would say, put my thinking cap on?' asked Adamsberg with a smile.

'That's it, chum.'

Raphaël and his brother went back home on foot at two in the morning walking in step at the same speed.

'I'm going home to the village, Jean-Baptiste.'

'I'll come on down after you. Brézillon's put me on a week's leave. It seems I'm in a state of shock.'

'Do you think the kids are still making toads explode with cigarettes up by the washhouse?'

'No doubt about it, Raphaël.'

LXV

THE EIGHT FORMER MEMBERS OF THE QUEBEC MISSION HAD GONE TO
see Laliberté and Sanscartier off from the airport on their 16.50 flight
for Montreal. In seven weeks, this was the sixth time Adamsberg had been
to the airport, and in six different states of mind. As they stood together
in front of the departures noticeboard, he was almost surprised not to
find Jean-Pierre Emile Roger Feuillet there; a good sort, old Jean-Pierre,
whose hand he would have liked to shake.

He walked a little way off from the group with Sanscartier, who wanted
him to have his special all-weather padded jacket with twelve pockets.

'Now look, it's special, because it's reversible. The black side's waterproof, snow and rain just run off it, you won't feel a thing. The blue side
makes it easy to spot you in the snow, but it's not waterproof. It'll get
wet. So depending on your mood you can wear it one way or the other.
Don't take this the wrong way, but it's like life.'

Adamsberg ran his hand through his short hair.

'I understand,' he said.

'C'mon, take it,' said Sanscartier, pushing it into Adamsberg's arms.
'That way, you won't forget me.'

'No chance of that,' murmured Adamsberg.

Sanscartier gave him a warm pat on the shoulder. 'Switch on your
lights, put on your skis and follow your nose, pal. All the best.'

'Say hullo to the squirrel on sentry duty for me.'

'Ah, you noticed him? Gerald?'

'That's his name?'

'Yup. At night he sleeps in a little hole in the drainpipe where it's been covered in anti-freeze. Cunning little fellow. And in the daytime he's back on duty. You know he had some woman trouble himself?'

'I didn't know that. I was in a hole too.'

'Did you notice he had a girlfirend?'

'Yes, I did notice that.'

'Well, his girlfriend gave him up for a while. Gerald was so upset he stayed in the hole all day. So back home I crushed some hazelnuts, and put them by his drain. After three days, he cracked and came out. The boss wanted to know who the dope was who was bringing Gerald food, so you can bet your boots I kept mum. I was already in his bad books over you.'

'And now?'

'He didn't stay off duty long, he's back on the job and the girlfriend's returned.'

'Same one?'

'Now that I can't tell you. With squirrels it's hard to tell. But, hey, Gerald I'd recognise him anywhere. Would you?'

'Yes, I think so.'

Sanscartier gripped his shoulder again and Adamsberg reluctantly let him go into the departure lounge.

'Come back and see us,' beamed Laliberté, with a hearty shake of his hand. 'I owe you one, and I wanted to tell you. Feel free to come over and see the red leaves in the Fall, and you could even go trail walking again: it's been exorcised now.'

Laliberté kept hold of Adamsberg's hand in his iron grip. Over the superintendent's face where he had never seen more than three expressions, bonhomie, rigour and anger, there now passed a reflective look which altered his face. There's always something else under the surface, like in Pink Lake, he thought.

'Know what I think?' Laliberté went on. 'We need a few of them in our job, cloud shovellers.'

He let go his hand, and disappeared after the others. Adamsberg watched as his massive back disappeared into the crowd. He could still see Sanscartier. He would have liked to take a sample of his goodness, put it on to a disk and isolate it, so that he could inject a little into his own DNA.

The seven other members of the squad were heading for the exit. He heard Voisenet's voice calling him and turned round, rejoining them slowly, holding the sergeant's thick jacket over his shoulder.

Strap on your skis and follow your nose, cloud shoveller.

Put all this in your pipe.

And smoke it.

Notes

'De la rigueur, de la rigueur et de la rigueur, je connais pas d'autre moyen de réussir' ('Rigour, rigour and yet more rigour, that's the only way I know to succeed') was a slogan in the television advertising for UQAM (Université du Québec à Montréal), for the years 2001 and 2002.

The Canadian DNA Data Bank is situated in the Ottawa headquarters of the Royal Canadian Mounted Police/Gendarmerie royale du Canada, but the 'annex' in Gatineau Federal Park is invented, and the episodes concerning DNA profiling in this novel are a mixture of the real and the fictional; they do not represent the RCMP's actual modes of procedure. The following article (which appears in both French and English) was drawn upon for details of DNA profiling procedures: Joanna Kerr, 'RCMP's DNA Data Bank Sets a World Standard', *The Gazette/La Gazette*, vol. 62, no. 5–6, 2000 (journal of the RCMP/GRC).

Translator's note:

Canadian French differs more in terms of idiom and vocabulary from the French spoken in France than Canadian English does from British or US English. The French characters here sometimes find the language difficult to follow, but the examples have necessarily been cut or modified in translation.

French police ranks, which were renamed some years ago along the same lines as the *gendarmerie* and the military, have been left in French. The hierarchy ascends as follows: *brigadier, lieutenant, capitaine, commandant, commissaire*. These are roughly equivalent but do not exactly correspond to the British ranks: (detective) sergeant, inspector, chief inspector, superintendent, chief superintendent, with the *divisionnaire* being equivalent to commissioner. As *commissaire principal*, Adamsberg is the equivalent of chief superintendent.

FRED VARGAS was born in Paris in 1957. A historian and archaeologist by profession, she is now a bestselling novelist. Her novels include *Have Mercy on Us All, Seeking Whom He May Devour* and *The Three Evangelists*.